# The Suitcase of Secrets

# The Suitcase of Secrets

Julie Fearn

Copyright © 2023 Julie Fearn.

The right of Julie Fearn to be identified as the author of this work has been asserted by her in accordance with the Copyright, Designs and Patents Act 1988.

A catalogue record for this book is available from the British Library

All rights reserved. No part of this publication may be reproduced, distributed, or transmitted in any form or by any means, including photocopying, recording, or other electronic or mechanical methods, without the prior written permission of the author, except in the case of brief quotations embodied in critical reviews and certain other noncommercial uses permitted by copyright law.

ISBN: 978-1-912882-75-5

Book cover image by LightSpeedDreams.net
Book design by Quantum Dot Press.

I dedicate this book to my father, Janusz Apoloniusz Pieczykolan Howerski – 1925 – 1984.

## A Free Story for You

If you'd like to stay in touch with me and my work, I'd love to meet you through my newsletter.

And you'll receive this free story!

www.juliefearn.com

# CONTENTS

## About this Novel

The story of *The Suitcase of Secrets* is fictional and grew from three sources: actual events, family stories - often invented to mask harsh truths and finally, imagined scenarios. My father was a displaced Pole who arrived in Northern England in 1946. As a family, we knew little of what happened to him during the occupation of Poland in WW2. He took his secrets to his grave. Many years after his death, I arranged the translation of documents belonging to him. Reading these provided the raw material for me to invent this story.

I would not have written *The Suitcase of Secrets* without the encouragement of Alan Stockdill, playwright and director of Talking Stock Theatre Company, Halifax. Nor would it have seen the light of day without the inspirational Lizzi Linklater, poet and founder of York's Pen2Paper writers' group, who provided thoughtful feedback and motivation. Instrumental to the process was Mia Botha, founder of Deadlines for Writers, an online program working to weekly deadlines. Many wonderful writers closely read the drafts. But I am particularly indebted to Anne Whitehead, Marijo Thompson, Peggy Rockey, Sudha, Nina Heiser, Sharon Hancock, and Graham Clift, whose suggestions improved my story no end. I say a special thank you to Katarzyna Ciszewska, who painstakingly translated the source material. Faded, tattered handwritten letters, certificates and ID documents were scanned and sent to her in Poland. Some had been written in pencil, but she persevered. Katarzyna and I shared a journey of discovery reading these, and I 'heard' my grandmother's voice for the first time. I thank David Howerski, my brother, for sharing his family research. Finally, I thank the wonderful city of Bradford for its rich cultural heritage, where my immigrant parents began their new lives and where much of this novel is set.

# PART ONE

## Roman 1940, Warsaw

Roman leapt from the tram as it swayed along its tracks in the freezing evening air. His boots hit the snow with a thud; he skidded to a halt at the sales kiosk, where people shuffled in a queue for the newspaper. Their white breaths billowed. Roman winked at the pretty young girl inside, who flushed and smiled. He laughed, performed a little jump, and then ran to the heavy doors of his family's apartment block. Roman had recently discovered what being handsome meant but did not dwell on it. Inside the building, he bounded two steps at a time to their first-floor apartment to thump on the door. Footsteps clicked from inside, and his older sister, Elouna swung it open and grinned.

'Roman, *you're* late home,' she said and waved a mocking finger.

They scampered down the parquet hallway into the drawing room, where the fire glinted off the Christmas decorations. The air filled with the sharp aroma of pine.

'I went to see Noam's family, but his neighbours said they've moved to the old town.'

Elouna turned to Roman. 'Papa said you shouldn't go there anymore. It's not safe.'

'I know, but I miss him at school.'

Elouna ruffled Roman's thick hair and chuckled.

'Come on, little-one, let's play a game of chess. See if you've learnt enough to beat your older sister?'

'Don't call me little-one; I'm fourteen now and nearly

as tall as you.'

'Sorry, it just slipped out.'

After flinging his satchel into his room, Roman slipped into a chair by the window, pulled one curtain open, and gazed into the street below. His father warned they should shut the curtains when the afternoon light died, but Roman adored watching the trundling trams and busy people hurrying around the city. Elouna set the wooden chessboard on a table and commanded Roman to consider his first move. While he concentrated, Elouna stood up to shut the green brocade curtain again.

'We don't want Papa to worry,' she said as she slid back down into her chair.

'Where's Mama?' Roman said as his hand hovered over the carved chess pieces. He hoped to guess Elouna's reaction to provide a clue to his intended move.

'I'm not sure. Maybe still at school. But Mama said nothing about a teacher meeting tonight.'

Roman looked up from the chessboard when he heard a key in the front door lock. By the clipped footsteps in the hallway, he knew it was their father rather than their mother. When the drawing-room door opened, a rush of cold air swept in with Ludwig, their father, whose face looked stung from the icy night air.

Elouna jumped from her seat and greeted him with a kiss on both cheeks.

'Oh! You're frozen!' she said.

'The trams are uncomfortable at this time of year.' Ludwig looked around the apartment.

'You've still got your hat on, Papa,' said Elouna.

Ludwig reached up and patted his fur hat. 'So, I have.' He removed it and scratched his scalp.

'Where is your mama?' he said.

'We don't know; she's not home yet,' Elouna said.

Roman saw a flash of worry flit across his father's face.

'Well, I'm sure there's a perfect reason. Maybe a school meeting she forgot to mention?'

Elouna nudged him towards the crackling fire where he stood and rubbed his hands together, light steam rising from his snow-dampened trousers.

'Are you hungry, my children?'

'Yes, a little, but we can wait.' Elouna glanced at Roman. 'Can't we?'

He nodded, although his stomach rumbled.

'Well, that's just as well as it's time for the broadcast,' Ludwig said. 'Sit with me.'

The three settled around the walnut-clad wireless to one side of the fireplace, where leaping flames licked the chimney's throat. Ludwig eased into a leather chesterfield that groaned as he sank. Roman and Elouna perched on a green velvet sofa opposite.

'As always, I will remind you not to let anyone, friends or relatives, know we listen to the BBC World Service... *because?*' He stared directly at Elouna to finish his sentence.

'Listening to outside broadcasts is forbidden; it's a punishable offence under the Third Reich,' she said, then threw Roman a solemn look.

He nodded. Roman knew they must obey this frightening rule. Ludwig turned the dial, and the wireless slowly hummed to life. Roman thought its pewter grill resembled a human face, the eyes and mouth illuminated from the filament inside. To him, it looked sad, curiously.

Roman listened to the radio, but his attention strayed to footsteps that sounded outside their apartment. Ludwig leaned forward and snapped off the radio. He pressed a finger to his lips. All three held their breath until the footsteps receded down the hallway. And when it was silent, Ludwig switched the set back on. The announcer reported an RAF raid on Manheim, Germany, had been successful. It was a retaliation for a series of devastating air attacks by the Germans the previous month over Bristol, Liverpool, and Southampton, which left those major British cities burned out and ruined. They savagely bombed Warsaw at the beginning of its invasion. Roman recalled the terror of those times, darting between blazing, falling masonry to get home, and people dying or lying helpless in the streets.

Ludwig clicked the radio off when the World Service broadcast ended, and all three sat in silence. Roman's fingertip traced crumbs in the crevice between the sofa seats from when he and his mother had eaten toasted rye bread the previous evening. His stomach lurched.

'Your mother is very late,' Ludwig said as he glanced at the mahogany clock on the mantelpiece that struck seven. He stood up and pulled at the bottom of his suit jacket. Then their phone shrilled in the hallway. 'Ah!' said Ludwig. 'News, perhaps.' He hurried to the phone. Roman and Elouna followed him to hang inside the oak door frame. 'Ludwig Kozynski speaking.'

Roman watched his father, who clung to the receiver with both hands as he turned his back to them.

'Are you sure?' Ludwig said, then listened some more. 'Yes, yes, I understand.' He leaned one arm on the wall behind the telephone table to steady himself while a muffled voice filtered from the receiver.

Elouna threw her arm around Roman's shoulders; he grasped her wrist, warm and momentarily comforting to him.

'There's just one problem.' Ludwig turned briefly towards his children. 'My wife isn't home yet.'

As more inaudible conversation followed, Roman's throat tightened. His father gently placed the receiver in its cradle and stood motionless for a moment, as though lost in a dream, then shook his head and clapped his hands together.

'Okay, children, we must go away for a few days. Let's pack.'

'What?' said Elouna.

Roman stood motionless, trying to comprehend. Ludwig hurried them back through into the centre of the drawing-room. He placed a hand on each of their shoulders and leaned in conspiratorially.

'A friend needs help; we must visit him.' He nodded at them with a strained smile. 'So, off you both go to pack immediately.'

'Where are we going?' Elouna said.

'Don't ask questions. Just do as I say. We leave tonight.'

'We can't just leave. What about Mama?' Roman

stood his ground against the gentle push of his father's hand.

'She'll meet us there. Now, get to it as quickly as possible.'

Elouna pushed Roman into his bedroom. 'I'll help you pack.'

She stretched up to grab his suitcase from the top of the wardrobe, pulled it clear, and threw it on the bed. The latches sprang open, and a layer of grey dust flew off the lid. She yanked open the wardrobe drawers and grabbed two red woollen jumpers.

'Here,' she said as she bundled them onto his bed. 'Pack these.'

Roman watched. His thoughts froze. His knees buckled. Everything happened too quickly for him to think clearly.

'Get your boots and socks,' said Elouna.

Then, hit by the urgency, Roman snapped from his confusion and grabbed clothes from the drawers. He stuffed them into the suitcase with shaking hands.

'I'm okay,' he said. 'I can do it. You pack your things, Elouna.'

Roman's heart raced as she hurried from his room. The sound of heavy footsteps, which thumped from downstairs, interrupted his attention. There were multiple people. Roman stopped what he was doing and crept into the hall, where he saw Ludwig huddled with Elouna. He ran and joined them. The sound of footsteps approached, then violent banging began on their apartment door. His father raised a finger in the air and motioned Roman to listen.

'Quick!' Ludwig whispered to them. 'Go to Roman's room and lock yourselves in. Do not come out until I say.'

Elouna darted towards Roman's room. He scrambled after her, skidding on the newly polished parquet floor. They sheltered, breathless, behind his bedroom door with their ears pressed against it.

'Open up. Open up!' a voice bellowed outside their apartment, accompanied by even louder crashing at their front door.

Roman could hear his father rushing around the apartment while the banging continued.

'You must open, now!' a man's voice roared.

Roman heard what sounded like repeated kicking. He whispered to Elouna to step back a little as he peeped out. His father stood behind the front door, straightening his jacket, while the wood shuddered from the blows delivered by whoever was outside. Finally, Ludwig smoothed his hair and slowly opened it.

The Gestapo rushed in.

Roman silently closed his bedroom door and told Elouna not to make a sound.

'Ludwig Kozynski?' a voice bawled.

'Yes, that's me.'

'Where's the rest of your family?'

Roman heard his father say they were visiting relatives out of town, and the thump of an assault followed.

'Men, search the apartment.'

Roman tiptoed to his bedroom window with Elouna in tow; her warm hand had turned cold.

'You escape through here,' he whispered as he eased

the window up as quietly as possible. Roman prayed the mechanism would not stick, as it often did. He needed it to open wide enough for Elouna to squeeze out. The window slowly yielded to his effort. Icy night air smacked him as he helped Elouna clamber over the window ledge to dangle her feet outside.

Elouna grabbed his hand and turned to him. He looked down to see a military truck parked beneath, but it appeared empty.

'I can't!' she said, glancing into the snowy street in terror.

'You must. It's the only way. Jump, and roll when you hit the ground.' Roman briefly kissed her cheek. 'I'll follow you,' he said.

They stared at each other momentarily. Roman's heart thumped in his gullet. Elouna slid from the icicle-covered ledge. Her skirt billowed as she plunged into the deep snow with a thud. Roman saw her lay there for a few seconds, stunned. Elouna scrambled to her feet, brushed herself down, and sneaked off into the night without a coat, but at least with boots. Roman pulled the window shut and turned towards his half-packed suitcase. His door flew open, and a Gestapo guard rushed in with his rifle at full tilt.

'Halt!'

Roman raised his hands as he had seen people do in the streets of the old town, where Jewish families were now forced to live. The guard glanced around the room and yanked the wardrobe open. Satisfied there was no one there, he turned to Roman.

‘Out! Out!’ He butted Roman in the stomach with his rifle.

As Roman staggered into the hallway, his father stood with his hands on his head; blood trickled from one corner of his mouth while a guard trained a rifle at his temple. Another ransacked their drawing room. He kicked aside the chairs at the table and smashed the chessboard with the rifle butt.

## Anya

Earlier that day across town, Anya Kozynska watched over her primary school pupils who scrambled into their boots, coats, and hats for the freezing journey home. She loved that time of day because the children looked happy and excited as they jumped up to pull their clothing from the brightly coloured wall hooks. Anya's gaze halted at the sight of Irena perched on the bench beneath the coats, struggling to lace up her clumsy-looking boots, far too large for such a small girl.

Anya approached her and bent. 'Do you need some help, Irena?'

Irena raised her head, her heart-shaped face flushed with embarrassment.

'No, Miss Kozynska.' She tugged at the top of one boot to tighten it. 'These were my brothers before me, and my mama says they have life left in them.'

'Indeed!'

Anya ran her hand over the toe of the boot and felt a lump at its tip.

'Let's just see what's happening here, shall we?' She slid her hands to the top, smiling.

Anya knew Irena's father died during the outbreak of the invasion, and her mother struggled to keep the family of three boys and two girls fed and clothed. Anya untied the laces, slipped the boot off, and probed inside. Her fingers prodded what felt like a wedge of damp paper at the toe. It had scrunched up to one side, causing Irena's foot to slide around when she walked.

‘Well, I can fix this for you.’

Anya watched Irena stare at her thin knees. ‘Thank you, Miss Kozynska.’

As Anya redistributed the padding, careful not to pull it out and embarrass Irena further, she said, ‘You know, I have some boots at home which belonged to my daughter, Elouna. She grew out of them a long time ago. I’m sure they’re your size. Shall I bring them for you tomorrow?’

Irena’s eyes widened. ‘But Mama might be cross with me.’

As she secured Irena’s laces, Anya said, ‘I will write her a note to go with the shoes. What do you say?’

Irena smiled and slid from her seat.

‘Come on, follow me.’

Anya walked the little girl to the outside door. She watched Irena clump through the thick snow, and her heart felt heavy for the girl’s future.

Anya pushed the door closed against the drifting snow and turned to see Mr Krause, the headteacher, striding towards her.

‘Miss Kozynska, do you have a moment?’

‘Why, yes, Mr Krause, of course.’

Krause’s small eyes flashed behind his steel-rimmed glasses. Anya had recently noticed him studying her intently as she went about the job she loved, but stifled her feelings of unease. He had never acted unprofessionally towards her, but she could not relax in his company. She and her family recently attended the school Christmas party, where Ludwig and Krause spoke of business matters and the political situation. She avoided Krause and chatted with the other teachers. Afterward, at home, she sought Ludwig's opinion of Krause.

'Hard to pin down,' he'd said.

Krause filled her with a sense of discomfort.

'Follow me.' He crooked a finger and hurried to his office. 'Sit down,' he said as he hovered nearby, arms folded over his skinny chest. 'Can you stay longer to assist me in checking the school finances tonight? I have a report to prepare for tomorrow morning for the school board.'

'Well, I…' Anya looked him directly in the eye. She saw Krause's pursed lips and arms tighten across his jacket. 'Of course, Mr Krause.'

'Excellent! I expected you would be at home with finances.'

Anya stared at him but said nothing as she sat down to attend to the ledger on Krause's desk. She wasn't sure exactly what he meant.

'Your husband's a business man. Or, am I mistaken?' Krause said, his head cocked to one side.

She adjusted her hair and breathed deeply. 'Yes, he is. So, what exactly am I required to do?'

Krause closed his office curtains and turned to Anya. 'Find evidence the bursar is stealing from me. I suspect he's Jewish, though he hides it.'

Her jump from the window shocked Elouna. But with every sense on high alert, she glanced around. Curfew had started, and the street was empty. The desolation and silence of the night struck her as eery. It was the first time she had broken the curfew restrictions, and extremely frightening. She knew anyone caught would be arrested. Some were immediately shot. Elouna needed to find somewhere to hide quickly. She set off toward a nearby park. The deep snow thankfully muffled her footsteps. As she ran, she was aware of semi-crouching to diminish her outline. Her rapid breaths steamed white into the night air around her head. As the park came into view, a spurt of energy added momentum to her rush. Thick evergreen bushes enclosed it. She slowed and headed to the densest section, squatting. As her breath steadied, Elouna noticed the sounds of a commotion that clattered through the still night. A shot cracked, and someone barked orders that echoed in the emptiness of the streets. Her stomach knotted because she guessed it had something to do with her father and brother.

The cold stung Elouna's hands. She glanced down to see them plunged deep in the snow to steady her position, a posture she had taken unaware. A vision of her coat and gloves on her bed flashed before her. Suddenly, an engine caught as it ignited, and the rumble of a truck sounded over the cobblestones. The vehicle roared past the bushes, and its headlights flashed through winter shrubbery. Elouna held her breath as fear prickled her scalp. She yanked her hands from the snow and tucked them under her armpits for warmth.

Elouna headed to the school where her mother worked. She stretched shakily from her hunched position and slunk off towards it.

When she arrived at the school, her whole body was trembling from the shock. It was impossible to process. The school was in darkness apart from one place where a dim light shone behind a curtained window. Elouna knew it was the headmaster's quarters from the Christmas party when he had shown her and Roman around and insisted his tree was the tallest in all of Warsaw's homes.

She crept past the window and around to the rear of the building. Her eyes had adjusted to the gloom, and she spotted a small open window. Elouna searched everywhere and found a litter bin tall enough to stand on to reach the ledge. She dragged it to the wall with as little noise as possible and clambered on top. The window opened into the school kitchen, and directly beneath was a draining board stacked with pots and pans. Elouna pulled the window open, and to her relief, the gap was wide enough to squeeze her slender body through in a crab-like manoeuvre. She slid down and planted a foot and hand between a skillet and a boiling pan. Her foot caught a pan that crashed to the floor. A brief silence followed where she held her breath and cursed in her head.

Someone yelled out, 'Who's there?'

Footsteps thundered outside. The kitchen door creaked open to a beam of light that swung around the room, carried by the headmaster, Mr Krause.

'It's me, Elouna Kozynska, Anya's daughter.'

He snapped on the light. 'What the devil?'

The brightness dazzled her. Despite that, Elouna completed her descent and jumped down.

'Help me, Mr Krause. Please,' she said as her knees buckled from the events of that night, and without warning, she crumpled to the stone-flagged floor before she lost consciousness.

When Elouna came round, Mr Krause said, 'Can you hear me?'

'Yes.'

She tried to sit upright but found herself dizzy and remembered she had not eaten since breakfast.

'Let me help.' Krause hooked his hands under her armpits and pulled Elouna to stand. 'Are you hurt?'

'No.'

He led her to the cook's table and eased her into a chair. 'You're alright now, Miss Kozynska.'

Krause eyed her damp clothes. Elouna felt as though she hovered above herself and watched. Nothing seemed real anymore. A short while ago, she and Roman played chess safely in their home before a knock on the door ripped their life apart. Elouna did not know why the Gestapo invaded their home or what happened to Roman and her father. And her mother was missing, too.

She cried.

Krause crossed the kitchen and drew the blinds down. 'I'll make some tea, and you tell me what's happened.'

He shuffled to the stove to prepare their drink. The red flame leaped to life as Krause lit the gas with a smooth taper. He jumped back. Elouna tried to compose her thoughts to relay the evening events to Krause, but an idea darted through her mind.

'Mr Krause, what time did my mother leave school tonight?'

Krause turned slowly from the stove. 'Why, my dear?'

'It's just, she hadn't arrived home before…'

He folded his arms. 'Before what?' Krause stared at her so hard she felt herself recoil from his gaze. 'Your mother left a little later than usual, but I can't imagine why she hasn't yet returned. Perhaps you're mistaken?'

Elouna's heart thumped at the base of her throat. She needed to tell someone what happened, or she would burst. Krause was her mother's employer, after all. She should trust him.

'We...' She hesitated, picturing the scene in her mind, and decided it wasn't safe to tell him about the forbidden radio broadcast. 'Some German soldiers burst into our home tonight. I think they took Papa and Roman away.'

Krause uncrossed his arms and rested his knuckles on his hips. 'Why?'

'I don't know. I escaped.'

'But why would they arrest your father?'

Elouna tried to catch the expression in his eyes, but the heat misted his glasses.

A silence followed.

'These are indeed strange times,' Krause said as the shrill whistle of the kettle sliced the air.

He poured the boiled water into a teapot and clamped the billowing steam beneath the cracked lid.

'I must find Mama.'

'I'm afraid you can't do anything now. It's curfew.' Krause returned to the table with their drinks. He set them down but remained standing. 'When you've had your tea, get some rest. Whatever has happened has given you a terrible fright.' Krause smiled and laid a hand on Elouna's shoulder. 'Tomorrow morning, I'm sure your mother will be in school, and everything will be fine.'

A grey fog cleared momentarily for Elouna, and a lump gathered in her throat. 'Do you think so?'

'I'm sure.' Cogs turned behind his eyes. 'I tell you what, you can take your tea, and I'll put you in the children's sickbay to sleep. There's a bed and a washbasin.'

She followed him down the cold corridor to a door he had to unlock. Krause motioned for Elouna to go inside. He flicked on a dingy light.

'It's more comfortable than it looks.' He pointed to a tiny bed. 'I'll see you in the morning. Goodnight.'

Elouna collapsed onto the bed and curled into a foetal position on the scratchy grey covers, too tired to climb inside. She scanned the room. A bright poster featured smiling boys with blond hair and blue eyes. It invited them to hike in the mountains with the Hitler Youth Movement.

## Anya

Anya hurried home from school that evening. Krause detained her for over three hours, going over school finance records that were in meticulous order, with no signs of fraud. Halfway through the task, she stopped to say everything looked fine. But Krause insisted Anya proceed as he wanted proof before he took action.

When Anya needed to use the lavatory, she requested Krause unlock the office door. On her return, she asked why he'd locked it. Krause commented a nosey caretaker often snooped around the office while emptying bins, and he seemed suspicious of his staff, which concerned her. Anya often overheard him quizzing staff members about colleagues. She evaded any questions he fielded.

Her thoughts brightened as she neared their apartment and saw the lights were on. It was late, and dinner plans would need to be changed to something less time-consuming than chicken soup with dumplings. At the outbreak of the war, their housekeeper fled to Finland, so Anya resumed responsibility for the daily tasks she didn't enjoy. She reached their apartment to find the door half-open.

'Strange!' she said, stepped in, and shut the door.

'Hello, I'm home,' Anya said. No-one answered. Anya crossed the hallway into the drawing-room, still wearing her coat and hat. The only sound was the tap of her heels on the wooden floor. By the window, two chairs lay overturned on the Persian rug. Chess pieces were scattered across the floor.

'Ludwig, Roman, Elouna!'

Anya's voice trembled. *Get a hold of yourself*, she thought; *they must have gone somewhere*. But the idea was absurd because they would never take such a risk at curfew unless there had been an emergency.

She ran into Elouna's room. A half-packed suitcase was sprawled across the bed. A dread pitted in her stomach.

'Anyone home?' she called out as she crossed back into Roman's room, praying they would be there playing a foolish prank.

'Please, God, let that be it.'

The curtains billowed inside Roman's room; the window was wide open, and snow gusted in. Anya pulled it shut with such force the noise startled her. On the bed-edge, a case was balanced and some of Roman's clothes were strewn on the bed cover.

'What on earth?'

Anya crumpled on the bed, clutched the onyx crucifix around her neck and muttered under her breath. She wanted to run out, shout, and scream, but fear weighed her down, and her legs would not allow her to stand. She gripped the bedhead to steady herself and halt the tremors that rippled through her.

Anya counted to sixty, twice, then hauled herself up. *I must phone Teofil*, she thought.

In the hall, she sat heavily on the chair by the phone, snatched it up to dial Teofil's number, and burst into body-quaking sobs at the sound of his voice.

'Something terrible has happened,' she said. 'Elouna, Roman, Ludwig, they're not here.'

'What do you mean, not there?'

'In our apartment, they've gone.' Anya caught her breath. 'It looks like they were packing to leave, but they've disappeared.'

She heard Teofil suck in his breath. 'Listen, Anya, you must keep calm; there's bound to be an explanation. Stay there. I'll make a few phone calls.'

'Who will you call?'

'Some contacts.' He paused. 'As soon as I have information, I'll phone you.'

Anya could hear a drawer opening as she spoke. 'But who are you calling?'

'It's best you don't know. Now try to keep calm. Don't rush to any conclusions. It will be alright.'

'But what if they don't come back tonight? What will I do?'

Teofil was silent for a moment. 'If that happens, you must act as though everything is normal tomorrow and go to school.'

'But…'

Teofil interrupted her. 'Don't draw attention to yourself. As soon as I know anything, I'll let you know.'

Anya crashed the receiver into its cradle and wandered into the drawing room, trying to calm down. She righted the fallen chairs, gathered the chess pieces, and placed them back in their box. She got on all fours, pulled the chessboard from under the table, folded it, and set it on the bookshelf. It was important for order to be restored, for her to erase the unbearable sight of disarray.

All thoughts of food left her; she felt unmoored from

routine. Anya flopped on the sofa, pulled a chenille cover up to her chin, and stared into space. She ran the day's events repeatedly in her head to see if a connection existed between what happened at school and her family disappearing the same evening. Anya contemplated for quite some time until a memory blazed and destroyed the looping thoughts. A few nights ago, she woke early to find Ludwig wasn't beside her. She slipped out of bed and located him hunched over his bureau, fiddling with something.

'What are you doing?' she'd asked.

Ludwig replied he was, 'Fixing the drawer.'

Anya questioned the hour, but he replied he could not sleep and was catching up on business paperwork.

'I wonder!' she said and flung the cover off to tiptoe to Ludwig's writing bureau.

She didn't know why she crept, but it felt safer. Anya had never looked through Ludwig's papers before or questioned why he kept them under lock and key. She assumed it was to do with business investments that were no concern of hers. However, she knew where he hid the key and dashed off to fetch it from his bedside drawer.

Anya held her breath. Her neck prickled as she eased the unlocked bureau open and pushed away the thought she might discover something she could not unsee. She lifted a thick pile of papers from the drawer and placed them on the bureau's top, then carefully pulled out the drawer to turn it upside down. Someone had taped a small notebook to the underside. Anya tugged it free, careful not to damage it.

She returned, trance-like, to the sofa, flicked on a floor lamp and stared at the notebook before she opened the pages. Her hand trembled. It was Ludwig's handwriting, but she could not decipher the coded content. There was a knock at the door. Anya jumped up, snapped off the light, and listened. She prayed they would go away.

Thump, thump, thump. Thump, thump, thump.

Then a voice, 'Mrs Koyzinska, is everything okay?'

Relieved, she opened the door to a neighbour holding one of Ludwig's shoes.

'Is this your husband's? It was outside my apartment.'

Anya closed her eyes for a second, willing the tears away. 'Yes, it is; he must have dropped it.'

She smiled stiffly and retrieved the shoe.

'We heard…'

But Anya cut her off. She was too frightened by now to trust anyone until she spoke with Teofil. 'Thank you so much. Goodnight,' she said, closing and bolting the door.

The following day was unbearable for Anya as she prepared for work. Her thoughts were fuzzy from lack of sleep. It was dawn before her eyes closed, but the sound of a speeding truck in the street immediately woke her with a jolt. Roman, Elouna, and Ludwig had not returned. To distract herself from a corrosive nagging anxiety, she searched for the shoes she had promised to give to Irena.

In the school yard, children hurled snowballs at each other. Some created ice slides on the compacted surface; their shrill laughter pierced the air. She had to act like it was an ordinary December day, so she hurried to the staff room. The aroma of burnt coffee filled the air as she opened her locker to search for lesson books. Two colleagues stood by the stove whispering. One flashed a glance across but looked sideways when Anya smiled at him. She had wrapped Irena's shoes in a brown paper parcel, tied with a red ribbon and written a note for her mother.

As Anya manoeuvred it into her locker, Krause's wolfish features appeared around the door. He strolled over and peered at the parcel.

'What's that?'

'Oh, just something for Irena'

Krause sneered; his piggy eyes flashed behind his steel-rimmed spectacles. 'God won't reward you for this. She's not here.'

'Oh dear, is Irena ill?'

Krause leaned one arm against the locker. 'No. Her family has gone away. To the country, I believe.'

'Oh, my goodness! That's sudden. Irena mentioned nothing when we spoke yesterday.'

'Children!' he said, then turned away to greet the other huddled teachers.

Anya crossed the room for a drink of water before she entered the class for the entire morning. She turned the tap and waited to see whether the water had frozen, but after a few thumping noises in the pipes, there was a gurgle as a small trickle emerged.

'They were arrested,' she heard her colleague whispering to the other.

Anya stood and sipped the cold water, her ears alerted for information.

‘They say she was hiding a family of Jews in her basement. They were paying her.’

‘Irena’s mother is such a little mouse. Who would’ve believed it?’

Anya felt herself stagger from the blow of information. One colleague looked up.

‘Is everything alright, Miss Kozynska?’ he asked.

‘Yes, fine, fine. I tripped on this uneven floorboard.’

She pointed to the floor with the toe of her shoe, smiled briefly, turned, and left with the parcel.

Irena’s chair remained empty through the first half of the morning. Anya tried to concentrate, but her mind continually slipped to what fate befell the little girl and her family. She prayed the rumour was unfounded. She had taken Irena’s parcel into the classroom as a talisman.

Just before the mid-morning break, Krause poked his head around the door, somewhat excited.

‘There’s a telephone call for you in my office, Miss Kozynska.’

Anya’s legs threatened to collapse beneath her. She leaned on the desk to steady herself momentarily.

‘Children, continue with your work. I’ll be right back.’

She snatched her bag and rushed after Krause to his office, too afraid to ask who was calling. Inside, he gestured to the phone laid sideways on his tidy desk. Anya grabbed it and pressed the receiver as close to her ear as possible. Her pearl earring crashed against the cup and sprang off. It rolled under Krause’s desk. He raised his eyebrows disapprovingly as though she were a naughty child.

It was Teofil on the phone. 'Anya, I have news,' he paused. 'Are you alone?'

She glanced at Krause, who hovered near but pretended to look out of the window, his hands sunk deep in his trouser pockets.

'No. Not really.'

'Okay, listen but say nothing.'

'Alright,' she said in a thickened voice.

Her mouth dried instantly; her tongue welded to the roof of her mouth and made it difficult to speak.

'The Gestapo have arrested Ludwig and Roman.'

Anya gasped. Krause turned sharply and stared at her. She exerted all her energy to compose herself under his glare and gripped the receiver so tightly the blue veins stood out on the back of her hand.

'I see,' she said.

'Elouna escaped, but I don't know where to. You must come home immediately; I'll be there as soon as possible. Make an excuse to leave now. Do you understand?'

'Yes, thanks for letting me know. And I'm so sorry to hear that.'

Anya placed the receiver back in its cradle as she fought the urge to cry. Krause's penetrating stare—one of someone who knew something and was seeking a giveaway reaction—terrified her.

'Well,' she said, smoothing her hand over her hair, then bending down to the floor for the lost earring, temporarily concealing her facial expression. 'My uncle is very ill, and I need to visit him.' She straightened up and clipped the earring back onto her lobe. 'I request a day's leave of absence. Unpaid, of course.'

Krause pulled his hands from his pockets, about to protest, but she rushed past him, apologised, and exited the room.

Anya fled back to the apartment from school, trying to absorb the details of the phone call from Teofil. The freezing winter air stung her cheeks as she overtook people on the icy pavements. Teofil stood smoking by their apartment door and hastily greeted her on arrival with a peck on the cheek. He placed a finger to his lips and shook his head. Inside, Teofil threw off his coat and scarf and paced up and down; his usual composure had slipped.

'Anya, I've spoken to one of Ludwig's friends.'

'Who?'

Anya stood, pulling her scarf back and forth through her palms.

Teofil stopped pacing. 'It's not safe to tell you this fellow's name, but…' He stared at Anya for a moment. 'He's more or less admitted Ludwig has connections with the Polish Underground.'

Anya clapped her hands to her breastbone. 'Oh, dear God.'

'Did you know this?'

She shook her head.

Teofil continued, 'He thinks someone's talked to the Gestapo about Ludwig.'

Anya sat down, winded, and rested her elbow on the chair arm. 'But who would do that?'

'People do all kinds of things these days.'

'Ludwig's put us in danger, Teofil. How could he?'

He moved to stand next to his sister and placed a hand on her shoulder. 'Ludwig is a good man. There must be a reason for his actions.' Teofil lifted her chin and stared directly at her. 'We must figure out a way to contact him.'

'What? How will we get word to the Gestapo Headquarters?' Anya pulled away and wound her hair into a coil at her neck.

Teofil sighed. 'I'll make some tea. We need to reflect before we do anything.'

When he returned with the tray, Anya sat at Ludwig's desk, holding the notebook. 'Take a look at this,' she said.

Teofil rested the tray on a coffee table and grabbed it to examine it.

'I found it taped under this.' She tapped the drawer with her hand. 'What do you think it might be?'

'Whatever it is, it's important enough to be written in code.'

She asked, 'Do you think it's the reason they arrested Ludwig?'

'It's impossible to know. We can't draw any hasty conclusions.' He scrutinised the notebook.

Anya rested her elbows on the bureau's open lid. 'Perhaps we should burn it. Get rid of it, if it's incriminating,' she said, staring at Teofil.

'Yes, but we must be cautious. What if its vital information for the underground?'

'But who could we show it to without endangering ourselves?'

As she said this, Anya prised the notebook from Teofil's hand. The two sat in silence, their tea steaming into the chilled apartment, and then a commotion in the street roused them from their thoughts.

'Teofil, I have an idea. Let's meet Ludwig's contact. The one you spoke to. Maybe he can help?'

'Talking on the phone's one thing, but meeting up? What if he's under surveillance? It's not safe, surely?' he said, fiddling in his jacket pocket, pulling out a pack of cigarettes. He lit one, then blew thin smoke rings into the air.

'You know Ludwig was successful in business after his army career.' She paused. 'Do you know why, Teofil?'

'I don't want to argue, Anya.' Teofil lifted his hand as if to halt the conversation.

'We're talking, not arguing. Ludwig was successful because he took risks.' Anya stood up and strode to the centre of the room, hands on hips, caught by her words but unwilling to back down.

'This is madness, Anya; why would a man we don't know help?' Teofil moved to the edge of his seat and rested his palms on his thighs.

'Because we have this.' Anya stared at Teofil, unflinching as she waved the little book in the air.

'Call him and we can meet in a coffee house later today.'

* * *

When Anya entered the venue, Teofil waved from a table where he sat with a young man with jet-black hair.

'This is Tadeusz,' Teofil introduced him.

Anya sat down. Tadeusz did not smile but nodded her

way.

'I was expecting someone older,' Anya said to Tadeusz, who shrugged and lit a cigarette.

'I don't have time for small talk. What's this about?'

Anya and Teofil leaned in; the dim overhead bulb spread their shadows over the oilskin cloth.

'The Gestapo have arrested my husband and son. We need to get word to them. Can you help?'

Tadeusz snorted and gulped his tea. 'Why should we do that?' He glanced around the room.

Anya thrust out her hand and grasped his forearm. 'Because I have something I think you wouldn't want to fall into the wrong hands.'

'Anya!' Teofil said.

Tadeusz stared at them both and shook his head. 'Whose side are you on, lady?'

'My family's.'

'Clueless,' he said. 'And dangerous. What is it you think you have?'

He shook his arm free from Anya's grip. She grabbed her handbag from her lap, placed it on the table, opened and peered inside.

'Oh, I can't seem to find what I'm looking for in this dim light. Could you help me?'

She pushed her bag towards Tadeusz. He didn't move but stared at her. Anya's hand was in the bag; her fingers worked the notebook to the lip. She tilted it towards Tadeusz, who glanced down quickly and then shook his head.

'Don't you want to take a proper look?' Anya said.

'Not really. I know what it is and suggest you burn it as soon as you get home.'

He nodded to them both, stood up, stubbed out his cigarette, and left. The doorbell rattled behind him.

Anya covered her eyes with her hands. 'Oh, Teofil, what do I do now?'

'I really don't know. But we must get back home before curfew.'

The moon hung low in the early evening sky, throwing sparse light onto the bombed-out buildings of the invaded city. Some were destroyed and others skeletal in form—gaped, crumbled and collapsed.

Anya sped home. An open-topped truck rumbled by her, then stopped. She stared at the men, women, and children huddled inside against the frosty night. A soldier approached her from the gloom.

'Halt,' he shouted.

She stood motionless instantly.

'Show me your papers.'

In her mind's eye, Anya saw them lying on the table in the hallway. She opened her bag and peered inside as her legs shook.

'Well?'

'I've left them at home; it's just down there.' She pointed. 'Come with me to see.'

'Do I look stupid?' He prodded her in the stomach with his rifle. 'Get in the truck.'

# Elouna

Dawn's light at the curtain's edge woke Elouna from a fitful sleep in the school sick bay. The previous day's events flashed through her mind, and she sat bolt upright to peer through the gloom. She listened for sounds of movement, but everything was silent. The urge to run was so strong she crept to the door and opened it as quietly as possible. There was a faint light at the end of the corridor but no sign of anyone being up. Mr Krause had been kind, but Elouna's instincts were to get out and return home to her mother, who would surely be there by now.

A dog barked as she sneaked along the hallway towards the kitchen. She stopped in her tracks. A shaft of light fell across the hall, and Krause appeared in his dressing gown and slippers.

'Good morning. Is everything alright?' he asked, hurrying towards her.

'Yes, Mr Krause, I'm looking for the bathroom.'

He caught up with her and grabbed her elbow to turn her in the opposite direction. 'The staff use this one,' Krause said as he pointed to a signed door.

Elouna stood her ground and forced a smile. 'Oh, Mr Krause, would you be able to phone my mother to tell her I'm on my way home? She will be so worried about where I am. I don't know why I didn't think to ask last night.'

'Well, it's very early, but I'll do that.'

He let go of her elbow and watched as she opened the bathroom door and entered. There was a sink, two lavatory cubicles, and a tiny top window frosted on the inside and far too small to squeeze through. The water taps were frozen. A thin sheet of ice layered the base of the sink. Elouna leaned down and rested her forehead against the sink's chilled edge to energise herself. She did not want to leave the bathroom until Krause confirmed he had spoken to her mother, so she pushed open a cubicle and sat down.

When the cook appeared, Elouna looked up from her thoughts. 'Oh, there you are. Mr Krause has contacted your mother, who is on her way. Do come and have a bite of breakfast while you wait.'

Elouna stood up and thanked her, following her into the kitchen. The first face she saw as the door opened was Krause's. He smiled with an air of satisfaction, then turned to two men standing off his right side.

'Miss Kozynska,' one said. 'We're here to take you to your mother.'

Roman and his father, along with other people captured, were driven to a building in central Warsaw reminiscent of a fortress to Roman's eyes. It was the Gestapo prison, Pawiak. The truck lurched into the courtyard and grunted to a stop.

'Don't be frightened, Roman,' Ludwig said, patting his shoulder.

A guard clambered into the truck, stood with his hands on his hips, and ordered them out. He herded the straggly group into the building. A bored-looking official took names and addresses; his desk was in front of a tall filing cabinet. The men marched up two flights of steps into a corridor of cells prodded by guards behind them.

'Halt!'

They clustered in front of the bars of a dismal cell that stank of urine and unwashed bodies. Roman glanced at Ludwig, looking for an answer.

'Why are we here?'

'It's a mistake. We'll be home in no time.'

A guard stepped in front of the men, pulled keys from his belt, and unlocked the cell.

'In you go.' He stood back, holding his rifle up.

The cell door slammed as the occupants bunched together. Ludwig pulled Roman close as they jostled through. A gaunt older man pressed against a damp wall and slid down slowly to sit and cradle his knees with his elbows. He beckoned to Roman, who looked at him quizzically. Roman glanced at his father, who nodded okay.

Roman bent low. The man shot out his skeletal hand and grabbed Roman's collar to pull him nearer.

'I'm done this time,' he said.

Roman saw defeat flash in his face, but then a slight spark lit his eyes.

'But you're not. Listen carefully.' His stare was so intense Roman was mesmerised. 'If you get to the bathhouse, a boarded section in the wall leads to a door that goes straight out to the street.'

'The bathhouse?' Roman repeated.

'Believe me, it's there,' the man said, then let go of Roman.

Hours passed, and Roman calculated it must be around midnight when a guard dragged the first occupant from the cell, wild-eyed. Incredibly, men dozed for a few minutes at a time, standing upright, their heads nodded to their chest. Ludwig encouraged Roman to rest his head on his shoulder to snatch some sleep. He dozed mere seconds before being startled awake by a gun-wielding guard who hauled Ludwig away.

'No!' Roman cried out.

A man whose face pressed close to Roman's shook his head. 'Don't protest, lad.'

Roman caught a whiff of his breath, like fetid rollmop. He glanced at the man's filth-encrusted nails that momentarily grasped his sleeve, guessing he was captive somewhere else for some time before here.

A slice of light cut through a high narrow window of the corridor at dawn as the sound of rapid footsteps approached. The cell door rattled open. An official with a long thin chin stared at the occupants. Roman tried to control his trembling legs with difficulty.

'You!' The man pointed his finger at him. 'Follow me.'

Roman pushed through the mass of bodies, his head light from hunger. One prisoner with an open wound on his forehead flashed him a look of pity. Roman wanted to drag his feet, but the official hurried him down uneven steps and into a basement complex full of unfamiliar sounds. Eventually, he halted and rapped on a door.

'Come!' a voice called out.

Inside the room, an overweight, balding man squinted at Roman. 'Sit!' He nodded to a chair in front of his desk.

Roman obeyed.

'Do you know why you're here?'

'No. No, sir.'

'Lieutenant Klunesberg, to you.'

'No, Lieutenant Klunesberg.'

Roman's legs jittered against the chair. He leant forward to bear his weight down on his knees to contain his fear.

'Your father, Ludwig Kozynski, is a traitor. Do you know what happens to traitors?'

Roman shook his head. He squeezed his eyes to force back tears that pricked there. Klunesberg pressed his fat lips together and gestured with a flick of his hand.

'We hang them.'

Tears leaked down Roman's cheeks.

'However, your father is a respectable man, I hear. But he associates with some bad apples.'

Klunesberg splayed his meaty hands on his desk, stood

up, walked around to Roman, and rested his hand on a shoulder. He leaned in. He reeked of alcohol.

'Do you know the names of your father's friends, those fools who aim to ruin our progress?'

The weight on Roman's shoulder increased as Klunesberg pressed down.

'I don't know anyone; nobody visits us these days.'

Klunesberg retracted his hand from Roman's shoulder and smacked the soft part of his temple with force. Roman rocked sideways in his chair.

'So, you want your father to die?'

'No, no! I don't know what you're talking about.'

Roman looked up as Klunesberg strode to his side of the desk. He slowly removed a gun from his holster and rested it on the glossy surface.

'Don't be a hero, young man. No one will remember you.'

'I don't understand.' Trembling, Roman wiped his wet cheeks with his sleeve.

Klunesberg reached for the gun, clicked it open, and peered into the barrel.

'Hmmm,' he said. 'Do you think it's loaded?'

'I don't know, Lieutenant Klunesberg.' Roman's voice cracked, but he maintained eye contact.

'We'll soon see. Let's pay a visit to your father.'

Klunesberg grabbed his phone, and a guard appeared to escort them to a basement cell within minutes. The heavy cell door opened with a bang. Klunesberg entered first. Then the guard pushed Roman forward because he hesitated at the entrance. Roman lurched and crashed into a bucket that clattered on its side. The rank contents spewed onto the floor where Ludwig sprawled, eyes closed—one was grotesquely swollen and bruising. Fragments of what looked like teeth were scattered over the floor.

'Papa!'

The guard yanked Roman's arm to hold him back. Roman yelped.

'Wake him up,' said Klunesberg.

The guard released Roman's arm and shoved him away. Hovering over Ludwig, he kicked at his ribcage. Ludwig groaned and rolled slightly to one side. He attempted to open his eyes, but only one obeyed.

Ludwig peered through the puffed slit. 'Roman.' His voice muffled through swollen lips.

Roman lurched towards his father, but the guard threw his arm out as a block.

'Let the boy go,' said Klunesberg.

Roman fell to his knees by his father's side. 'I'm here, Papa.'

He stretched his arm to touch his father's face, but the guard struck Roman with his rifle butt.

'It's time to talk about your friends in the Polish Underground, Kozynski,' said Klunesberg.

Ludwig raised his head from the floor, his voice thick. 'I know nothing about them. I've told you already.'

Ludwig tried to lift the rest of his body but cried in pain; he wrapped an arm around his ribs.

'You must think I am a fool who would swallow your lies like little sweeties handed to children.' Klunesberg turned and paced the floor. Roman watched his father watching Klunesberg. 'Kozynski, you know full well I will kill you soon. However, before that pleasure, I have a little surprise for you.'

Ludwig mumbled, 'I want no more.'

'Oh, you'll like this one.'

Klunesberg shot a look at the guard and nodded. He turned and exited the cell. The clack of his boots echoed down the corridor. A rat darted across the floor and vanished into the dank brickwork. Roman shuddered.

The only sound in the cell was Ludwig's ragged breath, magnified in Roman's ears. The click-clack of footsteps returned, and the door swung back. A shadow fell on the floor, cast by the dim corridor light.

'Here's your surprise, Kozynski.'

Klunesberg lifted his chin in the air and looked pleased with himself.

'Come!' he said.

Roman wanted to squeeze his eyes shut as someone staggered inside the cell, but he couldn't.

'Remove the hood,' Klunesberg said.

The guard obliged.

'God! No!' Ludwig cried.

'Papa!'

Elouna stumbled towards him. The guard leapt forward and smacked her in the forehead with his rifle butt. Elouna wobbled but remained upright. A trickle of blood ran from her hairline.

'Still don't want to talk, Kozynski?'

Klunesberg loomed over Ludwig, prone on the floor.

He drew his pistol and pointed it at Elouna's head.

'Please, let her go.' Ludwig's voice broke.

Klunesberg circled Elouna, waving the gun. 'She's lovely, your daughter. Yes?'

Elouna let out tiny sobs, her shoulders raised to protect herself.

'I could change that easily,' Klunesberg said with a sneer as he stroked Elouna's cheek with his gun.

Roman could not speak or hardly breathe as he watched.

'But maybe before I do, the guard here may not control his natural urges.'

Elouna slumped to her knees and lowered her head of disarrayed curls. Ludwig let out a furious roar that ricocheted off the walls.

'Elouna, Roman, I love you so much.'

'Very touching,' Klunesberg said. 'But I want to get home for supper.' He moved his pistol away from Elouna's face and swung it at Ludwig.

'Yes, yes, shoot me but leave my children alone, please, please. I beg you.'

Klunesberg sighed and slipped his pistol away. 'I'm tired and hungry now,' he said. 'That's enough for today.'

He marched from the cell. The guard shoved Elouna and Roman out of the door and slammed it shut.

Later that night, Roman strained on tiptoes to peer from the tiny window of his single cell. Down in the courtyard, a group of men jostled in a jagged line. They shivered and coughed. His heart leapt at the sight of his father amongst them, who bent forward, clutching his ribs with both arms. An army truck bumped through the archway and stopped. A soldier jumped down to the cobbles and glanced at the line of male prisoners. He spat on the floor.

'In the truck. Now,' the guard bellowed.

Roman glanced to the sky where the stars were so far away. The men shuffled to the truck; their breath misted in the freezing night air.

The truck arrived at the Gestapo prison at eight o'clock in the evening. Most of the people packed inside it whispered only amongst their group, avoiding exchanging information with the others. Who could be trusted? Anya thought it a sad gathering that comprised families and single men. She was the sole woman. A family wearing pyjamas underneath their coats caught her attention. She tried to imagine why they could not dress before being taken from their home. The mother pressed her two children to her stomach, her open coat wrapped around them. The father comforted a baby whose cries he muffled with a knitted shawl. What could this family have done to deserve such treatment? But a soldier interrupted Anya's thoughts, shouting orders to get out of the vehicle and follow him.

Inside the building, they were hustled up steps and into a cell with a barred front. Anya consoled herself she was in the same place as Ludwig and Roman, if Teofil's news was correct because there was only one Gestapo Headquarters in Warsaw. When the cell door banged shut, the new occupants huddled in their groups, avoiding eye contact. There was sufficient space for Anya to sit on the filthy floor; she fought her anger, slid down, and rested her back against the wall to close her eyes. The chill seeped from the dank floor and penetrated her coat to the marrow of her bones as she slept fitfully.

In the morning, she lifted herself from the stone floor with stiffened hips and brushed through her hair with grubby fingertips. Anya spat on a handkerchief and dabbed the corners of her eyes and mouth to freshen up. Everyone in the cell was awake, and the tension was palpable when someone entered the corridor.

'Anya Kozynska!'

A guard unlocked the cell. She stepped forward, easing past a woman and her whimpering baby, who was probably hungry. She wished she had something to offer, but the days of stashed treats were gone.

They marched her to the office of Colonel Schutt and ordered her to sit. Anya met Schutt's stare as the sound of the guard's footsteps faded into absolute silence. The stillness of the office intensified Anya's rapid heartbeat, which she tried to control with long intakes of oxygen. Anya hoped they were not as audible to him as they were to her. Colonel Schutt's glacial grey eyes seemed to penetrate her thoughts, and she was sure he could read them whirling around in her brain.

How long would it be before the notebook in her confiscated bag was discovered by his men? Even worse, how could she explain it?

Anya looked for a point in the room to fix her gaze on and keep control of her emotions for what might come next. As much as she ached to know what happened to Ludwig and Roman, she was simultaneously terrified harm might have come to them, and dread rose in her chest at what Schutt would say.

'You've had an interesting three days, Frau Kozynska,' Schutt said.

He stared at her, exaggeratedly examining his

manicured nails under the desk lamp. Schutt waited for a reply she did not give. A corner of his mouth twitched.

'Let me refresh your memory. Three days ago, we arrested your husband and son.' He glanced at a document on his desk, then back at her. 'Last night, we arrested you.' Schutt raised an eyebrow. 'Who do you think we arrested two days ago?

Her voice quivered as she answered. 'I do not know.'

Schutt snorted and flicked a fly from his desk with a glove. 'Really, is that so?'

He lifted the phone and spoke rapidly in German. Time slowed and appeared to stop as Anya and Schutt stared at one another. They waited for the knock on the door. It opened, and Elouna appeared around it with dishevelled hair and a ripped dress.

'Elouna!'

Anya blurted out before she erupted into tears and stood up from her seat to throw her arms around her daughter, who stumbled forwards and burst into tears. The two hugged each other, absorbing each other's sobs in a rocking motion.

'How nice to be reunited,' Schutt said. 'Guard, bring two glasses of water for the ladies.' The guard disappeared as Schutt said, 'Sit down, both of you.'

They obeyed him instantly and glanced at each other to comprehend the situation.

'Let me clarify for your benefit. I am in charge of all inmates here. There are many types, but most are political prisoners.' He paused and looked from one to the other, an eyebrow arched. 'It's my job to decide who leaves and who stays.' He nodded at Anya, then Elouna. 'And, who is transported to one of our labour camps. Do you understand me?'

They exchanged glances. Anya answered for both of them. 'Yes, Colonel Schutt. We understand.' She reached out for Elouna's hand.

Schutt observed the gesture and continued. 'My position does not mean I always approve of my colleagues' actions towards inmates. And I hope you, Elouna, have been treated properly in the short time you've been here.' Schutt turned his stare to Anya. 'Your daughter and I met earlier.' She held her breath, anticipating words she did not want to fall from his thin lips. 'We went to see your husband, Ludwig. And your son, Roman.'

Anya let out a gasp. 'Oh, dear God,' she said.

He leaned back and placed his hands behind his head. 'As I have been saying, I have discretion in how matters turn out.' He paused again as he watched Elouna, who recoiled in her seat. Schutt then addressed her directly. 'Elouna, my wife is unfortunately unable to care for our children.' Schutt smiled briefly at Anya. He continued, 'I have decided you will be their nanny.'

Anya jolted forward, she tried to stand, but Schutt held his hand up to her, shook his head.

*What is he up to*? Anya thought.

Elouna was too stunned to move.

Schutt's grey eyes shone like polished steel as he looked directly at Anya. 'Isn't that a favourable arrangement Mrs Kozynska?'

The door opened, and a guard entered with a jug of

water and two glasses. Elouna and Anya shot looks at one another before Anya broke the spell.

'That's a very kind offer, Colonel Schutt.' Her voice wavered, but she kept her nerve. 'But Elouna is not skilled in that area; she is training to be a musician.'

Schutt unclasped his hands and brought them down on the desk with a thump. 'Perhaps you are not clear, Mrs Kozynska; she will be whatever I say she will be, which could include dangling from the prison rafters.'

Anya leaned to squeeze Elouna's hand, her eyes wild. How could this be happening? 'But, what of Roman and Ludwig?' She turned to Schutt. 'Can you help them, too?'

He snorted. 'Trying to take advantage of my generosity?' Schutt's phone rang. He grabbed it and listened. 'Very well. Bring it here.'

A few minutes later, Schutt held the notebook from Anya's bag, reached for his gold-rimmed spectacles, and opened it. He scanned the contents and sat back, waving it in the air.

'We found this in your bag, Mrs Kozynska. Would you explain?'

Anya let go of Elouna's hand and moved to the seat edge. 'I don't know what it is. I've never seen it before.' She clasped her hands to her cheeks.

'Maybe your daughter knows what it is?'

'No, she doesn't.'

'Where had you been yesterday evening when we arrested you, Mrs Kozynska?'

She had to consider how much they knew of her movements. Would an outright lie make things worse? She decided on a half-truth.

'I met my brother, Teofil in a café. We were trying to find information about Roman and Ludwig.'

'But I hear there was a third person with you?'

'We met someone who said they knew their whereabouts, but it was a mistaken identity.'

'Really. Who was this man?'

Anya's brow prickled with sweat. 'I don't know, but he must have slipped that into my bag.'

She pointed at the notebook Schutt held between his finger and thumb as he rested his elbow on the desk. He brought his hand to lay it down. He stared at the book for a minute, then raised his head. The light glinted on his glasses.

'Well, that's a ridiculous story. I know very well this is a coded list.'

Anya shrugged. 'I don't know...'

Schutt cut in. 'We'll break the code. It's just a matter of time. But my guess is this belongs to your husband, and you would be a wise woman to say so.'

Anya said nothing. Elouna stared between Anya and Schutt; tears trickled from her eyelids and tracked down her dirt-smudged cheeks.

'We know he has dealings with the Polish Underground. Maybe you didn't?'

Anya fell silent.

'Very well. You will return to your cells while I decide what to do.' Schutt grabbed his phone.

# Roman

Roman's heart was heavy that morning as he trailed along with the group of prisoners. A miserable two weeks had gone by, and he had no way of knowing what happened to his father after he saw him bundled into a truck. He prayed his mother and Elouna were safe somewhere, because of rumours from the other prisoners the Germans would send the fitter amongst them to labour camps. Roman wondered which was worse for himself: starving in Pawiak, doing menial tasks, or the same elsewhere. He didn't know what a labour camp was. Few people did, so it was frightening.

The guard stopped outside the bathhouse. 'Halt! We'll keep you vermin free if nothing else.' He stared at the men and twisted his face into a grimace as he waved his gun at the entrance. 'You stink. In here. Undress, shower, re-dress, and out in five minutes.'

Roman's thoughts raced; the old prisoners' words about a panel in the bathhouse flashed in his memory. Here was his chance. Inside the bathhouse adrenaline pumped through him as he pushed through the group to tap on the walls while the others unpeeled their filthy clothes from reeking bodies. Roman's heartbeat pulsed at the base of his throat. He pushed at the panel, and it gave way. He crouched down to squeeze through.

Roman shielded his eyes from the sunlight, blinded after his confinement in prison. He desperately wanted to check over his shoulder as he hurried away from the prison and past the nearby new Ghetto wall. The street he was in ran alongside the walls and was busy with people out doing their daily business. Roman did not stand out in the crowd. One or two passers-by glanced at him, but everybody kept themselves to themselves these days in Warsaw. In Pawiak, prisoners wore everyday clothes. Roman appeared like any other young man dressed reasonably well, if not a little crumpled, on his way somewhere. The impulse to break into a run was so strong he muttered out loud.

Trams rattled along the main streets, and horses and carriages clopped on their way to the central market in full swing. Couples walked arm-in-arm, and Roman realised it was an ordinary day. He considered his options, which were by now limited in the extreme. Someone might spot him if he tried to return to his family apartment. As a family arrested by the Gestapo, neighbours who would fear for themselves, would ostracise them. Even at only fourteen, Roman had seen this happen to friends. He crossed the street parallel to the road where their apartment stood. Roman risked walking down the opposite side of the road to look up at the windows to see if the apartment was empty. He didn't yet know what he would do if it were but propelled by curiosity as potent as fear Roman took a chance.

As he neared their apartment block, everything slowed down, and his feet seemed to move as though pulled through deep, wet sand. He could feel his heart pound in his chest, hear the blood that pulsed inside his eardrums, and as a car passed him, it slowed down to less than walking speed. The window cranked open. Roman glanced through the corner of his eyes, afraid of what might be beside him.

A large grey saloon purred along.

'Excuse me,' a man's voice said. 'Can you tell me where the market is? I seem to have lost my way.'

Roman stopped in his tracks and turned to face the speaker. An elderly gentleman and his silver-haired wife sat inside the car, smiling at Roman, who felt his whole-body tremble. He gave them directions in a shaky voice. As he did so Roman spotted movement in his family home across the street. Two uniformed silhouettes were at the drawing-room window. Roman knew then his house had gone. The elderly couple thanked him and drove off. Although Roman's legs threatened to buckle at any moment, he rushed past his home and turned into a windy corner to make his way to Uncle Teofil's.

Teofil opened his front door a fraction and jumped back when he saw who it was.

'Come in, quickly,' he said. Reaching a hand out to pull Roman forcibly through the entrance.

When inside with the door locked and bolted, Teofil leaned back on the wall, exhaled noisily and wiped his brow with a sleeve. He stared at Roman with tear-clouded eyes.

'Dear God, you're safe. I can't believe it.'

He hugged Roman so fiercely he expected his ribs to crack. They made their way to the drawing room where Teofil poured out two large brandies and motioned Roman to sit on the leather sofa.

He handed a glass to Roman and asked, 'Does anyone know you're here?'

Roman shook his head and took a swig of the brandy

that instantly burned his gullet. He fanned his mouth. Teofil smiled briefly, then went to throw more fuel on the fire.

'Tell me what happened,' he said and returned to sit next to him.

Roman felt his cheeks flush from the brandy and his body relaxed. Teofil got up from the sofa as Roman spoke, peered out of the window, then drew the curtains even though it was still daylight.

'I'm afraid I don't know where your mother is right now, but I do know you're not safe in Warsaw. I must get you out as quickly as possible.

Roman reeled in his seat, wide-eyed. 'But, Uncle Teofil, how can we leave Warsaw?'

Teofil's face clouded. 'Roman, Roman, how it breaks my heart to tell you that I can't come with you.'

Roman's body went rigid.

'You must go alone,' Teofil said.

'Alone? Where must I go? I want to stay here with you until Mama, Papa, and Elouna come back.' His face contorted with confusion. 'I can hide in your back room. No one will know I'm here.'

Teofil shook his head, his face flooded with anguish. 'It's not safe. The grocer would notice if I bought more food than usual. Someone would see or hear you. I no longer know who to trust.'

Tears sprang to Roman's eyes, but he wiped them away with the back of his hand and straightened himself up on the sofa. They both sat silently for a while.

Teofil took Roman's hands in his. 'I promise you will

be safe. Some people I know can get you papers.'

'Papers?' Roman repeated.

'Yes, Roman, identity papers. We will change your name, and you'll be able to escape from Warsaw.'

Roman stared at his feet as his chin quivered. Warsaw was his home, and even though the Germans occupied it, he never thought he would have to leave.

'It costs money,' Teofil said. 'But I have it, and I know your mother and father would want you safe.'

'Would?' Roman said. 'Do you know where they are? I saw the Germans take Father away.'

Teofil passed a hand over his face. 'Roman, I don't know…' his words trailed off.

Roman saw the anxiety that twisted his uncle's expression. His world had cracked down the centre again.

'Don't send me too far away, please.'

Teofil pulled him close. 'No. I won't. We have relatives in Krakow, and they'll take you in. I promise.' Teofil gently cupped Roman's chin. 'This war can't go on forever, and then we'll all be back together.'

Elouna stared at the three-story townhouse as Colonel Schutt's driver pulled up at the kerb. She had known the previous owners, the Kauffman's, who traded diamonds and heard how the Germans bundled them into a truck bound for the old town to live with many other Jewish families in the newly created Ghetto so they could confiscate their home and valuable belongings.

Schutt turned around in his seat to stare at Elouna, bunched in the car's corner, grasping her knees.

'Don't be scared, little mouse,' he said. 'You will enjoy living here.' He motioned with a gloved hand to what lay beyond the window. 'Out you get. quickly,' he said, then laughed as Elouna pulled the door lever with a trembling hand.

It was a freezing night, and Elouna was glad Schutt provided her with a soldier's coat to cover her torn, grubby dress. He also produced some shoes. She forced herself not to wonder from where they came. Elouna could hear her father's voice, admonishing her for being grateful to a Nazi for something. As she followed Schutt into the house, she realised it was possible to hate and be thankful to someone simultaneously. Elouna knew her moral landscape had shifted and self-control would be critical to her survival. She felt her old self sprout an armour that needed to be worn at all times to conceal her true feelings. She was learning to survive in a hostile world.

A stout, short woman appeared in the hallway to receive Schutt's hat and coat.

‘This is Hilda,’ he said. ‘My housekeeper.’

She glanced up and down at Elouna, who straightened herself to stand as tall as possible.

The woman let out a small grunt-like humph and snapped, ‘Follow me,’ as she jerked her head at Elouna. She was nimbler than she appeared and climbed the two flights of stairs rapidly, stopping at a door that she yanked open, sneering. ‘Undress and wash.’ She pushed Elouna into the bathroom, followed her and grabbed her by the shoulders to look Elouna up and down once more. ‘I’ll bring you some clean clothes,’ she said, then stomped from the room.

Elouna’s head spun from confusion as she stood in the bathroom, worrying about what would happen next. Her hands trembled as she splashed cold water onto her face, glancing into the art déco mirror above the marble washbasin. Elouna’s face had drained of colour. Her stare fell to the black and white floor that was overpowering her senses. She felt sick. Although she wanted to shut her eyes to rest, she peeled off her ripped stockings and ran water into the roll-top bath. Its tumble echoed around the room as she stepped out of her slip and shivered.

A knock on the door made her jump.

‘Hello,’ she said.

‘It’s Hilda with your clothes.’

Elouna covered herself with her dress and opened the door to find a bundle of clothes, together with some shoes, placed on the floor. As she bent to pick them up, she heard footsteps clattering in the hall below and prayed they were Hilda’s and not Schutt’s.

He had not made his intentions clear, but Elouna found it improbable he wanted her to look after his children, who she had not yet heard or seen. She did not believe her mother consented to this as Schutt suggested, then scolded herself for the naïve thought her mother, or herself, had any choice. Schutt struck Elouna as someone who glossed over a ruthless nature with a veneer of politeness. Everything about him made her flesh creep.

After her bath, she slipped into the pleated skirt and plain white blouse. Hilda had guessed her size well. The lace-up shoes too fit comfortably. The outfit was simple and functional, and Elouna felt calmed by this. Perhaps she was to be a nanny, after all? But she could not tamp down the sense of dread that crept over her when Schutt peered at her through his steely grey eyes.

Hilda soon returned for Elouna's old clothes and ushered her downstairs into the dining room. Schutt was at a table laid for two.

'Sit down.'

Elouna fidgeted for a second, then slid into the chair opposite his; she folded her hands in her lap and raised her head to meet his stare.

'As you will look after my children, I wish to know a little about you.' He motioned to Hilda. 'Bring the first course.'

She performed a little bow and exited the room.

'Do you want children of your own?' Schutt stared at Elouna.

*Is this a trick?*

'Yes, when I'm a little older.' Her face flared at having

to talk about the subject with a stranger.

'It's good to have them when you are young, at your peak.' Schutt motioned towards her. 'As you are now.'

She nodded mechanically.

'You are musical, I believe your mother said?'

'Yes. I play the piano.'

Schutt leaned forwards. 'I see but my children are not musical, nor am I so there will be no music lessons here.'

Elouna flinched and looked away from Schutt. 'Colonel Schutt, you must tell me what my duties will be.'

Schutt raised an eyebrow and snorted.

Hilda brought in the first course of borscht and set it down. Elouna stared, her mouth bone dry.

'Eat!'

Schutt watched her as she dipped her spoon into the steaming liquid. Her hand trembled a little as she guided it to her mouth.

After a few spoonfuls Elouna said, 'How old are your children Colonel Schutt?'

'Four and six. Friedrich and Greta.' Schutt plunged his spoon into his bowl clanking it on the side. 'Excellent soup,' he said, smacking his lips.

After which they consumed their soup in silence until Elouna asked, 'Excuse me, but where is their mother?'

'Ah! Their mother.' Schutt pursed his mouth. 'She is in hospital. Unwell.'

'Oh, I'm sorry to hear that. Will she be there long?' Elouna looked down, afraid she had given herself away to Schutt.

'You want to go home already?' He pushed his bowl

aside and wiped his mouth with a napkin. The red stain made Elouna feel nauseous. She could feel tears pricking her eyes. 'Why do you assume you have a home to go to?'

Schutt crossed his arms and sat back from the table.

Hilda returned to collect the bowls. 'Are you ready for the main course, Colonel Schutt?'

He nodded, not taking his gaze away from Elouna, who pretended to cough so she could put her head down to hide her expression that was hard to control.

'So, you think your family is alive still?' Schutt reached for his glass of wine and sipped it.

Elouna fought with all her might to remain calm and not cry. In a tiny voice, she said, 'I hope they are.'

Hilda brought the food in and set a plate full in front of Elouna, who stared at the roast chicken dish; its sight stirred no appetite even though she had not eaten since the previous day.

'Eat!' Schutt said and tackled his meal with relish.

Elouna pushed her food around the plate and placed a small amount in her mouth. She chewed methodically, praying her suppressed appetite would return, but it did not. Elouna picked at her plate. Schutt continued to ravage his supper, slurping wine in between and becoming noticeably drunk.

'By the way, I've sent for your records.' He clattered his cutlery down on the sides of his China plate.

'What records?'

'Ha! You know very well what I mean. You are a beautiful young woman indeed, but you have certain features. And I wonder about your racial purity.'

‘My family are Roman Catholics from Poland,’ Elouna said, astonishing herself.

‘Really? Do you know where your parents were born, or your grandparents?’

‘Yes, in a small village east of…’

Schutt interrupted her. ‘Don’t bore me or flatter yourself. I will find out in time’ He pushed his chair back and stood up. ‘Finish your meal, then go to bed. Hilda will show you to your room.’

He wobbled out of the room and left the door wide open. Elouna put down the knife and fork as tears glazed her vision. In her head, she heard her father advising, as he had when he taught her to dive. “Focus, don’t be scared. You can do it.”

Elouna pushed away her plate of hardly eaten food, wiped her face with her napkin and waited for Hilda.

The room she slept in was an attic with a steep, sloped roof, so to stand up in most of it was impossible. It made her feel like a caged creature. Elouna lay in bed, looking out of the tiny curtainless window. The freezing night sky was clear and pin-pricked with distant stars. As she sank into sleep, a noise roused her; the creak of someone stealing up the stairs to her room. Elouna tugged the bedclothes to her chin as the door opened, and Schutt leaned inside the frame, a harsh light behind him.

* * *

Schutt climbed out of Elouna’s bed and lounged on the edge smoking a cigarette. She prayed he would soon leave. As he stared distractedly blowing smoke rings into the air,

Elouna tried to slow her racing mind down. Maybe, she could sneak out and get to Uncle Teofil's when everyone in the house was asleep? It was a risk because of the curfew, but then Schutt interrupted her thoughts.

'Don't try to leave here.' He turned his head, and the wolfish light in his cold grey eyes set goosebumps all over Elouna's skin. Schutt leaned towards her and laid his meaty hand on the bed cover, patting her thigh beneath it. 'Think of your family.'

*How should I take that?* Elouna's thoughts tumbled. Schutt took his hand away, stood up, walked to the door, and then turned.

'Be a good girl, and all will be well.' He snorted. 'Hilda will give you your instructions tomorrow.'

Elouna listened to Schutt descend the stairs, the sound of his unsteady footsteps thudding on the landing below and the creak of a door opening were amplified. Her hurt over the previous days erupted as she folded into great shaking sobs and tried to muffle the noise with a pillow. Humiliation and shock burned inside her. When her anger subsided momentarily, she slid out of bed to creak open the tiny window to release the smell of stale brandy and Schutt's sweat from the room.

Much later, she lay exhausted in a trance-like calm, almost looking down at herself from above. She asked whether her life was ruined. Yes, no, maybe? She knew she needed to fix her thoughts on one thing, a trick her mother taught her. She had little use for this until recent events had altered her world forever. How much had changed in such little time was impossible to comprehend, but she knew she must keep ahead of things.

Schutt's comment about her family repeated in her mind until she finally sank into a fitful sleep. But now and then, she woke with a jolt, sure she could hear the snores of Schutt slumbering below, feeling he could somehow hear and see what she was doing and thinking even in his sleep. She was aware this could not be the case, that she must fight the idea of him being God-like, all-seeing, and knowing. Eventually, she drifted off just as the dawn crept along the horizon.

Later the sounds of clattering pans and voices woke Elouna. The smell of fried meat drifted up the stairs. The previous night's events flooded her mind, and she was sick with dread for the coming day. She slipped out of bed and dressed as quickly as possible. Just as she was trying to straighten her hair with her fingertips, there was a knock on the door. Hilda's face appeared.

Startled, Elouna greeted her first in Polish, then German.

'So, you speak German?' Hilda looked Elouna up and down with a set mouth.

'Yes, I studied it at school.'

Hilda raised her eyebrows and humphed in what Elouna recognised as her contemptuous manner. 'The day begins; follow me.' She ushered Elouna down worn oak stairs to the kitchen, where she pointed to a cook's table in the centre. 'Sit!'

Hilda brought bread and fried sausage and stood over, arms folded, as Elouna eyed her breakfast that looked appealing but its smell made her queasy.

'You will address me as Hilda. It's the colonel's wish.' Hilda did not look pleased. 'Your job is to occupy the children during the day. As for the evenings, well! I'm sure you know by now what your duties are.' Hilda smirked. Elouna stared at her but was unable to say anything.

'Did you not wonder how the clothes I gave you fitted so well?

She found her voice. 'No. I didn't.'

'He has a favoured type you know: size, shape, colouring. He's very particular about acquiring a new toy. But not so when discarding it.' Hilda stood motionless, her hands on hips, glaring at Elouna, who fell silent again.

'He's like a child playing on a rug, amusing himself until he becomes bored.'

Elouna's throat constricted, so she could barely breathe. 'I don't know what you are talking about,' she said.

Hilda continued, 'I've *always* been with him. Your sort comes and goes.'

Elouna blushed deeply then. She looked down at her hands bunched in her lap, white and shaky.

'Anyway, the children are your concern now. You'll give them breakfast, then take them to school.'

Hilda raised her chin and glared at Elouna. 'Do you understand?'

'Yes, but I…'

Elouna avoided confessing her ignorance; she would learn to rely on instincts and intuition as she went along.

'But what?'

'Nothing.'

'Very good. You need a hairbrush, toothbrush, and so

on.'

Elouna pushed the plate away as she thanked Hilda.

'Don't thank me. Colonel Schutt expects his staff to be presentable.' She snorted. 'And that hair of yours is truly a disgrace.'

Hilda leaned in and snatched the plate from the table to Elouna's relief. Anxiety had robbed her appetite.

'Come with me.'

Hilda marched from the kitchen and into a nursery where two children sat playing. They looked up when Elouna entered; each said good morning in German and continued their game.

'Friedrich, Greta, this is your new nanny, Elouna; she will care for you.'

Hilda stood motionless and stared at Elouna, who realised it was her task to usher the children out.

'Where's the breakfast room?'

Hilda shook her head. 'Clueless. Follow me.'

She hurried into another room off the hallway. The children rushed to their chairs, wriggled onto them, and piled their plates from the food set out.

'Friedrich will overeat. Watch him, or he will be sick in the car.'

'The car?'

'The chauffeur will collect you at nine. And when you've dropped the children off, he'll drive you to the central market. Buy these for me.' From her pocket Hilda handed Elouna a shopping list written in German.

'And, don't let those Polish thieves steal your money. Barter with them.'

When the children were ready, they sat waiting for their driver in the hallway. A middle-aged man wearing a chauffeur's uniform appeared in the hallway at nine.

He lifted his cap to Elouna. 'I'm Hans, and you are?'

'Elouna.'

The children slid off their seats and rushed to the door. Hans opened it wide. They scrambled out and ran down the few steps to the car. Hans limped out.

'War wound,' he said over his shoulder.

Elouna wondered which war he meant.

The school was only a few blocks away, but Elouna guessed the children's father would not think them safe walking out in the Warsaw streets. As the car pulled up at a synagogue it was clear it had been converted into a school for the children of occupying Germans.

Hans told Elouna to take the children inside. As she passed through the entrance, she looked for doors as potential escape routes but remembered Schutt's veiled threats about her mother. Elouna needed a better plan and more time. She knew that much.

At the market, Hans carried her shopping bag as it filled up. One item on the list puzzled Elouna because she could not make out Hilda's handwriting. Elouna considered asking Hans but was afraid to trust him at that time. She was truly alone.

*Take it slowly,* she reminded herself.

Queuing for sugar, Elouna spotted a familiar frame near the front. She recognised the long neck and slightly protruding ears of Victor Zurek, a music teacher who had given her private lessons since the age of nine. Elouna stared hard at his back, willing him to sense her presence. The line shuffled forward; her heart beat faster. She glanced at Hans; afraid he would notice her change of mood to a slight excitability. Finally, Victor was served and turned to walk back down the shoppers' line. Elouna held her breath as he neared, and as Victor was parallel, she coughed. Victor looked up.

'Elouna!' Victor said.

She motioned to Hans, who was fiddling with the bag. Victor glanced at him, a little puzzled.

'Victor. What a surprise.'

'Yes!'

'I'm shopping for my new employer.' Elouna said in Polish. 'But how I miss my music lessons.'

'Oh, yes, of course, let's hope we can resume soon.' He lifted his hat to her, smiled and carried on walking.

* * *

After Elouna put the children to bed that evening, Hilda informed her she would dine with Schutt at eight. As she entered the dining room, Schutt was seated with a glass in his hand.

'Sit,' he said and watched her as she pulled out a chair.

'How was your day? Anything interesting to tell?' he said with a slight smile.

Elouna was silent; what should she say?

'Nothing at all?' he continued, reaching out to refill his glass from the crystal decanter. 'Hans tells me you had a conversation with a man at the market.'

Just then, Hilda came in with soups. As she set the

bowls down, she said to Schutt, 'The soup is missing paprika as Elouna forgot to buy some.' She glanced at Elouna. 'Isn't that so?'

Elouna remembered the item she could not decipher. 'I'm sorry, I meant to…' she trailed off.

'She was too busy chatting to a young gentleman,' Schutt said. He waved his hand over his bowl. 'Take it away. It's no good without paprika.'

Hilda smirked.

'So, who was this man, and what did you talk about?'

'Mr Zurek, he was my music teacher at home.'

'I see.'

*Think quickly,* Elouna admonished herself. 'He studied at the Berlin Music Conservatoire. And encouraged me to learn German, so I could study there later if I wished.'

'And do you?'

'Everything has changed now.' Elouna bowed her head.

'Yes, it has. You're here to keep me company and mind my children.' Schutt put his glass down, and his wolfish smile spread. 'My little filly.'

Hilda returned with the main course, a stew with dumplings.

As she put Elouna's plate down, Schutt said, 'Oh, that reminds me, I saw your mother today.'

Tears sprang to Elouna's eyes.

'Eat your meal.' Schutt motioned with his knife.

Elouna picked up her cutlery and sliced into a dumpling that puffed out steam. 'Where is she?'

'In prison. Didn't you realise I only took pity on you?'

Elouna tried to wipe the image of her incarcerated mother from her mind, but she could not.

'How is she?' She steadied her hand as she raised the fork to her mouth.

'Fine.'

They ate in silence until Elouna said, 'I wonder if I could write to her?'

Schutt studied Elouna for a while. 'Of course.' He continued to eat.

'Thank you.' Elouna let out a small sigh of relief.

'But you must write in German.'

'My mother doesn't speak German.'

'Not to worry, the prison guards can read it to her.'

Elouna nodded. 'Yes, yes, of course.'

Later, as she lay in bed hearing Schutt climb the stairs to her room, Elouna thought of Victor Zurek.

That night Elouna dreamt Victor rescued her from Schutt, and a sense of hope buoyed her into the next morning's duties. Hilda stood over a steaming pot of something she stirred, scraping the spoon along the pan bottom to make a grating sound. Elouna greeted her good morning and then grabbed bread and coffee from the table. Hilda didn't return the greeting but continued her task as Elouna watched clouds of steam spiral above Hilda's head and dissolve into the muggy kitchen air.

'Today, after you've taken the children to kindergarten, you're to collect some things from your parent's apartment,' Hilda said, still not turning to face Elouna. 'Hans will escort you.'

'What things?' Elouna said, then regretted questioning

Hilda when in one of her dark moods.

'I don't know. Hans will give you instructions. Now, hurry with your breakfast.'

Elouna gulped her bread down and rushed to tend to the children.

Greta stared sleepily from the covers as Elouna entered her room.

'My goodness, still in bed?'

Greta's room was warm and smelt slightly sweet. Elouna pulled the curtains back, and Greta whimpered as the light washed into the room.

'I don't want to go to school today. I want to stay with you.' She pushed her bottom lip out.

'Oh, dear!'

Elouna perched on the edge of Greta's bed. 'But you must go. Your father would be cross if he heard you say that.'

Greta sat up and rubbed her eyes with her knuckles as Elouna fetched her clothes from the wardrobe. She glanced at them and shook her head.

'I hate that dress. I won't wear it.' Greta threw herself back onto the pillows.

'But, it's a lovely dress.' Elouna watched Greta's lips tighten. Her chubby arms crossed over her chest as she lay stiffened. 'It makes you look so pretty. Like a princess.'

Elouna held the dress up and admired it.

Greta's eyes narrowed. 'Like a princess?' she repeated. 'But I want to look like a film star.'

Elouna fought the impulse to laugh. 'Well, film stars and princesses are alike.' She leaned over and took one of

Greta's hands. 'Your chauffeur will soon be here, and you don't want to miss breakfast, do you?'

Greta sat up, pushed back the bedclothes, threw Elouna a haughty look and flung out her stocky legs.

'Well, I care little for it, but I suppose I could wear it if you like.'

As Greta dressed, Elouna rushed to wake Friedrich, who was already up and playing with his green wooden train on his bedroom floor.

Later, when Hans entered the hallway to collect them, Elouna's hands broke out in a sweat. She examined his face for traces of emotion, something to give her an idea of how events might unfold on the trip to her family home. Hans greeted her and the children, making eye contact with them all as he smiled. She could detect nothing in his face.

'Off we go.' He raised his hat, and the children followed him to the door, elbowing one another to get ahead.

'Children, stop that,' Elouna chided, an edge in her voice.

As the car rounded the corner to the school, Elouna spotted a truck coming from the opposite direction. She turned to stare from the back window. The vehicle had no roof. Men, women, and children stood inside, swaying back and forth, in their coats and hats, layered against the cold winter day. She pushed the memory of her journey from her mind and looked away.

After leaving the children at the school entrance, Elouna desperately wanted to ask Hans if someone would be at the apartment when they arrived but she feared his reply. The car neared the avenue of townhouses and apartment blocks, interspersed with maple trees as people rushed about their business. Hans stopped the car, turned, and handed Elouna a list in handwriting with which she was unfamiliar. She would not have suspected a calligraphic style from Hilda, so it must be Schutt's.

'Here are the items Colonel Schutt wants you to collect.'

Elouna stared at the list, so nervous her eyes clouded, finding it hard to focus.

Coat, hat, dresses, blouses, skirts, underclothes, shoes, Bible.

'Don't run away,' Hans said.

Elouna wondered if that were a test or a hint, she could not work out Hans.

As she walked inside the building, she trembled so violently it was difficult to control her legs. *Just one flight of stairs,* she encouraged herself as she ascended.

Elouna's heart pounded as she turned the handle of their front door. It was unlocked. She pushed it open and stood on the threshold, looking into their apartment's hallway. Nothing was obviously out of place. The grandfather clock ticked loudly in the silence.

She took a deep breath and stepped inside, afraid to shut the door. As she tiptoed past the drawing room, she glimpsed a photograph of her family on the mantelpiece and her heart filled with pain. Her knees buckled as she staggered to her room, where her case lay open and empty on the bed. That terrifying night flashed through her mind; hastily packing before the soldiers burst in to arrest them.

But someone had unpacked her suitcase. She thought of her mother and slumped to the bed, covering her face with her hands as Schutt's list fell to the floor.

Elouna's thoughts hurtled as she opened her wardrobe. Picking out clothes under Schutt's requirements must be some type of test to follow his instructions and not deviate.

Elouna packed in a frenzy, then rushed to her father's study and sat at his writing table. A car horn pipped from outside, but she ignored it. She scribbled a letter to Victor Zurek, sealed it in an envelope, and shoved it into her coat pocket. Then she ran to her parent's bedroom to collect her mother's Bible. There was a framed family photo lying on her mother's bedside. Elouna grabbed it, hurriedly removed the photo and shoved this in her other pocket. She gulped down the air to calm herself from the crushing sensation in her chest. The car horn pipped again. Elouna grabbed the Bible and her case and hurried down to Hans.

'Not run off then?' he said as she manoeuvred into the car. 'With my leg, I couldn't catch you if you did.'

Elouna smiled weakly at him but wondered if she had missed an opportunity.

Hilda bustled from the kitchen to greet them as they entered Schutt's house, a look of excitement on her face.

'Give me your coat,' she said, thrusting out her arm.

Elouna set her case down on the parquet floor and struggled out of her coat, handing it to Hilda, who whisked it away.

That evening, Elouna told the children the fairy story of the Baba Yaga, a witch who lived in the Polish woods and stole babies when she could. She checked they were asleep before she trudged to her room and flopped onto her bed feeling guilty for frightening them with the old folk tale. It was almost eight o'clock. She had better tidy herself up for dinner before Hilda summoned her. Little more than a week had passed, but already there was a suffocating routine in place. Elouna rose wearily to wash her face when Hilda knocked on the door and entered. Her gaze flashed around Elouna's room as though she were looking for something.

'Colonel Schutt will dine alone this evening. Your supper is in the kitchen. When you've finished, you'll join him in the drawing room.' Hilda stood; her arms folded triumphantly over her bulk. 'Have you unpacked?' She coughed exaggeratedly.

'Yes, thank you.'

'Colonel Schutt will want to approve your belongings.' She turned on her heels and marched off.

Down in the kitchen, Elouna poked at her supper of meatloaf. Tears prickled her eyes, but she blinked them away, willing herself to stay composed and think of her plan.

At nine o'clock, Hilda threw open the door. 'Colonel Schutt wants you to join him now.'

Tired and upset, Elouna slunk into the drawing room. Schutt sat beneath a cloud of cigar smoke, a glass of brandy at his side.

'Ah! My little filly, sit down.' He patted the space next to him.

Elouna glanced around and took an armchair opposite him.

‘I see!’ he said, sitting up to balance his cigar in a sumptuous ashtray with the figure of a half-clad girl rising from its side like Venus from her shell. ‘Strong-willed. I admire a spirited girl.’ He swirled his brandy and took a large mouthful. ‘Now you have some of your things, you will feel more at home here?’

‘Yes, thank you.’ Elouna’s voice cracked.

‘However!’

Schutt reached out for his cigar, rolled it between finger and thumb, and sniffed the smoke wisps. He reminded Elouna of a hunting dog with his heavy jowls. Schutt leaned forward and retrieved an envelope from behind his back, like a children’s magician. A look of triumph crossed his face.

‘Hilda found this in your coat.’ He waved it in the smoke-fogged air. ‘Perhaps you would like to read it to me?’

Elouna shook her head.

‘It’s in Polish.’ Schutt tugged the letter from its envelope and unfolded it ceremoniously. ‘Shall I begin?’

Elouna said nothing.

‘I can read Polish.’ He glanced at her, then began. ‘Dear Mr Zurek, meeting you reminded me of how much I miss piano lessons. Please call by one evening to ask Colonel Schutt’s permission to continue with my music lessons.’

Schutt sat bolt upright and stared at Elouna. His grey eyes flashed under the lamplight. ‘So, you would like to resume music lessons?’

‘Very much.’ Elouna paused. ‘There’s a piano here.’

She gestured to the grand Steinway placed in front of the window.

'I see. And when did you intend to ask my permission?' Schutt crossed his legs.

Elouna rose from her seat; her hands balled at her sides. 'At dinner tonight, if you'd invited me.' She stood still and met his stare while her knees threatened to give way.

'Really!' Schutt laughed. 'Very well, little one. I will invite your Mr Victor Zurek to discuss this matter. I have his address right here.' He tapped his index finger on the envelope's front. 'Are you happy now?'

Elouna swallowed hard, opened her mouth, and was amazed a voice came out. 'Yes, I am thrilled. Thank you.'

Schutt shifted in his chair and produced the photo Elouna had smuggled from her home that afternoon.

'Hilda also found this.'

Elouna breathed in audibly and looked him directly in the eye. 'Please, let me keep it. It's nothing.'

'Yes, you have a point,' he said. 'It's nothing. You may keep it.'

Schutt smiled and threw back the remains of his brandy in one gulp. 'Just one more thing. It would be best if you didn't feel lonely anymore. Tonight, your belongings will be moved to my bedroom.'

Elouna slumped back in her seat.

'Hilda has made a fire in there. She will show you up now.'

# PART TWO

## Roman 1945, Italy

The smoke-filled air had stung Roman's eyes. Wounded, he slithered down the Italian mountain where mortar shells continually blasted. Shrapnel ricocheted from the rocks and the putrid stench of rotting bodies stuck in his nostrils. He'd smacked into an upturned tank, where Ivan's body slumped halfway out of the obliterated turret, fire-blackened. Ivan could not scramble from the inferno. Roman lay nearby, helpless and trapped amongst the rats scurrying over the corpses, until finally, after many torturous hours, they discovered him. On a stretcher, they moved him agonisingly down the slippery mountainside.

He had been in hell under the Mediterranean sky, fighting alongside the Allies to defeat Germany's invasion of Italy. And despite the unrelenting brutality of his war experiences in Italy, Roman's heart was captivated by the country where, at the end of the war, he'd settled to convalesce with other servicemen while his leg healed from shrapnel wounds.

Now, standing waist-high in the warm ultramarine sea, watching fish swim around his calves with his feet sunken into the soft seafloor, he was grateful to be alive. He fantasised about staying in Italy as the sun poured on his skin, turning it honey-coloured; the heat, light, and mountains all conspired to reach deep inside him to heal the terrible sorrow. Sunshine was life, growth, and optimism. The balmy nights and croaking cicadas soothed him when he woke to shout out from nightmares that plunged him into the dark days of the destruction in his recent past.

Now, Roman sat on a wall of the military barracks in the afternoon sun; riposo time was over in Ancona, and people returned outdoors. In the distance, he could hear the rattle of trucks on the war-destroyed roads, and the squeals of children coming out to play from their homes that still stood amongst the rubble and ravages of war. The noise of disputes filled the afternoon air. They routinely broke out at the water pump as women clambered for water to wash and cook.

A group of Polish soldiers passed him by.

One nodded to him. 'Are you coming to the meeting, Roman?' he asked.

Their army boots raised dust clouds from the heat-baked path as they walked.

'Yes.'

Roman limped over to them and fell in with the group. Recently the British government circulated a pamphlet to the Polish troops outlining their options in the post-war world. A meeting was being held for them all to discuss the implications. Roman read it and remained confused and unsure of what to do.

It was late afternoon but still hot. Although the shutters in the meeting room were closed to keep the sun out, the air was heavy with heat. Perspiration gathered on Roman's brow and prickled at the back of his neck, dampening his shirt collar. He stared at Tadek who stood in front of the assembled men. Roman knew Tadek was a well-educated

Pole who fought in the fierce battle of Monte Cassino and survived. This made him a legend and someone to take seriously. Roman was relieved it was Tadek and not some other lackey nominated to speak to them about such an important matter.

Tadek called the room to order. When the men quieted, he held up the pamphlet about the Polish Resettlement Corps that invited the displaced soldiers to join up to find alternative places to live if they did not want to return home.

'I'm sure you've all read this?' He smiled wryly and waved the pamphlet in the air.

'Well, I've read it too and note although they have given us options, the British Government recommends as many as possible should consider returning home to Poland.'

The men muttered and shuffled in their seats.

'Who wants to go home?' Tadek said as he placed a hand on his hip.

A man sitting near the front shouted out, 'Our homeland was gobbled up by communist Russia; how can we trust those bastards if we go back?' He stood and turned to the men sitting behind him as he shook his fist in the air.

The men erupted into hoots of agreement, stamped their boots on the floor, and began talking amongst themselves.

Tadek held up a hand to quiet them. 'Silence, please. If you don't want to go home, the British have offered us…' he paused and emphasised the next words, 'the opportunity to enlist in a resettlement programme to go elsewhere.

Questions?'

'Yes!' cried a man. 'Why have we been betrayed? We fought with the British Allies. Won! Now they have turned their backs on us. The bastards have accepted the Russian government of Poland as legitimate.'

Tadek nodded gravely as the crowd cried out in agreement. 'Your question is rhetorical, my friend.' His expression concentrated. 'A great injustice has occurred, and we must ask ourselves why we fought when the outcome is we have no home to return to.' He glared at the angry crowd. 'But we have to decide where we want to live; we can't turn back the clock.'

A sallow-skinned man raised his arm. 'Me!' He thumped his chest. 'I'm too old to start again in another country. I still have family back home so I want to return, take my chances.' The man's spine curled into the back of his chair as if minimising his presence.

Roman watched members of the audience glance at the older man, shake their heads at their shared plight, young or old. Their country no longer belonged to them. They were homeless.

Roman's friend Andrej raised his hand. 'I've heard at home there are still midnight knocks on the door and disappearances of enemies of the state.' He emphasised his words.

The crowd murmured in agreement.

Tadek continued, 'Yes, I have heard this too. Many of us fought against the Red Army in Poland. It's too risky to return now. They'll hunt us down.'

Roman flicked through the pamphlet as he listened to

the speakers. The booklet continually spoke of The Polish Question. He didn't feel like a question or part of an equation; he felt like an uprooted shrub, blown by hurricanes from place to place, needing hospitable land to settle in and throw out roots.

'What do I have to go back to?' Roman said to Andrej after the meeting as they walked back to their barracks.

Andrej shrugged. 'What do any of us have?'

'We're fucked!' Roman said.

Andrej stopped and grabbed Roman's shoulder. 'Don't say that. Have you had any reply from the Red Cross about your mother?'

Roman stared over Andrej's head, watching a butterfly flitting from bush to bush, never settling in its brief life.

He sighed. 'Yes, they traced her to a refugee camp. I wrote to the address they sent, but I've received no reply.'

'But Roman, that's good news. A refugee camp means she's alive somewhere. Where was it?'

'Germany,' Roman said, standing still.

'Jesus!' Andrej stopped and patted Roman's shoulder. 'How did she end up there?'

Roman blew his cheeks out, and shook his head. 'My friend, your guess is as good as mine. The last time I saw her was 1940, in Poland before the arrest.'

'You must keep looking.' Andrej turned and scrutinised Roman. 'The world's a large place. Don't give up.'

'I won't but I'm afraid of what I will find.'

They were both silent for a while as they walked on. Roman's hands were in his trouser pockets, his head down.

Andrej broke the silence. 'So, where do you think you'll go now? We have to make up our minds soon.'

Roman sighed. 'Well, I've heard quite a few Poles are settling in England. Maybe that's where my mother is. You never know.'

'It's good to be hopeful,' Andrej said, and they continued in the evening air suffused with the aroma of baked pines.

'Roman, would you consider going to England?'

'I don't know. Maybe. But what if I do and my mother's somewhere else, across another continent?' Roman stopped and looked to the sky. 'If only I believed in God, I would ask him to help me.' He raised his arms in a pleading gesture.

'But you don't,' Andrej said, patting him on the back. 'Anyway, God has lots of people to help, his hands are full.'

'I don't believe in anything anymore, you know.' Roman said.

Andrej sighed.

'But I have the chance to study here. I could learn the language, get a job, meet a girl, get married.' Roman smiled at Andrej. 'Maybe I could open a delicatessen and sell Polish food for the likes of us?'

'Follow your heart,' Andrej said.

'Maybe I will.' Roman thumped Andrej's upper arm and smiled.

Andrej laughed. 'Okay, try this. Which language would you prefer to learn, English or Italian?'

'Andrej, I'm so tired. I'll choose the easiest one.'

As they walked under the shade of the tree-lined path,

groups of young women hurried by, laughing and chatting, some pushed bikes by their sides.

'You know Andrej, these Italian girls fascinate me. They are more beautiful than our Polish girls.'

Andrej chuckled. 'Is that so? Well, you know what Tadek said about your dalliances.' Andrej mimicked and wagged his finger at Roman. 'Your studies must come first, Roman. There's plenty of time for romance later.'

Roman guffawed. 'I love Tadek. He's right, of course, but it's hard to sit behind a desk and study dusty old books after all the troubles. I want to be out there, living life.'

'Can't you do both?' said Andrej, peering into Roman's face, half smiling.

Roman stood still again. 'But we never know what tomorrow will bring, do we?'

'No, we don't, but before the war, can you remember what made you happy?' Andrej grabbed Roman's arm and pulled him along the dusty road like a naughty child.

'It's too long ago. I was a boy, pleased by the simple things in life: swimming in the river, picnicking in the forest with Mama and grandma. But, now I'm a man. I've seen too much. I only know the sun warms my skin, and I forget the pain for a while. That's all.'

They walked on in silence, broken only by the cicada's chorus and the sound of church bells ringing in the square.

'What have you decided, Andrej? Where will you live?' Roman said.

'Roman, I watched from behind trees while the Nazis massacred my family for no reason. I escaped to the forest; a band of us hiding, training for combat against them, but they caught us. You know the rest.'

'Yes, I do, but you haven't answered my question. Where will you go next?'

'Somewhere with no memories. Canada tempts me, but it's too cold. Many other places on offer are hot, so perhaps I should join the Resettlement Corps and go to Great Britannia. I can help you look for your mother if you go there.' Andrej laughed and threw a hand dramatically in the air.

Roman grinned, released momentarily from the agony of choice that was no choice at all in reality.

He slapped Andrej's shoulder. 'We can live in the countryside, raise chickens and find wives who will have babies.'

Andrej snorted. 'No! I want a job in a city, no manual labour for me. I have an accountant qualification to finish, remember.'

Later, Roman lay on his bed and carefully took out the photo he had salvaged. Now bent, torn at one edge, and creased, it showed his mother and father standing in a bustling street in Warsaw in 1934—his mother was draped in her deerskin coat, and his father was dressed in his Polish officer's uniform. In a gloved hand, his father, Ludwig held a large leaf that had fallen from an oak tree. It must have been autumn when someone took the picture. His parents smiled warmly at the camera. It was peacetime then.

Roman wished he could go back in time and place, but he knew it was impossible. Before he closed his eyes, he tried to imagine what life in England would be like, but there were no images to gather. Only a tumultuous cold, grey sea he had decided he would cross with Andrej.

## Roman 1946, Cannon Hall Resettlement Camp, England

'Hey! Roman, stop daydreaming; come on outside, we need you.'

Roman looked up from the letter he was composing. He studied English before leaving Italy for England, but it was much more complicated than he'd imagined. His mastery of English was slow, but in this letter, his thoughts had to be unambiguous. Roman stuffed the notepad under his mattress, swung his legs off the bed, and grabbed his greatcoat. The fabric was cold to the touch, so he warmed himself in front of the small stove in the barrack and rubbed his hands under the rising heat before he ventured outside to help.

The winter was extreme and relentless. English people complained and shook their heads. Six-foot snowdrifts were an everyday sight—one of the worst winters on record, everyone repeated. Even Roman, who had endured freezing winters in Poland, thought it was harsh. There was never enough food to eat, warmth to soothe the bones, or clothing thick enough to withstand the temperature.

Outside the hut, the frozen air stung the inside of Roman's nose as he breathed in. He pulled his hat as far down his face as possible without obscuring his view. Fat snowflakes plopped on his woollen gloves and glistened. It had snowed for weeks; each layer fell, melted a little, then froze again through the cycle of the day to create a compacted mass that resisted the thrust of a shovel and bounced it back to his chest. On the camp grounds, young Poles shovelled snow from the blocked path so vehicles could pass through with supplies and the inhabitants could make their way to and from their huts. Some men in the detail had broken away to build a snowman.

'I'll join you later when I've done some proper work,' Roman quipped as he passed them to grab a shovel and join the group that had erupted into song as they swung snow-laden shovels over their shoulders.

The sky poured out snow as the light drained from the Yorkshire sky. The men's efforts quickly covered under the heavy drifts. Roman leaned on his shovel and stared across the landscape. The white-out, relieved only by outline humps of dry-stone walls and bare black trees, was alien to him. But he saw its strange beauty under the thick glittering blanket.

Finally, when the light melted away and they could do no more work, the men returned indoors, their faces reddened and their throats dried from the frosted air. They scattered to their beds, tugged off their heavy damp coats, and discussed what they would do that evening. It was Saturday night, after all.

'Andrej, lend me your Polish-English dictionary.' Roman stood by his friend's bed, arms folded around his muscular chest.

Andrej blew smoke rings into the air as he lay on his bed. 'What's the hurry?' he said. 'Aren't you coming to the dance with us tonight?'

Roman blushed. 'Yes, yes, but I want to do this first.'

Andrej sat upright and smacked his forehead. 'Of

course, what a nincompoop I am. It's for her, right?'

'It's for my English studies.' Roman stepped back. 'I want Sunday afternoon free, so I'm doing it now.'

'Why? What are you doing Sunday afternoon?'

Roman didn't reply to his friend. Andrej tossed some books from his bed to uncover the dictionary. 'You know, Roman, you're the best-looking guy here, even if you're not very tall.'

Roman snorted.

'So don't bust your balls over love letters. Just walk right up to her and ask her to dance.'

'Shush, will you?' Roman said.

Andrej jumped up and scrambled to Roman's bed. He fumbled under the mattress, pulled the notebook out, flicked it open, read a little, and grinned.

'Guys!' He waved it in the air. 'Roman's got it bad; want to hear this? '

Roman rushed him and grabbed the book.

'Only joking.' Andrej shoved it against Roman's chest. 'Let's go out, and you can talk to your dreamboat face-to-face. Forget your love letter.'

When Andrej and Roman arrived at the Saturday night dance, it was crammed with young men and women who Roman had learnt lived in hostels and camps in the area. All were immigrants. Some from Ireland sought a less restricted life in England, away from the church's eyes. Some were refugees from the war: Poles, Lithuanians, and Ukrainians. They all worked in northern England's nearby mills and factories. Many had escaped dark pasts, that few (like Roman) talked about.

Andrej went to queue at the smoky bar while Roman looked around for the girl who reminded him of Maureen O'Hara, the exquisitely beautiful film star. The girl had attended the dance the previous week where he first saw her.

Andrej returned with the beers and grinned at Roman. 'Let's move to the edge of the dance floor and check the talent.'

He motioned for Roman to follow with a crooked finger. Roman sipped the warm beer that tasted sour on his tongue. Yorkshire men drank beer, and he would have to get used to the nasty stuff. A voluptuous blonde flicked her hair at him as he pushed through the chattering crowd and smoke-hazed air. She smiled and let out a low whistle. Roman looked away; he had no time to waste. His girl must be somewhere. He had to find her this week.

Since last Saturday night, Roman's thoughts dwelled on her image as she jived with a burly man who had looked keen. Roman saw her notice him at the side of the dance floor. And when she walked off at the dance's end, she'd looked Roman in the eye. Her gaze, like a searchlight, froze him to the spot. Nothing else existed at that moment. Time stopped. But then his legs became like liquid, and he couldn't move to follow her. He remembered how she lingered at the edge of the dance floor and looked puzzled. The intensity of his feelings was suddenly overwhelming, and he'd failed to act. But this week, he would approach her and speak.

Then the band played Glenn Miller's hit song Pennsylvania 65-000. His girl emerged from the swell and stood at the edge of the dance floor. She tapped her peep-toe shoes and shimmied a little. Her red crepe skirt flipped at her knees. Roman swallowed hard and walked towards her.

'Would you like dance, Miss?'

Her instant smile dazzled him; energy buzzed from every ounce of her being as he took her hand.

'What your name?' he asked.

'Bridget,' she said in a soft Irish accent. 'Yes.'

Roman steered Bridget through the crowd of dancers who twirled and kicked to the rhythm of Glen Miller's Pennsylvania 65-000. The high trumpet notes sent a shiver down his spine. Dancing was wonderful because it allowed him to place a hand on Bridget's waistline and pull her close without impropriety. *She's so beautiful*, he thought, as she spun and swirled in front of him, weaving her intoxicating magic. Roman could feel the heat of her body through her crepe blouse and smell the soap on her skin. He pulled her close, and she rested her warm cheek on his.

'Look at that!' Bridget said, nodding her head towards a couple performing a wild dance.

The man gripped the woman by her waist, threw her up into the air, and her skirt flew up to expose her bare thighs.

'My mother would have a fit,' Bridget said, and Roman laughed and twirled her around once more. 'It's called Lindy Hopping.' She smiled at him.

Then, prompted by the tune, she pulled away and kicked her leg out before the trumpet hit a final high note then fizzled out.

As they walked off the dance floor, Roman asked, 'Would you like drink?'

Bridget nodded, and her auburn curls bounced on her shoulders. 'Soda and lime, please.'

*My dream is happening right now*, Roman thought to himself.

'Find seat; I get drinks.'

He felt conscious of his Polish accent and limited mastery of the language. Some English girls wouldn't talk to him once they heard him speak, but Bridget seemed different.

Roman returned from the bar carrying their drinks and pushed through the hot crowd, searching for Bridget. When he found her, she smiled at him, and his heart somersaulted.

As he sat down, Bridget said, 'Did you know he died in 1944?'

'Who?'

'Glenn Miller.' She raised her eyebrows.

'1944 not good year for me,' said Roman then regretted his comment.

'Why?' Bridget asked. Roman shook his head and sipped the bitter beer. 'Nothing.' He wished they sold Vodka at the bar.

'Tell me, where *you* from?' Roman said.

Bridget looked shy suddenly. 'I'm from County Cork.' She paused. 'I'm Irish.'

Roman remembered seeing scrawled signs pasted in the dirty windows of rental rooms that read, 'No Irish, blacks, or dogs.'

'Where are you from?' Bridget asked.

'I from Poland, Warsaw.'

She hesitated for a minute. 'Is it cold there?'

An image of bombed-out buildings covered in snow flashed in his mind, but he regained composure.

'You have family, Bridget?'

'Yes, in Cork.'

'Why you here if still have home?'

Bridget narrowed her eyes and sipped her drink.

'I sorry.' Roman reached for her hand and squeezed it tight. Her skin was smooth under his fingers.

Bridget stared at him for a few seconds then said, 'Well now, where's *your* family?'

Roman shifted in his seat at the question he dreaded being asked, breathed deeply, looked into her eyes. 'I not know.'

Bridget's cheeks reddened in embarrassment and she lowered her head. She sat back and ran her finger along the rim of her glass.

'What do you mean?'

'We split up in war and not heard anything since.'

'Oh, Jesus, I'm sorry… I….'

Roman's face contorted. 'I not know what happen to my family, where they go.' He shrugged and forced a half-smile. 'But I not alone. I have best friend with me.'

Bridget relaxed a little and cleared her throat. Roman worried about upsetting her and had no wish to pursue the subject of the war further. He glanced towards the dance floor, searching for salvation as Andrej burst from the jostling crowd and waved at him.

Roman raised his hand. 'Over here, my friend.' He gestured for Andrej to join them. Andrej seized a chair, sat down, and beamed.

'This Andrej, we at school together.'

Andrej leaned over and clasped Bridget's hands in his, shook them, and nearly spilled her drink.

'Hello,' she said, and Roman could tell she approved of his vigorous friend.

Then the burly man from last Saturday night strode over to their table—the one Roman felt was too fond of dancing with Bridget. He had his hands thrust deep in his trouser pockets. The man nodded at Roman and Andrej, then leaned towards Bridget.

'Would you like dance?'

She nibbled her lip and glanced at Roman for approval. The man noticed their exchange.

'Just one dance, Miss. I no want marry you.'

He raised his hands to his shoulders with his palms outstretched. Bridget stood up slowly. Roman saw she wasn't smiling as the man lifted her hand dramatically in the air and led her to the floor.

'Bastard!' Roman said.

'Keep calm,' Andrej warned him. 'It means nothing. She likes you; I can tell by how she looks at you.'

He mimicked a woman fluttering her eyes and tapped his heart rapidly. Roman scanned the dance floor to track their movements; the lights in the centre of the floor pinpointed them. The smug bastard had placed a hand near the top of Bridget's ribs, too close to her bosom for Roman's liking. As he twirled Bridget around, the man shot a smirk at Roman, who flashed him a look of thunder as they swung away from his glare.

'Shit!' He pulled at his shirt collar; it was hot and hard to breathe in the smoke-filled atmosphere. 'I go for fresh air,' he said in English and pushed through the crowd to the red light of the exit.

Roman returned to find the man sitting opposite Bridget and a blonde woman had joined the table. She was pretty but not his type and wasn't a patch on Bridget, who didn't need make-up to attract a man. Roman pressed his thighs against the table edge and leaned forward as the man peered up at him under bushy eyebrows.

'What your name?' Roman said.

'Stanislav. Why?' he said in a thick accent Roman thought was Czech.

'Because, Stanislav, you in my seat. You go now.'

Roman gestured to him and placed his hands on the table, spreading his fingers and leaning forward. The Czech muttered something in his language but stayed put as he hooked an arm over the back of his chair, jiggling his fingers as he grinned.

Andrej spoke to Roman in Polish. 'He's a nutcase, be careful.' But Roman tried to stare the man down, regardless.

Then Bridget interrupted, 'Roman, this is my friend, Kay, from work.'

She pointed to the blonde woman, who swivelled in her seat to face Roman.

'Nice to meet you, Roman.'

The Czech laughed and mimicked her.

‘What so fucking funny?’ Roman said, but the man shrugged.

A fire flared in Roman’s guts and he swung a fist at him. The man toppled backward and his chair crashed to the floor. He looked startled for a second, then sprang up and hurled a punch at Roman. Before Roman knew it, they were locked in combat. Roman struggled to keep his opponent’s bulky frame jammed in a headlock as people scattered away from the commotion. Andrej grabbed Roman’s shoulders and dragged him off.

Roman heard someone shouting, ‘Out! Out, all of you.’

The bar attendant caught Roman by the arm and shoved him towards the door.

‘Please! I want tell her something.’ He pointed to Bridget who cowered by the wall, Kay’s arms around her.

‘Out, mate, before I call the bloody Police.’

The barman heaved Roman through the door. He skidded on the icy path and fell, palms smacking the pavement. Roman rolled over and groaned at his grazed hands. Above him, the stars winked in the night sky. They suddenly reminded him of home, of the Christmas eve walk his family always took through the glistening streets of Warsaw. Happy days and nights. Roman sighed and stretched out his arms. He stared up; his breath billowed white into the frosted air. Then he heard women’s voices and the tap-tap of shoes and turned to look. Bridget and Kay hurried from the dance hall with their coats wrapped tight.

Bridget jerked her head away when she saw Roman sprawled on the pavement. He heard Kay say, ‘The Poles are trouble, Bridget. Forget him.'

Soon Andrej staggered out. The barman stood behind him.

'Go home, foreigners,' he snarled with a final push at Andrej's shoulder. 'We don't want you here.'

Andrej plunged forward, arms splayed to balance himself and swore in Polish. He spat on the ground as he stumbled towards Roman. He plopped down on the pavement next to him. Andrej circled his skinny knees with his elbows and tutted.

'Look at you, stupid hot-head.'

He pulled out a pack of cigarettes from his jacket, shook out two, and flicked one at Roman's chest. The flare of the match lit Andrej's lean face as the sulphur invaded Roman's nostril.

'Your dreamboat just floated away, idiota.' Andrej patted Roman's leg.

* * *

Roman opened his eyes and wondered where he was until the familiar thin curtains reminded him he was in the hut. The black pot-bellied stove glowed orange at the edges of the lid, but frost still crisped the insides of the windows. He flung an arm over his forehead.

'Oh, no. What have I done?' Roman said aloud to no one in particular, thinking of Bridget hurrying away from him the previous night.

He scanned the room. Most occupants were up and out, with just a few still sleeping off Saturday night's indulgences. The door opened, and Andrej bounded in. He waved a letter in the air.

'This might be your lucky day.' He sat down and bounced on Roman's bed, shaking the metal frame.

'What?' Roman pushed himself up and peered at the letter in Andrej's hand.

'It's for you.' He handed it to Roman and sat back with his arms folded.

The Red Cross symbol on the envelope swam in front of Roman's eyes. His stomach flipped at the letter addressed to him.

'Go on then, open it.' Andrej nudged him.

'I daren't.' Roman sat up straight. 'What if it's bad news?'

'Then it would be a telegram.' Andrej smiled.

'How do you know?'

'I just do.'

Roman threw back the bedclothes, slipped his cold feet into boots, and pulled his coat over his pyjamas.

'I need a cigarette.' He tapped the letter on the back of his hand.

Andrej handed him a cigarette that he grabbed with a tremble. Roman inhaled once, passed the cigarette back to Andrej, and turned over the letter to tear it open. He read a few lines, slapped his forehead, and fell backward on his bed.

'What does it say?'

Roman stared at the ceiling for a few moments then read aloud in a shaking voice.

'Dear Mr Kozynski, further to your letter of 11 October 1946, we are pleased to inform you that the person you enquired of, Anya Kozynska, DOB 1905, Krakow, Poland, is listed as a resident of a Displaced Person's Hostel in Scotland.'

He dropped the letter to the floor and hid his face in his hands. His shoulders heaved. Andrej gently picked the letter up and continued to read its contents.

'She's in Scotland, man. That's fantastic! Unbelievable! And here's her address. Roman, you have a family again.' He hugged Roman, who could utter no words.

When finally released from Andrej's grip he said, 'The last time I saw my mother was in 1940, at breakfast. I was fourteen and she was thirty-five. Now I'm twenty years old so she will be forty-one.' Roman stared at his friend in disbelief.

'Never mind the maths, get dressed, my friend*; you* have a letter to write.' Andrej threw Roman's trousers at him and grinned insanely.

*To: Mrs Anya Kozynska, Beith Industrial Hostel, Ballochmyl, Scotland.*

*December 1946*

*Dear Mother,*

*I cannot express how happy the news that you are in Scotland makes me. So much has happened since we were last together. I have no information about Elouna or Papa, but I am praying you will.*

*I came to England in August 1946 on a ship from Naples. I had been fighting along with the British Allies. There were 2,870 Polish soldiers on that ship. The British arranged for us to go to many of their colonies to live, and I chose England, where it's cold and grey. And by some miracle, you are here as I hoped, but dared not say aloud.*

*I live in a Polish Resettlement Camp in the north of England near a place called Barnsley. Here we receive food and shelter in an old converted army base. The huts are primitive, but we have roofs over our heads. They provide basic education classes in English, Maths, and Geography. There is a coal mine where I and others work. I will tell you more about this when we meet. I can visit you only on a Sunday if convenient for you. All of this seems like a dream right now.*

*Your loving son, Roman.*

*NB: I will move to another location in West Yorkshire and start a new job in a textile mill next month.*

Roman re-read his letter, sealed the blue envelope, and slipped it into his jacket pocket to post the next day.

## Roman 1947, Saltaire Mill

'The buildings are even dirtier here,' Roman said as he jumped off the transport bus that stopped in a cobblestoned mill yard. There was a sour whiff in the air he could not identify.

Andrej grabbed his elbow. 'It's work, and we need it, so stop complaining.'

Roman snorted. They followed their employment officer, Stan, through an arched entry into a four-storey Victorian building.

'Wait there a minute, you lot.'

He pointed towards the foot of some steps where a massive glass window looked out onto a sloped road, darkened with rain and dusted with straggles of greyish fluff.

'I need to check you're all here. Don't want any escapees, do we now?' Stan chuckled to himself as he counted the line of Poles and ticked his sheet of paper.

'Alright, this way,' Stan said and heaved open an oak door opposite to herd them into a cavernous space. 'This is the spinning hall,' he told them.

Massive cast-iron pillars supported the beamed roof, and between them, giant machines thrashed up and down, attended by rows of mill workers.

'What's this?'

Roman caught fibrous fragments that drifted in the air as the thunderous noise battered out a rhythm. But Andrej couldn't hear him because of the din. Stan signalled they should keep pace with his clipboard held high. They followed him to the end of the long hall where huge wooden bays stood, packed to the ceiling with a clumped yellowish material. Men in long aprons scurried back and forth, tugged out wads, and hurled them into huge trolley bins.

'Line up here,' Stan said.

Then a skinny man appeared from behind a bay, rubbing greasy hands on his apron. He looked the recruits up and down.

'I'm your foreman now lads. My name is Mr Askew,' he said. 'I need five packers; the rest can go to the dye room.'

The men stood silent. No one knew what a packer was.

'Do they speak English?' He shouted over the heads of the group to Stan.

'Enough for you, Mr Askew.'

Askew grabbed some men from the line, including Roman and Andrej. 'I'm just bloody sick of repeating instructions.' He pulled his cap off and scratched his head. 'Follow me.'

Askew marched off, holding his hand up. Roman saw his index finger was missing at the knuckle.

They wound along stone-flagged corridors and into a dusty room where Askew barked at them to hang up coats and threw aprons their way.

'You'll work in packing. Do as your told—no funny stuff, or no pay. Now, let's get to work.'

They marched back to the bays.

Askew twinned each recruit with a packer and left the scene saying over his shoulder, 'Now I'll see what you're made of.'

Roman thrust his hand out to the fellow worker Stan had allotted him. 'I'm Roman.'

But the man stared at Roman's hand and planted his knuckles on his hips. 'Let's see if it's worth learning names.' He nodded at the high bay. 'It's wool, to spin into yarn. First, we take it to spinners.'

And with that, he motioned for Roman to join him and fill the bin. They worked quickly and silently. The air filled with itchy fibres which made Roman sneeze. When their container brimmed, the packer swung it around on its wheels to face the floor of pounding machines. He stood aside and pointed down the long aisles in front of him.

'Find a spinner with an empty bin, give him this and bring it back when it's empty.'

Roman set off pushing the heavy bin down one aisle. He heaved it along and peered into the containers lined up at the end of each machine but couldn't find an empty one. The spinning hall was almost a quarter of a mile long, Askew had told them. Roman's anxiety grew after passing a succession of bins with visible contents inside. Eventually, he stopped by an older man who flipped about his apron edges, searching for something in his trouser pockets.

'You need wool?' Roman said as the man stared at him with a smirk.

'Get you every time, they do,' he said.

'What you mean?'

The man adjusted his cap. 'Look.'

He pointed at the rows of machines in the next aisle

where a packer stopped at each bin, deposited some wool, and then trundled forward.

'There's no such thing as an empty bin. You just keep filling 'em up.' He returned to his work, laughing.

Roman's face reddened, and a sudden fury lit in his chest as he pulled a fat wad from his bin and hurled it into the man's container.

Roman glanced back at the loading area where his co-worker stood talking to another man. He tilted his head towards Roman, and they both laughed. Across in the next aisle, Roman spotted Andrej, head held high and tight-lipped.

Roman wanted to shout to him in Polish, 'Let's get the fuck out of here,' but the noise made it impossible for any voice to carry. Soon, Roman would find out the mill workers lip-read to communicate, creating another hurdle for him to overcome.

That morning, Roman fell into a rhythm that allowed his mind to escape from the repetitive task, and he wondered where Bridget was now and when his mother would reply to his letter.

*To: Roman Koyzinski, Greenbanks Hostel, Horsforth, West Yorkshire, England*

*January 12 1947*

*My Dearest Roman,*

*Tears fill my eyes as I write this letter. I have waited so long to write a letter you would receive and hold in your hands. Throughout the dark times, I have looked for you and written so many times to the Red Cross to find where you were. As your mother, I knew in my heart you were not gone from me. In times of great suffering, I have sought comfort in Jesus and begged him on my knees every morning and night that I would receive a message you were safe somewhere, no matter where it was in the world. When I had a telegram from Geneva to say you were in a displaced person's camp in England and looking for me, I could hardly hope against hope it was real and it was you.*

*The doctors assure me though I have been ill, I am getting better. You must come to visit me very soon. Sunday is a good day; any day is good, but I know you have work. When you do, you will need to catch a train to Glasgow and then a bus to Beith (pronounced Bis), which will take about an hour, and then it's a one-kilometre walk to the hostel. I will send you some money and the train times in a separate letter tomorrow. Tonight, I am too excited and must write back to you immediately before I have all the information you need to find me.*

*My son, with your beautiful dark eyes, do not lose hope of returning to our homeland. Things change all the time.*

*Look at what happened to us. Who would ever have imagined such things were possible? Maybe the Russians will not be in control for much longer. I'm a dreamer, just like your dear father, Roman.*

*I must go now. I am tired but so thrilled I will see you again. My heart is bursting with love for you. You will be a young man now, not the boy I knew.*

*Your loving Mamushka.*

## Roman

The train journey from Leeds to Glasgow was long, but Roman was so preoccupied with his thoughts he barely noticed the landscape. As it puffed into the city's outskirts, the surroundings were grey and damp with no sunshine.

Roman remembered the last time he saw his father, who was herded into a truck in Pawiak's hidden courtyard in 1940. He wondered what had happened to his father but dared not think about it too much. Things did not look good but there was always a glimmer of hope. He could still be alive? Miracles happened. He had heard from his mother after all this time. But sometimes, it was better not to know; for your hopes to remain suspended, rather than shot down by bitter truths. But he chided himself for this burst of dark thoughts. Perhaps his mother would be able to tell him something when they met. After all, she had mentioned his father in her letter.

Roman searched for an information kiosk when he arrived inside the smoky Glasgow station. His mother's letter said he must catch the bus to Beith. When he found the booth, there was a shuffling queue. There seemed to be no colour in the surroundings and the people looked pale and drawn. Roman had to fight off a heavy feeling that pulled his mood down as he moved slowly forward in the dismal line.

The bus journey out soon lightened his mood as it left the drab city and wound through the curved roads of small villages, ploughed fields, and blue-hued hills.

Upon arrival, Roman walked up the path to the

hospital. A vivid memory of playing chess with Elouna on that fateful night burned suddenly in his mind. Like him, she would be grown now, if she were still alive. Elouna would be twenty-four years of age. A grown woman. Perhaps with a family. The sharp smell of disinfectant shook him from his thoughts as he pulled open the heavy hospital door.

At the reception counter, his knees shook as he asked for directions to the ward where his mother was. As he neared, his thoughts raced. It was seven years since he had seen her. What if she didn't recognise him as a young man? So much had changed since he was fourteen. So much had happened. Then he worried what if he didn't recognise her? Roman was sick with fear as he pushed open the ward door.

A nurse at a table looked up and asked, 'Can I help you?'

Roman patted his chest as though he were breathless and stammered, he was looking for Mrs Anya Kozynska, his mother. He wanted to scan the beds that lined the ward but was too scared.

The nurse stood up. 'Follow me,' she said, leaving Roman stumbling behind her on shaky knees.

She stopped at a bed with a curtain drawn around it. The nurse turned to smile reassuringly at Roman and pulled it back. The curtain rattled on its metal hooks to reveal his mother propped up by pillows with her eyes shut.

'Mrs Kozynska,' the nurse said in a gentle voice. 'You've got a visitor.'

His mother's appearance shocked Roman. She was greatly changed by time and events. He watched her eyes slowly open. Her skin was grey and pinched. Her once thick hair now straw-like and streaked white at the temples. He recognised her immediately, but she was a shrunken version of what she had been. Tears filled Roman's eyes as he leaned toward her. Anya's voice was barely audible as she greeted him in Polish with tears forming in her eyes. It was clear she was now more fragile than he had ever dreamed. Roman realised with a heavy heart he could not ask his mother anything about the war, his father or sister at this visit. Pursuing answers from his mother as she lay attached to sickly yellowish tubes seemed heartless. Instead, he held her hand and sat down by her bed. There would be another visit.

## Roman 1947, March

Roman crossed over the foamy river that flowed beneath the iron footbridge and hurried up the slope towards Shipley Glen's summit, sucking in mouthfuls of clear spring air. Being outdoors after a week's toil in the mill was bliss. He would be with friends back home on such a day, fooling around on the Vistula River's banks, skimming stones and chatting up pretty girls that walked past in groups. But today, he was content to follow the track up through the woodland to the top, where the glen stretched ahead in mounds of bracken and heather to provide a sweeping view over the valley. A miniature train chugged up and down for those not willing to exert themselves, but Roman welcomed the challenge.

The scenery was rugged in the way Yorkshire people were. Ancient boulders littered the escarpment's edge, where sheep grazed amongst the high grass. The feeling of space and freedom invigorated Roman, allowing him to leave behind the working week. It took his new life up with tasks that seemed a constant struggle—learning to speak, read and write English with its impossible and confusing grammatical rules. Studying in the evening to pass the qualification to become an engineer, and working long, tiring shifts in the mill Monday to Saturday, had dulled his senses.

He recognised the curlew's distinctive call as he emerged from the wood's springy bluebell carpets onto the glen's plateau. Further along, a signpost showed there was a pub a mile ahead. English pubs were a novelty to Roman and his fellow compatriots because back home, cafés and restaurants were where people met friends to talk, eat and drink. But most English pubs sold only alcohol. Some served pickled eggs from giant glass jars that reminded Roman of laboratory specimens in school.

He followed as the path diverged down a slight slope to an old building that looked like a converted farm with a sign hanging above an arched door. Roman brushed his hair back from his face, cleaned his shoes by rubbing them on the back shin of his trousers, and strode in to the pub.

The contrast in light from the sun's brilliance to the thick dark gloom of the interior temporarily blinded him, but Roman made out a bar that curved into the room as his vision gradually adjusted. He headed across the worn, sloping stone floor towards it. Uneven oak stools surrounded wooden tables, and along one wall, a bench with wings at the sides stood next to a fireplace whose grate was cold and empty on such a pleasant day. Two pot dogs sat atop of the fireplace mantle, their cracked white and gold glaze thinly coated with dust. Roman disliked these ornaments, which usually adorned lodging houses' front rooms because they were dull. He missed the vibrant colours of the interiors of traditional Polish homes he had known, the tapestries, painted furniture, and colourful pottery.

After ordering a pint of bitter, a drink he gradually became accustomed to, Roman sat down at a table to a view through the window across the sheep-dotted glen.

He was thinking about his mother when he saw a young couple strolling towards the pub. His heart jolted.

There was no mistake. It was beautiful Bridget, who he had last seen hurrying away from the dance hall after his brawl with the Czech previously.

Since then, Roman had gone to work in Saltaire Mill and now lived in lodgings in nearby industrial Bradford. He often considered visiting the old dance hall to see friends from the mother country and at the same time look for Bridget to apologise, but never did. She was very pretty and of course she would be with another man.

He watched her wander through the door with a companion. Roman wanted to run away but had bought a drink and didn't want to waste it. Money was tight, and the simple pleasures in life were few.

To his relief, Bridget and her friend ordered drinks and sat down away from Roman on the bench with wings. They were deep in conversation and their line of vision did not take him in. But Roman could overhear snippets of the conversation, although their Irish accents meant he had to listen hard to make out individual words.

'I'm sorry I didn't reply to you, Ted. I had to think about what your letter asked.'

That was Bridget's voice, sure enough. Roman sneaked a look; her expression was concerned and perhaps a little uncomfortable. The man she called Ted was wan and wore spectacles. He looked very mild-mannered to Roman, who imagined him working in a library shuffling dusty books around all day. There was a pause in their conversation, and Roman looked away, not wanting to draw attention to himself.

A small group of people burst into the pub, and Roman

was glad of the distraction. They collected their drinks and sat nearby, laughing and joking. They had local accents, and Roman could hardly understand what they were saying to one another, but they looked jolly, and their mood lifted his spirits once more.

Roman gulped his beer down to leave before Bridget noticed him, but she glanced up as he hurried to the door. He saw her physically jerk, and then a flash of pink washed over her face as their eyes met. Roman lowered his head and scurried out of the pub door, wishing he had stayed in bed instead of going on this fateful jaunt. Now his feelings were churned up again.

Roman stopped dead in his tracks when he heard Bridget's voice call out to him from behind. What was she going to say? He turned and tried to smile innocently while his knees shook.

'Hello!' she said. 'It *is* you.'

As she stepped towards him, it struck Roman how lovely she was—her movements fluid, graceful as a dancer, in complete control of her body.

'It's grand to see you again.' Bridget stood before him, beaming.

Roman's face flared in shame. 'Not so grand last time we met,' he said.

To his surprise, she laughed, then said, 'Well, now, the English say Saturday night is for drinking and fighting.'

Roman relaxed. 'And what do Irish say it's for?'

Bridget grinned; her teeth were even and white. 'Much the same.'

He was now composed sufficiently to ask, 'What you

doing here?'

'I'm out with an old friend; he's visiting from Cork, my home town.'

'What kind of friend?'

Roman's English friends would advise this was too blunt a question. *Please don't get to the point straight away; it's off-putting*, they would reprimand him. He regretted his words.

Bridget flushed and smiled at Roman's question as he stood with his hands in his pockets, legs jiggling. His language skills were spiralling as he spoke.

He plunged ahead. 'He your boyfriend?'

'No. He's not. He *was*,' Bridget said, flicking a fallen curl from her forehead.

Roman snorted. 'Right now, he head this way.' He nodded over her shoulder, and Bridget turned.

Ted marched towards them, unsmiling.

'Roman!' Bridget leaned closer and whispered to him. 'Meet me at the funicular next Sunday at 1pm.' Then she flashed him a blinding smile, full of bravado and allure.

'The what?' he said, almost grasping her cuff.

'Bridget,' Ted called, 'is everything okay there?'

Bridget turned to him. 'Yes, this is a friend from the old hostel days. We're just catching up.'

Ted thrust his hands into his trouser pockets as he reached them. He glared at Roman.

'Ted O'Connell,' he said with a tilt of his chin. 'And who might you be?'

'I'm Roman.' He backed away. 'Be seeing you.'

Roman raised his hand and swung his knapsack over

his shoulder to set off on the uneven path. He was glad of the cool breeze as he rushed back down the road, a pounding in his chest. *What is a funicular?* he asked himself.

* * *

It took Roman half an hour to walk home after his encounter with Bridget. He wished he had a pencil to write the word funicular; instead, he kept repeating it. It was a strange word.

Roman hurried past the imposing black and gold gates of Lister Park and up Oak Lane towards his lodgings. A broad avenue with a name that amused him as there were no oak trees in sight, only buildings crammed together and some with grubby shops on the ground floors. Rows of terraced houses ran off the main road, a feature in this part of the country: the industrial north of England. He had learnt this in his English classes in the resettlement programme. Vastly rich mill owners built houses for their workers at the end of the last century. They had tiny paved yards where the family washing hung out and flapped in all weathers. All the buildings were now encrusted in black soot from years of industrial pollution. Roman found the environment dampened his spirits, particularly on cold, wet days when his thoughts turned to the majestic buildings of Warsaw and the clear delineation of seasons. Here it was possible to experience three seasons in one day under the ever-changing sky. As he climbed the hill, Lister's Mill tower rose and dominated the city's skyline.

But today was still warm under the spring sun, and

Roman's thoughts were full of his subsequent encounter with beautiful Bridget. He turned into the street where he lodged. Children played out on the road. They chalked on the pavements, hopped in and out of squares, jumped over skipping ropes, and were happy and content, it seemed. Nearly all the houses in the area had lodgers—immigrants like Roman, sharing rooms and working in the surrounding mills and factories. Roman's roommates were Tadek, Andrej, and Josef. There was no such thing as a room occupied by a single person; they packed all rooms to capacity. There was a large kitchen where the occupants gathered to cook and chat in their languages. The owners of his lodgings, Mr Svenski and his wife, secured a mortgage on a modest deposit funded from their lodgers' rents. Roman hoped to do this one day if he could not return home.

Roman burst into the kitchen searching for Andrej, who lounged at the table chatting with Katerina as she mixed the dough for pierogi dumplings, a favoured dish from home. Katerina had her hair pulled up inside a headscarf, her apron dusty with flour. She was laughing at something Andrej had said.

'Here's trouble!' Andrej said as Roman pulled a chair out to join him.

'How was your walk?'

'Great! Fantastic! Do you know what a funicular is?' Roman said, tugging off his rucksack and then his jacket.

'A what? No! What are you babbling about?'

Roman raced through how he bumped into Bridget at the inn on the glen, who proposed they meet at the funicular next Sunday.

'What a coincidence,' Andrej said. 'I wonder what she was doing up there?'

'I didn't get time to ask her. She was with someone who didn't look pleased to see me.'

'Really? Some intrigue, then.' Andrej winked at Katerina. 'I tell you what, let's look this funicular up.' Andrej rushed to fetch his English-Polish dictionary.

'Who's Bridget?' Katerina asked as she pushed back her fringe with the back of her floury hand and smiled at Roman.

Andrej returned with his dictionary and flipped through it.

Mr Svenski walked into the kitchen. He didn't smile at them as he usually did but sat down solemnly and placed his elbows on the table with his chin in the heels of his hands.

'Mrs Svenska received a letter from her aunt in Poland,' he announced. 'She'd written to find out her brother's whereabouts because she'd heard he returned to Lublin after the war but then nothing more.' His voice was grave.

Roman and Andrej exchanged looks. Roman feared what was coming next. So many of his friends had leads that suddenly went cold. Andrej put the dictionary down. Katerina stopped rolling the dumplings and turned around from the worktop to look at Mr Svenski, who continued.

'Her aunt writes those who return to their homeland…' He paused to emphasise, 'the Russians said they would welcome back with open arms, are being shipped to

Gulags. Mrs Svenska thinks this is what's happened to her brother.' Mr Svenski's eyes clouded with tears. Everyone was silent, with only the cries of children playing in the street drifting through the open windows until Mr Svenski said, 'But, we still want to return home.' He shrugged; his palms outstretched. 'Maybe one day it will be possible. But not now.' He appeared to shrink in front of Roman's eyes.

They were lost in thoughts of their homeland for a time until a Manx cat ran into the kitchen and sprang onto Andrej's lap. He stroked its arching back.

'Mr Cat, do you know what a funicular is?'

Roman looked up, smiled, and reached for the dictionary. After a few minutes, he said excitedly, 'It says here it's a train on a cable.'

He shook his head and passed the book to Andrej. Svenski woke from his thoughts and enquired about what they were discussing. He nodded when Roman explained and patted him on the shoulder. Warmth returned to his face.

'She means the small train at the foot of Shipley Glen for the day-trippers. That's where you're to meet her.'

Roman beamed at him and let out a whoop.

* * *

Roman counted off the days until Sunday came around. Walking to the glen required energy, but Roman possessed little appetite. His stomach fluttered as he forced down a breakfast of rye bread and salted dripping.

He brushed his demob clothes for the third time in a

row. On discharge from the forces, the government provided him with a suit, two shirts, a pair of shoes, two pairs of socks, a coat and some underwear. He had paid little attention to his wardrobe until now. After rent and bills, Roman saved the money he earned in the mill, hoping he could put down a deposit on a house one day. Now, he wondered if he would need to buy a new suit instead.

* * *

Roman adjusted the spotted red and white silk tie borrowed from Andrej for the date as he fidgeted on a bench at the foot of the glen. Andrej had bartered on the black market for this precious item and spent half a week's wages so he could impress the girls at the Saturday night dances. He said it was his lucky charm and Roman prayed it would work for him.

The funicular had two parallel tracks, one carrying passengers up to the top of the glen and the other down every ten minutes. As the open-air carriages rattled past one another, the passengers would let out a collective whoop which Roman heard repeatedly.

The trains came and went, and he became increasingly worried. Convinced he had misunderstood Bridget's instructions. There was also a small train station opposite the village mill on the other side of the bridge. *Had she meant that one? But it didn't run on cables, and she definitely said funicular,* he reasoned. She was Irish, and maybe that word meant something else to her. He became hot and uncomfortable but didn't want to loosen his tie.

Roman stood up and paced around the bench a few

times. Had Bridget meant to meet him at the top of the glen? Was it the wrong day? His mind played out many misunderstandings of the arrangement as time slipped by. Roman slumped back on the bench. He scanned the bridge she would cross to meet him. Every time a figure appeared, his heart leapt, but then he would see it was not Bridget, and his stomach would lurch.

Seven trains had rattled up and down the track, and Roman calculated at least an hour and a half had passed. He stood up slowly but suddenly sat back down and watched just in case Bridget would appear at the bridge. Another two trains came and went, and then it was time to accept, with a sinking heart, she wasn't coming. Roman stood up and kicked away some stones, scuffing the toe of his newly polished shoe. He loosened the knot of Andrej's tie and undid his shirt collar button. Roman walked hesitantly from the funicular and across the bridge, then rested on the railings watching a kingfisher dip across the water and dive for food. He trudged home.

Roman opened the front door at the house and crept into the hallway, hoping Andrej and Katerina would be out, saving him the heartache of telling them Bridget stood him up. As he reached his room door, he heard Katerina's voice from behind him.

'Roman, how was your date?'

He turned to see her standing at the foot of the stairs, her hair in curlers under a scarf and in her dressing gown, preparing for work the following day. Roman fought back the desire to cry because he was sure Bridget would be there to meet him. His heart had been soaring ever since she made their date.

'She didn't turn up,' he said as he attempted a weak smile that quickly made his bottom lip tremble.

'Oh, no. Roman!'

Katerina put her foot on the stair to climb up, but he held his arm in a stop gesture.

'I'm tired now. I'm going to rest.'

Later, Roman lay on his bed, turning the event repeatedly, when he heard the front door open, then Andrej talking to Katerina. Soon the noise of footsteps bounded up the stairs, and Andrej crashed into the room with a worried expression wrinkling his lean face.

Andrej listened to Roman's tale, not proffering advice or judgement as Roman repeatedly scolded himself for getting something wrong. Eventually, after letting him get it off his chest, Andrej suggested they go for a drink at their local pub. He reasoned although they had to work the next day, Roman needed to forget his sorrows, and it was still early evening.

It was packed when they entered the pub, to Roman's surprise. He guessed people were squeezing the last drop out of the weekend before the drudgery of the working week took hold. Andrej ordered drinks and searched for somewhere to sit. They spotted a space at the corner of a table where a group of men laughed raucously and banged their pint glasses down. Roman and Andrej perched on stools at the table edge. He noticed a young woman staring at him and Andrej as they talked. She sat with two others, playing dominoes.

'There's a redhead staring at us,' Roman said. He

nudged Andrej and nodded. ‘Over there.’

Andrej looked over. ‘Not bad at all,’ he said and grinned at Roman. ‘Come on, let’s cheer you up.’ Andrej motioned with his hand for the woman to come over.

‘Oh, no, don’t,’ Roman said. The woman whispered something to one of her friends, smiled over at Andrej, stood, and pushed through the jostling crowd to join them at their table.

‘Take seat,’ Andrej said, standing up for her to sit. ‘This Roman,’ he patted Roman’s shoulder. ‘He good looking boy but girl stand him up tonight. He sad.’

‘Oh, dear!’ the woman said as she peered at Roman.

‘It just mistake,’ Roman looked at Andrej, not the redhead. ‘I not want pity.’

The woman coughed. ‘Oh, I see, I…’ she hesitated before turning and saying to Andrej, ’Are you two Polish?’

‘Yes, why?’

She laughed at something, then said, ‘Me mam says to keep away from you lot.’

‘And why?’ Andrej nudged Roman’s shoulder, who stared into the foamy remnants in his empty glass, half listening.

‘She says you’re wild, you lads, you Poles.’

Andrej threw his head back, laughed, and rested a hand on Roman’s slumped shoulder.

‘Wild like bears?’ he winked at Roman, who looked up and straightened a little.

‘What?’ The woman shook her red curls.

‘Yes. It’s true. We wild like Wojtek?’ Andrej said.

‘Who’s Wojtek? What are you on about?’

'He bear, in army.'

Roman and Andrej exchanged amused glances as Andrej jiggled his legs.

'You're having me on, you are. There are no bears in the army.' She laughed.

'It's true.' Andrej grabbed her arm, and she looked surprised. 'He adopted as cub, make soldiers happy. Take him to Italy. Enlist him.'

'Enlist a bear?' she said.

'Yes, so he get rations.'

'I've never heard such poppycock in all my life. You must think I'm right stupid.'

'No. You not stupid. In war, crazy things happen.'

'Is that so?'

Roman saw merriment in her eyes, and his mood lifted.

'Honest. I have picture of him.' Andrej took out his wallet and pulled out a photograph that he slapped on the table in front of her. She leaned over to look. 'My name Andrej.' He pointed at the bear in the photo. 'And this Wojtek.'

'My name's Gillian, and you're a joker for sure,' she said as she examined the photograph.

Roman was now studying her intently.

The photo showed a group of soldiers surrounding a bear who wore a wide leather collar and chain. He balanced on his hind legs, paws around one soldier's waist. The pose was playful, and the onlookers smiled.

Andrej looked at Gillian. 'I not lying.' He jabbed at the photo with his finger. 'Wojtek!'

She burst out laughing. 'Well, I never.' She shifted in

her seat to look up at Andrej. 'Was he a mascot or something?'

'No! We enlist him. He carry ammunition for us. He like cigarettes and beer.' Roman scrutinised Gillian's look of amazement.

'Sounds dangerous, that does. Cigarettes and ammunition. Crazy! So where is he now?'

'Edinburgh Zoo, he demobbed like us. Sent to zoo.' Roman looked sad.

'Oh, that's a.... a shame.'

Andrej looked down at his and Roman's empty glasses. 'Gillian, we go to Polish club, have nice drinks. You see more pictures of Wojtek on wall.'

Gillian nodded toward her friends. 'But what about them?'

'They join us,' Andrej said, roaring with laughter as he waved to Gillian's friends.

'Come on, club near. Five minutes away.'

Gillian hurried off to speak to her friends, who looked across at the two men and giggled.

'Come on, Roman,' Andrej said. 'We drink with pretty girls and forget about Bridget.'

Earlier that afternoon, Bridget sat at her dressing table, brushing her unruly hair readying herself for her date with Roman. As a child, the family nanny had performed the ritual of one hundred strokes before bedtime to a protesting Bridget. But now those days were lost, buried under the rubble of misfortune.

On her bed lay a floral skirt and cream Broderie Anglaise blouse with a sweetheart neck she would top with the string of pearls her grandmother had given her the day she stepped onto the Cobh ferry to cross to England. She blushed when she recalled the shame of the pre-boarding inspection, how she and her friends had to strip to their shoes and socks to be inspected, by torchlight, for lice. Catholic girls of eighteen who would never be seen naked, even within the realm of family intimacy.

But she wiped this thought from her mind as she prepared herself for the meeting with Roman, whose surname she didn't even know. What would her mother and father think of such a liaison? She dabbed pillar-box red lipstick on and smiled at her image in the tiny mirror. Life was genuinely beginning, she felt as she stood up to slip on her blouse and fasten the mother-of-pearl buttons. Stockings were hard to get, so she wore white ankle socks with her shoes. She wondered if she should use an eyebrow pencil to draw a seam at the backs of her legs instead of the socks but thought this adornment should wait for a second date.

Bridget popped into the kitchen on her way out, where

the other girls were drinking tea and chatting in the hazy atmosphere of sunlight and cigarette smoke.

'Cup of tea now?' Kay held an empty cup out to Bridget mischievously.

'I don't have time, sorry. How do I look?' Bridget twirled.

'And who's the lucky fella?' Maura asked, looking Bridget up and down with mock raised eyebrows.

'Romantic Roman, I bet,' Kay chirped.

'Oh god, not a Pole. You be careful now.' Maura stood, shimmied over, and examined Bridget's face. 'You've got a lovely complexion, but why not try a wee dab of rouge?' She tickled Bridget, who squirmed and laughed.

'Be off with you.' Bridget turned and left them all singing, *Daisy, Daisy, give me your answer do*.

Bridget clomped down the wooden stairs in her wedge heels and opened the front door to a shimmering sunny day. She breathed in the honeysuckle-scented air. All her senses tingled.

Then a voice said, 'Morning, miss. Telegram for Bridget O'Keefe.' A young boy handed a tiny envelope over.

She held it in her hand and stared. Her mouth dried as she lowered herself to sit on the doorstep to read the message.

'Father very ill. Come home now. Georgina.'

Two weeks had passed since Bridget stood up Roman, and he had carried on with his life. This morning he felt the power in his legs as he cycled through the park to work, Andrej parallel to him. They chatted and laughed about their previous evening of high spirits at the local Polish club.

'See, I said you'd get over her soon,' Andrej said.

Suddenly Roman's heart weighed in his chest as he thought about Bridget.

'Race you there,' Andrej said and sped off past the lake, scattering blackbirds from the path.

Roman fell behind as he watched the ducks circling on the water, diving for morsels. Pigeons startled and flapped out of the leafy trees as he passed. The April sun streamed through onto his face.

As the mill clock struck eight, Roman rushed towards the entrance of the spinning shed but had to stand aside for Mr Askew and the foreman who helped a deathly pale man through, his arm swaddled in a blood-soaked cloth.

As Mr Askew passed Roman, he said, 'Don't stand gawping lad. Get on with it.'

Soon Roman's temples throbbed as he pushed the laden cart up and down the aisles of the spinning room. The fibre particles in the air incessantly rained and irritated his eyelids, which were puffed red from too many slivovitzes the previous night.

Mr Askew hurried towards him. 'That was a close call earlier,' he said, then patted Roman's shoulder lightly. 'Be glad you're not a spinner, lad. Now, I've got a job for you.'

Roman wished he'd eaten breakfast instead of staying in bed for an extra ten minutes. He was light-headed as he heaved bales of washed wool from the shelves that morning. He glanced at the massive clock hanging in the centre of the aisle. His stomach rumbled disagreeably. But it would soon be time to meet Andrej in the canteen. The English food served there was not to his taste, but it was hot and filling and would soak up the residual alcohol still firing in his system.

When the clock chimed twelve and with Mr Askew's permission, Roman rushed off up the stone stairs to the canteen. People clattered up and down in their work shoes. Roman had half an hour for lunch to queue, be served, eat, and take a toilet break before returning to his workstation. When he reached the line, it snaked back to the entrance. Roman caught sight of Andrej a few yards in front, who turned around and grinned at him.

'Spam,' Andrej mouthed, and they exchanged feigned looks of disgust.

As the queue moved quickly along the food counter, Roman saw Andrej step out of his place and rush to where Roman stood.

'Give me your place and find a seat for us,' Andrej said.

Roman glanced around; there were plenty of places to sit down.

'Why?' He raised his hands to his shoulders.

Andrej took a deep breath. 'Look, it's best that way. Take my word.'

Roman examined Andrej's worried forehead. Then he

leaned to the side and strained to peer down the queue. A young woman with brunette curls tucked inside a turban ladled something onto workers' plates as they filed past. Roman saw her smiling at the diners and was sure each man visibly jolted. Then he understood why Andrej wanted him out of the way.

'It's Bad Luck Bridget,' Andrej said as he placed his hand on Roman's arm, tightening his fingers.

'What do you mean?'

'Come on, whenever you bump into her, something goes wrong.' Andrej nodded.

'Find some seats.'

Roman stared at Andrej, his friend, who always watched his back, and had protected him from harm, then at Bridget, whose beauty floored him every time he laid eyes on her.

'No, I'm not running away from a woman,' Roman said and kept his place in the line.

A slight tremor rippled his arm when he reached Bridget and held out his plate. Bridget glanced up at him as she dolloped the pale-looking substance onto his plate. She froze.

'Dobry wieczor,' Roman said. *Good afternoon.* 'It's the Pole again.'

Colour rushed to her cheeks as she leaned toward him. 'Oh, Jesus, meet me after work. Let me explain.'

A wiry woman standing next to Roman nudged his back with her bony elbow. 'Come on, love, stop yakking. I want me dinner.'

As Roman moved off, clutching his plate, Bridget

called out, 'The gates, at six. Please, Roman.'

Roman found Andrej at a table, who was halfway through his food already.

'Well?' Andrej said. 'Bit of a surprise, eh?'

'What's she doing here?' Roman shook his head.

'Working, like us, I imagine.'

'Maybe it's meant to be, Andrej.' Roman said. 'It's fate.' He smiled and, before eating, said, 'She's asked me to meet her at six.'

'What for? You dumbo.'

'To explain.' Roman shrugged and stared at his plate.

'Why bother? She's a teaser.'

Andrej wolfed down a forkful of spam and mash, then gulped down his glass of water. Drops trickled down his chin.

'What do you think this spam…' he emphasized the word, 'really is?' He jabbed his fork into a piece and lifted it for inspection.

'Search me.' Roman cut into the glistening pink substance. 'Could be anything.'

They exchanged looks.

'Hmm,' Roman said. 'If it was a pig, it was very ill.'

'Anaemic even?' Andrej said. 'Or maybe it was just boiled with some added glue.'

'Oink, oink,' Andrej said, then he snorted.

'Oink, croak, oink,' Roman repeated, feeling hysteria rising in his chest.

Suddenly, he wanted to laugh and cry simultaneously. And before he knew it, he had put down his cutlery and was convulsed by uncontrollable laughter as Andrej continued to make piggy noises between bursts of laughter himself. Tears streamed down Roman's cheeks as he doubled up, choked with emotion while the people around stared at him and Andrej and nudged one another.

'Fucking crazy Poles,' someone said.

Then Roman stopped, slapped his chest a few times as though to tamp down something, took a swig of water, and stood up. 'Time to get back to work,' he said.

* * *

At the end of that day Roman leaned on the mill gatepost, his stare fixed on the outside clock as people streamed out on foot and bicycles. He thought, *she better not take me for a chump*. Roman watched the workers hurrying away in tight groups like ants. Then someone touched his shoulder. He turned and Bridget stood before him; her eyes sparkled from inside, and the sun behind formed a halo around her auburn hair.

'I'm so glad you're here,' she said. 'I've been trying to find where you live since I returned.'

Roman crossed his arms over his chest. 'Returned. Where you been?'

Bridget tugged his jacket sleeve and played with the buttons on the cuff. 'Come on now, let's take a walk. It's a gorgeous evening.' She smiled at him and kept her gaze fixed on his.

'Why you think I go for walk with you?' Roman leaned towards her, wanting to smile. 'You stand me up. Remember?'

'Please, please, come on, let me explain.' Bridget

beckoned.

The day's heat absorbed by the cobbles rose in a hazed shimmer. Yellow-billed starlings flitted around the rooftop of the mill and gathered to swoop off in search of supper. Roman and Bridget crossed the small bridge and scrambled down the grassy slope to the canal towpath.

'So, what happen?' Roman sneaked a sideways look at Bridget and saw her expression altered as they walked on.

'My father was very ill. I had a telegram on my way to meet you.' Bridget glanced at him. 'I had to go home to Cork straight away.'

'Oh, I see.' There was a silence then. 'I sorry. He better?'

Bridget kicked away a stone as she walked. 'No. He's not.' She stopped walking. 'He died.'

Roman halted. 'Oh, that very bad.'

He turned towards Bridget and folded her in his arms. She nuzzled under his neck for a short while, then pulled away, dabbed her eyes with a handkerchief from her sleeve, and blew her nose noisily.

'Sorry,' she said. 'They call me Nellie the Elephant at home.'

Roman laughed, even though he was not sure what she meant.

'Let's sit,' Roman grabbed her hand and led her towards a grassy stump, where they settled themselves. 'How he die?'

'You don't beat around the bush, do you, Roman?'

He raised his hands as though surrendering. 'Sorry, my English not good.'

Bridget touched his arm. ‘It’s okay, it is. He had a stroke.’ She shook her head. ‘He drank too much you see.’

‘You very sad now?’

She paused for a while, and they watched a laden barge chug by. The wash rippled towards the canal edge where damselflies flitted in the swaying grass.

Bridget broke the silence. ‘I don’t know, it’s strange. It’s nice to be back here. Away from Ireland, away from the Church.’ She put her hand to her mouth. ‘Oh, I’m sorry, I didn’t mean to sound callous… you must think I’m terrible.’

Roman let out a hearty laugh and hugged her close, stroking her cheek with his thumb.

‘No, I understand, you free from past now. We good match.’ He turned her face upwards and planted a soft kiss on her lips.

She pulled back. ‘Well, I never. *You’re* a forward one.’

‘Bus go forward, time go forward. What you mean?’

Bridget smiled at him. ‘It’s just an expression.’

She picked off the grey flecks of wool that had settled on his jacket, then rested her temple on his shoulder.

‘We go dancing Friday night? Cheer you up.’ Roman squeezed her tight and caught the scent of her breath: sweetened tea.

‘Yes, that would be lovely.’

‘No standing up this time,’ he said, then regretted sounding insensitive. ‘You be my girl now?’

# Bridget

Bridget stared at her porridge; the glutinous mass cooling in the bowl made her stomach churn. She gagged and ran out to the bathroom with hands clasped over her mouth. Back in the kitchen, she leaned against the sink and covered her damp face with her pinny.

'Sit down, and I'll get you a fresh cup of tea,' her friend Kay said, getting up to heat the kettle on the ancient gas stove.

'I don't know why we have to have porridge for breakfast, it's summer now. And it tastes horrible,' Bridget said.

'Honey, it's called food rationing and is preferable to powdered eggs, don't you agree?'

Kay lit the gas flame for the water and returned to her seat. Bridget uncrossed her arms and reached in her pocket for her cigarettes. She pulled one from the pack and examined it.

'Even this makes me feel poorly today.' She passed the cigarette to Kay. 'Here, you have it.'

Kay snatched the cigarette and lit it. The sulphurous flare from the match head hit Bridget's nostrils. She turned around and threw up in the sink.

'Jesus Christ, Bridget.'

Kay jumped up, caught Bridget by the elbow, and guided her out of the kitchen to their shared room. She settled Bridget on her bed and went to fetch a damp cloth. When she returned, Bridget was crying. Kay pulled a chair up to the bedside, leaned over Bridget, and placed the cool flannel on her glistening forehead.

'Is something wrong, Bridget?'

'No. No. It's just, I can't really face food right now.'

'Why's that, love?'

Bridget shrugged.

'What have you and Roman been up to these last few months?'

Bridget remained silent.

'You can tell me.' Kay's fine-boned face was open and kind.

'I can't, Kay.' Bridget paused and turned her whole body towards the wall. 'I'm so ashamed,' she said in a low, whispery voice.

The sun poured through the window while Bridget moved her hand back and forth over a patch of eiderdown where hot rays saturated the cover.

Kay said, 'Jesus, Bridget, you're not, are you? Really?'

Bridget turned to see Kay's eyes screwed into a squint. 'That bloody Pole.'

'Oh, God. Kay, believe me. It's not his fault.'

'Christ almighty. Oh, girl.' Kay leaned and pushed Bridget's hair back from her forehead. 'Have you seen a doctor?'

Bridget snorted. 'No. How can I? I'm supposed to be a good catholic!'

'Never mind about that now, Bridget. You have to. How far do you think you are?'

'About three months.' Bridget said.

'Well! You didn't waste any time, did you?'

The two fell silent, with only the sound of the ticking

clock on the bedside table. The atmosphere in the room was dense and suffocating. Kay rose to open the window to the sounds of children playing in the street below, cries, and laughter.

'Tag! I got you,' a young boy shouted, and then a girl squealed and giggled.

* * *

The summer of 1947 was scorching— it seemed to Bridget the weather threw off the grey blanket of the war years. She rode the bus to meet Roman at the foot of the glen the following weekend. They would walk out there rather than meet in stuffy pubs or sneak to his lodgings.

Bridget sat bunched up to the window and tried to lose herself in the journey. Aromas from the streets breezed through the open windows. The distinctive smell of sizzling beef fat wafted from the fish and chips shops on most street corners. The bus trundled through rows of terraced houses, all blackened by years of soot. The signs of daily life were evidenced by washing that flapped on outdoor lines as small groups of women gathered by whitewashed doorsteps rocking prams, talking animatedly, while children tugged at their skirts. Even as the sun shone fiercely, the surroundings always seemed dark.

Bridget thought of Ireland's fresh, clear air and of going to the beach with her brothers and sisters winkle picking when they were young. Their lips salted and tingled as they meandered on the long journey home. And later, after her father ruined everything, they were forced to move and live in damp, cramped rooms in the backstreets of Cork. Her only sense of freedom was when she was with her friends on the busy city streets. She had hoped to escape that life.

The bus conductor's voice crashed into her thoughts. 'All off for Shipley Glenn.'

As she walked to their meeting place, she spotted Roman waiting and broke into a trot. His hair looked glossy and freshly cut, and his jacket was hooked over his shoulder by a finger. He laughed as she rushed into him.

'Is it train ride or me you excited about?'

Bridget hugged him and then let go. 'The train!' she said.

Roman grinned and grabbed her hand. 'Come on, no time to waste.'

The funicular sat idling while passengers filled the rows of small wooden seats. Then the train set off, and as it chugged slowly up the wooded hillside, Bridget watched some butterflies flit between the wildflowers which lined the side of the track. Fat bumblebees swayed unsteadily in the air; their legs laden with pollen. Everywhere life bloomed and flourished, she felt overwhelmed by the sudden abundance of things.

At the top of the hill, the train jolted to a stop. Roman climbed out and offered his hand to Bridget. He bowed to her and smiled. Bridget took his warm hand as she stepped from the carriage onto the grass where the sun's rays beat down. A slight breeze ruffled her dress about her knees, and Roman leant in to kiss her.

'You beautiful today,' he said, and they set off on foot towards the plateau hand in hand.

They reached a wide flat rock, and Roman sat down, inviting Bridget to follow. He laid back and cradled his head in his hands as he stared at the clear expanse of sky.

'No dark cloud today,' he winked at Bridget.

Sheep bleated in the background as Bridget scanned the valley below; the smoke rising from mill chimneys seemed at odds with the glorious summer day.

'What you think about?' Roman asked Bridget, twiddling a grass stem between his tongue and teeth.

She turned to speak to him, and his beauty suddenly overwhelmed her. He shone.

'Oh, this and that,' Bridget said as she regained composure.

'You quiet today. Not like you.'

'I'm fine. Really, I am.' Bridget smiled at Roman, who leant upon his elbow, spitting the grass away.

'Something wrong. Tell me,'

Bridget examined her knees closely for a while.

'What is it?' Roman sat upright then and put his hand on her arm that circled her knees.

She felt her face prickle. 'I went to the doctor.'

Roman's face changed immediately, 'Why? You not ill. You look like rose in full bloom.' He raised his hand in the air, fingers spread out.

Bridget breathed in. *I have to tell him, and then it will all be over. He'll run away. I know it.*

'It's just, I've been feeling a little sick in the mornings.'

She turned to face him and examined his expression for signs of comprehension. He held the tip of his nose between finger and thumb as though about to dive into a river.

'Has it gone away?'

'Has what gone away?' Bridget felt a chill pass through her.

'Sick feeling?'

'Oh, no. Not yet.'

'Doctor give you medicine?'

'No.'

'He do nothing?'

'Yes, yes, he did… he did something…' She paused and looked away. Her face burned, and tears formed in the well of her eyes. 'Roman, he took a blood test.'

'Blood test. What for?'

*Here goes,* she thought. 'The doctor thinks I might be… I could be… pregnant.' Bridget buried her face in her hands and cried.

Roman's arms encircled her as he pulled her into his chest. He kissed the top of her head and gently peeled her hands from her face.

'Why you cry? It good news.'

Bridget looked up at him. 'How is it good news, tell me?'

Roman pulled away and knelt on one knee. With one hand, he took Bridget's hand and placed the other on his heart.

'Bridget O'Keefe, you marry me.'

Bridget opened her mouth, but the words dissolved in her throat.

Roman's expression collapsed. 'You no want to?' he stammered.

'I might not be… you know… well, pregnant.'

Roman pulled his hand away. 'When you know?'

Bridget grabbed his hand back and grasped it tight. 'Next week.'

'You not love me?'

Bridget rubbed her thumb across the back of Roman's hand. 'I love you. It's just all happened so… so quickly.'

'Life happens fast. You no answer my question,' Roman said.

'We hardly know one another. I don't even know what happened to you in the war.'

Roman put his hands on Bridget's cheeks and cradled her face. 'Nothing happen to me. I fight, stay alive, and I here now.'

'You don't understand, Roman. I can't tell my family. They'll never speak to me again through shame.'

'Why?'

'It's a sin, out of wedlock. I can't ever go home again.'

'Even if married?'

'They'd know.'

'How they know? Tell lies.'

'I can't.' Bridget shook her head. 'I just can't.'

'Can't marry me or can't tell lies?'

Roman let go of her and stood upon the rock, surveying the lush valley below. 'If you pregnant, I have plan.' He turned to Bridget. 'Good plan.'

Roman sat back down on the rock and took Bridget's hand. He had a plan of sorts, and this was a chance he was willing to take. It amazed him how suddenly he knew what he wanted from life, how an alternative path had opened up and beckoned him to explore.

'Bridget, what most important thing in life?' Roman screwed his eyes up.

Bridget looked up into the summer sky. Roman raised his gaze too to watch the fragile strands of clouds that drifted and mingled high above in the blazing blue.

Bridget turned to Roman. 'I don't know. Well, I haven't really thought about it.' She shook her head and smiled. 'I'm sorry.'

Roman grinned, and the tension lifted from his brow. 'I have. I had time to think. Most important thing is family.'

He watched Bridget consider his statement. She closed her eyes for a few seconds and squeezed them the way a child might try to make a magical wish when blowing out their birthday cake candles.

'Roman, my family are, well, important to me. But I had to get away from them. It wasn't straightforward you know.'

'You no love family?'

'Yes,' she paused. 'But not all of them.'

'Who you not like?'

Bridget looked at Roman. 'You know unconditional love isn't always possible.'

'What you mean?'

'Well, I love them in my way, but there's more to life than your own kin. There's an entire world.' She gestured to the scenery and then laughed at herself. 'I'm not well-travelled, but coming to England was the start of a new life for me. Away from home.'

'You lucky you still have home.'

Bridget bit her lip. 'I'm sorry. I didn't mean to offend you.' She traced a crack running along the rock's surface where green moss sprouted and ants darted in and out.

Roman shuffled closer. 'Bridget, in war, I lose contact with family.' He looked into her eyes and fixed them with his stare to drive home this most crucial truth. 'After war, I come to England and think my family could be dead.'

'Oh, Roman, that's terrible. It is so, so, unimaginable.'

'But!' His dark eyes misted over. 'I kept writing to Red Cross, and one day, just after I met you letter come from them to say mother she alive and in refugee camp in Scotland.' Roman turned away and wiped his shirtsleeve over his face.

'Oh! Roman.' Bridget threw her arms out and hugged him until he pulled away. 'That's wonderful. Absolutely wonderful.

'I can't breathe,' he said.

Bridget laughed at his jest, then returned to the subject. Her voice trembled as she asked, 'Why didn't you tell me about your mother earlier?'

Roman paused. 'I thought Red Cross letter mistake. Couldn't believe it true. I had to see her first. Then when I do, she so ill. I fear she might die.' His chin trembled.

'After I escape, I go to house, but no one there so I not

know what happened to her.'

'What do you mean after you escaped? Escaped from where?'

'In Warsaw, from Gestapo prison. They arrest us, but I escaped.'

'Hold on, arrested... who was arrested?'

'My father, me, then sister.'

Bridget let out a held breath. 'But why? Why were you arrested?'

A thin man walked past with an Alsatian dog that tugged on its lead toward Roman and Bridget. Roman flinched and pulled his legs back.

'Keep voice down.' Roman put his finger to his lips. 'You don't know who listen.'

'It's okay, Roman. We're in England. You're safe.'

'How you know?'

'I just, I...' Bridget trailed off.

He continued, 'We arrested because my father listen to outside radio broadcast.'

The sound of a brass band playing in the cricket ground below reached their ears. Saturday afternoon entertainment was very English, thought Roman, but it reminded him of something else, of marching bands and arms flung rigid in the air.

Bridget said, 'What do you mean an outside broadcast?'

'In occupation, Polish radio run by Nazis, but can tune World Service.'

'Roman. I feel out of my depth with you. I just can't imagine...' she trailed off.

Distant chimes of church bells echoed through the valley as Roman smoothed Bridget's hair that fluttered in the warm breeze.

'People not know what it like. Everything turned upside down. If you manage to live, you hope your family did.' Roman paused. 'But maybe not.'

'I'm trying to piece this together. How did your mother end up in Scotland?'

'After war finish, she in refugee camp in Germany.'

'In Germany? What was she doing in Germany if you were Polish?' Roman watched Bridget blush.

He shrugged. 'I don't know. We lost contact. Big gaps.'

'But she's in Scotland now?' Bridget patted the base of her throat and breathed in.

'Yes!' Roman snorted. 'Refugee camp. But she been very ill. In camp hospital.'

An owl glided over the valley's edge and dipped suddenly into the long grass.

'Oh, I thought owls only came out at night,' Bridget said.

'Surprise element, that's how they hunt.'

They sat in silence for a while then Bridget spoke. 'Roman, that's a lot to take in in one go.'

Roman moved back slightly.

Bridget took his hands in hers. 'You know we Irish are famed for weaving stories, but I've got nothing on yours.'

'What you mean, you think I lie?'

'No. No.'

The sounds of children's laughter pierced the air as they ran free on the glen.

'You want hear my plan now?' Roman grinned.

'Yes, please. I'd almost forgotten about that,' Bridget said, then giggled and looked relieved.

'I write my mother letter say we visit her. We have surprise.'

'Visit her? Are you sure? You said she's still very ill.'

'True but time running out.'

Bridget flinched. 'But what surprise? You don't mean, I, I can't announce my condition to...'

Roman threw his head back and laughed. 'No, not that. We tell her we get married soon. Make her happy.'

'Roman, heavens. I haven't even said yes to your proposal yet. My thoughts are whirling in my mind.'

'It easy. Say yes and everything fall into place.'

Bridget laughed. 'Where would we live?'

'I have Polish friends; we can rent room in Polish house. I speak with them.'

'But we can't marry in a church,' Bridget said.

'Registry office fine. Cheaper.'

'How romantic.' Bridget leaned in, tickled his ribs, and laughed.

Roman pulled Bridget up by the hand. 'Let's walk, clear head. Go home, then I write letter to mother.'

She giggled. 'What a cheek. You're so sure I will say yes, aren't you?'

Roman pointed to a young couple pushing a baby in a pram. 'How you think they get pram up here?'

Bridget smiled at him. 'God knows, must have struggled up this rocky path.'

'Good exercise. You like being mother, I know.'

Roman hugged Bridget. ‘When you have no family, you lost. We be family now? What you say?’

‘I’m going to think about it.’

‘Be quick. I want post letter to mother tomorrow,’ Roman said and kissed Bridget.

'Orsfield Common.'

The bus conductor's flat northern voice announced, to Bridget's astonishment, it was her stop. The ride home whizzed by in a flash as she tried to settle her mind on what to do for the best. Her key clicked in the lock, and she pushed the door open. The smell of fried bread clung in the hallway and reminded her of home and the blue haze ever-present in the kitchen at mealtimes.

Kay sat at the kitchen table reading when Bridget entered. She put her book aside and smiled.

'How'd it go, gal?'

Bridget sat down opposite Kay, her eyes wide. 'I can't believe it.'

'Oh god, what's happened?'

Kay grabbed Bridget's hand across the table and stroked it between hers.

'I told you not to mess about with those Poles. They're trouble, they are.'

Bridget withdrew her hand and pulled back a little.

'Oh, Holy Mary, mother of God, he didn't?' Kay stared intensely at Bridget, whose chin quivered.

'Didn't what?' Bridget said.

'Deny it, like they usually do?'

Kay let go of Bridget's hand, pulled out her cigarettes to offer Bridget one, and lit one herself. She blew smoke from the side of her mouth.

'No, thanks.' Bridget waved the cigarette away and then burst in to tears despite her intentions.

'Oh! the flaming fecking bastard,' Kay said.

She stood and hurried around the table to comfort Bridget. Kay circled Bridget's shoulders, knocking over a salt cellar that rolled off the table and crashed down—glass and crystals sprinkled like frost across the floor.

Bridget felt the warmth of Kay's arms on her neck, and calm settled onto her. She shook her head, then pointed to the salt.

'You're supposed to throw that over your left shoulder for good luck now, not on the floor!'

'Another time, honey.'

Bridget laughed for a short time, but then her shoulders heaved and shuddered inside Kay's embrace, and tears trickled down her face.

'Kay,' she said between gasps, 'Roman's asked me to marry him.'

Kay removed her arms and slumped into the chair next to Bridget. She stubbed out her cigarette.

'He never!' Then she stretched her face into an exaggerated expression of total surprise and leaned in close to Bridget's face. 'Oh, my God. That's just, just great,' Kay said. 'It's wonderful, Bridget!'

Tears gathered in Kay's eyes, and she dabbed them away with a lace-edged handkerchief whipped from her skirt pocket.

'Fancy that!' She threw her arms around Bridget and squeezed her. Then jumped up to put the kettle on. 'Let's celebrate.'

A girl from the lodging house breezed into the kitchen. 'Have you seen my powder compact?' she asked. 'I can't find it anywhere, and my mammy gave it me.' She slid into a chair at the table and glanced from Bridget to Kay. 'What's going on here now?'

'Nothing,' Bridget said. She straightened herself and wiped her cheek with her palm.

'Don't pull the wool over my eyes. There's an atmosphere, alright.'

'There's atmosphere everywhere, young lady,' Kay said. 'Now, me and Bridget are just making a cup of tea, and we're off for an early night.' She nodded to Bridget, who quickly stood up.

'Goodnight, Nancy,' Bridget said as she left the kitchen with a smile.

Bridget pulled the thin curtains tight in their room and ensured the door was firmly closed.

When Kay brought their drinks and sat on her bed, Bridget said, 'I want to keep this quiet for the time being. I don't know what I'm going to do.'

Kay had moved her cup to her mouth but stopped at Bridget's announcement, tea suspended in mid-air.

'Oh, Bridget, what are you talking about? I mean, what else can you do in your position?'

Bridget sank back onto her bed, stretched out, and pushed her shoes off at the heels with her toes. They clopped to the floor.

'I don't know, Kay. It's just, I came here to make a new life for myself, to get away from babies and useless husbands for a while.' She laid her forearm over her forehead and sighed.

'But Bridget, not every man is like your father. I'm

sorry for what I said earlier about Roman. I thought, you know…'

'No. I don't know. What did you think, then?'

'Well, I thought he would say, "are you sure it's mine?" like they all do and try to wriggle out of it.'

'Well, he didn't.'

'Bridget, I've got a feeling he's a good man, or he wouldn't have asked you to marry him.'

'If he meant it, that is.' Bridget turned on her side to stare at Kay, her mouth pulled down at the sides.

'Of course he meant it, girl; that would be a terrible thing to do if he didn't,' Kay said.

'How do you know he meant it?'

'What's wrong Bridget?'

'Oh, Kay, I know I love him. God, he's so kind, but…'

Kay moved to sit back on Bridget's bed. 'But what then, sweetheart?'

'It's just, what do I actually *know* about him or what happened to him in the war?'

'Why does it matter so much? We all have pasts of some kind,' Kay said.

'Well, it's a big step marrying someone you know hardly anything about.'

'Why are you so suspicious of him Bridget?'

Bridget sat up rigidly. 'I'm just worried about everything. That's all.'

'There was a knock on the door. Kay looked at Bridget and sprung up to answer. Nancy stood outside the door with a posy of sweet peas cradled in a white napkin, tied with a green string bow.

She handed them to Kay, peeped inside the room, and said, 'They're for Bridget. Left on the doorstep, they were.'

Kay took the flowers and examined them before handing to Bridget. The neat handwriting on the napkin's edge read: *To Bridget, my darling.*

'Thanks, Nancy,' Kay said and shut the door.

They heard Nancy humph from behind.

Bridget breathed in the flowers delicate scent.

'That's so romantic,' Kay said and sat back on her bed. 'And to be fair what are your options, honey?'

Bridget rested the flowers on the bedside table. 'Oh, I don't know, fall down the stairs. Take a hot bath and lots of gin.'

'No! Bridget. No. That's not for you.' Kay paused and peered sternly at Bridget. 'If you're not sure about Roman, you could have the baby adopted.'

'Oh, Kay, that's awful. You know those mother and baby places are hell. Those nurses look down on you like they never had a lustful thought.'

'Yes, maybe, but you can't be a single mother here in England. And you can't go back home now. How would you survive? God, Bridget, you know the shame of it.'

Bridget sat up. 'Kay, I love Roman, you know that, but I feel forced into a snap decision.'

'Choice is a luxury, Bridget. Get your head on,' Kay said.

Bridget stared at Kay as though seeing her anew. Like Kay knew something she didn't.

'But what if he turns out to be like my father?'

'Well, do *you* think he's like your father?'

'No, that's why I love him. He's strong-willed, straight to the point, and says what he thinks. My father was a weak man. Cowardly. God, he used to hide in the wardrobe in thunderstorms.'

Despite the seriousness of the conversation, Kay laughed. 'Oh, Bridget, he was a bit of a character, your Da. I remember him almost sucking up whiskey from a spilled bottle on the carpet one time.'

Bridget put her hands to her throat. 'Less of a character, more of a ruinous, selfish bastard.'

'Don't speak ill of the dead now,' Kay said. 'Are you afraid Roman will take to the drink or something?'

Bridget considered the question for a moment. 'Now Kay, him and his friends like their vodka, for sure.'

'Oh, Bridget, they're young men. They've been through rough times. They're bound to let their hair down now and again.'

'Ted didn't let his hair down,' Bridget said, 'and he was training to be a doctor. I could have been his wife.'

'But you turned him down, Bridget. Why was that?'

Bridget lay back down and rested her elbows across her cheekbones. 'Well, I got on with Ted. We talked and talked, but when I look at Roman, it's like he's lit from the inside, glowing. Looking at Ted was like looking at my brother. Homely.'

'But Bridget, that wears off, you know. Then what?'

'A life of babies, nappies, and housework, I suppose.'

'You know most girls *want* to get married.' Kay raised her eyebrows.

'I do too, Kay, but when I'm ready, on my terms.'

Kay was silent, then said, 'How far are you, if you don't mind me asking?'

'About three months.'

'The clock is ticking.'

There was a knock at the door again.

'I'll get it this time,' Bridget said.

When she opened the door, Nancy stood in her pyjamas and curling rags, wearing an excited expression.

'Bridget, your boyfriend's at the door. He says he has to see you.'

'Oh my God!' Bridget said, looking at Kay wide-eyed.

Bridget ran a brush through her hair, dabbed lipstick over her mouth, and rushed from the room, pushing Nancy aside on the landing. Downstairs, the front door was open onto the evening street, and Roman sat on the step. She saw him swivel around at the sound of her footsteps and jump up. He held something in his hands.

'Sorry, it's late to call but here's letter I write to my mother. I read to you,' he said.

The moonlight broke through the trees and covered everything with a lustrous hue.

'But I haven't said yes to your proposal yet, Roman.' Her voice had a musical tinkle.

Roman looked at Bridget as he held the letter up in his hands, which trembled slightly. 'Listen anyway.'

She shook her head gently. 'But how can you read it in the half-light? You know you can't come inside; the landlady would go bonkers.'

Roman grabbed Bridget's hand and led her to the soft yellow pool of light that fell from the street lamp. He stood beneath. Moths flitted and batted off the low-fizzing bulb.

'Here, I can see it now. It in Polish. I translate.'

'Of course,' Bridget said and took a step back to watch him read.

Roman cleared his throat and began.

*'Mrs Anya Kozynska, Ballochmyl Hospital, Beith, Scotland.*

*Dear Mother,*

*I hope you better, soon out of hospital. I miss you very much, too many years of separation. I like visit soon because of excellent news to tell.*

*My heart full with love. I sit by you, hold hand, tell to face.*

*Leeds Glasgow train run every day. My English now better reading bus and road sign. I been industrious, you find out.*

*Write soon, let me know when can visit but must be Sunday. I work all other days in mill. I save money, be sensible like you say.*

*Your loving son,*

*Roman.*

What you think?' Roman said, moving towards Bridget and grabbing her hand.

'But you haven't mentioned me?' she said with a grin.

Roman laughed and kissed the side of her head, tugging her into his body as she slid her arms around him.

A couple weaved past on the other side of the street, chattering, laughing raucously, and bumping into one another, obviously drunk. A dog barked somewhere, and a baby's cries floated from an open window.

'They should be in bed for work tomorrow,' Bridget said.

'Make hay when sun shines!' said Roman, proud of his mastery of the English phrase.

'What's going on here?' a voice interrupted.

Bridget's landlady stood on the doorstep, a grey dressing gown pulled tight around and belted with what looked like plaited string. Her arms folded.

Bridget flashed a look at Roman. 'I'm just helping Roman with a letter to his mother.'

Bridget signalled for him to put the letter away. She let go of his hand and backed away a little towards the door where the landlady stood glowering.

'Is that right? Well, can't you do that at a decent hour, young lady?'

'I'm sorry, I….'

'And I told you girls, no gentlemen callers.' The landlady glared at Roman.

Bridget stopped on the path, her feet firmly planted, hands on her hips. A thought popped into her mind as she looked at Roman and then at her landlady.

'And I expect he's one of them foreigners, as well?' she said, peering at Roman through narrowed eyes.

He flashed his brightest, widest smile at her and winked.

'Actually, he's not a gentleman caller as you referred

to him,' Bridget said and crossed her arms, a fire flaring in her eyes.

'I don't understand you, Miss O'Keefe,' she said. '*Surely*, you're not saying he's your brother or some such nonsense?' She laughed, and her belly wobbled under her dressing gown.

Bridget shot a glance at Roman and smiled. 'This is Roman, and he's my fiancé. He's no foreigner to me. And…' She paused to grin at Roman. 'We're going to be married very soon.'

There was silence for a minute, then Roman whooped and rushed towards Bridget, tears in his eyes. But the landlady stopped him by shouting, 'No! Get in with you, young lady, and no more of this bloody nonsense.'

She motioned Bridget forward with her plump hand and shut the door after her with a bang.

Upstairs in her room, Bridget looked from the window to see Roman still standing on the path below, smiling as though his face might crack.

# Roman

When Roman received a letter from his mother, he read it three times before he rushed down to the kitchen to find Andrej sitting with Katerina drinking Russian tea with lemon and sugar—a Saturday treat given the rationing of sugar. Roman grabbed a chair excitedly and sat down.

'Listen, my friends. Life is delightful.' He held the letter, ready to read, in unsteady hands.

'You need a cold bath,' said Andrej and winked at Katerina, who chuckled at Roman's enthusiasm.

Roman read from his mother's letter: 'How wonderful it will be to see you again, my darling son. I am so excited you have good news for me, and I am even more excited because I have good news for you. I will tell you everything when we meet, but I will allow you to give me your news first.'

Roman slapped the letter lightly and laughed. He read, 'I have news from your sister, Elouna who is alive and well and would like to see us when it's possible.'

Roman looked up, and his face crumpled. He dropped the letter and sobbed into his chest, head bowed.

'Oh, Roman, that's wonderful news.' Katerina rushed to put her arms around his neck and squashed his head to her side.

Andrej jumped up from his seat. 'Roman, Roman, why the tears? It's time to celebrate your marvellous fortune. You have a beautiful fiancée and a good mother, and now the news that your sister is alive.'

He placed his hand gently on Roman's shoulder. 'Let's

celebrate, my dear friend.' Andrej's voice quivered a little.

Roman lifted his teary face and smiled at Andrej and Katerina. Andrej was right. Could life become any more perfect for him? Yes, it could.

'You're right. I am indeed very fortunate.' He wiped his hand over his face and stood up. 'Now, let's tell Bridget the glorious news, and then all celebrate at the Polish Club.'

* * *

Roman found it impossible to sleep the night before the train to visit his mother in Scotland. It was humid, and no matter how wide he opened the bedroom window, there was no air or breeze to cut through the heavy night. Roman didn't want to wake the others, so crept downstairs for a glass of water. He paced around the kitchen, the linoleum floor warm under his bare feet. His stomach fluttered and grumbled in equal measure, but he could eat nothing because nerves dried and contracted his throat and mouth. Roman tugged open the kitchen window and leaned his elbows on the sill. His head poked out into the claggy night. Roman gazed at the inky sky; the moon's light illuminated the rooftops of the rows of silhouetted terraced houses. It would be a few more hours before threads of pink streaked from the brightening horizon when the birds would pip, chatter, and trill in their dawn awakening. He saw a thin fork of lightning flash from the sky far away and closed the window in case of an oncoming storm. After more pacing, he tried to read a newspaper, but his thoughts would not stay fixed on anything, and when an hour had passed, Roman returned to bed and eventually fell into a fitful sleep where he kicked and jerked through obscure nightmares.

Roman's heart thudded at the base of his throat as the train pulled into the smoky Glasgow station. He wondered how his mother would have changed since his first visit and tried to imagine her sitting in bed with some colour in her cheeks. He had brought Polish rye bread and salami from the continental shop in Bradford Market. The items had cost him almost his full rations, but he knew his mother craved the food of her homeland. He mused how things had turned full circle, and now he brought food to her. He would look after his mother and keep her safe, as well as his new family-to-be.

The walk from the bus stop to the hostel flashed by. Then, as Roman looked up, a dark building with opaque windows loomed in front of Roman, signposted the hostel's hospital. The smell inside made him nauseous as he entered it, and he gagged. Images of injured and dying men, screaming and crying, flooded his mind, and Roman fought to push them down and think only of his mother, Bridget, and their future. He found his way to a reception window and, after a few enquiries, made difficult by the thick Scottish accents of the staff, was directed to her ward.

He reached the entrance and looked around the ward of women. Some sat up, and some laid down, all very pale-skinned. Roman spotted his mother, and a lump formed in his throat, making him want to swallow rapidly. Anya raised an arm and waved feebly. His footsteps sounded extra loud to him as he rushed towards her bed.

Anya had a knitted shawl around her thin shoulders.

As he approached, Roman thought about how much older than her actual years she looked. She was forty-three but could easily have been mistaken for a woman in her late fifties. Looking at her as he neared, he realised his mother must have suffered terribly. He hoped at this visit she would be able to tell him a little about what had happened during the war years.

Roman collapsed into the stiff bedside chair and choked. Tears trickled down Anya's hollowed-out cheeks as he leaned over and kissed her still-soft forehead. Roman grabbed her hand to hold between his. It was cold and clammy in his grasp.

'Mama, you look well.' His voice quivered.

Anya's face broke into a half-smile and her dark eyes flashed beneath pale eyelids.

'You're such a terrible liar, Roman. The doctors have almost given up on me.' Her smile disappeared, and her forehead creased into tracks.

'Don't say that. Please,' Roman pleaded. 'I can't bear it.'

'My son with the beautiful black eyes, tell me your good news.' She stared at him with such warmth that his heart felt like it would burst from his chest.

'I will! Mama. But first, what of Elouna?

'She's fine, Roman. You must tell me *your* news first. I insist.'

Roman stroked his mother's hand and recounted breathlessly about Bridget, how they met and were to be married.

'It will be very soon,' he said. 'And you will be well

enough to attend. It will be a big Polish party, with dancing, singing, vodka, and, of course, some fighting.'

His mother laughed, coughed and squeezed his hand.

'Who knows, maybe we can all live in the same place here in England soon,' Roman said.

Anya smiled. 'Yes, in the country, with chickens. I'd like that. I can teach your bride to cook Polish dishes.'

Roman grinned and pulled his chair even closer to her bed. 'Now, Mama, tell me your news of Elouna from the beginning. Everything.'

Anya took a deep breath and winced slightly. 'A few weeks ago, I received a letter from Elouna. She'd been searching for me through the Red Cross since the war ended.'

Roman shifted so near he was almost sitting on Anya's bed. His eyes shone, and it took him some time to speak. As he did, his voice wobbled with emotion.

'That's amazing.' He wiped damp eyes with his cuff. 'I can't quite believe it. I thought she must be…' Roman broke off, unable to voice his thoughts. He shook his head as though to free it from those dark ideas. 'So, tell me, where is she now?'

Anya studied him for a while, then cleared her throat. The clatter of hospital life went on in the background. Moans, groans, curtains hastily pulled shut. 'Elouna is on her way to England, with her children.' Her voice was a whisper

'Her children!'

'Yes, she married.'

'I can't believe it.' A huge grin lit his face.

Anya looked down at the starched white bedclothes and scrunched them in her shaky hands. Thin blue veins streaked their backs and stood out against her pallid skin.

There was a long silence before she said, 'She's travelling from Germany.'

Roman shifted in his seat trying to piece together what might have happened. 'What was she doing in Germany?' His grin dissolved.

Anya cowered slightly and released the bedclothes, raising her hand in the sterile air.

'Many incomprehensible things happened during that terrible war.'

Roman stared at his mother as the words fell heavily on his ears. Their meaning stirred a dread in his belly and parched his throat. His eyes narrowed. 'What happened to Elouna?' Roman hardly dared to breathe as he waited for her to answer.

'People had to make harsh choices during that time. On the spur of the moment. No time for reflection.' His mother looked at him in a plead.

Roman nodded. 'Yes,' he said, encouraging her to continue but not wanting to hear what she might say.

'Roman, there's something you must understand,' she said. 'It's hard to grasp, but Elouna married a German officer during the war…he took care of her, you see.'

'A German took care of her? Are you joking?'

Roman could see the panic in her eyes. He dropped Anya's hand and stood up. His hands clenched tight by his side.

'I don't believe it. It's not Elouna; it must be an

imposter or something. Show me the handwriting of this letter.'

'It's not an imposter, Roman. It's Elouna.'

'It can't be. These things happen all the time now, people pretending to be someone else. How can you say it's not just a stranger looking for a new identity?'

'Because, Roman…' Anya paused and looked away from Roman as she said, 'I was with her for a short time.'

'With her, where?'

'In Germany. When he was posted back from Warsaw.'

Roman threw his hands in the air. 'God, my head is about to explode. Elouna married a German officer who she met in Poland?'

'Roman, it was how she survived.'

'No! Please tell me I'm having a nightmare. What are you saying?' He smacked his forehead with his palm.

Anya wrung her hands. 'Please, try to listen. Let me explain the circumstances to you.'

'No. There can be no explanation. I don't want to hear it. You're traitors… collaborators…both of you. I…' Roman turned and stormed towards the ward door, swearing in Polish.

He heard Anya call after him. 'Come back, Roman, please. I need to tell you what happened!'

Roman ran from the hospital to the bus stop, unable to believe his mother's words. His whole body trembled, and he had to sit down on the grass verge to try to calm himself, head in hands. On the bus, he counted the fare into the conductor's palms. Roman's hands shook violently. The conductor nodded and picked the coins from Roman's palm. 'Bad day, eh?' he said.

Roman tried to imagine what circumstances could have led his mother and sister into such betrayal on the route back to Glasgow. To marry a German was the act of a collaborator. He could not imagine how Elouna could have been coerced into this and concluded it must have been a consenting act. And his mother with her while *he* had suffered so? All that time, he had secretly grieved, thinking they must be dead, and there they were, living with the oppressors—the brutes, the monsters. His thoughts imploded, and rage deep within him bubbled to the surface. Roman clenched his jaw and fists in the act of attempted containment.

The street to the station, shielded by tall buildings, was without sun and its greyness overwhelmed Roman, deepening his mood as he hurried along. He passed a pub door where shouting and high-pitched laughter teemed out. Roman turned into it. The gas-lit interior was dank and fuggy. He pushed through the cram to order a pint of bitter plus a double whiskey. Settling into a seat, Roman knocked back his whiskey in one. The table strewn with sticky empty glasses, overflowing ashtrays, and a crushed cigarette pack disgusted him. A man opposite with translucent, shrivelled skin lifted his glass to Roman and smiled a toothless smile. Roman nodded to him, picked up the pint that he downed quickly, and then ordered another.

In a far corner, a bulky man gripped a spindly man with frizzed red hair in a headlock. His arms flailed like windmill sails while the crowd at that table laughed, wheezed, and waved their glasses in the blueish air. A scrawny woman draped in a fake leopard coat smoked outside on the pavement and relayed something to each man who stepped past her into the pub.

On his fifth set of drinks, Roman realised he was ravenous. He regretted hurling his bread and sausage gift for his mother over a wall as he rushed to the bus stop. His former self, who had endured months of gnawing hunger, would not have believed him capable of such an act.

Roman scrambled from the pub and headed for the train station, his mind in a blaze of fury and confusion. He staggered into shop windows on the way as passers-by stepped aside. Roman had time to kill before his train and stumbled towards a bench to smoke. A man plopped down next to him and asked for a light. Roman leaned in and struck a match that flared and fizzed, suddenly making him nauseous.

'Thank you!' The man smiled, revealing a gleaming gold incisor.

Roman pulled back. Unwanted images sprang into his mind.

'Don't get gold teeth,' he warned the stranger. 'Germans pull out.'

The man drew away. 'You being funny, pal?'

'No! It true.'

He stood and walked away from Roman. 'You're crazy,' he said.

Then Roman was right behind him, one arm around his neck, dragging him down in a headlock.

Roman shouted, 'You not know what they do!'

The man struggled, but Roman held him in his grip,

overcome by the images of piles of blood-smeared gold teeth. Soon people crowded around them. Roman swore in Polish and English but would not let the man free until the police burst onto the scene. Roman heard their whistles before he saw them sprinting toward him. Two men with ruddy faces who stopped nearby. One raised his hands in the air.

'Come on now,' he said as he edged slowly towards Roman. 'Let him go, why don't you, laddie?'

Roman felt his mind go blank and released the man who staggered away from him, coughing. The policeman grabbed Roman's arm.

'You're coming with us.'

He hauled Roman away, shoved him into a van with bars at the rear windows and slammed the door. The van careered around for a while before it stopped somewhere. The doors opened. Roman was yanked out and dragged up steep stairs into a police station.

'You can cool off here, pal,' said the policeman who bundled him into a bare cell with a floor mattress and bucket in the corner. The place reeked of piss, stale sweat and alcohol.

Roman fell into a deep sleep despite the surroundings, exhausted by his day.

In the morning, an older policeman entered the cell.

'Good morning.' He glanced at Roman, then the cell. 'It's not very comfortable here, is it?'

Roman laughed, thinking, what could this man ever know about the places he'd slept? Bug-infested, disease-ridden, putrid, reeking of shit and death.

‘Been in worse,’ Roman said.

The policeman smiled. ‘Okay. I’m Sergeant McManus.’ Roman liked him. ‘Now, come this way, laddie.’ He led Roman to a small room with an iron desk and chair and invited him to sit. ‘You caused a bit of a disturbance yesterday evening. What happened?’

Roman couldn’t fully remember but knew it had started when he talked with his mother. ‘I visit mother in hospital. We fall out.’

‘I see, but you attacked a stranger in the street for no reason?’

Roman shook his head. His thick hair fell over his forehead. ‘I no remember.’ He pushed his hair back with a grubby hand. The dirt under his nails reminded him of different, far away days he’d rather forget.

Sergeant McManus stared hard at Roman. ‘I know you lads have had it rough.’ He paused, but Roman said nothing. McManus continued, ‘My daughter was engaged to a Pole but broke it off because he was volatile. You know what that means?’

Roman nodded. ‘Like Mount Vesuvius.’

McManus laughed. ‘Well, the man you attacked doesn’t want to press charges, so you’re free to go after a few checks. Is there anyone I can contact to vouch for you?’

Bridget woke to the sound of knocking on her door, then Nancy peeped her head around it. *Oh no,* Bridget thought, *she wants me to go to Sunday mass with her*, but when she saw Nancy's expression, she jolted.

'What is it?' Bridget said, rubbing the heels of her palms into her eyes.

The previous evening's excitement about Roman's visit to his mother that day had led her and Kay to tip down a few glasses of beer, more than they had planned, and now she was heavy-headed.

'Bridget, the police are on the doorstep, and they want to speak to you,' Nancy said, eyes wide in amazement behind her thick spectacles.

'What!' Bridget threw off the bed covers and reached for her dressing gown discarded over a chair.

'Oh, God, do I look a fright, Nancy.' She tugged at her hair, a cloud of tangled curls waving breezily about her head.

'You look just fine,' Nancy said with a suppressed smirk. 'What do you think they want?'

'I don't know.' Bridget pulled on her dressing gown, belted it, and ran downstairs barefooted.

The door was open, and two police constables stood on the doorstep. One flipped through a notebook, and the other looked at Bridget as she arrived dishevelled in front of him, slightly breathless.

He cleared his throat. 'Miss, are you Bridget O'Keefe?'

Bridget's knees buckled as she leant on the chipped

door frame for support. She spotted a couple saunter past and peer in at the spectacle of the police at the Irish girls' lodging house. They shook their heads and tutted. *Be damned*, Bridget thought.

'Yes, I am. What's wrong?' Bridget looked for signs of how serious things were from one to the other.

'It's nothing to worry about,' said one constable, then looked to the other with the notebook and nodded. 'We just need to confirm some details with you.'

Bridget opened her mouth to speak but stopped as she heard footsteps behind her. She turned her head to see Nancy standing right behind her, trying to lean over her shoulder.

'Nancy, please can you bring Kay down here for me?'

'Can *I* help at all?' Nancy stood firm.

'I need to talk to the policemen. Please, just do as I ask.'

Nancy huffed and stomped off upstairs to wake Kay.

The constable continued. 'Miss O'Keeffe, do you know of a man named Roman Kozynski?' He pronounced Roman's surname a syllable at a time as though speaking to a child.

'Yes! Yes, I do. Why?'

'We'll get to that soon.' The constable stared at Bridget as his colleague scribbled in the notebook. 'Mr Kozynski says you're his fiancée.' He looked scornful. 'Is that so?'

Relief washed over Bridget, and her knees were suddenly more able to support her. 'Yes. I am. We've just become engaged.'

'It seems he's got himself into a spot of bother.' He

coughed. 'And as he's a registered alien, you need to vouch for him so we can release him from jail.'

'From jail?' Bridget repeated with disbelief. 'What is he doing in jail?' Her face clouded over.

'He was arrested in Glasgow.'

'Arrested?' Bridget said mechanically and looked from one to the other.

'Yes, arrested. If you could report to your local police station and take your passport as a means of identification, we'll take it from there.'

The constable gave Bridget a piece of paper with the station's address then they both turned and strode down the path. Bridget moved back into the hall to see Kay walking towards her with her arms outstretched; she looked prepared for the worst possible news.

'What's happened? What is it?'

Bridget felt herself crumple into Kay's arms. 'Roman's been arrested. I've to go to the police station.' Her head lolled forwards.

Bridget slid out of Kay's grasp down onto the linoleum floor in a swoon.

Later, when Bridget had recovered, she and Kay stepped out into the morning sunshine and made their way to the police station. Bridget had never been inside a police station, and her pulse raced as she approached the building with its intimidating sign above the entrance.

Bridget had made a point of wearing her white lace gloves to match her summer sandals and was glad the fine material absorbed the dampness that spread across her palms. She reported to the reception desk, where the clerk told her and Kay to take a seat. The wooden bench was hard. Soon a policeman appeared from the echoey corridor with a file clutched under his elbow. He approached them with rapid steps and a closed expression.

'Which one of you is Bridget O'Keeffe?'

'I am,' Bridget said. 'And this is my friend, Kay O'Brien. Can she come with me, please?'

He nodded his head wearily. 'This way, ladies.'

They followed him down the dimly lit corridor into a stuffy room.

'Take a seat,' he motioned.

They sat at a table as he slapped the file down and flipped it open.

'First, can I see your passport please, Miss O'Keefe?'

Bridget handed over her passport, trying to keep her hand from shaking. He took his time scanning the contents.

Eventually, he said, 'Okay, everything seems in order here.'

Then he checked some file details while Bridget held her breath, hardly daring to look at Kay. The policeman looked up at Bridget with a frown.

'Mr Kozynski was arrested last night for disturbing the peace.'

He stared at Bridget for a time. Though she wanted to flinch under his gaze, she kept her nerve.

'What happened, please?'

He sighed, shut the file, and placed his hands over it.

'The Glasgow police will give you the details. However, before he's released, they need to speak to someone who can vouch for him.'

‘I can do that.’

Bridget glanced at Kay, who nodded, and then smiled at the policeman who ignored her.

‘You can phone from the office. Follow me.’

* * *

‘Hello, operator, please, can you put me through to Glasgow Central Police.’

When the connection was made a woman said ‘Yes, who’s speaking, please?’

‘My name’s Bridget O’Keefe, and I’ve been told to phone this number in connection with Roman Kozynski who I believe is with you.’

‘Hold on, please, I’ll just fetch the Sergeant.’

The line went quiet for a while then Bridget heard a man’s voice.

‘Sergeant McManus.’

Her voice trembled. ‘Hello, my name’s Bridget O’Keefe; I believe you want to speak to me about Roman Kozynski.’

McManus’s voice softened. ‘Aye, I do. You must be the wee Irish lassie he told me about.’

Bridget let out a breath of relief. ‘What’s happened? Please tell me he's alright.’

‘Yes, he’s fine, but I’m afraid we had to arrest Mr Kozynski for disturbing the peace near Glasgow Train Station.’

Bridget breathed in. ‘Disturbing the peace?’

‘It seems he was upset…’ Sergeant McManus coughed, ‘after visiting his mother. He was drunk, swearing, and frightening folk.'

'But… he went to see his mother to…' Bridget paused. *Oh no,* she thought, *his mother's displeased with our plans.* She continued. 'Roman went to give her good news.' Just then, a thought occurred to her. 'Do you know if he actually got there?'

'Yes, he did. He couldn't remember exactly what occurred, just that they fell out.'

Bridget was silent.

'You know, Miss O'Keefe, we've had lots of Polish lads here and the Italians. They're excitable, aren't they? But after all they've been through, it's not surprising, is it?'

'Roman's a good man, Sergeant McManus. He's not a troublemaker. He works hard, and we're going to be married soon.'

'I can tell all that, Miss O'Keefe, just from talking to him.' He paused. 'Now you've vouched for him and the police have checked his registration card, we'll release him. We're satisfied he's not a threat to anyone. But please, would you meet him at Leeds Train Station and make sure he gets home safely?'

Relief swept through Bridget. 'Yes, of course, I can do that. Do you know what time Roman's likely to arrive back?'

She flashed a wide smile at Kay, who stood by her side listening, her hand on Bridget's shoulder.

'Hold the line and I'll check the timetable.'

As soon as Kay and Bridget were out of the station, Kay lit a cigarette and blew an enormous white smoke plume that hung in the humid air.

‘What do you think happened?’ Kay said.

‘Oh god, Roman’s mother must have said no.’

‘Don’t be daft. His mother’s not marrying you, is she? He is. It’s not up to her, anyway.’ Kay grabbed Bridget’s arm and linked her.

‘But what else would they fall out about? I don’t understand it.’

Kay glanced at Bridget as they walked along. ‘You don’t know what went on. Wait till Roman gets back, then you can find out. Stop worrying, my girl.’

‘Oh no, look who’s heading this way *now*.’ Bridget motioned at Nancy, who fast approached from the opposite direction.

‘Don’t tell the nosey cow a word,’ Kay said and tightened her link with Bridget.

Nancy waved and cantered towards them, her enormous bosoms heaving up and down.

‘What’s happened?’ she asked when she reached them, looking hungry for gossip from one to the other.

‘Nothing,’ Bridget said.

‘Absolutely nothing,’ Kay repeated, then puffed on her cigarette.

Nancy narrowed her gaze. ‘But I heard the police mention Roman this morning. I did.’ She crossed her arms over her chest.

‘You must have misheard. Now, we have to get going,’ said Kay.

Nancy’s mouth twisted into a grimace. ‘You’re a bit late for mass, you are,’ she said as they smiled at her and walked away, waving.

When they were out of earshot, Bridget said, 'Oh, Kay, what if he doesn't want to marry me now?'

'Bridget, I told you to stop making up stories, you silly mare. What time's his train arrive, anyway?'

'Seven o'clock tonight. I can't stand the wait.' She tried to halt her trembling lower lip.

'To those who wait, good things come. Now, girl, we're off to the Sunday matinee: Bing Crosby, Bob Hope, and Dorothy Lamour in The Road to Rio. It'll be fun.' Bridget raised a weak smile. Kay looked at her. 'You only have a few hours to wait.'

* * *

Bridget stood on the platform as the train puffed into the station, billowing out clouds of steam into the vaulted iron roof, high above. The train groaned to a halt by the enormous green buffers at the track's end, then suddenly, the doors flung open, and passengers piled out onto the platform.

The train was packed, and a wave of people swarmed towards the crammed exit. Bridget searched the crowd for Roman, a film of dampness across her palms. Then she spotted him as he emerged from the mass. He waved when he saw her. She noticed his rumpled clothes, but her heart still flipped over and over. They hugged; his unshaven face prickled against hers. Bridget squeezed his arm as they exited and headed for the bus to Roman's lodgings.

As the bus pulled away from the bustling city centre, Bridget glanced at Roman, who stared out of the window, his full lips sucked in.

'Roman, how's your mother?' she said, then held her breath.

He didn't turn toward her. Instead, he shifted his legs towards the bus side. 'I don't want talk right now.'

He continued to stare out of the window, and Bridget noticed tears trickled down his cheeks that he sporadically wiped with his jacket sleeve.

'I'm sorry,' she said.

Roman put his hand on top of hers and rested it there, and Bridget noticed a tremor.

When they arrived at his lodgings and walked into the kitchen, Andrej and Katerina sat at the table, playing cards. The air clouded with Katerina's incessant cigarette smoke despite the open window and the breeze fluttering the net curtains. Andrej stood up, pulled Roman towards him in a crush-like motion, and spoke rapidly in Polish. Katerina placed her cards down and listened intently, leaving her cigarette to smoulder in the ashtray.

Bridget watched Roman fling his arms around wildly as he spoke to Andrej, whose eyes narrowed to a barely perceptible slit. He nodded intently. Roman stopped and choked back sobs twice, and Andrej patted his shoulder gently, his brows deeply furrowed. Bridget saw a mixture of what looked like rage and hurt animate Roman's face, and he looked to Bridget like a wounded animal.

'What are they saying?' Bridget asked Katerina, who raised her hand in a halt-like gesture, her stubby nails painted letter-box red.

'He'll tell you himself.' She smiled briefly at Bridget and then resumed listening to the exchange between the two men.

Suddenly, Roman looked at Katerina; he broke off speaking to Andrej and said, 'Katerina, this private. Take Bridget to your room for while.'

Katerina looked surprised but smiled stiffly at Bridget, who was irked. She followed Katerina out of the kitchen and up the narrow stairs. Half an hour passed, and then Andrej knocked on Katerina's door to say they could return to the kitchen.

There, Andrej said something to Katerina in Polish. She nodded, and her mouth turned down at the sides. Bridget offered to make tea for them all and was lost in thought until the shrill whistle of the kettle pierced her world. Roman and Andrej sat at the table as Katerina returned and placed a bottle of vodka and four small glasses down on the pale green oilskin cover.

'He need it,' she said as she looked across at Bridget with a tight smile.

Katerina unscrewed the cap and poured giant slugs of clear liquid into the glasses. She handed Bridget one, nodded to the air, raised hers, and said, 'na zdrowie!' *cheers.*

The three Poles threw their drinks back in one gulp and slammed their glasses down. Bridget took a sip and coughed, excusing herself. She reached for her cup of less punishing tea. Whiskey was one thing, but vodka was quite another.

Roman pulled his chair close to Bridget's and encircled her with an arm. 'Put hair on chest.' He cleared his throat, smiled at her, then said, 'Mine, I mean!' They all laughed, and Roman spoke again in English. 'My mother very ill.' He addressed Bridget directly. 'Can't attend wedding.' Roman paused and glanced at Andrej as he continued to speak. 'I upset. I angry, drink too much, and get in trouble with police.' He smiled at Bridget.

Her face flushed as she remembered Sergeant McManus's words about a fall out but felt unable to ask questions because the atmosphere crackled with static.

They sat in silence for a short while, then Roman said, 'Andrej, fill glasses, we toast Bridget and I getting married.'

Bridget felt a rush of relief, chased by a wave of anxiety at his words. She desperately wanted to be alone with Roman to find out what had occurred in Glasgow and if it was her fault something had happened. Did he tell his mother she was pregnant? Was *that* what the upset was all about? Without knowing the actual circumstances, her mind spun wild theories, which featured her as the source of conflict. She needed Roman to reassure her, to tell her the truth. But it was clear at that moment the three had closed ranks and locked her out of their secret.

She politely sipped her vodka for the toast. At least Roman was unharmed, and she could relax a little. Then he and Andrej resumed the quick-fire conversation in Polish. Katerina got up to busy herself at the sink.

Eventually, Bridget stood up, defeated. 'Well,' she said, fussing round for her bag underneath the table.

It must have slipped off the chair back where she hung it. She was embarrassed and bewildered at the turn of events. When she found her handbag and retrieved it, she leaned toward Roman to kiss the side of his head as he continued to talk with Andrej. He raised his hand in her direction to acknowledge her presence.

'I'll leave you to sleep. We can talk tomorrow,' said Bridget, pulling her cardigan close.

Roman stopped talking briefly, turned to face Bridget, pulled her down towards him, and kissed her cheek.

'Yes, that good idea. We talk then.' He smiled, unwound by the vodka, released Bridget, and turned back to Andrej, who re-filled the glasses.

* * *

Bridget's thoughts whirled in her head as she walked back home, dazed. She was close to exploding with frustration. She hoped Kay would be there for her to unburden herself.

Bridget flung open the front door and ran into the kitchen. Nancy looked up from the table where she sat knitting. Her elbows jerked up and down, resembling a demented butterfly.

'Oh!' Bridget said and hesitated, 'is Kay in?' She wanted to cry and scream at the same time.

Nancy plonked her work on the tablecloth noisily and pushed her bottle-thick glasses back up her long nose. She stared at Bridget; Nancy appeared to be assessing the question, deciding what to say.

'She's out with Beryl. They've gone to the flicks,' she said after a pause.

The cased wooden clock ticked loudly in the background.

A sly smile appeared as Nancy picked up her work and

resumed the clickety-clack of the sharp needles. She kept her head down. Bridget knew most picture shows didn't finish until ten o'clock, and it was now only eight. She looked at Nancy, who did not lift her gaze from the red wool hat she knitted.

Bridget sat down heavily and dumped her handbag on the tablecloth. Nearby, an empty plate scattered with toast crumbs lay abandoned. Nancy, the nibbler. She wished she could phone her sister, Georgina but knew she could never confide her shameful and confusing situation to her or any member of her family. She was utterly alone in this.

Nancy looked up and scrutinised Bridget, who stared back, folding her arms over her bolero cardigan. It had been a demanding day for her, but she would not tell Nancy her sorrows.

'What's wrong, Bridget?' Nancy placed her knitting back down on the table and rested her overworked elbows.

Bridget shook her head. She was trying to fight off her emotions. 'Nothing,' she said, but tears trickled down her cheeks.

One slid off the tip of her nose and plopped onto the table, disturbing a fly that took off with a loud rattle.

'Shame Kay's not here. I expect you would want to tell her.'

Nancy then pursed her lips but reached out slowly for Bridget's hand, at which point Bridget crumpled into a sobbing heap. Nancy moved across to comfort her as Bridget wailed like an injured child for some time. She reached for her handbag when she had expelled enough emotion to regain a measure of control. Nancy then removed her freckled arm from Bridget's shoulder and peered into her face, a little too close for Bridget's comfort because she caught a whiff of Nancy's fish supper.

'Shall I make a cup of tea, or do you want something stronger?'

'Tea would be grand, Nancy.'

Bridget dabbed her eyes with the corner of her folded handkerchief, trying to keep from blurting out what had happened at Roman's earlier.

While Nancy made tea with her back turned, she asked, 'Is it Roman that's upset you?'

Bridget flicked open her hanky and blew her nose loudly. 'No, it's not. In fact...' She sat up straight, stared Nancy directly in the eye, and said, 'He's asked me to marry him. Didn't you know?'

Nancy twisted around; her face contorted by scorn. 'What?' Her gaze bored into Bridget. 'Why would he do that? He hardly knows you?'

Bridget recoiled. Nancy quickly finished preparing the tea and rushed to sit back down. She pushed the half-knitted hat to one side.

'Oh, I didn't mean to sound unkind, Bridget. I'm sure he's nice, even if the police were looking for him yesterday.'

Bridget stared steadily into Nancy's green eyes; a strength suddenly radiated from her core. She stretched her spine as far as possible. Three inches taller than Nancy anyway and now further enhanced, she looked down at Nancy as she spoke.

'They weren't looking for him, Nancy. They were

looking for me.'

She reached for her cup with a stable hand and drew the steaming contents towards her lips. Her eyes fixed on Nancy's.

Nancy pulled back from the table and surveyed Bridget. 'Are you in trouble?'

Bridget took a sip of the hot liquid and placed her cup back down with a clink. She leaned in and reminded herself to hold her breath when Nancy replied to avoid the stench.

'What do you mean, Nancy?'

'You know what I mean. Don't play all innocent with me.'

Bridget exhaled loudly and leaned back a little. She enjoyed herself as the burden of hurt she felt lifted.

'If you mean in trouble with the police, no. Absolutely not.' Bridget grinned at Nancy. A sense of triumph filled her.

A flash of irritation crossed Nancy's face. She placed her hands on the table and steepled them as she forced a smile. Nancy resembled an infant teacher, unable to coax the truth from a resistant child.

'The *other* kind of trouble,' Nancy said. She raised her chin as her eyebrows advanced upwards to her forehead.

Bridget laughed at her then. 'I assure you, Nancy, I'm not in *any* kind of trouble.'

Nancy humphed, stood, and snatched up her knitting. 'Well, I'm off to bed.' She paused, 'I hope Kay doesn't stay out too late.'

Then she exited the kitchen dramatically and banged

the door shut, causing an empty envelope to lift on the table with the sharp breeze.

At ten-thirty, Bridget heard the front door open and light footsteps in the hallway.

The door creaked open, and Kay appeared as Bridget snapped on the light and sat up. Kay perched on the edge of Bridget's bed, pulling off her headscarf.

'Well, what happened then? Do tell.'

Bridget relayed her encounter with Roman, between tears and sobs. 'Roman was very upset and said his mother was too ill to attend our wedding. But he didn't mention a fall out like the policeman did'.

'Maybe the policeman got it wrong? Kay said as she stepped into her pyjama bottoms and slid into bed.

'I think there's something he's not saying.'

'Now, don't jump to conclusions. If Roman's mother is gravely ill he would be distraught, wouldn't he? Especially as they've only recently made contact again.'

'Yes, I know, but what if it's because she doesn't approve of him marrying a foreigner?'

'A foreigner!' Kay repeated. They looked at one another and laughed; the tension dissipated from the air. 'Bridget, you know how families are, don't be so suspicious, put yourself in his place. There's lots going on for him. Tomorrow, you should visit him and say you'd like to visit his mother with him when she's well enough.'

'But what if he refuses?'

Kay sighed and turned over. 'He won't. Trust me.' She smoothed the worn quilt on her bed.

The following morning Bridget woke early; she

played the day ahead in her mind. It culminated in a visit to Roman's lodgings if she missed him at work. Some days he would forego eating in the canteen. And instead, he and Andrej ate their food outside on the mill wall as Andrej whistled at pretty girls, and Roman laughed at him.

It was a long day for Bridget. Roman made no appearance at work. The clock handles climbed laboriously up and down the hours until half-past five came, and Bridget rushed off to tidy her hair before the walk to Roman's lodgings.

As she rapped on his door, Bridget crossed the fingers of one hand and prayed Roman would open it. Presently, she heard footsteps in the hallway, and the door pulled back.

'Dobry wieczo, Bridget,' Andrej said. *Good evening.* He gripped the side of the door.

'Is Roman here?'

Andrej looked at Bridget; a thought darted behind his eyes, but she could not interpret it.

'No, sorry. Roman out.' He shrugged.

Bridget's stomach cramped. 'Can I come in to sit for a moment? I've walked from the mill.'

Andrej sucked in his breath and pulled the door wide for Bridget to enter. She followed him to the kitchen, where she slumped down on an old-style dining chair. Andrej ran the cold tap for a short while, filled a tumbler. He snatched a seat opposite Bridget.

After drinking the water in one go, Bridget wiped her face.

'Andrej.' She hesitated. 'Can I ask where you and

Roman met?'

Andrej jerked back a little. 'At school. In Warsaw.'

'Oh, so you've been friends for a long time?'

He nodded his head but said nothing.

'Were you in the war together?'

'What you mean?' Andrej shifted in his seat and moved one shoulder away from the table.

'You know, in the Polish forces?'

He cleared his throat. 'We split up at beginning of war but meet later on.'

'Where did you meet?'

He gestured with his hands. 'Sorry, Bridget, I have somewhere to be. You stay here. It up to you.' Andrej stood up, bowed his head, and hurried out.

Bridget rested her thumping head on the table, exhausted from the efforts of the last two days. Then, the door opened, and Katerina poked her head around it.

Bridget looked up. 'Katerina, do you know where I can find Roman? I need to see him.'

Katerina shook her head. 'Sorry, not seen him today.' She stood for a moment before she said, 'I go now. Take care.'

Bridget realised she was famished because it was now seven o'clock. She stood up, pushed back the dampened hair stuck to her forehead, and left the house for home. As Bridget stepped out into the noisy street, Roman appeared by the gate. She saw him frown as she rushed towards him.

'Shall we go for a walk, Roman?'

Her appetite vanished with the excitement of being near him. Suddenly, she noticed it was a sunny evening, and the birds twittered and chattered in the trees.

Roman held her hand. ‘Bridget, I tired. Long day today. I need sleep.’

He kissed her forehead and turned towards the door.

‘Roman, please tell me what’s wrong. I don’t understand why you’re like this?’ Bridget clung to his hand as tears misted her vision.

Roman pulled his hand away. ‘I not like anything. I tired. We meet Sunday, go somewhere.’

He blew a kiss and disappeared into the house.

Bridget collapsed onto the garden wall and sobbed. She felt a hand on her shoulder and raised her head to see Katerina standing in front of her.

‘We crazy Poles, hard to understand, yes? I walk you home.’

The two set off in the heavy evening air.

Roman had taken Bridget out to the market town of Knaresborough. He said it was to escape the fug of the nearby mill towns. His boots slipped once or twice as he descended the narrow path to the river's edge that Sunday afternoon.

'Careful, Bridget.'

He turned as she stepped gingerly on the dilapidated stones where dandelions sprung through the crevices.

'I'm grand,' she said. 'Oh, look!' Bridget pointed at cygnets that flanked their mother, gliding along the riverside near brightly painted row boats for hire.

Roman hopped into one of the wooden boats at the riverside as the swan family darted off, leaving little washes behind them. He stretched his hand for Bridget, who tottered into the swaying boat and lowered herself onto the seat.

'Alley up!' Roman said, then plunged the oars into the water and propelled the boat down the river with light strokes, his shirt sleeves rolled up to the elbow, muscles flexed beneath his tanned skin.

As he rowed towards an arch of the famous Knaresborough viaduct that towered twenty-four metres in height, Roman stopped. He settled the oars in their cradles and gazed up at the castellated wall of the magnificent structure.

'Remind me of Italy,' he said, waving his hand at the vista.

The viaduct stretched across the deep gorge where

roofs peeped from behind the trees, and cobbled lanes spiralled down to the market square.

Bridget craned her head to take in the view; her neck veins protruded.

'I've never been there,' she said. 'But I've seen photos of the Vatican.'

'It beautiful, Italy.'

Roman unhooked the oars and splashed them into the river that rippled at the bank's edges. An emerald dragonfly bounced the light as it darted over the surface and disappeared into the feathery grass.

'What did you do in Italy?' Bridget said.

'Fought with British allies.' He pointed to a heron that had glided to land at the river's edge; its feet planted; its wings flapped slowly as though it was not sure whether to stay.

'Where were you stationed?'

'I don't like talk about war.'

He let go of one oar and splashed water at Bridget playfully with his hand. She shrieked and placed her hands over her head.

'My hair!' she said, then laughed.

After the boat ride, they strolled along the river edge before settling in the long grass to sit down. Roman laid back and gazed up at the sapphire sky. A tiny patch darkened and moved towards them.

Bridget leaned in and placed a hand over Roman's chest; she fingered a loose shirt button and cleared her throat.

'Roman, please tell me what happened when you

visited your mother, why you fell out. This is the first time we've been alone since your return, and it seems you've been avoiding me.'

'Why it matter?'

She leaned closer. Her shadow fell across the lush tamped grass at Roman's side.

'I know it upset you.' Bridget paused, then looked directly into his black-brown eyes. 'And I need to know why. We can't have secrets between us, Roman.'

Roman sat up and rolled down his sleeves. A chill tinged the air as the sky dimmed.

'Katerina, she say tell Bridget. She smart.' He glanced at Bridget. 'But it not good story.'

Bridget sighed. 'I guessed that much, sweetheart.' She grabbed his hand and held it tight as the heron flapped over them on its journey again.

After a while, Roman said, 'When you treated bad like vermin by someone, you hate them.' His eyes screwed up as he stared back at Bridget.

She put her finger to the tip of her nose and hesitated. 'I'm not sure I understand you. I thought you were telling me about your mother?'

Roman was silent.

Bridget shuffled on the ground. 'Are you saying your mother mistreated you?'

'No. I mean Germans, who else?'

Bridget nodded. 'Oh, sorry. Of course!'

'When you eat dead dog because you starving.'

Roman jerked his head away, not wanting to see Bridget's reaction. He looked down at the grass bank where a spider made its way through; its long high legs moved mechanically.

'When home city bombed to rubble, family taken.' He turned back to Bridget, his face horribly twisted. 'You hate who did it with strength of Goliath.' Roman yanked a clump of grass, held it tight in his fist, and shook it. 'Then mother tell me something about Elouna – it unbelievable.'

Bridget reached for him, unfurled his fingers from the strangled grass, and held them in her palms.

She cleared her throat. 'Slow down a little. I'm lost.'

'How to say?' Roman's face crumpled. 'Big blow, in hospital mother tell me Elouna… never mind. It not important.'

Roman watched Bridget's puzzled expression.

He pulled his hand away and thumped the ground. 'I hate them all.'

'But Roman…,' Bridget softened her voice. 'You can tell me.'

Roman squinted at Bridget. 'Let's drop subject.' He was silent again.

'Roman, you've found your mother now. And your sister, that's truly wonderful.'

'But not father,' he said.

'No. Not yet, but anything is possible.'

'Maybe.'

'Please promise you'll revisit your mother soon and sort out whatever it is.'

'I think about it.'

'Things are never what they seem, Roman. Even I know that.'

‘I need time to take all in before next visit.’

‘Don’t leave it too long,’ she said.

They stayed until a fat raindrop plopped onto Roman’s forehead. He stood and pulled Bridget up.

‘Time to go.’

The skies unfastened as they ran to the path, and warm, heavy summer rain pelted down. It drenched them in seconds.

Roman and Bridget arrived back. Their clothes clung to their youthful bodies after the downpour. Roman watched Bridget shaking her wet hair out and thought they were in their prime with so much ahead. Happiness flowered in his heart as he dashed to his room for towels. On his return, when Bridget ruffled his hair, he flung his arms around her and kissed her, repeating, ‘I love you, I love you, I love you.’

The kitchen door flew open, and in burst Andrej.

‘Excuse interruption, but there’s telegram for you.’

He thrust an envelope towards Roman, who slung his towel around his neck and frowned. He tore open the envelope and rapidly read the sparse words.

‘My mother very ill.’ He turned to Bridget. ‘We must go see her now.’

* * *

They boarded just as the shrill whistle blew, carriage doors slammed shut, and the train chugged off, hooting. Roman clutched Bridget’s hand; their knees touched as both stared out the window at the houses and fields that flew by.

‘We set wedding date now. Invite Mother.’

Bridget snorted. 'I think we need to visit the registry office first.' She squeezed Roman's arm.

He looked out of the window, his eyes misted, as hills rose and fell; villages appeared and disappeared, and their odd names flashed briefly on the tiny platforms. *I can leave the past behind*, Roman thought. *I can and I will*. He turned back to Bridget, her pretty brow creased in thought.

'I apologise to mother.' He held up Bridget's left hand. 'Buy you ring. Write Elouna.' His voice cracked.

Bridget kissed the side of his cheek. 'That sounds like a wonderful plan, darling.'

Thoughts raced through Roman's mind like driven storm clouds.

Halfway through the journey, the train hooted, and the carriage plunged into darkness as they entered a tunnel. Towards its end, the train screeched and ground to a stop when only a pinpoint of light could be detected.

'What's happening?' Bridget peered through the gloom.

People chattered as the train guard advanced through the carriages.

'Nothing to worry about, just a temporary delay.'

'Why?' someone asked.

'Overheated engine, I'm afraid.'

The train was stationary for half an hour. Roman left his seat and paced up and down the aisle. He visited the toilet three times, and his insides churned like butter.

Eventually, it set off again.

On the approach to Newcastle, Roman blurted, 'Hurry!'

As the train chugged across, he looked down from the bridge to the dockside, where cranes swung back and forth. The workers looked like ants, scurrying around anonymously. Roman checked his watch and crossed and re-crossed his legs. It had been over six hours since he received the telegram. *For Christ's sake, move it,* he thought.

At the North-South border, the red sun slid behind the sea. Grey waves rolled in and smashed at the base of the rocks. Above the bays, clusters of houses teetered.

'That woman stare at me,' Roman whispered to Bridget.

'What woman?'

'Her, with stupid hat.'

Bridget looked over at the woman staring out of the window.

'She know I foreigner. She not like me.'

'Don't be ridiculous; she's probably admiring your handsome face.'

'No,' he said. 'Something else.'

Bridget said, 'Roman, look at me. You're just feeling very on edge right now.'

* * *

They pulled into Glasgow station. Roman stood by the carriage exit. He pushed the door open before the train halted, and it swung back with a bang. Roman had one foot on the edge of the step, prepared to leap down as soon as possible. Bridget held onto his shoulder in restraint.

Before they left, Andrej lent Roman two pounds,

equated to a week of his wages for their fares and insisted they take a taxi from the station to the hospital. An unaffordable luxury in their present lives.

In the taxi, Roman rested his elbows on his knees and covered his face with his hands.

'I can't stand it.'

Bridget leant her head on his shoulder with a hand on his juddering knee.

But just past Glasgow, an accident halted the flow of traffic.

'Stop!' Roman said to the driver, who turned to him in surprise.

'What?'

'I run rest of way. Not far.' Roman grabbed the door handle and moved to get out.

Bridget pulled at his arm. 'No! You can't. Just wait a little longer.'

'We never fucking get there.'

'Roman!'

He saw her cheeks colour at his crude language.

'How much further is it?' she asked the driver as she tugged Roman's hand away from the door handle.

'Nearly there, lassie.'

The car moved again. It crawled forward, and suddenly, the jam cleared, and the taxi sped off.

Bridget asked for the ward directions at the hospital as Roman circled behind her. He muttered in Polish. When they reached the ward, Roman spotted a priest who stood over a patient; the curtains were half-drawn around the bed.

'Please, God. No,' Roman said as he hurried down the

ward.

Bridget's heels clicked rapidly behind him.

A nurse turned from the bed as the priest closed his Bible. She recognised Roman and nodded gravely. The nurse moved to the bottom of the bed, drew the curtains with a loud swoosh, and approached. Her shoes made soft sucking noises on the floor. Roman stood rigid. He hooked his arm through Bridget's warm elbow and leaned against her. As the nurse reached him, she said, 'I'm so sorry, Mr Kozynski, she's gone.' She steered him and Bridget from the ward. Roman stumbled between them.

'We'll go to a quiet place,' the nurse said gently to Roman. But her previous words were ringing in his head. *She's gone.*

'I have some of your mother's belongings. And letters she asked to make sure you received. When you're ready. We'll have a cup of tea first.'

## Roman a Few Weeks Later

His mother's battered leather suitcase with its dirt-encrusted monogram, AK, lay gaping on the foot of Roman's bed. A hungry monster to him. Its contents had been vying for attention, but he had avoided the task. What would he find? He stared at the newspaper clippings, folders stuffed with papers and certificates, bundled letters, identity cards, and a tarnished silver-plated knife. Where should he start? Roman picked out a bundle of letters and slowly untied the frayed string. They unravelled in a slither across the bed spread.

*Warsaw. 1941.*

*'My Dearest Mama,*

*I received your letter today via Victor and am so relieved I know where you are, even though you are back in the Gestapo prison on some concocted charge. I have repeatedly begged Schutt to tell me your whereabouts, but he insists there is no need for me to know. He uses this as a weapon to keep me in check, amongst other things.*

*I am so sorry to hear they dismissed you from your post at the school and cannot see any reason apart from the Head, Mr Krause, knowing of our family's misfortune and using this as an excuse to settle old scores over his rivalry with Papa. I hear much of this goes on these days, and it is virtually impossible to trust anyone apart from your own family.*

*Although I am still officially Schutt's children's nanny, he has moved me into his bedroom. Mama, my face burns with shame because he has taken me as his mistress. I can write to you in Polish because Victor sneaks my letters out. But I dare not share my inner feelings about my situation here. Oh, Mama, in another life, I might have married Victor. I adore him, and he is so kind, brave and handsome. I have been sweet over him since my first music lesson at home, and I now realise he is not much older than me.*

*I have a small measure of persuasion over Schutt. I do not fully understand why apart from his infatuation with me and his need for me to admire and fear him. I will tell him I know you are still in Warsaw and without means of support. And ask if he could take you into his household to cover the role of the children's nanny. It has become clear that it is not my forte, and they are not so fond of me. They regularly side with Hilda, the housekeeper, on dispute matters and play up at bed times. Hilda runs to Schutt, telling tales about my incompetence. Last night, there was no soap in the bathroom. I asked her where it was as I knew I had bought some at the market earlier, but she swore blind I had forgotten it. She then told Schutt his children were not clean because of me. But enough of my petty struggles. I'll take over the role of housekeeper to get rid of that dreadful woman. That way, you and I will be together. I dare not think of the future, and everything now can only be day-by-day. Within a few months, I have gone from being a dreamy seventeen-year-old with romantic visions of my future as a famous pianist to a person seeking to turn every opportunity to their advantage, no matter how low they must stoop.*

*I have repeatedly asked Schutt about Papa's*

*whereabouts, and each time he brushes me off with the excuse that they have sent him somewhere to work and the paperwork is lost. I pray to God every night to keep Papa safe wherever he may be.*

*Schutt drinks lots, and sometimes he loses his guard; I overhear things while talking on the phone or with friends after dinner. Mama, please forgive me if this is not accurate. It is what I heard him tell his friend, in person, after a long night of cognac and cigars. Schutt was furious because a young man, who I believe to be Roman, escaped from the prison, which embarrassed Schutt and did not go down well with his superiors. A rival ensured the information went up the line to the Führer, and Schutt believes he must watch his back.*

*Could this be Roman?*

*Mama, I will work on Schutt with my plan and in the meantime, keep safe and keep your spirits up; we will be reunited.*

*Yours, your ever-loving daughter, Elouna.'*

Roman looked up through the open window of his room to the outside world, where the clatter of shoes on cobbles signalled the mill shift was over for the day. People hurried home excitedly, chattering. They looked forward to the small pleasures of their evenings. Above the terrace rooftops, the sun appeared from behind a slate grey cloud, and its silver rays speared across the sky. There was a tap on Roman's door, and Andrej poked his handsome head around. He glanced at the suitcase and scratched his head.

'Bridget's downstairs to see you.' He smiled.

Roman dropped the letter from his fingers. 'I don't know what to make of this, Andrej.' He shook his head. 'I can't take it in. I'm bewildered.'

Andrej perched on the edge of Roman's bed, his long legs splayed out, ending in scuffed work boots. He nodded to the letter. 'What is it?'

'Here, read it for yourself.' Roman handed it over.

While Andrej read, Roman stomped up and down his room. His hands stuffed into his trouser pockets. He would stop and peer at Andrej intermittently in search of his reactions to the contents. When Andrej finished, he folded the letter and carefully placed it back in the suitcase. He stood to put his hands on Roman's shoulders and, with a loud intake of breath, said, 'Listen to me. We all did things outsiders would never comprehend. Only *we* know why we had to. Take your time, don't rush to judgement. Now, Bridget is waiting for you downstairs. Come.'

Roman sighed. 'Just one more thing.' He reached for the knife and handed it to Andrej, who turned it in his hand to examine the inscription.

'Bergen-Belsen Officer's Mess?' Andrej said. 'What the fuck?'

Roman shook his head from side to side.

# PART THREE

## Bridget, Bradford

Bridget stepped off the bus onto the wide pavement outside the Bradford Registry Office, followed by Kay. Trolleybuses rattled past the building, an imposing Victorian structure with a grand pillared entrance. Passers-by stood aside for them in the yellow haze of the mid-afternoon sun. Bridget looked nervously up and down the street while Kay fussed with the cream crepe rose pinned in Bridget's hair.

'How do I look, then?'

'Beautiful, radiant. A summer flower in full bloom.'

Bridget laughed at Kay's exuberant mood. She knew Kay was happy for her and had taken Roman on as an honourable, reliable man. They were her future now, and she was sure life would be kind to them all.

'Kay, you know, to be honest, I've never really dreamed about a big white wedding with all the palaver. Do you think I'm odd?'

Bridget gestured to her pale grey post-war suit embellished by her hand with lace-trimmed cuffs and collar.

Kay lit a cigarette and passed it to Bridget for a puff, and she took one.

'Yeah, you're a real screwball,' she said, then plucked the cigarette back out of Bridget's white-lace gloved hand and took a deep drag, pluming a fat smoke cloud into the still summer air that hung like a genie.

'What time is it now?' Bridget said.

She wiped away imaginary fluff from her shoulders as nerve-driven cramps wobbled her insides.

'Three-thirty, lovely. Shall we go in?'

Bridget's legs shook. 'I can't remember what I'm supposed to do, Kay.'

Kay took her arm. 'It's okay. We go inside, tell them your name and the time of the ceremony, and then they'll do the rest.'

'Okay.' Bridget heard her voice sounding parched, and she coughed to clear her dry throat.

Kay stubbed her cigarette on the entrance wall; its sparks splintered to the ground. She pulled Bridget inside by her elbow. The entrance hall of the registry office was dark, oak-panelled, and cool in contrast to the outside temperature. Red plush chairs lined the walls on either side for the wedding guests to wait their turn. At the end of the hallway, a set of double doors adorned by ornate brass handles were closed tight as another couple was becoming one in wedlock, judging from the sign on the wall. "Engaged", it read, and Bridget suddenly wanted to laugh, thinking *not for much longer*.

Bridget and Kay stood around and looked for someone official before a man with a clipboard stepped out of a side room and advanced toward them. He smiled courteously and brushed a rogue strand of hair from his shiny forehead.

'Good afternoon, ladies. Which party are you with, please?'

'Bridget O'Keefe and Roman Kozynski's marriage at 3.45 pm,' Bridget said as she raised her chin and looked at him directly. 'I'm Miss O'Keefe.' She thought, *I'm getting married, but I'm not having a proper wedding, and I don't mind.*

The man smiled and introduced himself as the Assistant Registrar. 'Mr Kozynski is here, and we're just going through the registration formalities. If you'd like to follow me, we'll complete yours, and then we can begin.'

'I don't have anyone to give me away,' Bridget blurted; her voice wavered as she followed him. 'My father's ill, and my family can't make it from Ireland.'

Kay linked her arm. Shame set Bridget's face ablaze as her eyes filled up.

'That's perfectly alright. I can fulfil that function should you wish. The Superintendent Registrar will perform the marriage ceremony, and I assist him.'

He opened the door of a side room and beckoned them in.

* * *

Bridget heard the registrar say, 'You may now kiss the bride,' as she watched Roman lean towards her, grinning from ear to ear, then settle his full lips onto hers. He squeezed her hand, where his mother's gold wedding ring circled perfectly on Bridget's finger.

It was four o'clock precisely. As the wedding group stepped out into the street, the Cathedral bells from the bottom of the hill rang out across the deep valley. A small group of people followed, including Nancy, who rushed past them to turn and scatter paper cuttings over them like confetti. Bridget and Roman laughed and kissed.

Kay grabbed Nancy by the elbow. 'Come on,' Kay said.

‘Let’s find you a nice young Polish man.’

Nancy giggled excitedly and patted her chest at the neck of her pink dress that clashed with her fiery red hair.

As Bridget and Roman walked to their party, fragments of shredded paper fell from their clothes. Bridget noticed people smile as they passed them. Weddings made people happy with their promise of beginnings and happily-ever-after endings.

At the entrance to the Polish Club, Roman held the red door open for Bridget to pass through. Inside the bar room, newspapers cut into wedding decorations hung from the ceiling and the ornate Victorian light fittings. Balloons tied to the backs of chairs danced in the air. Bridget spun around straight into Roman’s chest; her eyes clouded with tears.

He hugged her tight and said, ‘Congratulations, Mrs Bridget Kozynska.’

Earlier, Roman had instructed her about Polish surnames, the masculine ending in Ki and the feminine in Ka. She thought it might take some time to become accustomed to it, but her new name sounded pleasing to her ears, if not a little exotic in its difference from Roman’s.

The background babble from the wedding party was a mixture of Polish and mainly Irish-accented English to Bridget’s ears as she surveyed the guests carrying glasses from the bar and jostling around to find friends. In the room's corner, she spotted a table piled with food. Katerina and Andrej had offered to take care of refreshments at the party, and Bridget expected a few sandwiches because no one had any spare money. She turned to Roman in amazement at the spread. Roman laughed and hugged her.

'Katerina and Andrej been busy. Guests donate.' He gestured to the table laden with various loaves, cheeses, salamis and sour-barrel gherkins. 'How you like?' Roman said.

'It's beyond belief, Roman. So generous.' She raised a hand to cover her mouth.

'And centrepiece—Polish cheesecake Katerina make.' Roman pointed to the circular cake as he beamed at Katerina, who made a slight bow.

Bridget moved close, delighted at the tiny silver candles that adorned it. 'Thank you so much, Katerina, it's beautiful.'

Bridget watched from her seat as their guests devoured the food quickly; alcohol helped spur appetites, but feeling hungry all the time was commonplace in the years of food rationing. When the spread had vanished, Roman's friends stacked some tables to clear a modest space to dance. Someone had brought a portable gramophone and a few records of popular dance music.

Andrej stood on a chair and bellowed out, his face flushed with the heat and excitement of the afternoon, 'Ladies, gentlemen, raise glasses to happy couple.'

Cheers of nahzdroveyay and sláinte filled the room. *Good health.*

'Now, bride, groom, dance.' Andrej gestured.

Roman encircled Bridget's waist as he whirled her into the dance space. Glenn Miller's Moonlight Serenade floated through the air.

She leaned her chin on Roman's shoulder while they

smooched and thought of their first dance that snowy December and how life sprang surprises. As they twirled, Bridget noticed a ruddy-faced man talking to Nancy, who stood on the sidelines awkwardly. As he spoke, Nancy nodded and continually pushed her glasses back up her nose.

Bridget whispered to Roman, half-laughing, 'Guess what, Nancy has a suitor.'

'Good! Always someone for everyone.'

He grinned, and the depth of his compassionate nature captivated Bridget at that moment.

She thought to herself; *I'm truly blessed.*

After end-to-end dances with Roman's friends, Bridget excused herself to visit the powder room. She found Nancy busy in the faded surroundings, dabbing her perspiring face from her compact.

'Nancy, I see you have an admirer.' Bridget smiled at her.

Nancy clipped her mirror shut and dropped it into her handbag. She turned around and leaned against the basin edge.

'Oh, Bridget,' she said, a slight frown creasing her still glistening forehead. 'He works on a farm somewhere called Greengates Village.'

'That's grand.'

'But I can't understand a word he says.'

'Oh, I see,' Bridget said. 'Is he Polish?'

'No. He's *Yorkshire.*' Nancy looked helplessly at Bridget.

'He said to me: if thou were me wife, I'd mostly tell

thee to put coal in 'ole.'

Bridget laughed though she didn't know what that meant either.

'I just kept nodding and saying yes, but he looks at me queer-like.'

Bridget moved towards her and laid a hand on Nancy's pinked forearm.

'You'd be surprised how much we can say without words.' Bridget's face flared as she realised how that sounded.

Nancy's eyes widened behind her bottle glasses. 'Well, you're a brazen one.' She fixed her gaze on Bridget's belly. 'That's a swell swell,' she said in a mock American accent.

Bridget stepped back and sighed. 'Okay, Nancy, see you later.' She exited the room, clicking her tongue.

Bridget sat down in the crowded bar and dabbed her face with her hanky, which was increasingly damp from heat and tears. Kay shimmied to sit beside her and pushed some empty glasses to the table's edge.

'You're not flagging already, are you, Mrs K?'

Bridget leaned toward Kay. 'No, I'm fine, but that Nancy's a cow. She's guessed.' Bridget lowered her voice. 'She knows I'm,' she mouthed the word pregnant silently.

Kay pushed Bridget's hair away from her forehead. 'Ignore the silly mare. Everyone else does. It's none of her business, anyway.'

Bridget wrung her hands. 'I know, Kay. It's just I feel ashamed. I really do.'

Kay took a comb from her handbag and tidied Bridget's billowing curls from her face. 'Bridget Kozynska, you're not the first and won't be the last, so get on with it. We're in England now, and the holy father priests aren't breathing down our necks. We're free from all that.'

Bridget smiled weakly and looked to the floor. Kay grabbed her hands and pulled them towards herself.

'Look, you're moving to Bradford and nobody knows how long you've been together, so keep it that way and concentrate on your new life.'

Bridget watched Kay glare across the room to where Nancy stood with the ruddy-faced man who wore a flat cap in the local style. As he spoke, Nancy nodded in Kay's direction. Kay lifted her hand and waved to Nancy.

'Shut your feckin mouth, you ye frustrated hag,' she said, and Bridget collapsed in a fit of laughter, knocking over an empty beer glass that rolled off the table edge and smashed on the floor.

## Roman 1948, Mrs Hawanska's Rooming House

Roman hauled his mother's suitcase from under the bed, where it lurked. It was a Pandora's box that he steeled himself to delve into slowly. The late afternoon brought an intricate layering of frost on the outside window of their bedroom, and beyond it, the laden sky flushed blood red, feathered with navy streaks as the sun dipped below the horizon.

He held a torn letter from his mother's belongings, never posted.

*'I owe my life to God. From 1945, before I moved to this Scottish camp, I taught primary school subjects to displaced people in the German camp. The place was too horrible for words; it had been Bergen-Belsen Concentration Camp in the war, but it became a clearing house for displaced persons after the liberation. Nobody knew what had happened there until the war ended. Then, only dribs and drabs of unbelievable things leaked out. The British who liberated the camp burned the huts because it was riddled with Typhus. It was still a filthy hellhole when I lived there.*

*I volunteered to be transported to England because God told me, "Go there!" But the idea troubled me as it's such a foreign place. But as soon as I signed the form, straight away, I felt better. Now I know it was an order from God because He sent you to England first and me later. He wanted us to be together.*

*I can now work in the textile factory. My primary duty is*

*to pack bobbins, but it is easy. I can stand and sit if I want to, but I will tell you more when we meet.*

*In November 1945, I was gravely ill and spent a lot of time in different hospitals because I had kidney tuberculosis. Finally, in January 1946, the doctors said they must remove my right kidney. "Otherwise, there is nothing left to do with that woman. She goes to the ground." But I prayed to stay alive, and dear God kept me here because I wanted to see my most precious son, Roman.'*

The letter ended; Roman put it down and stared into the dark sky. So many questions spun in his mind, so many images he fought back in terror and bewilderment. He grabbed his coat from the bed, which acted as a blanket in the freezing nights, and hurried downstairs.

Bridget sat in the shared kitchen of the rooming house, warming herself near the stove, the one source of decent heat in the chilled place. She looked up at Roman.

'I can feel the baby kicking,' she said, her hands against her strained belly. 'It's wonderful.'

Roman kissed her on the forehead and pushed back a fallen curl. 'I go with Andrej for drink. Be back soon.'

'But it's freezing outside.'

Roman sighed, 'I trapped all day in mill. Stuffy, can't breathe, be back soon.'

* * *

'Let's go here.' Andrej pointed to a pub sign from which icicles dangled. Roman read out loud, 'The Oddfellows

Arms. Wonder what that means,' he said. Roman expected the pub to be empty on such a bleak evening and looked forward to talking with Andrej about his mother's letter without fear of being overheard. It cleared the mystery of the Bergen-Belsen knife—she'd taught there herself a refugee, nothing more.

He stepped through the door into a fog of cigarette smoke; the aroma of stale beer and poorly washed bodies invaded his nostrils.

'Smelt worse,' he said to Andrej as they pushed through the crowd of men to the bar.

When seated, they raised their glasses. 'Na zdrowie – *cheers* to dog piss!' Roman said, and Andrej guffawed, almost spilling his beer. Two of the many things they missed were Vodka and Polish beer.

Roman relayed the contents of the letter he had read earlier. 'I don't understand how she ended up in a German camp. Even though it was a clearing place for refugees.'

Roman looked at Andrej, who was staring intently at a man slouching on a bar stool, his profile silhouetted by the gas lamps on the wall.

'Are you listening?' Roman asked.

Andrej turned to him. His hand shook perceptibly as he picked up his glass. 'Yes, yes,' he said, then took a large swig of beer that deposited a froth moustache on his upper lip.

'What is it?' Roman said, shifting in his seat.

Andrej's lips were downturned, and his eyes glowered. 'Him, over there. He looks like….'

Roman stared over at the man Andrej pointed to, and

memories hit him full force, blasting his sense of security into smithereens.

'The dentist,' Roman said.

They grabbed their glasses and took large gulps.

They stared at the man on his stool as he slowly finished his drink. He ground his cigarette with a boot-heel into the sawdust-covered floor and spat. The dentist pulled on his woollen cap, wrapped a tattered scarf around his neck, and bid the barman farewell.

Roman and Andrej followed him out of the pub into the deep snow that fell heavily in fat frozen flakes. They quickened their pace as best they could in the deep snow. When they were close, Roman shouted to the man.

'Hey you - need some pliers?'

The man darted into an alleyway between the terraced houses. Roman followed quickly, his fists bunched at his sides, his boots plunging in and out of the creaking snow.

'Remember us?' Andrej said as he caught up.

The man turned and shrugged through his bulky coat. He held out his hands as though the question puzzled him.

'Don't know what you're talking about. You must think I'm someone else.' He took a step back as Andrej approached.

'Don't give me that shit,' Roman said as he caught up with him.

The man was startled for a minute and tried to run, but Andrej seized him by the shoulders and pushed him to the ground.

'You've mistaken me,' the man said, recoiling in the snow.

'No, we haven't, and we remember what you did in that camp.'

'I've never been in a camp. I swear you've got the wrong person.'

'If you have a double, bad luck, mate,' Andrej said.

'Here's for old times, you bastard,' Roman said as he swung a kick into the man's stomach. The dentist curled in a ball and covered his head with his arms. 'No, please.'

'Now, who's chicken?' Andrej said as he kicked the man in the ribs. He cried out.

Roman aimed one more kick and held his arm out to block Andrej from further action. Sweat covered his brow.

'Leave the vicious dog in the gutter, where he belongs. Come on, let's go.'

Roman looked at the man, balled up and whimpering in the snow, and spat before turning away.

'Rubbish, that's what you are. Scum!' Roman said.

They hurried away from the alley where the man lay, coughing and spitting into the snow. With the weight of history on their shoulders, they walked home in the silence of the snow-blanketed night.

Roman crept up to his and Bridget's bedroom and softly perched on the edge of the bed to pull off his soaked boots. *Idiota!* he said to himself. He should have done this outside the room not to disturb her. Bridget's shape moved, and her hand emerged from beneath the bedclothes.

'You're late, Kozynski,' she said and rolled over to click on the bedside lamp.

Roman blinked at the glare and smiled at her. 'Can't put coat on bed tonight. It wet.'

Bridget hauled herself up and rested against the bedstead. ‘Pass it here; let me be the judge of that.’

He tugged off his coat and handed it to Bridget, who heaved it across her knees and ran her hands over the surface.

‘It’s damp, but if we lay it dry side down, we’ll benefit from the weight.’ She pulled her hands away to wipe them on the bedspread. ‘Oh, my God. Roman, what’s this?’ Bridget said, gawping at her blood-smeared hands.

‘Nothing, we helped someone who fall in snow. Cut themselves.’

‘Cut themselves in the snow? Roman, tell me what happened.’

He looked at Bridget wide-eyed. So focused, so fiery, so full of life. Her arms were outstretched, and she looked beautiful when she was cross.

‘Okay. Me and Andrej in small fight.’ He tried to smile at Bridget, but her face remained set.

‘Jesus Christ, Roman, you know you’ve got to be careful, kerb your temper. You’ll be in court, and then you know what happens next. They’ll deport you to Poland, to the Russians. And what will become of the baby and me?’

Bridget covered her face with her hands and gasped for breath. Roman shuffled towards her and cradled her in his arms. ‘Nothing will happen. We safe. I promise.’ Just then, someone knocked loudly at the front door.

‘Who could that be at this hour, Roman? It’s after 11 pm?’

Roman sat rigidly on the bed, afraid to think.

Suddenly, Bridget cramped over and grasped her

stomach through the bedclothes.

'Oh, my God, Roman, I think… the baby's coming.'

'What! It too early.'

'Tell that to the baby,' Bridget said and yanked herself further up the bedstead. She threw off the blankets. 'Oh Jesus, my waters have broken. Roman, you need to phone an ambulance.'

Roman jumped up from the bed, pulled his coat from Bridget's hands, and flung it on.

'Make sure you've got some change, Roman; I don't know if the emergency calls are free.'

Roman checked his pockets, jingled some pennies, and bent to kiss Bridget on the forehead.

'I go now. Ask Mrs Hawanska sit with you 'till back.'

'Oh Jesus, Roman, what about whoever's at the door now? Are you sure you're not in any trouble?'

'No! I not.'

Roman planted a quick kiss on her forehead, then rushed out of their room to Mrs Hawanska's, whose door was open. He peeped in, but her room was empty. He descended the stairs two at a time as he heard voices from downstairs.

In the hallway, a Polish man he knew by sight from the mill was standing, a gloved hand resting on the door jamb, speaking heatedly with Mrs Hawanska. Roman breathed a sigh of relief; it was irrational, but he was worried it would be the police, somehow rapidly divining he and Andrej left an injured man lying in the snow earlier.

'Sorry, Bridget's having her baby now! I'm going to the telephone. Mrs Hawanska, will you sit with her, please?'

Mrs Hawanska swivelled around to Roman, 'Ach, what am I supposed to do first? He says he wants to speak with you. I've told him no, it's late.' Her expression was one of pure annoyance. 'Do you know him?' She said as Roman pushed past her towards the door.

'No!' He glared at the man up close. 'Move, please.' He could smell his beery breath.

The man shifted and folded his arms. 'Okay, but I'll be back to talk with you, Kozynski, about a matter this evening.'

'Fine. Now piss off.' Roman's nose was almost touching the man's as he eyeballed him.

The visitor shrugged, turned and trudged off down the icy path. He swung the gate with such force it bounced back with a metallic clang from its concrete post, and snow jolted from the wall.

Roman ran the two streets to the public phone box and yanked open the door to call the emergency services. When he put down the receiver, Roman realised he'd been so busy working all hours to save for the baby the hospital's whereabouts were unclear to him. He had visited only once with Bridget. Mrs Hawanska would know. He hurried back through crisped snow that now resembled a blanket of tiny, scattered diamonds which crunched pleasingly under his boots.

Roman saw Bridget grimace as he burst through the door; his face felt flushed from rushing, even in the freezing temperature. Mrs Hawanska had helped Bridget pack her hospital bag and got her dressed, ready to leave for the hospital. Bridget was lying down on the bed, panting. Mrs Hawanska dabbed her forehead with a cloth and held Bridget's hand.

Soon, when the ambulance doors closed, Roman waved at Bridget on a stretcher and could not stop the tears from running down his cheeks. If only his mother could have been there with them.

He tried to sleep but found it impossible as he fretted about Bridget and the baby coming early. After repeatedly getting his legs tangled in the blankets from turning every few minutes, he sat up, snapped on the lamp, and swung his legs out of bed. He bent over to locate his mother's suitcase from beneath the bed. His head swam with beer, little food and lack of sleep. Roman took a deep breath to steady himself before hauling the case out by the tattered handle. It would provide distraction. However, he couldn't face another letter right then. *No more surprises,* he thought. He shuffled the contents and selected a faded, manilla folder stuffed with papers. A certificate caught his attention. It was a yellowed, raggedy-edged document headed Testimonium Copulationis. The certificate was written in Latin in blue calligraphic script. He could remember enough Latin from his school days to make out it was his parent's marriage certificate from 1922. The certificate identified his parents, Anya Sobotnika and Ludwig Kozynski. *Okay, he thought, no surprises there.*

He put this aside and examined a similar document dated 1889, again in Latin script. It certified the marriage of his mother's parents. Then his eyes caught his maternal grandmother's surname before she entered the Sobotniki family. Her name was Stefania Frank. Roman had known her only as Grandma Sobotnika. A thought formed in his mind, one he did not want to unleash. He slid the document carefully into the suitcase. Enough.

Roman fell back on the bed. Memories of his grandmother flitted in his mind. She was tiny, a bird-like creature with dark shiny eyes, a full mouth, and wild black hair. He remembered her pale skin from working in his grandfather's shop all hours that transformed to a beautiful nutty brown when they visited their forest summer house for holidays.

A single sparrow's song pierced the silence with its shrill whistle and softer chatter to signal the start of the dawn chorus as Roman finally drifted asleep.

At seven-thirty, Mrs Hawanska knocked on his door and woke him; she carried a cup of tea, to his absolute surprise. She had made it clear she was the house owner and not a landlady who would never perform menial tasks for her tenants, such as tea in bed.

'Roman, you need to get up and telephone the hospital to find out how Bridget's doing.' She shook his shoulder as though he were still asleep.

Roman grabbed the tea with shaky hands. 'Thank you, Panne Hawanska; *Mrs.* How long will it take, do you think?'

Mrs Hawanska stood with her hands on her hips and laughed. 'Oh, my! There's never one the same as the other. Who knows?' She bent slightly to pull the blankets from his bed. 'Up you get.' She smiled at Roman. 'Today will be a wonderful day.' She winked at him and left his room humming.

When washed and dressed, Roman hurried to the local phone box. The massive drifts halted the local traffic until the city corporation's bulldozers rumbled out to clear the roads. Snow covered everything and created a sense of tranquillity; the only audible sound was his footfalls plunging in and out of the crunching snow.

As Roman's phone call connected to the labour ward, he had to repeat his question twice. The nurse on the other end could not understand his accent, which annoyed him. He had lived in England for three years and considered his English now advanced enough for straightforward communication. People needed to listen. After all, he had to struggle to understand the thick local accents of Yorkshire people. Eventually, after many repetitions and her going away and returning, she informed him that Bridget was still in labour and to phone back at teatime. Roman slammed the receiver down and felt an impulse to kick the booth walls but resisted. *I'm tired,* he thought. *Better get back, grab breakfast and go to the mill. Work will take my mind off this.*

The walk to work was arduous. The streets were full of people who struggled in the snow. Many trudged in the middle of the road, and the absence of traffic created a curious holiday-like feeling. A camaraderie had emerged, and people smiled and waved at one another as they passed.

Roman clambered the weathered stone stairs to the canteen at lunch break when the man who had visited his home the previous evening appeared. He recognised Roman and halted on the top step. When Roman reached him, he grabbed Roman's lapel.

'We need to talk, comrade.'

Roman pushed his hands away. 'I'm not your comrade, and I don't want to talk.' He tried to shove beyond the man who stood in his way. People were trying to pass them on the stairs, eager to get their food.

'Follow me,' the man said and tripped lightly down the stairs, his shoes clattering on the stone. Roman tramped after him in annoyance. His stomach rumbled from hunger.

In the main yard outside the mill, the man beckoned Roman through wrought-iron gates to the rail yard that carried goods back and forth to the city. He huddled into an alcove, lit a cigarette and offered Roman one, who refused.

'Okay!' the man said. He took a deep drag on his cigarette and blew smoke into the frosty air. 'Someone saw you and your friend in the alleyway with "the Dentist".' He stared intently into Roman's eyes.

'I don't know what you're talking about,' Roman said. 'Now, I want to eat before my shift starts again.'

The man eyed Roman coolly. 'You know what happens to Poles who come to the attention of the police, the courts? The British deport them home. It's not as nice as England yet.'

'Why should that bother me?' Roman's legs felt weak, but he masked it by stamping up and down, pretending to keep his feet warm.

'He's been to the hospital, you know, just a few broken ribs.'

'Who?' Roman said, kicking a lump of coal-stained

snow against the wall.

The man laughed and passed Roman a leaflet. 'Turn up tonight at this meeting. You should join up.'

Roman read the leaflet's heading: The Polish Communist Party of Great Britain Call to Action.

'Why should I do that?'

'Because,' the man said, flinging his cigarette butt into the snow with a fizzle. 'We'll keep you and your friend's secret for you.' He tapped his nose, turned, and sauntered away in the stained snow.

'But my wife's in hospital having a baby,' Roman called after him.

'Too bad,' the man said over his shoulder.

The rest of that afternoon at work, Roman ran through the implications of ignoring the stranger's instructions to attend the meeting that evening. If the man was serious and Roman didn't turn up, would he report him and Andrej to the police? How could he prove it was them who beat up the ex-guard? They could deny it, two against one.

But both were registered aliens, meaning they carried identity cards with them and must report to the local police station every two weeks to provide information about their daily lives. Any misdemeanour on their part could result in instant deportation back to Poland. Even though the British Government had finally agreed to the Polish Resettlement Act of 1947, it was also keen to rid itself of war refugees.

Roman knew the official story manufactured by the Russian communists who now governed Poland was that they welcomed post-war nationals back home. But was Poland still the home they had known before the war? The other story that leaked out via letters from family and friends in Poland was that the Russians were carting thousands of people, including returners, to labour camps, or worse, because they had opposed them during the war. Roman realised he must attend the meeting to throw the man off his track to avoid this terrifying fate. Later at work, he sought Andrej out to tell him and begged him to come along just for one meeting. Andrej agreed.

When the mill siren sounded at 5.30 pm, signalling the end of the working day, Roman headed into the deep snow to find a phone box. His call connected to a nurse in the labour ward who informed him that Bridget was still in labour but not yet in the delivery room.

'Can I visit?' he asked.

The nurse advised Roman to phone again at about 9 pm.

Later that evening, he and Andrej found the building where the meeting of the Polish Communist Party of Great Britain would take place. It stood on the corner of a run-down street opposite waste ground full of mounds of rubble and the odd abandoned pram.

Inside was an ancient tavern with low ceilings and muddy-coloured, buckled walls. Roman enquired at the bar about the meeting's whereabouts. The bartender, a giant of a man whose rolled-up sleeves exposed tattooed arms that resembled ham hocks, nodded towards a door. Roman and Andrej went through it. It led to a staircase that sloped to one side. At the top, the floor also tilted dizzyingly towards an open door where Roman heard voices. He and Andrej shuffled in. The room was dark, lit by softly hissing gaslights. About fifteen men sat around tables littered with beer glasses. Most wore hats and coats, some scarves, even though the room temperature had climbed above freezing because of their generated body heat.

Roman spotted the man who'd invited him, weaving between tables and heading his way. When he reached Roman, he slapped him on the back, then turned to Andrej.

'Glad you made it.' He held out his meaty hand. 'Allow me to introduce myself. I'm Joseph Kowalski.'

With that, he motioned to them to take a seat at a table of three other men; heads bowed in conversation.

Joseph sat down next to Roman and offered him a cigarette. Roman accepted it. Joseph lit it, then placed the matchbox back in his bulged coat pocket. For a second, Roman imagined he had a gun but then realised his pocket was stuffed with propaganda leaflets.

'See that man over there?'

Joseph pointed to a stocky man, about forty, with a ragged scar that ran from beneath one eye down to the corner of his mouth, holding court with a group of rapt younger men.

'Tadeusz Godowski,' Joseph said.

'He's the brains behind our cell. Smart. Shrewd. Ruthless.' He eyed Roman, who kept his face as unreadable as possible. 'Look at his hand,' Joseph said.

Roman stared. As Godowski talked animatedly now and then, one arm flew into the air to illustrate a point. At the end of the sleeve, a hook glinted where his hand should be.

‘Not pretty, eh?’ Joseph said. ‘So, we can’t send him out to talk to people. He scares the shit out of them.’ He laughed.

‘Is that a fact?’ Roman said.

‘Yes. We need pleasant-looking men like you and your friend. To help spread the word.’

‘What word would that be?’ Roman said.

Joseph leaned in; his ice-blue eyes shone. ‘The glorious Soviet Republic must one day take over the West. Banish capitalism and oppression forever! We must rebuild our country and contribute to the communist struggle for victory against the world's domination by capitalism. We owe it to the Polish state to support the fight and return to our motherland.’

Roman took a deep breath in and stubbed out his half-smoked cigarette. ‘I’ve had enough of fighting.’

‘Me too,’ Andrej said.

‘But this is the ultimate cause, requiring the ultimate sacrifice.’

‘I don’t quite understand your logic, Kowalski. On the one hand, you’re threatening Andrej and me with deportation to Russian-run Poland yet insisting we tell others they need to return for the cause. It makes little sense.’

Kowalski smiled. ‘Ah yes, at the moment, Poland is in a transitional phase; it is not yet truly communist. In the way that Marx and Lenin intended. We must work towards returning when it has fully become a communist state.’

‘Sorry, I’m lost,’ Roman said. ‘But now you’ve explained it to me, can I go to the hospital to visit my wife, who's having a baby?'

'A true comrade must subjugate his personal needs to the needs of the collective. No. You must stay to listen to Tadeusz Godowski speak. He will enlighten you both.'

Roman sighed and glanced at the clock on the wall. It was 8 pm. At eight-fifteen, Kowalski bustled around the room, reminding men to order more drinks at the bar before Tadeusz's speech.

'No interruptions,' he said.

As Roman followed the men down the uneven stairs into the saloon bar, Andrej whispered to him, 'I have a plan. You hold back. I'll spill my beer on someone, start a commotion, and you slip out the side door.'

Roman glanced around the thick smoke for the exit. He edged towards it and when he heard someone say, 'Watch it, idiot,' he scrambled out in search of a public phone box.

As Roman approached the red phone box, someone was inside, their outline visible through the ice-crusted windows. Outside the box, a man stamped his feet, arms tucked under his elbows, and his breath puffed into the frozen air. He nodded at Roman as he trudged up to stand behind him. Roman remembered the English were fanatical about queues; if you tried to jump, they went berserk. One of the few times he'd ever witnessed them break out of their polite shells to complain in public.

The man turned to Roman. 'She's been in that box for ages, mate. Must be on with her mother.' He snorted. 'Must be made of money an' all.'

'I knock on window?' Roman said. 'My wife having

baby. I need phone hospital.'

The man shrugged. 'It's up to you, sunshine.'

Roman edged around him and rapped on the window. Through the frost-glazed glass, he glimpsed a woman in a headscarf turn to peer at him, then she turned back and huddled closer over the telephone. He knocked again, but she ignored him.

'Is it your first?' the man asked Roman.

'Yes.'

'Tell you what, when lady muck's finished, you can go before me.'

'Dziękuję,' he said before he'd realised, then smiled at the man. *Thank you.*

Five long minutes passed before the young woman stepped out of the phone box and glared at the two men.

'Call yourselves gentlemen,' she said and stomped away in the snow.

She struggled in her fur-lined ankle boots that looked insubstantial to Roman.

His hand shook as he dialled the hospital number and waited to be connected to the labour ward. When a nurse answered, Roman, heard a tremor in his voice.

'It Mr Kozynski. Has Bridget had baby yet?'

'Just a moment, love, I'll find out for you.'

Roman tapped his fingers on the side of the telephone to relieve the tension that mounted in his chest. Soon the nurse returned to the phone.

'Mr Kozynski, congratulations, you have a son.'

Roman folded with emotion. 'A son,' he repeated.

'Yes. A healthy boy.'

‘I come hospital now?’

‘Your wife’s well but tired. It’s better to let her rest and visit tomorrow morning.’

‘Okay.’

Roman felt he was floating above himself, looking down at this fortunate young man with a bright future. He pushed the booth door open and grinned at the man, who was still stamping in the snow.

‘I have son!’

He lurched towards the man and tried to hug him. The man took a step away but relented and patted Roman’s shoulder.

‘Well done, lad,’ he said.

‘It miracle.’

Roman sprinted off into the midwinter night.

## Roman, Christmas Eve

Roman sat by the cot, gently rocking it with his foot and marvelling at Janek. He nestled inside a red armchair Katerina and Andrej had rescued from the basement, recovered, and given to them as a wedding present. It was their first Christmas together as a family. Roman stared out the window at the snow that had fallen all day and covered every sharp edge with a soft, glistening coat. The snow absorbed all sound and reflected the light, so that afternoon, Roman imagined himself wrapped inside a wonderland, far from harm and hurt.

Roman knew down in the shared kitchen of Mrs Hawanska's, the final touches to the Christmas tree were made by Bridget and Katerina. Since September, the residents saved money to buy a tree. That week they also pooled their ration provisions to provide a Christmas dinner for the whole house. They had agreed it was best to wait until the late afternoon of Christmas Eve to purchase the tree. Most shoppers had gone home, but a few trees would still be left for sale. So when Katerina and Mrs Hawanska had hurried to the market and the clock ticked towards closing time, the price of the remaining trees dropped. Even though the ones left would be scrawny and shedding needles, it was nothing they couldn't fix.

Roman peered into the cot, handmade in the traditional Polish style and loaned to them at Janek's birth. They would hand it back later when they had saved enough to buy a small bed. Janek lay asleep with his arms resting above his shoulders. Pink fingers curled like petals at dusk.

His silk-soft face flushed bright red as his breaths puffed into the air. Roman stood and stole quietly out of the room and down the stairs. As he opened the door, Katerina and Bridget stood back admiring a small tree laden with glittering handmade decorations, red ribbons, candles, and a string of Christmas lights. Roman's throat constricted as the memory of childhood Christmases overcame him for a moment. But he composed himself quickly, crossed the room, and placed an arm over Bridget's shoulders.

'Where lights from?'

He released Bridget and bent to pull a single one towards him to inspect. It was a miniature Chinese lantern of red and white opaque glass. Next on the green plaited cord came a frosted snowman with a jolly black hat. On it went, each decoration was different from the previous one.

'Don't touch!' Katerina said. 'They're Mrs Hawanska's pride and joy.' She eased Roman's hand away from the lights. 'If you damage any, she'll evict you.'

Roman laughed and stepped back.

'Is Janek sleeping, Roman?' Bridget said, her hands moving to her hips.

'You not trust me?'

She stared back at him. 'Not always.'

'Hey, let's gather around for drink and switch on tree lights?' said Katerina.

She didn't wait for an answer but slipped out the door, saying she would round up the house residents and Mrs Hawanska.

Soon, the fourteen residents bunched in the warm kitchen with their glasses of Polish cherry brandy held high as the ruby liquid glinted and swirled in the light. Mrs Hawanska instructed Roman to plug in the tree decorations carefully. He winked and bent to switch them on. Nothing happened, and the room fell deadly silent, but suddenly the lights tinkled, flickered, and burst to light to a collective, 'Ahh!' before the toast to Wigilia was made: the Polish Christmas Eve feast. Roman and Katerina talked about the traditional fish dish they would have eaten back home that night.

'Maybe next year we can afford it?' Roman proposed another toast to their health and good fortune in this new land.

He stared around at the smiling faces, cheeks pinked by the drink and heat from the fire. Bridget looked so beautiful as she sat by the glowing coals. The soft amber light illuminated her graceful profile, and her curls shimmered as she turned her head to speak to Mrs Hawanska.

Bridget returned to their room before Roman. She told him she wanted to check on Janek. When Roman went up later, he found Bridget lying on the bed on her side, gazing at Janek, who slumbered in his cot. Bridget had insisted earlier that evening they would have candles light their room before they went to sleep because it was Christmas Eve. She had collected unwanted fabric pieces from the mill and told Roman she would cut them into the shape of miniature Christmas trees that now hung across the window frame. She had repurposed a few sequins by removing them from the skirt of her treasured best dress and had sewn them onto the decorations that twinkled in the soft glow of the candles.

'It look beautiful,' Roman said as he crept in and sat beside her.

Bridget yawned. 'The cherry brandy has gone to my head, Roman.'

He was silent for a moment as he gazed around at the scene. 'There letter from Mother, about Wigilia, in suitcase. I read now?' he paused as he considered his following action.

'Yes,' Bridget murmured as she closed her eyes.

Roman held the letter in trembling hands. Previously he had opened the letter, glanced at the first sentence, and dropped it back in the case, unable to face the contents, but this evening seemed right. His mother had written the letter some time ago. Just before he had found her whereabouts, she must have kept it, hoping to send it one day but changed her mind. He could understand this.

*Ballochmyle Hospital, Scotland, 24th December 1946*

*My Dearest Roman,*

*Tonight, it is Christmas Eve, Wigilia in Polish. My son, you must never forget your language even though you must learn a new one to get along in this cold, foreign place where the sun never shines. How can I describe my feelings on this awful Christmas Eve here as I look around at the grey walls, white beds, and sad, pale faces of the others, their thoughts as far away as mine?*

*Tonight, my mind returned to happier Wigilias when snow*

*fell quietly from the sky, and the wax candles twinkled on Christmas trees in all the houses. After supper, do you remember we would walk from our apartment to the square where the colossal Christmas tree glittered and climbed high into the sky? Your father would point to the North Star and tell you the Wise Men used it to find Jesus on the first Christmas Eve. And he would say that when you were brought to us, one bright cold night, another star shone out from the others. And then the angels let you fall gently from it, and your tiny wings dissolved into little clouds as you came to Earth. Then we knew you were blessed. But now, there is sadness instead. I have so much to tell you. I fear I cannot do so to your face before it is too late. But once you know these things, I can fly away in peace, over the clouds, the trees, and the deep seas, to Jesus, who will not judge me harshly for my actions.*

*A few weeks ago, my brother wrote to me about what happened to your father, Roman, and how it angers me that they denied him a funeral. As an ex-Cavalry Officer of the Polish Army, this was his right. But for him, there was no ceremonial music, wreaths, or goodbyes. The Germans took him from Pawiak Prison, where we were all held during that fateful autumn of 1940. They drove him through the dark, destroyed city after pushing him and the other prisoners into wagons, throwing in shovels, and tapping their machine guns with impatience. They took away many men that night. To make a point to the Polish people never to oppose the Nazis. Not to organise behind their backs or fight against their plans. The Germans tried to turn the Polish into cowards like themselves with their guns, dogs, prisons, starvation, propaganda, and sheer lies. But your father was not a coward and worked with the Polish Underground. Even though this jeopardised our family, it was the right thing to do. We must accept this.*

*When the prisoners arrived in the forest in the dead of night, they had to dig a massive pit. Some men just stood and cried. And when these poor souls had finished digging, the Germans shot them all and pushed them in. Some were not dead. Roman, every day in Bielany, these tragedies happened day and night. Thankfully, the bodies are now recovered and lie in a memorial grave in Warsaw, but this is not enough. It will never be enough. It broke my heart, Roman.*

*I could do nothing for your dear father, but at least Elouna was saved. But I could not help you and deeply regret this. However, I heard you escaped that dreadful prison and prayed that Teofil would help you escape Warsaw. He, too, had connections with the Polish Underground. But the Germans murdered Teofil as well. I found this out much later. My soul cannot rest until you revisit me.*

*Your loving Mamushka.*

Roman placed the letter on the bed and turned to speak to Bridget, who was exhausted and asleep. He felt an odd numbness. And he was glad she had not heard the letter's contents. How could she comprehend such terrible things? He wanted to keep Bridget safe from knowing how brutal the world could be. He inched slowly to the edge of the bed to stand, trying not to wake her. Roman held the eiderdown where it hung over the bed and carefully covered Bridget, tucking it beneath her as she slept. He tiptoed to the cradle and bent down to kiss Janek's warm forehead, then blew out the candles as the scent of the snuffed wax filled the air. Roman collected his coat and crept from the room down the stairs.

Roman closed the front door as quietly as possible, pulled his coat collar up, and set off in the deep snow with no destination in mind. He needed only to be occupied, fixed on putting one foot in front of the other. The freezing wind blasted snow in his face and stung his cheek raw.

Roman wished he'd grabbed his scarf, but it was too late to turn back. He had hoped no word about his father meant there was still the slightest chance he was alive somewhere. After all, his fears that his mother had perished were unfounded. He had found her. Many people turned up years afterwards with extraordinary stories of how they survived. Deep in his heart, he believed this to be true of his father. Roman knew he could not contemplate the worst even though, with reluctance, he had told Bridget that his family were lost when they met. He hoped to find them all or they to find him. He thought of his family as somewhere out there in the world until otherwise proven. And they were, or at least his mother and sister had been. The pain to him of his sister's actions was searing, but at least she was alive. There were so many layers of hurt in life it was sometimes unbearable, and he needed to escape the torment. His vision blurred by the driving snow; Roman stumbled but kept going and tried to quicken his pace even though the effort of plunging in and out of the thickened snow with sodden boots strained painfully in his thighs. Snow piled in a helmet on his head that he shook intermittently. Freezing clumps slid down his neck inside his coat collar to settle on his shoulders.

Roman lost all sense of time as his thoughts hurtled round in his mind. When Janek grew up, how would he ever be able to tell him what happened to his grandparents? Why would a father burden a young heart with this terrible knowledge? He stumbled, fell to his knees, and his bare hands plunged into the freezing snow. Then it hit him hard in the pit of his stomach why his mother had not posted her letter telling him of his father's death. When he last visited her, she said she didn't know what had happened to his father. Her lies were to shield him, her son, from the bleakest truth she thought he could not hear. Or bear. She chose deception.

Roman thought back to the night Bridget went into labour as he struggled to stand up in the engulfing snow, his hands numbed. He'd stayed up late drinking and went to the Catholic church in the morning before work to tell God what he thought of Him. His worst fear had visited him that long night. What if Bridget and her baby died? If again he lost his family? He'd sat in a pew and observed the interior's false finery, the polished silver, chandeliers, and paraphernalia, all a façade to him. A rage inside him broke, and he shouted into the dusty air, 'Why do you let us suffer?'

His words echoed around the ancient stone walls. Then soft footsteps signalled another presence, and a priest slid alongside to sit by him.

'My son, are you in trouble?'

Roman shook his head. 'Not me. Entire world.'

'I see,' said the priest in a calm voice. 'Can you tell me about it?'

Roman turned to him and grabbed his sleeve. The priest did not pull away. 'Why you believe old man in sky with white beard, watch terrible suffering and do nothing?' The priest stared intently at Roman, who said, 'You really believe in fairy tale or just good job for you?'

Roman searched the priest's face for traces of deception. The faintest twitch at his lip's corners, a quick drop of the gaze, a flash of something, anything, but the priest's face remained utterly still.

'My son, it's a calling from Him, Himself, Almighty God.'

Roman released the priest's arm and snorted. 'You know nothing.' He stood.

A voice from the fog pulled Roman out of his thoughts of the past, and a light shone in his direction.

'And who do we have here?' said someone from inside the swirled white mist.

A dark mass emerged, and Roman recognised it was a policeman who held a torch. He swung the beam around the snow at Roman's feet as though looking for something. Then concentrated it on Roman's face, who held an arm up to shield his eyes from the glare.

'What you up to, sonny?' he said to Roman.

'I get fresh air.'

'It's two-thirty in the morning. And it's Christmas Day.' He stared at Roman.

Roman shrugged.

'You're a foreigner, aren't you? Got your ID to hand?'

Roman sighed; patted his pockets but knew he had left it at home.

'No. I forget.'

'Okay, sunshine, I think we need to take you to the station.' The policeman grabbed Roman's arm and blew his shrill whistle for help. It pierced the frozen silence.

'I do nothing wrong. Just walk. Very sad tonight.'

The policeman blew his whistle again. 'Save your breath; my mate will be here in a minute.'

'Who is that, Santa Claus?' Bridget heard Mrs Hawanska say as she padded down to open the front door.

Bridget looked at the clock on her bedside table, it was 3.30 am on Christmas morning, and Roman was not by her side.

'What have I done to deserve this life?' she heard Mrs Hawanska say.

Bridget was out of bed, into her dressing gown, and halfway down the stairs when she heard a man's voice say, 'Sorry to trouble you at this hour, but can I speak with Mrs Bridget Kozynski?

'Kozynska,' snapped Mrs Hawanska. 'You'd better come in.'

She gave Bridget a stern look as they collided at the door to the kitchen. The policeman followed them in. He explained they held Roman at the station for being out without an identity card in the middle of the night and asked to see Roman's card.

'What do you think he was doing, Mrs Koyzinska?' said the policeman as he scrutinised Roman's picture on his card when Bridget returned with it.

Bridget looked at Mrs Hawanska, who leaned against the sink and shrugged.

'I do not know. We lit the tree, toasted Christmas, and went to bed. Then I fell asleep.'

'Toasted, you say? Was there alcohol involved?' The policeman stared intently at Bridget as though her reply would be a revelation.

‘A glass of Wisniowa,’ Mrs Hawanska butted in. ‘Would you like one, as it is Christmas?’

He sat up straight and tugged his lapels. ‘Err, no, thank you, I’m on duty.’ He snapped his notebook shut and stood up. ‘Okay, I’m satisfied this is the same man.’ He pointed to Roman’s card lying on the table with his photograph. ‘He’ll be released and back home for breakfast.’ As the policeman reached the kitchen door, he turned to Bridget. ‘Just make sure your husband doesn’t make a habit of wandering the streets in the middle of the night.’

‘Merry Christmas,’ Mrs Hawanska said to his retreating figure.

* * *

The following day Bridget was in the kitchen with Janek on her knee talking to Mrs Hawanska when she saw Roman’s face appear around the door. He hung his head low and hesitated on the threshold.

‘I’ll prepare vegetables,’ Mrs Hawanska said. ‘You two talk.’

Bridget looked down at Janek and smoothed his wispy hair. ‘Do we want to talk to Dada?’ she said.

‘Bridget, I sorry.’ Roman looked so remorseful Bridget couldn’t help but smile at him.

‘Okay! Janek, it’s time for your nap.’

She stood up, and Roman followed her to their room. As Bridget settled Janek into his cot, she said, ‘Roman, you have a son and a wife now.’ She turned to Roman. ‘We have bills to pay. What were you doing out on the streets and getting arrested by the police?’

Roman pulled her towards him and held her. Bridget felt the warmth of his body through his clothes. He must have run all the way home from the police station.

Bridget leaned away. 'Can I depend on you, Roman?'

'Bridget, last night I had big shock.'

Bridget's eyes widened.

He continued. 'I read letter from mother. One she wrote me but not post.'

'Oh, I...' She put her hand to her mouth. 'I'm sorry, I remember now. I fell asleep.'

Roman eased her down with him to sit on the edge of the bed. 'It say my father died in war.'

'Oh, Roman, I'm so sorry.' Bridget searched Roman's face. 'Your father is dead, after all?'

He wiped his dampened eyes with his sleeve. 'But it long time ago now. At beginning of war.'

'Oh, how sad for you. Do you know what happened?'

Her voice was almost a whisper as she watched Roman turn his face away. He was silent for a while. Janek stirred and cried. She moved to his cot, took hold of one of his hands, and sang gently.

'He die in Prison.'

Bridget looked up from the baby. 'Oh, Roman, that's so awful.'

Roman stood up. He moved to Bridget and Janek. 'But today is day for celebrations. New family. New life. No tears.'

Roman took Bridget in his arms and kissed her upturned cheek.

Christmas day passed in a warm haze; the aroma of

dinner hung in the air until late afternoon and mingled with the sharp smell of the pine tree. Bridget watched wine, spirits, and conversation flow between the joyful residents. When the candles finally puckered to wisps of smoke, Bridget took Janek upstairs. Tired but happy, she lay on the bed with him, dozed, and later heard Roman tiptoe into their room. She opened her eyes as he picked Janek from her side and laid him in the cot, whispering to his son in Polish. Bridget closed her eyes, turned over, and fell asleep, still in her clothes.

On Boxing Day, the snow was even deeper, having fallen all night, and walking outside was a task not to be taken lightly, but Roman insisted he needed some fresh air. Bridget fretted a little but realised she had to trust him and try to understand he had come from difficult circumstances. She waved him goodbye as he set off to visit Andrej.

Roman and Andrej struggled in the snow to the park. They laughed as they slid around, threw snowballs at each other that exploded on impact, and covered their coats with fine white dust. Roman's ears were so cold he could hardly feel them, and he suggested they go to the Polish Club for a drink before returning to their homes.

Inside, men jostled and laughed, temporarily free from work constraints. Roman ordered drinks with brandy chasers. They settled into his favourite corner, where he could survey the room.

'So, when will you find yourself a good wife?' Roman said to Andrej with a grin.

'Oh, you giving me advice now? Andrej nudged Roman in the ribs. 'No rush. There's plenty of time,' he said.

'Time has a habit of running out.'

'Roman, you're a decent man but also a pessimist.' Andrej smiled. 'A man like me must ensure he marries the right girl to spend the rest of his life with.'

Roman sipped his drink and studied Andrej. 'My friend, the happiness you will experience when you love a wonderful woman and have your own family is unimaginable. Far, far better than running around with different skirts.'

Andrej winked at Roman. 'Is that a fact? One for the road?'

As Andrej stood, Kowalski appeared, spread his hands on the table and leaned close to Roman.

‘That wasn’t a smart move last month, Kozynski. Stupid to leave the meeting – but we’re watching you.’ He glared at Roman, who said nothing as he lifted his drink to drain the dregs.

‘Really?’ Roman said. ‘Then you’ll know I visited the police station yesterday and had a chat with them.’

Kowalski looked confused. ‘A chat about what?’

‘Poles, stirring up trouble. Maybe I even mentioned your name.’

Kowalski looked between Roman and Andrej, who stood rigid with two empty glasses in his hands.

‘You’re bluffing,’ Kowalski said. ‘You wouldn’t dare.’

‘Why not? I have nothing to hide.’

Kowalski guffawed. ‘That’s not true, and you know it. We all have things to hide. Things that would make people change their minds about us.’ He folded his arms over his chest.

‘Well, we will see.’ Roman said.

Kowalski’s jaw tightened. ‘I hear you have a beautiful wife and a baby boy.’

Roman stiffened. ‘So?’

‘I was thinking of visiting them for a chat.’

Roman hoisted himself up, his face inches away from Kowalski’s. ‘Stay away from my family, Kowalski, or you’ll regret it. I promise.’

‘Are you threatening me?’ Kowalski moved slightly back.

Andrej banged the empty glasses in his hands down onto the table.

‘You need to listen to my friend,’ he said.

Kowalski removed his hands from the table. He took a step back. 'Well, don't think this matter has ended because you want it to.' He sneered at them, turned on his heels, and pushed back to the bar.

Roman looked around to see if anyone had noticed their exchange. No one seemed to care.

Andrej huffed. 'Did you really mention him to the police?'

'Wish I had.' Roman picked up the glasses. 'My treat,' he said and weaved through the crowd.

Roman waited his turn at the bar. At its other end, Kowalski talked animatedly with an unknown man. He glanced at Roman and whispered something to the stranger who looked over.

Roman nodded to them and held a glass up. 'Cheers!' he said in English, then ordered drinks.

Later, when he returned home, Roman mounted the stairs two at a time. A sense of panic emerged beneath the beer haze. Bridget sat on the bed, rocking Janek in her arms and singing a song to him in Gaelic. Roman plopped down next to them and flung his arm around Bridget.

'You've been to the Polish Club,' she said as she pretended to look cross.

'Darling, promise me, if strange man come to house, don't let him in.'

Bridget jerked back. 'What strange man?' Janek screwed his face up at this disruption and let out a howl.

Roman stroked her hair. 'Any strange man. Be careful.'

Bridget stood up and rocked Janek gently in her arms. 'Roman, I'm not sure drinking is good for you.'

Roman laughed and fell back on the bed. He shielded his face beneath his arms. 'You good for me. I know that.'

Bridget moved to the window jigging Janek softly in her arms and looked out. 'Roman, a man is standing across the road.'

Roman leapt up to see. Below the street lamp, a figure huddled in a coat and blew smoke rings into the freezing air as he stared up at their window.

## Bridget 1950

Bridget waived goodbye to Roman as he again dashed off late for work with a piece of bread clutched in his hand. He spent most nights out and was secretive about where he had been. In their increasingly cramped room, she dressed Janek for a day out. As Bridget fastened his coat buttons, she noticed they were straining. Janek grew out of his clothes quickly, but Bridget worried about asking Roman for money for new things. Overtime at work had dried up, and the three of them had been living at a bare minimum. At times like this, she missed her family and the close community ties she had known. As they were called, big coats were handed down or passed on between people so nothing was wasted and money not spent.

Bridget had written to Kay a few weeks previously to suggest a visit. That morning Bridget fretted about catching the bus to Kay's house. It was five miles out of town in an area she was unfamiliar with, where the Corporation was completing a housing estate.

She repeatedly pulled Kay's letter from her pocket at the bus stop to check the address and instructions.

Bridget stepped onto the bus's platform and asked the conductor, 'Is this the right bus for Thorpe Edge estate?'

'It is, lass,' he said, helping her fold the cumbersome pushchair and placing it underneath the staircase before taking her seat with Janek.

She wore ankle socks instead of stockings that day, and the rough bus seat prickled behind her knees as she sat.

'Will you tell me when to get off, please? I need the

stop before Greengates Village.'

'Certainly.'

The conductor wound a small red handle on the ticket machine and out puttered a bus ticket. He handed it to Janek, who smiled and clutched it with a giggle.

On arrival, Bridget followed Kay's instructions and cut through an alleyway from the main thoroughfare to a large circular road full of corporation houses, some of which were still under construction on the estate. Each property was semi-detached with a garden area front and back. One or two homes that had been built first sprouted fledgling lawns.

As she walked along the pavement to Kay's house, Bridget noticed that the doors of the homes were painted uniformly in a sequence of blue, red, yellow and green. She manoeuvred Janek's pram down the path of number five and knocked on the green door. It immediately flung open to reveal Kay holding a baby. Kay stood aside and beamed. Bridget untied Janek from his pram and helped him over the doorstep, still unsure of his footing at almost two.

Soon they were seated with a pot of tea in the dining room. Bridget felt the atmosphere tingle with the excitement of so much to catch up on.

'I was so delighted to get your letter, Bridget. It's almost two years since we've seen each other.' Kay stretched her hand and squeezed Bridget's arm. 'You look wonderful.'

Kay poured steaming tea into china cups with decorated saucers. 'These are my best. A wedding present from my in-laws. It's the first time I've used them.'

'Lovely.' Bridget opened her handbag and pulled out a packet of cigarettes. She offered Kay one, who shook her head.

'I've given up for a while. Too expensive.'

Bridget lit her cigarette and puffed on it. She grinned at Kay. 'Sorry.'

'How's Roman these days?'

Bridget grimaced. 'He drinks a lot.'

'Well, you knew Roman liked a drink with his pals when you married him.' Kay crossed her legs, her feet clad in mule slippers that she jiggled.

'I did, yes, but...'

'Is everything alright?'

'I'm not sure. Roman's changed.' Bridget blew cigarette smoke out of one corner of her mouth.

'What do you mean?'

'He used to work lots of overtime to save money so we could get a mortgage. But now he says the company have cut back, but I don't think that's true.'

'I see,' Kay said. 'I might have one of your cigarettes if I can?'

Bridget nodded and passed her packet over. 'They're strong - Capstan Full Strength.'

'Crickey Bridget.' Kay lit up.

'He's out late most nights with his Polish friends. He comes home blind drunk and starts…' she stopped herself.

'And starts what?'

'Ranting. Raving, on and on about who he can't trust and whose out to get him.' Bridget shook her head.

‘Oh, goodness. How long has that been going on?’

‘Well, it was the Christmas Janek was born. This stranger turned up looking for Roman. Roman said he didn’t know him. But soon after that, he started going out nearly every evening.’

‘Going where?’

‘That’s what bothers me. Roman said he and Andrej joined a chess club when I pressed him. He said they were training for a big competition.’

There was a knock on the door, the crack of it opening, and a booming female voice said, ‘Are yer home?’

A tall woman with red hair, tucked into a roll and pinned up, poked her head around the door.

‘Oh, you’ve company, Kay.’ She moved to the table and took a seat. ‘How lovely. Is this one of your old friends from back home, then?’

Kay laughed, and Bridget noticed tiny crinkles beneath her eyes that disappeared as soon as her smile went.

‘Bridget, this is Gillian,’ Kay said. ‘Gillian, this is Bridget. Cup of tea, Gillian?’

‘Pleased to meet you, Bridget.’ Gillian smiled broadly at Bridget, who liked her immediately because of her steadfast but warm gaze.

‘Bridget has just been telling me about her husband, Roman, learning to play chess. He and his friend Andrej.’ Bridget heard an unexpected edge in Kay’s voice.

‘Bloody hell. Well, I’ll be damned.’ Gillian looked from Kay to Bridget. ‘It’s not them two Polish fellas I used to know. I went to the Polish Club with them a few times when we all worked at Salts mill.'

Bridget's eyes widened.

'That Roman, he were a looker alright.' Gillian winked at Bridget. 'But he were swooning over an Irish lass back then.' She stared at Bridget. 'Were that you, love?'

Bridget laughed. 'Ah now, yes, it was.'

'Well, I never,' Gillian said.

Janek sneaked from under the table and pushed into Bridget's knees.

'And whose that then?' Gillian said.

Janek hid his face in his mother's skirt. Bridget pulled him onto her lap, took out a hanky, spat on it, and gently rubbed a smudge from his cheek.

'This is Janek,' she said to Gillian. 'Roman's son.'

Gillian stretched out her arm to rub Janek's chubby knee. 'Hello, bonny lad.'

Kay coughed. 'Anyway, as you said, Bridget, Roman and Andrej attend many chess tournaments these days?'

Bridget shifted in her seat and redistributed Janek's weight. 'That's what he says. But I don't believe it anymore.'

'Chess! Fancy, leaving a pretty young lass like you alone. Bloody hell. He must be mad,' Gillian said.

'What do you think he's doing, Bridget?' Kay stared steadily at Bridget, who swivelled a wriggling Janek to the floor.

'All I know, Kay, is he can't keep running around with his Polish mates, getting blind drunk, coming home frightening Janek and me.' Tears sprung to Bridget's eyes, and she wiped them away with her starched white cuff.

'Oh Bridget, lovey, there must be an explanation. Roman's a good man,' Kay said, handing her a frilly handkerchief.

'I'm sure there is. But I've been thinking of visiting my mother in Ireland. She's not well. Maybe I'll take Janek with me.'

'You're not leaving him, are you, Bridget? Not so soon.' There was a heavy silence then Kay grabbed at Bridget's knees.

Bridget stood and crossed to the dining room window. Children played contentedly in a field beyond the garden fence. They had no visible toys but were happy, circling, jumping and inventing games for themselves.

'No, I'm not leaving.' She paused. 'Just warning Roman he needs to change his habits.' Bridget continued to stare out at the children. *They're happy here,* she thought, a*way from traffic and the dirty city.*

'I'd better be going now. Glad to have met you, Bridget.' Gillian said.

'Me too. There's the tea to make.'

Bridget decided to walk home. 'I can save the bus fare for my trip to Ireland, 'she said as she asked Kay for directions.

Her journey back required pushing Janek's pram up a steep hill crossed by a bridge where steam locomotives rattled back and forth. On one side smoke puffed from the chimneys of simple terrace cottages. They led to a church, then a cemetery where gravestones sagged and leaned into the shifting ground. The new estate sprung pristine from green fields on the other side of the bridge. It climbed up the hill past a new school, shops, wide roads planted with springy saplings and grass verges. Bridget enjoyed being away from the smoky city centre, the feel of the space and light, and she thought about the future in a new way.

## Roman

The pub was full of men cooling off after a long day's grind. Roman and Andrej sat in their favourite seats where they could observe the room, always on alert. Roman detected a frown on Andrej's face and noticed his jaw clenched. Roman took a large gulp of his pint and wondered what was coming.

'I bumped into Bridget yesterday in town.' Andrej paused and peered intensely at Roman, who nodded but said nothing.

'She said you've been out lots lately,' he continued.

'I've been busy, this and that, you know.' Roman gestured with a hand and smiled innocently.

Andrej put his drink down. 'No, I don't know. And if you don't mind me saying, neither does Bridget.'

'I'm not sure what you mean?' Roman looked away from Andrej; his palms began to sweat.

His best friend had fixed him with such a look that he dreaded what he was about to say.

'Don't lie to me, Roman. I'm the only person you can't tell lies to.' Andrej took a large swig of his pint, swirled the liquid around, and set it back on the table. Froth clung to the inside of the glass forming elaborate patterns beneath the rim.

'Bridget's unhappy,' Andrej said.

'No! She isn't,' Roman said but avoided Andrej's eyes.

'Bullshit! She told me she's sad because you're out all the time with me and the lads, playing chess.' Andrej left the words to hang in the air while he continued to glare at

Roman.

'It's none of your business.'

'Oh, it is if you involve me in your deception.'

'I'm out helping the party; you know I can't tell her.'

'Rubbish! I thought we'd established they're as frightened of us as we are of them, so they have no power. Roman, don't use them as an excuse.'

Roman pulled a tobacco pouch from his pocket and rolled a cigarette. Slivers of tobacco clung to the tips of his dampened fingers.

Andrej swivelled towards Roman. 'I'm Janek's godfather and your best friend. So, tell me why you're running around with those no-goods instead of taking care of your family?'

A woman wearing a floral pinny over her dress popped her head around the saloon door and searched the room for someone. Andrej pointed at her with his glass.

'See her, looking for her husband most likely. You don't want Bridget to end up like that, do you?'

Roman remained silent but shook his head.

Andrej grabbed Roman's tobacco and rolled himself a cigarette. 'Whatever it is, you're doing Roman; if you don't stop now, I'll tell Bridget our secret, I swear.'

Roman grabbed Andrej's arm. 'You can't. She won't believe you. She just wouldn't.'

'Why not, Roman? You think you don't look the type—you, the handsome Polish man with those mysterious eyes.'

Roman squeezed Andrej's arm even more tightly. 'Please, I beg you. How could she love me then? She must never know.'

'Well then, will you cut the nights out drinking with your party pals?'

'I'll try. But you know, drinking helps me calm down. And forget'

Andrej spluttered his drink. 'That's not what Bridget says, Roman. She says you act like a maniac.'

## Roman 1943, German Camp

Roman lay on the bug-infested bunk he shared with Andrej. The men beneath were still asleep but cried out now and then in different languages. Roman tugged the grime-encrusted, rough blanket over his shoulder; one finger poked through a hole, and he cursed. Andrej shivered and tried to pull it back. The door swung open, and an officer marched in, followed by a soldier with a gun slung over his shoulder.

'Out of bed, now,' the officer shouted into the fetid air.

Suddenly, men stirred; those more able scrambled from their bunks immediately. Roman and Andrej were first, standing to attention in their ragged clothes. The men lined up by their bunks for the officer to walk past them. He glanced briefly at each man and stopped when he reached Roman and Andrej.

'You, and you,' he said. 'Guard, take them away.'

Roman's legs shook as he glanced at Andrej, who stared back with a dumbstruck expression. 'Not even time for a chunk of stinking black bread,' Andrej whispered to Roman as they followed the guard.

Outside the hut, the guard marched behind Roman and Andrej with his rifle pointed at their backs. Their broken-down shoes plunged in and out of the putrid mud with a squelching sound.

'We're going over there,' said the guard.

He motioned to a single-storey building behind a high fence that everyone referred to as the shower rooms. A thick, dark, acrid smoke belched incessantly into the air from its chimneys, covering everything in the vicinity in fine ash. Roman knew of the rumours but had tried not to think about them until now.

'Let's run for it.' Andrej whispered.

'No, it's no use.'

Roman knew that the guards who led straining Alsatians trained to attack and kill patrolled the perimeter fences. They would hold back from shooting until the dogs had had their fill. Often the bullets were no longer needed.

'Shut up, or I'll shoot,' the soldier shouted and prodded Andrej in the back with his rifle. 'Get a move on.'

As they neared the building, Roman saw a line of people herded inside, shuffling close together, occasionally turning to catch the eye of someone behind. But they were roughly shoved forward by the guards surrounding them.

As he neared the dishevelled group, Roman felt a strange calm envelop him. *At least I have my friend with me,* he thought. *I'm not alone.*

Their guard ushered them past the line of people entering the building and led them around the back into another entrance. Roman walked through the door into the vaulted chamber, and the stench hit him so hard he creased over and wretched, but his empty stomach did not obey the physiological command, and after a few dry wrenches, he straightened up.

'You'll get used to it,' the soldier said.

He led Roman and Andrej to what at first looked like a mound of rags, but as they neared, Roman realised it was a pile of bodies heaped together. A wave of nausea overcame him again, but his gut did not react so violently this time.

A man appeared out of a corner wearing a tattered guard's uniform slightly too large for his scrawny frame. He leered at them. Roman recognised him as a camp guard he saw patrolling regularly. He was Polish and carried a rifle across his chest.

'Traitor,' Roman said under his breath.

'All yours,' the soldier said to the guard, turned, and marched away.

The guard looked Roman and Andrej up and down. 'Healthy specimens, I see,' he said, then laughed.

*Compared to the others, we are,* Roman thought.

'Come with me.'

He beckoned to them with filthy fingers and retreated into a corner where boxes stood piled. Roman and Andrej tramped behind him as they stole anxious glances at one another. Roman noticed Andrej's face had gone near translucent if it was possible for him to be paler than he was already. The months of hard labour, watery gruel and tiny scraps of stale black bread had drained them of vigour and colour.

The guard took two pairs of pliers from a shelf in the nook and handed one each to Roman and Andrej. He smiled at them from a mouth of greyed, broken teeth.

'These are your work tools,' he said, hooking a finger at them to follow him back to the corpse pile.

The guard halted when they reached it and swung his rifle over his narrow back to bend down. He struggled to pull a corpse from the tangle by its head. Its glazed eyes stared out from the shaven head. The guard pulled open the mouth and rooted inside.

'Jews like gold teeth,' he said, then laughed. 'A way to store money on your person.'

Roman watched him bend closer, the body obscured by the guard's back. He heard a soft sucking sound then the guard turned around with something between the pliers.

'This is your job now. Check every one of them for this.' He brandished a gold tooth at them for a second, then tossed it into a cloth he had laid on the ground.

'We store these over there,' he said and motioned to the corner with the boxes, 'and extract the gold later. That's a good job to get.'

Roman stood rigid; his eyes widened with terror, and his thoughts raced uncontrollably. He shot a look at Andrej, who had staggered back with an expression of absolute horror on his face.

'Don't like dirty work?' the guard said, moving towards Andrej to jab the rifle in his ribs. 'That's fine, my friend. You have a choice.' He looked from Andrej to Roman, then laughed. 'Stay here and do the job, or join them. It's simple.' He pointed to the pile of bodies.

Roman returned home that evening, shaken by his encounter with Andrej in the pub. Bridget must never know what he had done to stay alive. He had entered a place where the concept of choice was an illusion, an unreachable fabrication. It was another world that most people did not know existed. One that ordinary people could never, ever imagine. It had been a nightmare world where humans obeyed their most primal instinct to stay alive, no matter how, because the urge to live for just one more hour or day was the most vital impulse ever to pulse through your body.

Earlier, he had sworn to Andrej he would extricate himself from the clutches of the Communist Party. They agreed if Kowalski went to the police about the dentist incident, they would deny it and tough it out. Andrej had reminded Roman that he could not bear life without Bridget and Janek. They were his reason for living. Andrej would support him in creating a new life far from the horrors of the old one.

Their room was empty when Roman entered it. Bridget had tidied up, but it looked different somehow. Roman spotted an envelope on the bedside table addressed to him. He walked dreamlike towards it and picked it up; his hands trembled as he slit it open. Letters had a way of bringing him grief as well as happiness.

*'My Dearest Roman,*

*My mother is ill, and I have taken Janek to meet her, her beautiful grandson. We will catch the bus and then the ferry to Cork. Katerina has lent me some money for the fares.*

*I am sorry I could not wait to tell you in person, but there is no time to lose, and I did not know when you would return from your chess playing. As soon as I arrive, I will write to you. Please take care of yourself.*

*I love you dearly, Bridget.'*

Roman looked around the room. Bridget's case was gone. Janek's pushchair, too. He ran to the wardrobe and yanked it open. Empty metal hangers clinked where the few clothes Bridget owned had hung. He slammed the doors and fell back onto the bed with his hands over his eyes.

'No, please, no. Bridget!' he cried out.

## Bridget 1950, Ireland

Bridget sat in the kitchen of her sister Georgina's house in Cobh, County Cork. Georgina was at work because she owned a ladies' clothing shop on the main street. Bridget's mother sat across from her with a sleepy Janek nestled on her knee.

'Jesus, it's a killer of a journey, buses, trains, the ferry, heaving Janek and a case on and off.' Bridget looked at her mother, whose weary eyes stared back in anticipation. 'But we're here now.' Bridget smiled and leaned forward to touch her mother's knee.

'Would you make a cup of tea, Bridget, milk for the boy, and some toast? Then we can put him to sleep for a while.'

Bridget got up and surveyed the kitchen for the necessary things.

'Hasn't Georgina done well for herself,' she said as she filled a kettle to boil on the gas cooker rather than an old-fashioned range.

Her mother laughed, a croaky laugh born of years of incessant smoking. 'She was always up to something, selling stolen sweets to other kids in the playground. Making money.'

Bridget set the tray on the table and then returned to the cooker to make toast. 'Well, at least her endeavours mean she can look after you now.'

'I don't need looking after, and I'm not yet sixty. *I* help Georgina!'

'Of course, that's what I meant.'

The aroma of toasted sourdough filled the kitchen as Bridget sat to lather hers and Janek's in butter.

'You know we still have rationing in England, and this stuff's rare as hen's teeth.' She pointed to the butter dish with her knife before cutting some toast into quarters and passing it to her mother. 'Would you give Janek this for me?'

'He's fast asleep now. You should put him down; he can eat later.'

Bridget bit into her bread. The butter slowly dripped off its edge and trickled down the inside of her wrist.

'In a minute,' she said, catching the butter with a finger and licking it clean.

'You know Georgina has a woman to keep this house tidy,' her mother said. 'Imagine that. Wasting good money, I would have done it for free.'

'I'm sure. But it's good of Georgina to let me and Janek visit, isn't it now?'

Bridget's mother paused her food poised mid-air. 'Is everything all right with you and that husband of yours?'

'Grand.'

Bridget stood to lift Janek from his grandmother's knee and tiptoed to the room where they would sleep after their long journey. Above the bed, a large, battered cross dominated the wall, and beneath it, a picture of the Virgin Mary in a flaked gold-leaf halo stared beatifically out into the unknown. Bridget laid Janek down, slipped the quilt over his slumbering body, and crept to the window. Her fatigue fought with her curiosity. Roman's words ran through her mind; *I can sleep lots when dead.*

Georgina's house looked over rooftops down to the harbour, where Bridget saw boats that plied up and down. Both colourful fishing boats and large commercial vessels traded in the busy port. St Colman's Cathedral imposed itself over the town as the buildings leading down to the quay came into view. Its enormous spires reached high to point their fingers at heaven, to remind everyone God watched them. And the priests could be seen scurrying along in their flapping robes in the streets, pockets jingling with coins, in and out of everyone's business, taking note. The priests would condemn her marriage if they had known the circumstances, but they would not, and neither would her family.

Months after her wedding, Bridget wrote she had married; it had been a very simple affair as money was tight. She hadn't received a reply to her letter until over a year later when her sister, Georgina, wrote to say she had moved from Cork City to Cobh to start a business, and their mother now lived with her. The letter gave the new address and included some money that Bridget had put aside.

She returned downstairs.

'Now you've finally come to visit, do you have a wedding photo to show us?'

Bridget heard both sarcasm and suspicion in her mother's tone, who sat at the table peeling potatoes, slicing them, and dropping them into a bowl of cold water with a plop.

'Things are very different in England,' Bridget said and slid into a chair beside her. 'They're rebuilding after the war. There's little money, rationing, housing shortages....'

'Well, why did you stay there then? Why not go on to America to make your new life like your brother?'

'Mother!' Bridget rested her hand on her arm while peeling potatoes. 'The simple truth is I fell in love, and we married quietly and cheaply.'

'Many a fool's fallen in love,' she huffed. 'I just hope he can give you a better life than we could, whoever he is?'

She was silent for a while as she continued her task with short sharp movements. Huffing now and then until finished. Her mother dabbed her hands on her pinny and asked, 'Is there a photograph of this wedding now?'

'A friend of Roman's took photos at the reception, but he got very drunk.' Bridget laughed. 'We all did.' She stared at her mother and shook her head. 'I'll never take to vodka. Anyway, Roman's friend, *the photographer,* fell into the canal on the way home. He was lucky he didn't drown.'

Bridget's mother glared at her with arched eyebrows and pinched lips. 'Jesus, you're the spit of your father with his tall tales.' She stood up from the table and grabbed the bowl of potatoes. 'I better get these on the stove soon.'

'I have a photo of Roman and Janek from our first Christmas together. I'll fetch it.' Bridget hurried to her room and prayed her mother would not enquire too closely about the dates of events and why she had married so quickly.

Bridget sprung open her case and searched for the photo of her, Janek and Roman with his arms around her shoulders, beaming. Behind them, the Christmas tree in Mrs Hawanska's kitchen twinkled. She thought to herself what *a lovely photo*, then lay beside Janek, closed her eyes, and fell asleep.

Bridget woke later when Georgina touched her arm resting on the bed's edge.

'Bridget, wake up; it's teatime.'

When Bridget opened her eyes for a second, she did not know where she was, but then she heard Janek's giggling voice coming from the landing. The door opened, and Janek walked in, holding his grandmother's hand.

'Mummy, we have rabbit stew for tea.' A tattered teddy tucked under his arm.

Bridget sat up and pushed the hair from the sides of her face where it had sprung free from the grips. Roman called it her wild Irish hair, but she called it a damn curse.

Georgina leaned in and hugged Bridget. 'It's lovely to see you, and your little man is great. Now, Janek, you've to be a big boy and look after Granny while your mammy and me go for a brief drive out.' She winked at Janek.

Janek looked from Bridget to his grandmother with a frown. 'Come on, little man, we'll see if the bread is ready, and we can have it with our tea.' Grandma turned him gently by the shoulders, and they padded from the room.

'Georgina, I'm so tired with all the travelling. Can I just sleep a little longer?'

Georgina moved away from the bed. 'Of course, you must have been travelling for hours. I'm so excited to see you and want to show you my car. That's all.'

'You have a car, my goodness, how wonderful.'

‘It’s for the business, really.’ She looked at Bridget, who could hardly keep her eyes open. ‘I tell you what, we’ll drive to Cork and have afternoon tea at the Bridge Restaurant tomorrow. You get some sleep now.’ Georgina pulled the satin eiderdown over Bridget’s shoulders. ‘We’ll keep some supper warm for you.’

Bridget caught Georgina looking at the floor and bend down to pick up something. It was the Christmas photo Bridget dropped when she fell asleep. Georgina hurried to the window to scrutinise it in the fading light of early evening.

‘Bridget! What a handsome fellah you have.’ She whirled around just as Bridget closed her eyes with a smile. ‘I wouldn’t leave him alone for too long if I were you. What a charmer.’

* * *

Georgina stood in front of her dark blue Ford Thames van with O’Sullivan’s Ladies Wear logo in gold script on the sides.

‘Come here,’ she said to Bridget, ‘and I’ll take a photo of you by the carriage.’

Bridget thought carriage a little grand but suppressed her smile. She took the photo then the sisters climbed into the front and set off for Cork City. It was clear Georgina was proud of her achievements.

As the van bumped along the winding country roads, Bridget was deciding how much she would reveal to her older sister about her reasons for visiting the family after such a long time away. Having left England this time without planning what she would disclose about her married life, she was torn between wanting her move to England to appear successful and admitting she could not cope. When she contacted them two years ago, her family had been shocked at the news of her sudden marriage, and then afterwards, she had kept them at a distance, afraid they would somehow guess the circumstances. The idea of an all-knowing being seeing into everything still haunted her from her Catholic upbringing.

She would divert attention away from herself at this moment. 'I haven't met Eamon yet,' Bridget said to Georgina, who had wound down the window and was shooing some hens vigorously from the road with her free hand.

'Get off the fecking road, will ye!' Georgina turned and smiled at Bridget. 'Can take the lass out of Cork, but not Cork out of the lass,' she said.

A farmer appeared from behind a berried hedgerow, shook a stick at the van, and broke into a wide grin as he approached the now halted vehicle.

'Mrs O'Sullivan, I take it this is your sister? Now young Bridget, you're not on your way back already, are ye? Before we've properly met' The farmer gave Bridget a wink. He'd reached the car and leaned in through the open window to rest his elbow caked in dried mud on the ledge.

'We shan't be going anywhere if you don't get your hens back in the field now, Murphy.'

He laughed. 'They're just having their daily stroll.' He continued to lean in and grin at Bridget.

'We'll drop by for a cup of tea and a craic soon,' Georgina said as she started the engine. 'We're just off to Cork for afternoon tea.'

Murphy lifted his cap, scratched his head, and moved back to let them pass. The hens had, by then, crossed the road and entered another field.

'I'll be seeing you.' Under his breath, he muttered, 'Georgina and her Cork city ways.'

'I was asking about Eamon,' Bridget said as they drove on. Suddenly feeling pushy and not very Irish in her abrupt reminder of the subject of their conversation. She'd forgotten the Irish habit of meandering around before getting to the point of something.

'Oh yes! Well, you'll meet him this evening. We have a grocery shop in Cork, and he's still running it. He comes back to Cobh at the weekends.'

Bridget felt her face flush. She hadn't meant to pry so indelicately. 'Oh, that's a grand arrangement,' she said, feeling even more embarrassed.

Georgina snatched a look at her and laughed. 'It is! But he'll be handing over the shop's running to someone he's training and working here helping me to manage the Cobh store.'

Bridget managed to say, 'I see.' Still feeling as though she had intruded.

'Eamon and I get on just fine, don't you worry,' Georgina said. 'So, what about your fellah, the handsome one?'

'I'll tell you all about Roman when we're having our tea,' Bridget said, breathing in loudly.

As the car descended the main road into Cork, Georgina said, 'Shall we park on Bridge Street? It's changed little since you left, but there's a new department store, and it's full of beautiful things.'

'What's it called?'

'Pennies. They sell coloured suede gloves and furs. It's a treat to visit.'

Bridget considered quipping that she had little money for such fancies but stopped. Instead, she stared out of the window as they approached Bridge Street. Two young women strolled along, arm-in-arm, in skirt suits and hats, wearing suede gloves and carrying little clutch bags beneath their elbows. She remembered her and Kay's days of freedom in Cork when everything seemed uncomplicated. Then her thoughts returned to Georgina.

'I don't know how you manage with three children and the shop; you must be run ragged.'

'Well, now, I have the woman help and mother lends a hand. You know it's true that the more you do, the more you can squeeze in.'

Georgina signalled with her arm and steered the car alongside the curb to park. She clicked off the engine and peered at Bridget. 'I'll not be having any more if I can help it. I think I've squeezed enough out and in'. Georgina snorted and grabbed her handbag from the floor.

Bridget coughed; her older sister was bold, so sure of how her life would be. It was overwhelming.

'And I don't care what the church says!' Georgina climbed out to wait for Bridget to stumble from her side.

The restaurant was as Bridget remembered when she

worked there before she left Cork. Its massive bay-fronted windows looked onto the busy main street and were crammed with customers guzzling afternoon tea. The silver cake stands glinted in the afternoon sun. Pristine white linen cloths adorned the tables with hand-made lace doilies between the gleaming cutlery.

They entered through the double doors, and a server in a black dress and frill-trimmed apron glided over and asked seating for how many.

'Just a table for two, please. We've left the boys in the pub!' Georgina winked at the waitress.

Bridget thought the waitress hesitated in her response for a second, but then she giggled.

'This way, please, ladies.' She led them to a secluded table beneath an ornamental set of steps to the upper floor and motioned for them to sit.

'Can we have an upstairs balcony table, please?' Georgina opened her purse and pulled out a banknote.

'Oh yes, of course, madam. This way, please.'

They followed the waitress up the gold-railed staircase, where diners sat in front of wrought-iron balconies that looked down to the pavement below. The waitress pointed to an empty table by the window.

'Please, be seated, ladies.'

She disappeared to return shortly with two menus on glazed cards.

'Fond memories, eh?' Georgina said, grabbing the card.

Bridget smiled as she thought of her and Kay, surveying the evening clients on their shifts, searching for handsome unattached men who didn't dress like farmers. Bridget had decided she would marry a poet and Kay a film star.

'Innocent, long-ago days,' Bridget said.

'And now?'

The waitress returned to take their orders.

Bridget looked to Georgina, who said, 'Afternoon tea for two, please.'

She handed the waitress her menu card and looked intently at Bridget. 'Well?'

'Keep this secret, Georgina; I think I've married my father!'

Georgina pulled a face. 'What do you mean?'

'Roman, he drinks too much.' She fell silent, worried she had opened up a chasm that would not close quickly.

'Men like a drink, Bridget. It gets them out of the house and out of our hair.' Georgina folded her arms.

'I know, but…' Tears sprung to Bridget's eyes. Georgina passed her a linen napkin, and Bridget dabbed her eyes with the starched cloth. 'I'm not sure I can take any more.' Bridget clutched Georgina's hand.

Georgina sat back. 'Come now, if every Irish woman left her husband because of his drinking, there'd be no more families in Ireland.'

Bridget kept her head down. 'I haven't left him,' she said.

'That's good to hear,' Georgina appeared relieved. 'He works to pay the bills and keep you both, doesn't he?'

Bridget sniffed. 'Yes, he does, but no overtime anymore because he's out with his friends too often.'

'Do you need money? Is that it?'

Bridget shook her head. 'No, it's not.'

'Well, what then?'

Bridget put the napkin down and glanced around before she said, 'I'm scared of him. He has these rages and gets out of control.'

'What do you mean?'

'Well,' Bridget hesitated for a moment. 'When he comes home drunk, it's like he's someone else. He rants the Russians are after him because they know.'

'The Russians? Know what?'

'I've no idea. Roman accuses me of having a secret affair with Kowalski.' It's madness, Georgina.

'Whose Kowalski?' Georgina leaned back on her chair.

'Someone who works with Roman. Kowalski visited our house once when Roman was out, and when I told Roman he was agitated, he later became suspicious and accused me of encouraging Kowalski.'

'Did you? I mean, by accident, you know.'

'God, no. Kowalski gave me the creeps. He scared me. He kept saying, what if something were to happen to Roman? Who would take care of Janek and me?'

'Did you tell Roman this?'

'Yes! I did, but he mixed it all up and threw it back as though I were saying I would run off with Kowalski.'

The waitress appeared with the food and set it down. Bridget straightened her posture and patted her face with her hand.

'It's warm this afternoon. Would you like some iced water?'

'Yes, please,' Georgina replied and reached for the cakes.

'There's something else,' Bridget said. She looked at the fluffy cream cakes, but her appetite had deserted her. 'Roman has these nightmares. He screams and shouts in Polish, then wakes up in a terrible state. I don't know what on earth to do.'

Georgina took a bite of her cream éclair and placed it gently onto the china plate. 'I've met no Polish people, so I don't know what they're like.'

She glanced at Bridget, picked up her éclair and continued eating, staring straight ahead.

Bridget poured them tea and reached for a slice of iced apple cake.

'I tell you what; we won't say anything to Mother. You can stay as long as you need to, but you will have to return to him at some point.' Georgina reached and patted Bridget's arm. 'Does he know where you are now?'

Bridget shook her head as tears once more filled her eyes. 'No, I said I was going to Cork because my mother was ill.'

'Do you think he'd try to follow you?'

'He can't. Roman doesn't have a passport. It's at the Polish Embassy in London.'

Georgina looked puzzled.

'And he can't go anywhere without the police agreeing.'

'Why not?'

'It's just how they treat immigrants.'

Georgina shook her head. 'Now, let's eat this smashing

food.'

Later, Bridget and Georgina arrived back to find their mother asleep on Janek's bed; she clutched the teddy close to her chest.

Bridget gently shook her shoulder, and she woke to say, 'My goodness, I must be more tired than I thought; taking care of little ones is quite exhausting.'

The three of them went down to the kitchen and left Janek sleeping, tired from his day with Grandma.

Bridget made a pot of tea and sat at the table where the photograph of Bridget, Roman, and Janek still lay. Georgina picked it up and waved it in front of her mother.

'Look what a grand catch our Bridget has.'

Their mother nodded in recognition. 'Very fine.' She looked at Bridget with a long stare. 'When did you say you two were married? I've quite forgotten now.'

Bridget looked at her. Her mother looked at Georgina, who smiled brightly.

'And remind me, girl, was it a church wedding?'

Bridget set the teapot down and wafted at the steam rising from the spout.

'We decided it would be more economical to marry in a registry office.' She sat down and fussed with the cups.

'More economical!' Her mother scowled before she said, 'Well now, it must have been a passionate business, what with Janek born so fast afterwards.'

Georgina coughed. 'I'll pour the tea now. Bridget, one sugar or three?' she asked.

'One, please. I must be very fertile then, like you, Mammy.' Bridget sat straight in her chair and stared directly at her mother.

She didn't reply. She just shook her head, took a sip of the too-hot tea and let out a little whimper.

'And now you're here without Janek's father. Mr Passionate.'

Bridget put her head to one side and fiddled with her hair. 'He's working away for a while, so I thought it would be a good time to visit.' Her cheeks flushed pink.

'I have an idea,' said Georgina. 'Let's have a family get-together. You can introduce Janek to the rest of the clan.'

Bridget audibly breathed in. 'Oh, no, I don't want a lot of fuss and bother.'

'Why ever not?' her mother asked, raising her chin. 'Since when has spending time with your dear ones been fuss and bother?'

'It isn't. It's just a big gathering that could be overwhelming for Janek. He's not used to lots of people all at once.'

Her mother shook her head and tutted. 'Only a few years away in England, and now these standoffish ways of yours.'

Bridget rested her elbow on the table and rubbed her forehead with her fingers. 'I don't expect you to understand, but I just need a few quiet weeks here, that's all.'

Their mother finished her tea quickly. 'Well,' she said, 'Who am I to understand the young ones of today?' She glared at Bridget for a second. Bridget looked away. 'I'm tired, so I think I'll go up and leave you two to it.'

Her mother stood from the table. Bridget noticed she leaned on it, and as she did, something like a wince passed over her face. She collected her crocheting and left silently.

When she'd gone, Georgina said, 'Bloody hell, she's a keen hunting nose.'

Despite her sadness, Bridget laughed. 'Georgina, I hate lying, but I'm too ashamed to tell her the truth.'

'What truth would that be now, Bridget? The truth about Roman and you or why you were married so quickly and not in a Catholic church?'

Bridget looked at her sister, whose severe expression did not seem judgemental.

'Both.' Bridget said, then sighed. 'It wasn't easy in England either, you know. It might not be a Catholic country, but being pregnant before you're married is shameful. I had to hide it as much as possible, Georgina.'

Georgina passed her hand over Bridget's arm, which cradled her chin.

'I can imagine,' she said. 'So, who else knew?'

'Only Roman, his friend Andrej, Kay, and Katerina.'

Georgina spluttered, 'Not that many then?' Her face broke into a smile.

'And this terrible girl called Nancy, who threatened to tell my boss and have me fired.'

'Jesus, it sounds just like home to me.' Georgina stood from the table and gathered the cups. 'It's been a long day; let's get some sleep. Things will be fine, I'm sure of it.'

## Roman 1950, England

Roman had hardly slept all night. Just as he dozed off, a loud knock on his door startled him from his dream. He opened his eyes to see Andrej standing in the door frame, waving something in his hand.

'Roman, there's a letter for you. It went to your old address.'

Roman sat upright and flung off the bedcovers. As he scrambled from the bed, he asked, 'Is it from Bridget?'

Andrej looked at the envelope to check, then said, 'Not unless she's in Scotland.'

'What?' Roman had reached Andrej by now and grabbed the letter from his hand. He stared at the postmark and the name of the sender: Mrs E Schutt.

'I don't know anyone called Schutt.'

'Sit down and open it,' Andrej said, then plunged onto the bed to smoke a cigarette while Roman sat down slowly to open the letter.

*Hill Top Cottage, Forfar, Scotland*

*Mrs Elouna Schutt.*

*October 1950*

*Dear Roman,*

*You cannot imagine how hard it has been to track you down, and I pray this letter reaches you before you move on again. How the war changed everything for us, how we fled to keep safe, only to find we were not. But I believe you are safe now, as am I.*

*There is so much to explain, which is impossible to put in a letter because it would turn into an unbelievable book. However, I can outline the main events, and if we meet face-to-face, we can discuss these events. I know Mother told you of some things that happened.*

*Roman, I was forced to marry a German during the early war years after our arrest. I hated him, but I could not leave. He disgusted me. I endured all of his pig-like behaviour until the war ended. It was chaos after April 1945, and I managed to escape from him with my two children. We found ourselves in a refugee camp in Germany, where I began my search for mama and you. Miracles happen and I found out that Mama was in Scotland, England, and I managed to travel there. I am finally near to you now. If you receive this letter, please write back to me. I desperately want you to visit my children and me. I think of you every day, Roman.*

*With love from Elouna*

Roman sat in his chair for a while, staring into space. He smoked a cigarette distractedly. Andrej lay on the bed and waited for him to say something. When Roman had finished his cigarette, he stood up and crushed the butt in the ashtray on the bedside table. He turned to Andrej, who swung his legs off the bed to sit upright.

'Well – who is it?'

Roman looked at him with such force Andrej put his head down.

'You won't believe this. It's from *my sister*, Elouna or Mrs Schutt as she is now.'

'Your mother warned you.'

'No, she didn't warn me; she told me – there's a difference.'

'You didn't get the full story before she died, Roman. Who knows what happened?'

'Who cares? It seems the women in my life feel it's fine to abandon me when I need them the most but reappear and want to be friends like nothing has happened.'

'What does her letter say?'

'She wants to see me, *to explain*.' Roman crumpled the letter and threw it in the waste bin.

'Another cow is changing her tune to suit her.'

'Roman, that's harsh.' Andrej stood to retrieve the letter from the bin. 'Can I read it, please?'

'Why bother yourself with more lies?'

Andrej unfurled the letter and began to read.

'She still thinks I'm her little brother who'll come running.'

Andrej nodded absently at Roman's remarks as he focussed on reading.

'She doesn't know I have a family.' Roman sneered. 'Who has now also abandoned me. It's the pattern of my life.' He slumped back into his chair and covered his face with his hands.

Andrej looked up at Roman. 'Stop feeling sorry for yourself. This development might prove in your favour. Listen to me.'

## Bridget Ireland

*Dear Roman,*

*I was so pleased to receive a letter from you. I am sure you can imagine how much I miss you. Janek often asks, 'Where's Dada?' out of the blue. It makes my heart heavy. So, it is truly terrific news that your sister Elouna is in Scotland with her children. It must be so wonderful to have some family near you again. I understand how important family is to you because you lost your's young.*

*I am now staying with my sister, Georgina, who has given me some paid work in her shop. Mother lives with us and is in much better health but has asked if I can stay a little longer to help Georgina. As Janek now calls her, Granny takes care of him while I work. Granny adores him, and they have become very close. Although she has other grandchildren to dote on, for her, Janek is special. His dark eyes must remind her of her eldest son, Connor, who departed Ireland to live in America. Older people often live in the past, and it seems this is what she is doing. I am not sure this is always for the best.*

*Living here in Ireland again has reminded me of why I wanted to leave in the first place. My family drags me to mass on Sunday as it is not permissible to miss church. I don't believe half of them are devout, but everyone keeps up a pretence as they still fear the Catholic Church.*

*Although I am busy at the shop and with Janek, I have had a chance to consider my life in England with you. Being away from a situation allows a person to view it from another angle. My thoughts have led to the following. I can no longer tolerate the way you behave.*

*The drinking and abrupt mood swings frighten Janek and me. You are only one step away from harming us, albeit accidentally. Therefore, I will only consent to return to live with you in England on one condition: we move out of the Polish community, and you break ties with your past. I believe your history is at the centre of the problem, and I insist you leave this behind. You have shared little with me, so it is easier for us to put everything behind us, including Andrej and Katerina, at least for the time being, so that we can establish a new life.*

*You might remember I visited Kay, who lives on a housing estate away from town, owned by the corporation. I have been in touch with the City Corporation by letter and found we can apply to rent a house there. We qualify as a young family unable to afford to buy our own home. The houses are unfurnished; if they offer us a tenancy, it's for life. There is no landlord or landlady setting terms or snooping. The Corporation is the landlord. You would not be alone living on this estate as your friend, Gillian, who knows you and Andrej from Saltaire Mill, lives across the road from Kay. It's a small world, indeed.*

*Roman, you need to know I have a choice to continue living here permanently. Doctor Ted O'Connell has offered me the job of housekeeper. He is well-respected in the community, and his father knew mine. I would need to give up my job at Georgina's, but the position would provide Janek and me security and a permanent roof over our heads.*

*However, if you agree to my conditions of return, which I believe is the best for our family, please write to the address below to obtain the housing application form. Please fill in your details and send the form here. I will complete and return it straight to them. If you find the application difficult to fill-out please, ask for help from the corporation. Finally, my darling Roman, if they offer us a home, I will return to England, to the gloomy north! And we can visit your sister Elouna.*

*All my love, Bridget*

*The Bradford Corporation*

*Housing Division*

*The Town Hall*

*Bradford*

*West Yorkshire*

Bridget stood by the kitchen sink; she stared out the window into the gardens beyond, where the tree leaves had turned to autumn golds and burnished reds. Chestnuts had fallen from the tree at the end of Georgina's Garden, their spiked jackets split, and the dark shiny nuts lay waiting to be harvested to roast on the fire. Bridget regarded autumn as a time of hidden treasures.

Her thoughts turned to her first autumn in England with Roman when she was newly married and pregnant with Janek. Friends introduced them to an English custom called Guy Fawkes night. This event originated in the seventeenth century. It was a failed attempt by a small group of Catholics who tried to blow up the protestant king's Westminster palace. Over the centuries, it had mutated into Bonfire Night, where communal fires blazed on common grounds, fireworks exploded in the sky, and people gathered around to celebrate something unclear. Bridget and Roman were to attend the mill's bonfire and arrive about six-thirty when the mill manager would ceremonially light the fire.

As they approached the colossal bonfire silhouetted against the dark sky, Roman turned to Bridget with a look of dread on his face and stopped dead in his tracks.

'Bridget, there's someone on top of bonfire.'

Bridget peered through the crowd. She could see the bonfire mound composed of a variety of dismembered tree branches, broken bits of planks, odd sticks of furniture, and a couple of wrecked mattresses, their springs bursting out of them. At its pinnacle, a figure stood, head bowed to its chest - dressed in an oversized coat and cocked hat.

Roman grabbed Bridget's hand. 'We go now. It not safe.'

'Roman, it's not a person. It's just a Guy Fawkes. It's the tradition.'

He pulled her around and yanked her in the opposite direction. One of her shoes slipped on the uneven ground, and she stumbled forward, hands splayed outwards for a fall. Roman caught Bridget before she toppled over.

'Steady on Roman. I nearly broke my neck.'

'We must run, now!'

She held his arms to stop him from running off. 'Sweetheart, you've made a mistake.'

'What?'

‘I’ve seen kids pushing them around in prams saying “penny for the guy”. It’s like a scarecrow. But they throw him on the fire.’

Out of the dark, Andrej and Wanda appeared, waving their hands.

‘You’re going wrong way,’ Andrej said. ‘You’ll miss fun.’

He pulled Roman around to face the fire and tugged him along with Bridget to where the people gathered. The mill manager stepped forward to ignite the bonfire; flames licked at its base, crackled, and spat out tongues that ascended towards Guy Fawkes. They crept up its legs, flared in the barrelled chest, and engulfed the head that flopped forwards and then rolled off in a ball of fire. The crowd cheered.

Roman turned to Bridget. ‘It dummy, you right,’ he said.

They leaned into one another and watched the flames leap, twist, and curl, turning solids to ash.

Later, they walked home through the night air heavy with the aroma of smoke and the aftermath of spent fireworks. The smell of English autumn that Bridget never forgot.

She looked down into the greyed dishwater that had gone cold as she lost herself in thought. It was autumn again, and things had changed radically from two years ago.

‘Penny for your thoughts,’ a voice said behind her.

Bridget turned around to smile at her sister. ‘Just thinking about English life and Penny for the Guy.’

'What's that?'

'Never mind,' Bridget said, rubbing her water-crinkled fingertips on her apron.

'Isn't it about time you heard from that Roman of yours?' Georgina said.

Bridget sighed. 'It is. If only life were delivered to plan.'

Georgina was silent as she dried the dishes from the drainer, stacking them methodically in the cupboards.

'Is there anyone you could telephone? To ask after him?'

'Not really.' Bridget sucked her lips. 'We have to communicate by letter. Anything else is too expensive.'

'I'm sorry,' Georgina said.

Bridget brightened. 'I suppose I could ring the mill, but they would only pass on a message if that. And what would I say? Ask Roman to write to me. The people we know don't have house phones, Georgina.'

'Well, I'll keep my fingers and toes crossed for you.' Georgina turned and faced Bridget, who toyed with Janek's dummy taken from her pocket.

'But remember, we have lunch at Ted's on Friday, and he'll want to make arrangements for the housekeeper position. I know he's kept it open for you, but you must decide soon.'

Friday came. Bridget peered from the car window as Georgina pulled outside Ted's house, bumping the car over the uneven driveway. Peat smoke curled from one of the chimneys into the fogged autumn air. Ted stood at the entrance of the grey stone building and ushered them inside. His smile strained before he led them into the dark hallway.

'Where's Janek?' Ted asked as he took their coats.

'He's with Granny. They're making soda bread for our tea.'

Ted's footsteps rattled on the parquet floor as he opened the door to the drawing room. He held his pale hand towards a dark green sofa opposite the fireplace. 'Do take a seat. Lunch will be soon. It's nothing fancy as I'm not the greatest cook.'

'Oh, I'm sure it will be lovely,' said Georgina.

'Would you like a cup of tea?'

'Tea would be fine,' Bridget said, and Georgina echoed.

Ted slipped from the room, and Bridget cast her gaze around. The furniture was oak, ornamented, and solid. There were plenty of fragile China objects to dust, she noted. And silver to polish. These were furnishings handed down through the generations that made her feel depressed with the weight of tradition.

'Well, now, isn't this comfortable,' said Georgina settling into the horsehair stuffed sofa popular in the previous century. 'Janek would do fine, I'm sure.'

'Hm,' Bridget said. 'He'd have to be on his best behaviour with all these delicate trinkets.' She nodded to a display case of obscure objects. Everything looked brown and misshapen to her.

After their lunch of veal cutlets and over-boiled potatoes, Ted gave Bridget a house tour. He began on the top floor, where the bedrooms for Bridget and Janek were situated. Janek had never had his own room, and Bridget wondered if he would be frightened sleeping alone. As Ted opened each door, he stood stiffly outside, directing Bridget to inspect the beds and cupboards. The beds looked soft and welcoming, but Bridget thought the rooms were a little damp and chilly.

'Is everything satisfactory?' Ted said.

'Yes. Fine.'

They descended to the floor below in silence where Ted's bedroom, the guest rooms, and bathroom were. Again, Ted stood outside the doors as he summoned Bridget to enter and inspect the interiors. Because of their history and the job he was offering, she felt unsure of how to act towards Ted. But pushed this to the back of her mind to concentrate on the security the situation would offer. She noticed Ted paid particular attention to showing her the kitchen and highly organised pantry where he had labelled all containers and jars. In the scullery just off the kitchen, Bridget stared at the vast stone sink with its built-in copper wash tub. She thought of her childhood and the family maid at her chores on wash days. Early that morning the maid would light a fire underneath the copper pot that would burn throughout the day. Many times, Bridget watched the young maid working in the scullery, dodging great wafts of steam from the pot as she heaved the washing around with a heavy club-like appliance. And as the stages progressed ruddy and sweat-drenched from scraping clothes back and forth across the rubbing board. Her forearms purpled and hands roughened from the mangle and coarse starch. Ted was well off enough to buy a modern washing machine but must consider this a squandering of his resources Bridget concluded.

When the house tour was complete, Ted ushered Bridget into the garden. In England, Janek played indoors or in a stone yard that she did not think was very safe, but terraced houses had no gardens. He pointed at a swing. 'Janek will like that.' Bridget smiled. 'Yes, I'm sure he will.' As Ted proceeded, he named the herbs in Latin and then the rows of vegetables planted in the kitchen garden area. He steered Bridget towards the swing by the elbow.

'Please sit down for a moment.' He gestured to the child's swing.

Bridget glanced at it and laughed.

'It's sturdy enough,' Ted said.

Surprised by his request, she obeyed his instruction.

'Bridget,' Ted began. 'I very much hope that you will accept the offer of employment and you and your son will come to live in my house.' He adjusted his tie.

Bridget detected an air of discomfort in his suddenly formal phrasing. He continued, 'As you know, the post of housekeeper attracts a small salary plus free board and lodgings. I would set out your duties in writing, which will change depending on the season and my workload.'

'Yes, I quite understand.'

Ted cleared a rasp in his throat. 'Now, to another matter. Most people here do not know we were betrothed before you moved to England.'

'Don't they?'

'I think not.'

Bridget thought Ted was a little naïve about how much

people knew of others' lives.

'Therefore, I think it would be best to stay that way.' He began to fiddle with his earlobe.

Ted fixed Bridget with an intense gaze. He cleared his throat again, waiting for her verbal response she suddenly realised.

'Oh, of course, Ted. I'm sure that's the sensible approach.' She paused. 'But you know how people gossip. It will probably come to light at some point. But we have nothing to hide.'

Bridget unlocked her fingers and spread her hands over her skirt, her elbows rising like butterfly wings.

'But looking ahead following the dissolution of your marriage, you and I can never...' He turned his face away as he said, '…be man and wife. Despite any resumption of….'

Bridget jerked forward. 'I expect to be *your housekeeper* and nothing more, Ted.'

He ruffled. 'Of course. Good. I'm thinking only of our futures and reputations.' Ted locked his arms behind his back.

'Reputations?' she repeated slowly.

'Bridget, you must understand I am a country doctor. A figure of respectability in this community, and nothing must alter this.' He loosened his arms and straightened his jacket at the sides. 'Well, that's that. I'm pleased the matter is clarified.' Ted turned sharply and hurried back to the house with his head down.

Bridget remained on the swing, stunned. She wondered if she had heard him correctly. The phrase “despite any resumption” rattled in her head. Had Ted assumed she would become his mistress while acting as his housekeeper? Why had he felt the need to make it clear marriage was out of the question? She had not been thinking along those lines at all. Bridget was still waiting for an answer from Roman about her conditions for a return to England. Any residual feelings she had left for Ted had been extinguished in a blaze when she met and fell in love with Roman. Her face burned in shame at the realisation of her folly. She had been pursuing a path in Ireland half-heartedly and dishonestly, out of touch with her inner feelings.

Everything swung back into focus for Bridget. She stood up from the swing and pushed its seat with such force it banged violently against the posts with a clatter.

‘Damn your respectability,’ she said to herself.

Bridget could not look Ted in the face back in the drawing room. Her emotions boiled. She did not sit down but stood and glared at Georgina, hoping she would read her thoughts. Georgina was busy admiring an ornamental clock.

‘Georgina, Ted has served a nutritious lunch for which we must thank him. I have toured the house satisfactorily, been advised of the duties, and now it’s time we return home.’

She didn’t wait for Georgina to answer or for Ted to respond; instead, she rushed to the hallway, yanked her coat from the stand, and marched out to fume in Georgina’s car.

Georgina scrambled in five minutes later. ‘What was

that about, Bridget? It was very rude of you to storm off. I was so embarrassed for Ted.'

'Rude! Rude of me? You have *no* idea. He just proposed I become his low-paid skivvy and mistress.'

'He *what*?' Georgina said, cranking the engine to life as she stared wide-eyed at Bridget.

'Ted's assumed that I've left Roman for good. Which I have not.' Bridget glared at Georgina.

'I've said nothing to him, Bridget. It's clear you're still thinking things over.'

'I am, and it's just as well because I'm surrounded by wolves in sheep's clothing.'

'What are you talking about?'

'It seems I'm not good enough to be the country doctor's wife, but I'm perfectly suited to be his mistress. God, Georgina, I'm so insulted I could strangle him.'

'Steady on, Bridget, you know how things are here with the church. At least Ted's thinking about the future.'

'No. Ted's thinking of his future, me and Janek are simply appendages.'

Georgina released the handbrake. 'Whatever you do is your choice, Bridget. But it's time to make up your mind. And, for heaven's sake, be realistic. It's not fair to keep people dangling.'

The car jolted off.

Bridget swivelled in her seat to face Georgina as they bumped away. 'I have made up my mind. I'm returning to England.'

'Holy Jesus!' Georgina smacked her forehead with her palm. 'Why the hell did you get Ted's hopes up then?

Pretending to want the job if you'd already decided?'

Bridget burst into tears. 'I hadn't. I've been waiting for Roman to make up his mind. But it's not that straightforward, Georgina.'

## Bridget 1951, England

Roman finally sent Bridget the money to travel from Ireland back to their hometown, Bradford. It had taken a few months for him to save. The last stage of their journey was by train. Bridget watched Janek enthralled as he perched on her lap and gazed at the surrounding strangers. After eating the remains of the egg sandwich his granny had prepared and wrapped in greaseproof paper, Janek dozed off, comforted by the train's rocking motion. It was early December, and the weather was bitterly cold but bright. The train chugged past snow-buried fields, where sheep bundled together, their pelts piled with hardened snow. They sheltered behind the dry-stone walls to stave off the freezing winds and waited for the farmer's sheepdog to herd them into pens. Bridget mused the Yorkshire landscape had a bleak beauty in winter. One she would come to love, she hoped.

She and Janek would arrive back around sunset. Before the train pulled into the station, it squealed into a pitch-black tunnel that seemed endless. The smell of soot-laden smoke seeped into the carriages and caused some occupants to cough. A young man swaddled in a heavy coat stood and slammed an open window with a bang. Janek jumped and opened his eyes. He stared up at Bridget, a little puzzled.

'Mummy, where are we?'

'It's okay. We're almost home. And Daddy is coming to meet us.'

At the mention of his father, Janek sat upright and

beamed at an older lady sitting opposite. She smiled, her face breaking into a network of fine wrinkles. Yorkshire people were friendly, at least.

The train emerged from the tunnel into a low light and puffed into the station. Bridget could feel her heart thump against her breastbone. Her stomach flipped as she thought of Roman waiting for them on the platform. The train finally stopped with a series of metallic screeches. It's doors flung open, and people clambered to exit. Bridget remained in her seat until the crush died before she hauled her suitcase and climbed from the carriage with Janek. She heaved the bag down first, then Janek.

'Dzien Dobry, darling.' *Hello darling*- Bridget looked up, and there Roman stood with his arms outstretched and eyes glistening.

The setting sun flooded the station with a pink glow that sifted through the glass canopy. Bridget stared at Roman, transfixed. Light burst out from within him. His dark eyes shone. His face radiated a luminosity, and a halo formed around his head impossibly cast from the beams of the overhead lights. She drew towards him by forces she could not withstand, her body energised in his presence. They collapsed into one another's arms. Janek snuggled between their legs as his hands grasped his parent's knees.

Bridget felt Roman's shoulder heave as they hugged.

'I love you, Bridget.' He managed to say. 'I miss you so much. Never go again.'

'I won't. I love you too.'

'I lost without you.'

Roman pulled away from her. He swept Janek up and

hugged him tight to his chest. Janek squealed as his father hoisted him onto his shoulders. Janek's bobble hat toppled off his head, and Bridget caught it before it fell to the ground.

'Give me suitcase,' Roman said.

They pushed through the crowded platform, through the doors into the city that hummed with the noise of people headed home for the evening.

On their walk from the station to the bus through the swelling fog, Roman said, 'We go collect belongings from Mrs Hawanska's, say goodbye. Andrej drive us to new house.'

Bridget scrambled onto the packed bus and secured seats. She cleared the misted window with her bare hand, and the coldness shocked her. She wished she had gloves in her coat pocket rather than her suitcase in the luggage compartment.

'Roman, please look in my case for gloves for Janek and me?'

He grinned and pulled a pair of red and white mittens from his coat.

'Present from Katerina. She knitted.' Bridget took the gloves, examined them with a smile, and pulled them onto Janek's reddened hands.

'Colours of Polish flag,' Roman said.

Bridget gazed at him. 'How very thoughtful of Katerina.'

Janek turned his hands in the air as he admired his mittens, then stretched towards Roman, who grabbed and squeezed his fingertips through the wool.

‘Polskie rękawiczki,’ Roman said. *Polish gloves.*

Janek giggled.

When they arrived at Mrs Hawanska’s, Bridget hovered behind Roman at the front door, unsure how they would greet her because she was taking Roman away from his community. It also troubled her that her demands for their move would isolate Janek from his heritage, but she could think only of the immediate future for now.

Mrs Hawanska greeted them cheerfully in her cluttered hallway. Behind her sat three cardboard boxes and one suitcase with Roman’s mother’s deerskin coat balancing on the top. Bridget studied their meagre worldly possessions and remembered the childhood move after her alcoholic father had ruined the family. They were forced to move from their three-storey Georgian home to two rented rooms in another city far away from their former life. She knew what it was to be ripped from a place of safety and plunged into an alien one devoid of comfort and privacy. A shiver rippled through her because she had vowed never to put herself in the situation her mother had ended in, having to scratch a living from more or less nothing. But life did not go to plan, and they were beginning a new life. Mrs Hawanska must have read her thoughts because she snapped Bridget out of her gloom by handing her a bulging string shopping bag.

‘Here’s tea, milk, sugar, bread, margarine, and Polish sausage. So, you not starve.’

Bridget thanked her in Polish. She inwardly scolded herself because almost everyone had started from scratch after the war.

They hugged one another before Andrej and Roman loaded their belongings into the trunk of a Ford saloon car that Andrej had borrowed from a friend. Bridget's case wouldn't squeeze into the trunk, so she and Janek sat beside it as the car crunched away.

They waved goodbye. Mrs Hawanska, a diminishing figure, stood on her doorstep, wiping her eyes with her apron's hem. Bridget turned from waving and stared ahead as the car's headlights hit the dense fog that created the impression that they existed only in the present, the future, and the past, obscured by the thick grey mass.

In the front seat, Roman rooted in his coat pocket for something. He turned and waggled a piece of paper in the air.

'This our tenancy agreement with Bradford Corporation.'

He waved it at her, then tucked it back into his coat pocket, chuckling and humming.

Half an hour later, the car stopped outside the house. The fog had lifted, and Bridget recognised the corporation estate where she had visited Kay the previous summer. Roman jumped out of the car and flung the door open for Bridget and Janek. He grabbed her elbow as they walked up the path together.

'English man home his castle.'

Lamplight illuminated the path in an amber glow, and the houses were outlined against the dark sky. Smoke floated from the chimneys. The scene evoked a sense in Bridget. That of being home and safe.

Roman flourished the keys dangling from a string: one

for the front and one for the back door.

'Two entrances.' He laughed.

Roman lit a match to find the centre of the lock, delicately placed the key in and turned it with a slight crunch. The door opened. Bridget heard him seeking a light switch before the match fizzled out.

'I carry you over threshold?'

'No, it's fine, sweetheart.'

The house was cold from being empty as Bridget stepped in.

'Mrs Kozynska, we have electricity.'

Roman flicked the light switch on and off, grinning. He pulled Bridget into a room off the hallway where a large window without curtains looked onto the garden. *All I need is a sewing machine,* she said to herself.

'This sitting room,' Roman said.

'It's a good size.'

A fawn-coloured fireplace enclosed a pristine empty grate. Not yet used. The wind rattled faintly in the chimney breast.

Her gaze fell on three orange crates topped with cushions arranged in front of the hearth.

'Did you bring those?' Bridget patted her throat. Emotion rose at the sight of the makeshift seats.

'Furniture for now. Follow me.' Roman went through to the next room.

'Here we have dining room.'

Bridget stared at the bright red and white linoleum floor. *Cheerful. Modern*, she thought. Ted's gloomy house flashed in her mind.

‘I can’t believe how lucky we are,’ she said, her voice quavering.

Roman spread his arms out wide and grinned. Bridget had worried he would resent the move away from his community. But the gamble had been worth it. Roman was delighted.

‘Next!’ Roman rushed Bridget into another room. ‘Here we have kitchen, gas cooker, sink, draining board, cupboards, pantry, and stove to keep warm.’

Tears sprang to Bridget’s eyes at the sight of the newness of everything.

‘You have own kitchen now, can cook Polish food.’

‘I’ll need to find out where the shops are first.’ Bridget cleared her throat. ‘Roman, I have a confession to make.’

His face darkened. ‘What you mean?’

‘I don’t like Polish sausage.’ Bridget waited for his reaction.

‘Why you no say before?’

‘I was afraid of offending you.’

‘Don’t forget your little one!’ Andrej burst into the kitchen. He tugged Janek behind him.

‘I put boxes in sitting room. You want cases there too?’

‘Yes!’ Roman said, bending to swish Janek up. To Bridget, her son looked exhausted.

‘This our new home, Janek.’ Roman hugged him. ‘You have own bedroom. Like little prince.’

Janek laid his head on his father's chest and sucked on his glove.

The tour continued with Janek resting on Roman’s shoulder. Proudly, Roman showed Bridget the immersion heater that would allow them to take a bath whenever they wanted instead of stand-up washes on cold winter mornings. They had their own bathroom and toilet they didn't have to share with anyone else, which they had both despised. There were three bedrooms, an outside toilet, and a coal shed in the back garden.

*I believe I've saved him,* Bridget thought.

As they descended the stairs, with Janek now fast asleep, Bridget said, 'Roman, where will we sleep tonight? We don't have beds yet?'

'No need beds.'

Andrej had prepared a coal fire that crackled pleasingly downstairs in the sitting room. Its dusky aroma filled the air. Roman handed Bridget Janek and tackled one of the cardboard boxes from which he yanked out woollen blankets and feather pillows that he spread on the bare floor.

'Oh, my god, Roman, aren't you going to sweep it first?'

'Already did, earlier this week.'

He laid his coat down with a pillow at the collar.

'Pass Janek.'

Roman gently settled him on the coat, pulled the blankets over, and tucked his slumbering body in.

Andrej picked up the string bag of food and danced to the kitchen, whistling.

'Tea! Sandwiches!' he called out to them in a mock English accent. 'Make yourselves at home!'

Andrej returned, ferreting plates, cups, and cutlery from their boxed belongings, friends had donated and Mrs

Hawanska packed. Andrej brought their supper in ceremoniously, a kitchen towel flipped over his shoulder. He kissed them both on the cheeks and bade goodbye to drive back through the cold night. Peeping the horn as he rumbled off.

Roman eyed the supper set before the fire. He jumped up and flicked off the electric light.

'What are you doing?' Bridget said.

'Little romance.'

'We can't eat by firelight.'

'Don't have to.' Roman produced a candle in a glass jar from one of the boxes, lit it and set it next to the food. It's wavering yellow light enough for them to see.

Soon, Bridget snuggled under the blankets alongside Janek. Before getting in, Roman pulled Anya's deerskin coat over the three of them. Bridget found his hand beneath the bulky warmth and tugged it to her as she squeezed his fingers tight.

'We're going to be just grand,' she said as she stared out of the window at the velvet sky.

## Bridget 1951, Summer

Bridget watched Roman in amazement as he struggled through the door carrying a rocking horse. How had he brought it home on his scooter? Roman planted it in the middle of the kitchen and beamed at her.

'For Janek! What you think? Is nice?'

She stared at the white, red, and gold horse. *Yes, it was gorgeous, but what about the cost?*

'Roman, it's wonderful, but I'd rather the money spent on a carpet for the living room.'

'Carpets. Pah! It not for you anyway.'

Bridget turned to face him and placed her hands on her hips. 'We've lived here for over a year, and I'm fed-up tripping over that horrible rag rug in there.'

Roman pulled off his donkey jacket. 'I hate jacket. In Italy, we ride bikes with no jacket, just fresh air on skin.'

'Don't change the subject now. Please don't buy anything without talking to me first.'

'You mad at me?'

Bridget watched him stride into the hall to hang up his jacket. He hovered there a short while before he rolled up his sleeves and returned to the kitchen, where Bridget bristled, pushing her hair back with her forearm.

'Yes, I am mad at you. We have hardly any spare money. We buy furniture on hire-purchase, for goodness' sake. Otherwise, we would still sit on orange crates and eat off our knees. Now you've squandered money on that.'

Bridget pointed her knife at the rocking horse and returned to the sink to continue peeling turnip.

'You drop water on floor, now slippery.' Roman reached over to Bridget to grab a dishcloth, and as he did, he planted a quick kiss on the back of her neck.

She pushed him back with her elbow. 'Stop it! And that's not the floor cloth.'

Roman sighed exaggeratedly and threw the cloth back onto the draining board. 'Why you always pick on me?'

Janek ran in just then. He looked at the rocking horse and stopped dead in his tracks.

'For you!' Roman said, swept him off his feet, and steered him into the seat. He gently rocked the horse with one hand as Janek shrieked with joy.

'Roman, are you listening to me?'

Roman continued to rock Janek. 'Yes, I listen, but Bridget, children not remember carpets.' He turned to grin at her. 'Tell me what colour carpet you had as child.'

Bridget huffed and turned her back again. The day had been sweltering, and it was almost unbearable in the kitchen cooking supper.

'You need to be more responsible, that's all,' she said.

'I work all hours to put food on table, clothes on backs. You no right to talk to me like this.'

After they had eaten their evening meal in silence, Roman stomped out into their garden to his makeshift greenhouse to examine his broad beans and smoke a cigarette. Growing his food was one of Roman's passions.

Later, Bridget followed him outside to gather the washing from the clothesline. As she unpegged the sheets and smoothed the indents of pegs from the corners, she inhaled the aroma of newly dried laundry. To lie down on cool, crisp sheets was one of her pleasures. She would change Janek's bedding and get him ready for sleep.

As soon as Janek sunk into his pillow, tiny pearls of sweat blossomed on his brow. His mouth turned down as he passed a sticky hand over his face.

'I'm boiled, Mummy!' he said.

'I know, chicken, it's so hot tonight. I've opened all the windows.' Janek turned his head and tried to kick away the blanket. 'Okay, you can sleep with just a sheet tonight.' Bridget removed the cover and pulled the crisp cotton sheet to his waist.

It was still light, but he was tired from the day and fell asleep immediately. Bridget remained on the edge of the bed, watching his chest rise and fall. She smoothed away the dampened hair stuck to his forehead and marvelled at his luxurious dark lashes that curled from his eyelids threaded with tiny blue veins. A detail that had amazed her when she first held him in her arms and studied his perfectly formed features. His skin looked like it had been sprayed with mist and dusted pale pink. A sense of contentment unfurled inside her. Bridget was glad of her return to England and Roman.

Tomorrow she would photograph Janek and Roman for Georgina and her mother to prove she had made the right decision. And she would persuade Roman to return the rocking horse to the shop. They would use the money for a deposit on the much-needed carpet. All would be well.

Later, when it was dark, Bridget and Roman retired to bed. The air in their room was laden, and there was still tension between them, both silent as they undressed.

Before he tumbled into bed, Roman yanked open the window and left the curtains undrawn.

'In hope of breeze,' he said.

But the night was airless and heavy.

Around midnight, Bridget woke to a loud rumble and Roman screaming in Polish. He flailed his arms frantically in the air. A shattering boom erupted, followed by flashes of forked light. Bridget struggled to grab Roman's shoulders to shake him out of his dream. Roman opened his eyes mid-scream. He was stricken with terror.

'Bridget, we got to get out. Germans invading.'

'What!'

'I hear guns.'

'No, no. It's a thunder storm, Roman….'

'We must leave now. Hide in forest.'

'You've been dreaming, darling. It's okay.'

Bridget scrambled out of bed. She ran to the window. Intermittently, the night sky was cleaved, then illuminated by jagged lightening over the rooftops, followed by low, loud rumbles, then booms that shook the house as the storm closed in.

Roman jumped out of bed and rushed to grab Bridget's wrists. 'Listen, stupid woman, it German invasion. We pack things, warm coat, boots. Bread, money, run.'

Bridget struggled away from his death-like grip. 'Roman, It's just a storm. The war is over.'

A massive bang clapped overhead. Roman dropped to the floor.

'Get down,' he said. 'Keep down. Crawl, they no see us.' He turned around quickly to check on her, then scrambled on all fours to the closet, where he pulled out a suitcase. 'We hide in forest. I done it before, many months.'

Bridget followed Roman. She sat up on her knees as she reached him. 'Roman, love, there are no forests here. Honestly, it's….'

'What you say crazy woman?' He grabbed her shoulders and shook her. 'Do as I say.'

'I'll fetch Janek. You pack,' Bridget scuttled on all fours out of the room.

At his bedside, Bridget sat on the warm linoleum floor and hugged her shaking knees. Janek jolted awake as lightening flashed at the window. He cried out.

She clambered in beside him and cradled his head as they lay trembling.

'It's God's moving his furniture around. That's all it is.'

Bridget pulled the sheet over their heads and clutched Janek. 'It will pass soon. You're safe, sweetheart. Safe.'

The storm crashed and raged outside; lightning flashed across the walls as it passed directly overhead. Bridget peeped out of the sheet when the thunderclaps began to reduce their frequency. A lightning streak illuminated the doorway where Roman crouched—wearing a winter coat and boots. A suitcase at his side.

'Get up. We go, now!' He sprang to the bed and yanked away the sheet. Janek cried out and curled further into his mother's body.

'Roman, we can't go anywhere in this storm. We're staying here.' Bridget grabbed the sheet and tugged it back. 'It's dangerous.'

She tried to struggle away as Roman grabbed her by the arm and dragged her out of bed. She held onto Janek as both tumbled onto the floor. Janek yelped out in shock.

'Oh, Janek, are you hurt?' Bridget sat up and patted his arms and legs for any source of pain.

Roman crept over and examined Janek. 'He fine,' he said, then pulled Bridget to her feet.

She winced in pain and looked down to see her ankle swelling.

'Oh no! I can't go anywhere, Roman. I can't walk.' She lent on Roman's back, slowly put her foot down, and then screamed as a burning pain seared through her foot.

'Woman, you no understand. Germans will break down door. Shoot me, Janek. Rape you.'

'Oh, for the love of God, there are no Germans. Please, Roman, you're scaring us all.'

Roman pushed her away, and she fell back onto the bed with a cry. He bent down to pull Janek's jumper and trousers on and struggled in the dark with his socks and shoes. Janek stopped crying and instead shivered from head to foot with fear.

While Roman dressed Janek, Bridget eased off the bed to the floor. Holding her injured ankle off the ground, she shuffled towards him on her bottom.

'Roman, I can move. I'll come downstairs with you.'

Roman slammed the case shut and swept Janek up as Bridget shuffled after them. He tiptoed down the stairs to the kitchen.

'I get bread.'

When Bridget reached the bottom stair, she hauled

herself to the front door, stretched to unlock it, yanked it wide, and yelled out for help. Roman rushed back to stop her, but she placed her good leg over the threshold to prevent him from closing the door. She screamed with all her might.

Across the road, an upstairs light went on where Gillian lived.

Bert, Gillian's husband, flung open a window and shouted, 'What's going on?'

'Help me!' Bridget bellowed. 'Please, Bert, Gillian.'

Roman shouted over her. 'We no need help. Bridget fell,' as he tried to pull Bridget back into the house.

'No! Help me, please. I need an ambulance.'

The hall light lit up at Gillian's as Bridget held her breath. Bert and Gillian appeared and ran across the street; their dressing gowns flapped as they approached.

Janek whimpered beside Bridget as she watched Bert and Gillian rush across the road.

Roman crouched over her and muttered, 'Gowno, gowno, gowno.' *Shit. Shit*

'What's happened?' Gillian said when she reached Bridget and bent down to her. Roman moved aside with a grunt. She held Bridget's face in her hands, examining her. 'Are you injured?'

Bridget clapped her hand over Gillian's arm. 'Yes, yes, I fell. Get an ambulance. I've hurt my ankle.' The fear was palpable in her voice.

Gillian nodded at Bert, 'Love, phone an ambulance.'

Bert glanced down at his night clothes. 'Like this, in the middle of the night?'.

Gillian waved her hand. 'Doesn't matter. Nobody will see you.'

Bert frowned.

'It just bump, no need for fuss,' said Roman.

'Roman, get me some water, please.' Bridget shot a glance at Gillian. Roman hesitated but turned on his heels towards the kitchen.

'Something's wrong with him. Get an ambulance quickly.'

Bert hurried off to the phone box in the next street. Roman returned with a glass of water, sloshing some on Bridget as he passed it to her.

'Why are you wearing winter clothes, Roman? It's bloody boiling.'

He didn't answer Gillian. He whispered something to Janek, who quietened.

Gillian settled next to Bridget on the doorstep and put her arm around her shaking shoulders.

'Out my way,' Roman said, pushing Gillian aside. Bridget turned. He ran off, Janek crooked under one arm and the case in the other.

'No! Stop!' Bridget yelled after him. 'Roman. Don't.'

'What the blazes?' Gillian stood up. 'What the hell is happening, Bridget?'

Bridget dropped her face in her hands and rocked herself back and forth. 'He's gone mad. I don't know. He was ranting about the Germans invading.'

'You what?'

'It was the storm. It set something off.'

'What do you mean?'

'It sounds crazy, Gillian, but he said we'd to hide in the forest…from the invasion.' Great sobs heaved out of Bridget's chest. Gillian smoothed her hair from her face.

'It's all right. The ambulance will be here soon. They'll know what to do.'

'Can Bert look for them when he's back?' Bridget said.

She pulled away from Gillian and tugged her hair at the roots, shaking her head in small side-to-side motions. 'Oh, God.'

'Yes, I'm sure he will.'

'What if he hurts Janek? He's not in his right mind.'

'Oh, he wouldn't, surely, not Roman.'

'He might go to Andrej's.' Bridget felt relief for a split second.

'That's a long walk in the middle of the night,' Gillian said. 'Oh, look who's here.'

Bridget heard the puffing of breath and looked up to see Bert. 'They're on their way, the ambulance,' he said, bending to rest his hands on his knees before he straightened up to look around. 'Where's Roman?'

'He's done a runner – with Janek,' said Gillian.

The sound of an ambulance bell clanged as it veered into the street and rumbled to a halt at Bridget's house. A man jumped down from the cream-coloured vehicle and the driver soon after.

'Now, who's the injured one?' he said as he approached the huddled group.

Gillian and Bert moved aside to let him kneel to examine Bridget's ankle.

'Can you wiggle your toes?' Bridget obliged. 'Good.

Let's get you inside to inspect.' He signalled his colleague, and they supported Bridget to the ambulance as she hopped on one leg.

Bridget told the man what had happened between bursts of tears as he examined her ankle.

He nodded reassuringly as he wrapped her foot in a crepe bandage. 'It's a strain, a bit of a nasty one. I think you should come into the hospital tonight.'

'Oh no! Will I need to stay?'

'I shouldn't think so, but it's best to check it's not broken.'

'Do you need your handbag or anything?' Gillian asked as she stood by the ambulance doors peering in.

'Yes, please.'

'What about your husband and son?' the paramedic asked. 'Do you want us to call the police? It might be a good idea from what you've said.'

Bert and Gillian grimaced at one another before Gillian dashed to fetch Bridget's bag.

'What shall I do, Bert?' Bridget said. 'I just want them back safe.'

"'It might be for the best to involve the police. Roman's done nothing wrong, after all.'

Roman hurried along the road carrying Janek. Checking behind him now and then that no one followed. They would hide in the woods, he decided. It was a twenty-minute trek but would provide shelter. He stopped to shift Janek from under his arm to sit in the crook of his elbow.

'Where are we going?' Janek asked, whimpering now and then.

Roman followed the footpath that curled beneath the bridge to access the woods. He knew the route well because they had walked it often since their move, usually in the light. But it was now after midnight, and carrying Janek and a bag, he had to tread carefully to scan the ground for obstacles to avoid falling. The path wound into the dense summer woods. Roman headed for a place they sometimes used as a picnic spot. It was a massive shoulder-high rock with one side worn into an enclave-like shelter. They could sleep there until morning and then move on to escape from the Germans. Raindrops plopped off the tree branches as Roman thwacked them aside. Occasionally, a twig cracked in the distance or bushes rustled, and Roman would stand stock still, listening hard until confident there was no one there. He pressed on, proud of his navigational instinct until the rock came into view under the gleam of the half-moon. When they reached it, he set Janek on his feet.

Roman pushed a lit candle into the mossy earth to survey the area. The flame barely wavered in the still night, and he saw the ground was thick with nettles and dock leaves. Roman dropped to his knees and ripped the weeds away in clumps to clear a spot to sleep. His hands stung from the nettles interlaced with the dock leaves, but Roman kept clearing. A stream tinkled nearby, and he contemplated finding it to rinse the sticky green substance from his hands, but it was too risky to leave Janek. He laughed at himself then and remembered the misery of his past: hunger, beatings, witness to executions. What was a little stinging in the fingers compared to that?

In the clearing, he spread his coat on the rain-sodden ground. It would become wet, but Roman couldn't think how else to protect Janek from the damp night. He laid his son on the coat's silky lining. 'Get some sleep, little one,' he said. Janek rubbed his eyes before turning onto his side and curling up foetal-like. Roman sat for a while, turning his head toward the faintest noise, but the only constant sound was of owls hunting. Eventually, he settled down to sleep.

Later, Roman snapped awake. It was dawn, and a pinkish light rose behind the trees. There was an audible thudding coming from nearby.

'Wake up, Janek, wake up.' He shook Janek, and the coat felt damp and cold under his hand.

Janek turned and groaned something inaudible. There was a loud snap, and two police constables emerged crouching from the bushes, creeping towards him. They spotted him and straightened up.

'Roman Kozynski?' one said, stretching his arm behind him to stop his colleague from moving further.

Janek sat up, blinking, staring at the police officers.

‘Get up, Janek. It’s time we go.’

Roman kept his gaze fixed on the police as he stood up slowly. Janek wobbled to his feet.

An officer moved forward a few steps. ‘You’re not in trouble. We need to check you’re both alright. Your wife Bridget, she’s worried about you.’ He raised his hands in a surrendering gesture.

‘I worry too. Thought Germans coming last night.’ Roman pulled Janek behind him. ‘You no hurt my son.’

The policeman shook his head. ‘You must be hungry by now, the two of you?’ ‘Why not come with us for a nice warm breakfast.’ He smiled at Janek.

‘It trap,’ Roman said.

‘No, you’ve got it all wrong. We want to get you home safely.’

Roman bent towards his bag. The constable sprang forward, grabbed one arm, and twisted it behind Roman’s back. The other swung a pair of cuffs and clamped Roman’s wrists. They held him between them and pushed Janek away, who cried out.

‘Leave him,’ Roman yelled. He kicked at them and stumbled to the ground. One policeman sat on Roman’s legs to restrain him.

‘Just come with us. It’ll be okay.’

As they dragged a struggling Roman to his feet, Janek screamed and shrieked. His face coloured to a furious red.

‘Janek, it okay, we go to mummy.’

Bridget heard car tyres crunch to a halt outside; fearing the worst and anticipating the best, she scrambled from bed. Events of the previous night had whirled in her mind, and not until dawn broke had her exhausted mind slowed down enough to drift off. She limped downstairs to answer the thumping.

Two constables stood at the door. One looked very young to Bridget; she thought he seemed a little uncomfortable and feared what he might be about to say. The other, a portly older man, addressed her calmly. 'Mrs Kozynska, may we come in?'

Bridget guided them into the living room, realising she was wearing her nightdress. 'Please sit down,' she said. 'I just need to go upstairs for my housecoat.'

When she re-entered, the police stopped mid-conversation. Bridget sat abruptly on a chair, desperate to grab a cigarette but too scared to let any more time pass without finding out what news they had.

'Have you found Roman and Janek?'

'Yes, we have,' the older one said. He flashed a smile that disappeared as quickly as it came.

'Where?' Bridget's voice cracked.

'In Greengates woods. They'd slept there.'

'Oh, my God!' Bridget stared from one to the other. 'They slept in the woods?'

She could think only of the danger Roman had put Janek in and how frightened he must have been.

'Are they okay?'

'Yes, but we've taken them to the hospital for a check-up.'

Bridget stood up to grab her cigarette packet from the mantlepiece. Her hand juddered violently, and she steadied it with the other. She flumped back down in the chair, leaving a little trail of smoke.

The older policeman coughed. 'We understand your husband had some type of episode last night. Can you tell us about it?'

*Oh Christ, what will I say*, she thought.

'Well, we'd had a bit of an argument - about something.'

'I see; what happened?'

'Silly, really. He'd bought Janek a rocking horse that we couldn't afford.'

'Were you worried about how he acquired the money?'

'No, nothing like that. I was cross.'

'You were cross because your husband bought his son a present?'

Bridget waved her hand. 'He was upset.'

'Does he often '' get upset''?'

'No. But there was that thunderstorm, and Roman had a nightmare…'.

Bridget took a deep pull on her cigarette and held the smoke in her lungs for a few seconds before she exhaled. 'He ran away.' She didn't want to mention the Germans; it frightened her.

The constable glanced at his younger partner, who looked embarrassed, then checked his notebook.

'Mr Kozynski told us he thought the Germans were invading.'

'It was a bad dream,' Bridget searched his face. 'That's all.'

He consulted his notes. 'Under the circumstances, Mr Kozynski had to be examined by a doctor. Whose opinion is that it's best if Roman spends a few weeks in a specialist hospital.'

The young constable grunted.

'What kind of specialist hospital?'

'A mental asylum.'

The air crackled with tension.

'Asylum! But, Roman, he's not….'

The policeman interrupted. 'It's a voluntary stay. To monitor him until he's stabilised.'

Bridget stood up, brushed the front of her housecoat, and flung her cigarette into the blackened grate.

'Has Roman agreed to this?'

She tried to turn, but her legs became liquid at the knees. Bridget slumped onto the mantlepiece, light-headed from the nicotine coursing through her system before breakfast.

The constable rushed to steady her. 'Sit down, Mrs Kozynska. You've had a bit of a shock. Would you like some water?'

She shook her head.

He sat down and continued. 'To answer your last question, he's agreed to this.'

Bridget thought a snort escaped from the young officer. Her sense of reality floated away.

'Where is this place?'

The fledgling officer finally spoke. 'It's nearby, Menston Mental Asylum.'

'Never heard of it.'

'It's just a few miles from here.' The portly officer assured her. 'There's a regular bus service and visiting for relatives on Saturday afternoons.' He flipped his notebook shut.

Bridget's thoughts whirled off in all directions, full of what-ifs. 'What about Janek? Where is he?' She buried her head in her hands.

'Janek's waiting at the hospital for you to collect him. He's seen a welfare officer who said he's ready to come home.'

'Welfare officer?' She shook her head. 'I can't *believe* this is happening.'

The older officer stood to put his helmet on, then handed Bridget a slip of paper. 'This is the hospital ward number. If you telephone, you can visit Roman after you've collected your son. We'll leave you to make arrangements.'

'What? Is Roman in there now? I thought you'd bring him home first, so we could talk.'

The younger man stood, and they turned to leave. Bridget followed them in a daze.

At the front door, she said, 'My husband's a good man. He fought in the war. I'm proud of him.'

Bridget watched them hurry to their black Wolseley, bound to attract the neighbour's attention. She glanced across the road to see Gillian at her kitchen window. Bridget crossed the street in her housecoat. Unless she talked to someone, she would collapse with anguish. Gillian opened her door.

A few days later, the bus rumbled to a stop near the hospital gates. The conductor shouted, 'Menston Asylum', and rang the bell. It was a shock for Bridget to hear this out loud, but she remembered there was also a Menston village, so it was necessary to let the passengers know which stop this was.

Bridget wriggled to the edge of her seat as a middle-aged couple opposite her stood first. She shuffled behind them to the exit. As she stepped from the bus, a cyclist sped past on the pavement and turned left at a set of enormous gates as his coat flapped behind him. The gates opened onto a drive that swept up to a bend where the cyclist disappeared from view. The middle-aged couple vanished at the curve a few yards in front of Bridget. And when Bridget reached this spot, a Victorian building with an imposing clock tower at its centre loomed into sight.

Bridget shuddered at the look of the place. She had visited the library and found it was built in 1888 and opened as The West Riding Paupers' Lunatic Asylum. In the 1920s, the hospital changed its name to Menston, that of the nearby village. She rang the bell as the instructions requested. Someone slid open a small rectangular panel in the door and asked for her name and reason for being there. Unable to eat anything that morning, she was lightheaded as she replied.

'Hold on a minute,' the mysterious voice said as Bridget heard footsteps and people talking.

After waiting anxiously for a time, the door cracked

open and pulled back to reveal an orderly in a grey uniform who beckoned her inwards. The ornate nature of the interior surprised Bridget with its marble floor, Grecian columns, and dramatic staircase. Such grandeur seemed out of step with the building's purpose. However, a distinct smell pervaded her nostrils, akin to boiled cabbage and carbolic soap, and as she looked more closely, pale green paint peeled off the walls in strips. The orderly made no conversation as he marched in front of Bridget down a long corridor to a set of double doors where a plaque read "Dr P Highroyd". He knocked.

'Come!' an imperious voice called from inside.

Bridget was ushered inside by the orderly. 'Mrs Kozynska,' he said and cleared his throat.

A diminutive man with wiry hair sat behind a mahogany desk, almost obscured with papers and open books. He looked up and motioned Bridget to sit.

'Dr Highroyd, pleased to meet you, Mrs Kozynska.'

He stretched out his hand, and Bridget had to stand and strain across the desk to reach him. Her handbag slipped from her knee, making things awkward as she grabbed it. Dr Highroyd folded his short fingers together and leaned his elbows outwards on the desk in a gesture intended to increase his physical presence. He was a tiny man. As he spoke, he looked mainly over Bridget's head and seemed uncomfortable meeting her gaze for more than a few seconds. He told her Roman was now stabilised and resting. What appeared to be troubling him was not uncommon.

'Since the war, many ex-servicemen have been treated here for mental instability.'

‘Exactly what do you mean by mental instability?’

Silence followed as the doctor leaned back, swivelled his chair towards the window and crossed an ankle over a knee. His brown Oxford Brogues were highly polished.

‘You will have heard of shell shock. Many men suffered this condition during World War I.’

‘Yes, I have.’ Bridget paused. ‘Is that what you think is wrong with Roman?’ Her face coloured as she considered she had suddenly betrayed Roman.

A short silence followed. ‘Not exactly,’ he said as he swung his chair to face the window. Bridget noticed a shiny bald patch beneath his springy hair. He must be in his late forties, she decided. Then chided herself for having such frivolous thoughts at such a time. He continued his diagnosis, appearing to address the window. ‘Shell shock victims suffered debilitating tremors; they shook constantly. Some never returned from their deranged minds.’

He swivelled again to peer at Bridget, who nodded but remained silent, waiting for the connection he was making to be made clear.

The doctor continued. ‘There’s a mental instability afflicting some men who served in this war. It’s not shell shock, but there are similarities. It's likely the effect of being in extreme situations that strain the nervous system. We don’t consider it a permanent condition and have been able to give curative relief with the help of Electro Convulsive Therapy.’

‘I’m sorry, Doctor, but what is electro-conv… whatever you just said?’

He turned his chair at an angle again. Bridget stared at his noble profile wishing he would sit still. Perhaps he was a ball of nervous energy, unable to contain himself.

'ECT, as we call it for short, is a treatment that began in the 1920s to help with various mental disorders. The patient is administered a mild electric shock to the brain. Here and here.' He pointed to his temples. 'Just a few minutes for a few sessions. We have found this treatment rids them of their bad memories.'

Bridget remained rigid. She dared not voice her immediate thoughts, which were that it sounded brutal and excruciating. She wanted to ask what the name of Roman's mental disorder was, but the doctor was racing ahead, talking about treatments.

'There is sometimes a side-effect: the patient loses some of their memory permanently. But overall, after a few months in the hospital, they can return to their daily life.'

Bridget sat forward and gripped her handbag. 'What does losing *some* memory mean? Will Roman recognise me, his son, his friends?'

Silence followed her question. She wondered if he was telling her the truth or deciding on acceptable answers.

'We are unable to make a prediction. Should your husband not respond positively to ECT, the treatment would likely be to lobotomise his brain.' Doctor Highroyd swung back to face Bridget but continued addressing the air above her head.

Bridget glared at him, swivelling back and forth in his chair. He spoke another language.

'What is Lobotomise, may I ask?'

He glanced at his watch. 'A tiny section of the brain that produces the emotions is removed. Surgically.' He briefly met her gaze.

Bridget let out a cry. 'No! I don't believe it. Are you telling me Roman has agreed to these treatments?'

'Mrs Kozynska, your husband is here as a voluntary patient and must agree to a course of treatment if he is to stay. I can tell you he's agreed to the ECT. And we will start this very soon.'

'But what if he changes his mind?'

'I don't think it will come to that.' Dr Highroyd stood, extending his hand to Bridget. 'The nurse will show you out and explain visiting arrangements. Thank you for seeing me today.'

He picked up a small bell and rang it. A uniformed nurse entered the room briskly, took hold of Bridget's elbow, and steered her from the office.

# Roman

I woke up in the woods with Janek and don't remember how we got there. The police came and took Janek away. They brought me to this place, and now the doctor talks about voluntary treatment. Voluntary means not compulsory, I'm sure. I can't fully absorb what the doctor says to me right now. He's finished speaking and turns away from me as a man in a blue uniform appears and tells me to come with him.

Bridget, Andrej, I need your help. Where are you?

We walk down a long corridor with a marble floor and doors to each side. It smells horrible. Worse than the hospital Mother was in, much worse. Men pass us in nightclothes, but I'm sure it's daytime. Some amble along the corridor laughing. Some stand statue-still and gaze into space.

Now I'm in a large dormitory, packed with beds, virtually side-by-side. There's only a tiny space between each so that a person can squeeze through. Many of them are empty. Some men lie asleep or stare up at the high ceiling. It's noisy. Two men in pyjamas stand in the aisle that runs down the middle of the dormitory. They shout, gesticulate. One throws a punch at the other. No one attends to them. I know what kind of place this is. I have to get out.

The man who leads me says his name is Tom. He's a ward nurse, and this is the admissions ward. Tom stops by an empty bed and hands me blue pyjamas and slippers. He tells me to take off my clothes and put these on. There's no room for curtains between the beds. Tom folds my clothes into a pile at the end of the bed and says he'll take care of them later. I slide my bare feet into the rough grey slippers. They're too big. Tom tells me it doesn't matter, just get into bed. I sit on the edge, but he insists I must lay under the covers.

Tom hands me a paper tumbler, then a blue pill. Take it, he says. There's a coldness in his eyes. It'll help you relax after all the excitement.

I ask what it is. Tell him I'm fine now, and I don't want it. A sedative, Tom says. Lithium. Never heard of it, but I place it in my mouth and swig back some water. Smile. Lie down. When Tom's out of sight, I spit out the pill. Hide it in my pyjama pocket. Close my eyes. Pretend to sleep but listen. Someone stumbles into the bed on my left side. I turn and open my eyes. A gaunt man with a shock of red hair lays there and shakes his head from side to side. His arms are out over the cover; they stretch rigid. Hands purple. Time to shut my eyes. Think.

I must have dozed off. Tom's back. He grabs my feet under the covers, tells me it's teatime, and throws a dressing gown at me. Across the ward, men rise, shuffle to the door, and file out. We snake down the corridor, led by another man who opens a double door into a canteen. People sit at the first seat they come to robotically. Orderlies reach over their shoulders and slam down plates of something white and brown, mush-like. Spoons clatter as everyone eats—eyes dart all over.

After the disgusting food, they herd us into a washroom. Sinks line one wall and toilets the other. At the back, a door opens to a room where three baths stand side-by-side. A man with a wild beard wanders towards it, but an attendant stops him. The door slams shut. He's told tonight's not bath night. He screams and flings himself to the floor, and kicks out. Bits of food hang from his beard.

While no one watches, I throw my pill from earlier down the sink, look in the tin mirror, and smile.

Filing back to bed, I spot a telephone on the nurse's desk. Tom comes back with another pill, a different colour, orange. To help you sleep, he says. I smile and oblige as before. Later, when it's in my pyjama pocket, I crush it with my fingers in case there's a pat-down before bed, like in the camp. I retrieve my hand to see some fingertips are stained. I lick them clean. The taste is so bitter it makes me gag. I try to work up a saliva ball to swallow the scratchy residue and remove the disgusting taste. My attempt takes several goes. The after-taste sits on my tongue, but there's no water nearby. Asking for some would draw too much attention.

Time passes slowly, but I keep my resolve. I concentrate on recalling the image of Elouna's letter to me. I visualise her Scottish address. Her beautiful script appears clear in my mind's eye. Elouna lives in Forfar, Angus. I repeat it over and over, and it calms me.

I turn to look at the patient on the other side of my bed. A boy, maybe seventeen. Ruddy cheeks, shaven head. One arm is limp over the edge of his bed. Blue and yellow bruises along the forearm. A splint on three fingers.

Wiggling my toes keeps me occupied and alert. Later, when it's dark, the nurse at the desk gets up to leave the ward. I pull the covers back and slide out barefoot. My mind amplifies the thump of my heels on the floor, but I continue. Grab the phone. Dial. Ask the operator for the number of Mrs E Schutt, Forfar, Angus. She tells me, and I repeat it silently as I slink back just as the nurse barrels through the doors. He senses something and walks down the middle of the ward. The torch beams flash across the beds. My heart pumps at the base of my throat. His torchlight continues to fly around the dormitory. Nothing is out of place. He walks back to the desk with a grumble.

## Elouna

Elouna heard her phone ring as she was out in the sloping garden, pegging washing on the line. The day was gusty. Through the flapping laundry, she could see the purple and brown mountains; snow dusted their peaks. Few knew she now lived in Scotland, so the call must be important. She scrambled indoors to answer it, leaving a dress half-pegged on the line and tugged by the wind.

'Mrs Schutt, I have a collect call on the line. Will you accept the charges?'

'I'm sorry, what is collect call?'

'Oh, it's when you pay for the caller's charges.'

'Strange. Who is this caller, please?'

'It's a Roman Kozynska.'

'Oh, my God.' She palmed her cheek. 'Yes. Yes.'

Then collapsed onto the telephone chair and grabbed its edge to steady herself.

'Elouna, it's Roman.' A grown man's voice whispered from the phone. Elouna didn't immediately recognise it, but she knew it was Roman.

'I have little time. Please get me out of this place, or I will perish. You must contact Bridget.'

'Roman, is she your wife?'

'Yes.' Roman gave her the address. She heard rapid footsteps, then shouting in the background of the call.

*'Hey you, what are you doing?'*

Sounds of a scuffle followed, and the phone went dead. Elouna dropped the receiver; it slid over her knees and clattered to the floor. Her whole body shook.

Bridget opened the door to see a beautiful brown-eyed woman standing there with two blond children, a boy and a girl. She held a Gladstone bag and smiled.

'Taxi wait for us.' She motioned behind her to where a car sat with its engine running. The driver blew smoke out the window.

'Elouna! It's you. Oh, my God.'

Bridget flung the door wide, and Elouna stepped in followed by her two children. She dropped the bag down and grasped Bridget's hands in hers.

'I wanted to meet you in better times.' Tears clouded her eyes as she held Bridget close. 'These are my children, Olli, nine, and Flora, seven.'

'What lovely names you have.' Bridget bent down to the children. They glanced at their mother and said, 'Very pleased to meet you, Aunty Bridget.'

'I teach them English,' said Elouna, who followed Bridget into the living room, where Kay and Gillian sat rigid on the sofa with Janek wedged between them.

Bridget saw the look of admiration flash over their faces as they greeted Elouna, whose delicate, asymmetrical features resembled those of a film star.

'And this is Janek,' Bridget said.

Elouna bent and leaned in to hug him as a sob emerged from her. She squeezed him and stood back up.

'Dzien dobry – *Hello* Janek. I'm Aunty Elouna.' She fanned her teary eyes and said, 'He look like Roman, and his grandfather, Ludwig.' Elouna patted her chest and smiled at Bridget.

Kay and Gillian ushered the children into the dining room for sandwiches and milk.

'Now we must go to Roman. Kay and Gillian will take good care of all the children. They're my good friends.'

'Thank you for your telegram,' said Bridget as they settled into the taxi's back seats. 'Menston Hospital, please,' she instructed the driver. Bridget outlined what had happened for Roman to end up in the hospital and what Dr Highroyd said.

'I didn't like what he told me when we met, but he said Roman had agreed to stay there for treatment.'

'This not true. Roman sound desperate on phone.'

'I'm so glad he phoned you, but how did he know where you lived?'

'Good memory of letter I sent him.' Elouna smiled and reached for Bridget's hand. 'We sisters-in-law now,' Bridget said, and they both laughed.

The taxi arrived outside the hospital's driveway in thirty minutes. Elouna paid, rebuffed any contribution from Bridget, and scrambled out first.

'Do you think we should've phoned to say we were coming?' Bridget said, her stomach fluttering wildly.

'No! We surprise instead,' said Elouna. 'And when we there say you have appointment.'

They marched up the drive towards the bend, arm in arm.

'But I don't.'

'Not problem, insist they make mistake not you!'

'I'm sure I can do that.' Bridget huffed out of breath

from keeping pace with Elouna, taller than her with long legs.

They reached the bend, and the hospital swung into view.

'What place is this?' Elouna said.

She snatched a glance at Bridget, shook her head solemnly, and tutted loudly.

'No place for Roman, for sure,' said Bridget.

They climbed the steps to the imposing entrance with pillars on each side and a locked door. Bridget thumped on it, and soon the hatch with a grid opened. Bridget gave her name and insisted she had an appointment with Dr Highroyd. After some discussion with colleagues, an orderly opened up, and Bridget and Elouna pushed past him and clattered to the reception desk, where a nurse sat flipping through a ledger. She looked up as they reached her and smiled stiffly.

'Mrs Kozynska, is it?' she said, still searching for the elusive appointment entry.

'Yes, and this is my sister-in-law, Mrs Schutt,' said Bridget. 'I have an appointment with Dr Highroyd, as I told your colleague.'

The nurse glanced at the book again and stared at Bridget, then Elouna. 'I'm afraid I can't find your appointment anywhere.'

The two women looked at one another. 'So?' Bridget said to the nurse. A man came running towards them, shouting something incoherent. He wore only one slipper and a gaping dressing gown. A male orderly ran behind him, grabbed him by the belt and pulled him back down the corridor. The distraction provided time for Bridget to compose herself. 'I beg your pardon?' Bridget said, her voice steady. 'I have an appointment, and my sister-in-law has travelled far to attend it with me at great expense. Someone must have made a mistake.'

Elouna nudged Bridget with her elbow. 'We see doctor now?' she said innocently.

'If we don't, I will complain to the health authorities.' Bridget glared at the nurse, who shrank back a little.

The nurse stood. 'Excuse me for a moment.' She walked off, her heels clipping sharply on the marbled floor.

'What do you think she's doing?' Bridget said.

Elouna shook her head. 'We wait. It good.'

The nurse soon returned and told them they were lucky because Dr Highroyd was in his office and had agreed to see them despite no appointment in their records.

'Follow me,' she said, and the three hurried down the echoey corridor that smelt of vomit and disinfectant.

They reached the doctor's office, and the nurse knocked.

'Come,' said a voice.

Bridget's knees buckled as she stepped in, but Elouna grabbed her elbow and steadied her to the desk, where she sat abruptly.

'Doctor, good day. I'm Roman Kozynski's wife, and this is his sister. We've come to take him home.'

Bridget stared at the doctor and waited for an outburst. She imagined her father looking down at her from above, as amazed at her audacity as she was. But Elouna's presence had given her strength.

The doctor's expression changed. 'There's been a misunderstanding,' he said with a forced smile. 'Roman discharged himself a few hours ago.'

'What!' Bridget twisted to face Elouna. 'How can that be? He begged for us to come for him. He phoned his sister in Scotland.'

Elouna sat upright and kept her gaze fixed on the doctor's face.

He leaned back in his chair. 'Ah yes,' he said. 'The phone call. Let me explain. When we heard Roman making a call from the nurse's station, we asked what he was doing. You see, patients aren't allowed to use the phone unassisted. I'm sure you can understand why. But Roman was agitated and said he wanted to contact his family to leave our establishment.' He paused and folded his hands together on the desk.

'And?' said Bridget.

The doctor was silent for an unnerving moment. Bridget could hear the blood rushing in her ears. 'We explained that his stay was entirely voluntary and that if he did not want to proceed with the treatment we had discussed, he was free to leave.' The doctor gave a little snuffle; his head twitched slightly, then continued. 'We suggested he wait for you to take him home if he had been in contact, but he was eager to leave and discharged himself this morning.'

'So, you're saying he's left the hospital?' said Bridget.

'Yes. The ward nurse escorted him to the external bus stop and left him there.'

'Did he have money?' Elouna asked. Bridget put her

head in her hands.

'We returned his belongings from the admission—a bag and a coat. That's all I am aware of.'

'Oh no. He'll be heading home, and I'm not there to greet him. We must hurry back.' Bridget stood up.

'Mrs Kozynska, just a moment. Before you leave, I suggest that Roman needs treatment, as I advised you at our previous meeting.'

'You did indeed.' Bridget stood clutching her bag, praying he would let her go soon.

'Roman was very agitated when he arrived here but soon became calmer and realised things had gotten out of control in his mind. Therefore, my recommendation based on a prognosis of mental instability following a trauma, most likely originating from the war, is he would benefit from daily sedatives to calm his nerves. And I will refer him to our new talking therapy, which we are trialling at Leeds General Infirmary. I will contact his GP.'

Bridget glanced at Elouna for confirmation. Her mind was still whirring.

'That's good,' Elouna said.

'Yes, it is. Thank you so much, Dr Highroyd,' Bridget said.

She breathed a massive sigh of relief before heading out with her sister-in-law, arm in arm.

* * *

When Bridget and Elouna returned home, it was late afternoon. The early September air was tinged with a chill as their children rushed down the path to greet them and clambered for their mothers' attention. Gillian and Kay stood on the doorstep and looked anxious, stepping aside to let them into the house.

Elouna offered to make supper for the children and hurried into the kitchen while Bridget explained what had occurred to Gillian and Kay. They left, saying she must ask for help if needed.

After supper, they sent the children to play in the living room as Bridget and Elouna converged at the dining room table to talk.

'He should be home by now,' Bridget said, clasping and unclasping her hands. 'The hospital's not that far away. I'm so worried.'

Elouna took a hand. 'Have faith. He be home soon.'

'Elouna, I've been thinking of what the doctor said about Roman. I know so little of what went on in the war. Roman won't talk to me about it.'

Elouna withdrew her hand. 'It hard sometimes. What he tell you?'

'Nothing!'

Elouna shifted in her seat and smoothed her dress over her knees.

Bridget continued, 'Roman told me he'd escaped from a prison in Warsaw and feared his mother had died during the war but didn't give up hope. At the end of the war, they made contact. Roman was so happy. He visited and something happened, but he wouldn't say what. Then he was arrested in Glasgow. It was awful, Elouna.'

'Arrested for what?'

'Drunk and disorderly. Roman wouldn't tell me what

happened, so I let it go.'

'Ah, I see. Sometime that best way.' Elouna reached for a cigarette from a packet in her bag.

'And then your mother died. We were on our way to see her, to tell her we were getting married.'

Elouna nodded her head. 'She mention this to me.' Her face was unreadable as she flicked her lighter.

'But Roman changed after that. He became very secretive and flew off the handle at the slightest thing. His friend Andrej knew something but wouldn't tell me either. I think there must be a big secret.'

Elouna took a deep breath. 'I'm sorry, but I know little about Roman's war years, Bridget. You must ask him.'

Bridget realised Elouna was unable or unwilling to fill in the missing pieces. A feeling of dread gathered in her stomach.

'I'll make a fire, then put Janek to bed before yours go up.'

She couldn't look at Elouna in case her inner turmoil broke out on her face. Bridget swept Janek from the sofa where he had dropped off to sleep and carried him up to his room.

How much time had passed, Elouna was unaware of as she lifted her head from the table where she had fallen asleep after the uncomfortable conversation with Bridget. But it was now dark. She jumped up, flicked on the light, and hurried into the living room. It was empty. Bridget must have put Ollie and Flora to bed, as well as Janek. Elouna hoped Bridget didn't think her a bad mother.

She listened but couldn't hear any sounds from upstairs; perhaps they were all fast asleep. Bridget had lit the fire earlier; the coal burned dark red in the grate as the embers shifted.

A key turned in a lock, followed by light footsteps in the hall. The room door slowly opened, and in crept Roman, wearing a winter coat. He dropped his bag when he saw her. 'Elouna! It's you.'

Elouna held her arms wide. She took a step towards him. 'I'm so glad you contacted me.'

Roman suddenly stepped back and stumbled onto the sofa.

Elouna dropped next to him and took his hands. 'There's so much we need to catch up with.'

Roman sat up. 'Where's Bridget?'

'Upstairs, sleeping. Please, can we talk first? It's important.'

Roman let go of her hands. 'You're sure Bridget and Janek are okay?'

'Yes.'

'Where to start?' He stared at her intently.

'You contacted me. That's a beginning.'

'Blood is thicker than water.' He shrugged – a wry expression on his face. 'I was desperate.'

'What happened – why were you in that terrible hospital?'

'Too much happened to me,' Roman said.

Elouna pondered – she had waited a long time. 'Can I tell my story.'

'About why you married a Nazi?'

She winced. 'I had to live with that pig Schutt to survive. Many people would not understand this. Why didn't you kill him in his sleep or run away? they would ask. But how could I with small children? I had to stay until the war ended.'

'You were forced?' Roman looked bitter. Unconvinced.

Elouna thought for a while. 'Do you remember Victor Zurek – my piano teacher? He tried to help me escape, but Schutt found out, and Victor *disappeared.*'

'I'm sorry to hear that,' Roman said, looking at Elouna through narrowed eyes.

'Bridget asked me about your war years. It's hard to keep secrets.'

'You should know.'

'Why don't you tell her the truth?'

'What do you mean *the truth?* What has she said?'

'Nothing! Only she told me you won't talk about your past.'

Roman breathed in loudly, 'Or of yours.' His face clouded over. 'It's true, Elouna; Bridget is ignorant of these things.'

'You should tell her. She's your wife.'

Roman pursed his lips. 'The English can't understand our past. But they are quick to judge. How can I explain the Germans put me in a camp and later forced me to fight in their army?'

'Bridget doesn't know about your conscription?' Elouna clasped her hands together.

'No. I can't admit it. An English person would say, but surely you had a choice.'

Roman stared at Elouna, long and hard. She could see his emotions tugging this way and that. A miniature war breaking on his features. He covered his face with his hands; the only sound in the room was the clock ticking.

Roman lifted his head to speak. 'You know what choice I had: do as they tell you or die. That's not a choice. I did what I could to survive. Unless a person has been in that situation, they don't know you will do anything for one last day, hour, or minute - that the desire to live overpowers everything else. They can push you to the limits of perseverance, but you won't fall until forced.'

'Bridget loves you, and she would understand if you shared your story.'

'Elouna, I can't take that risk. You don't know the shame of being associated with the Germans here. If anyone found out, I would be knifed in an alley.' Roman stopped talking and stood up.

'When mother told me about you, *my sister* marrying a German, the hurt was unbearable.'

'Roman, unless you unburden yourself to Bridget, the hate and guilt will poison your soul. I have seen this many times since the war's end. I have watched people going mad with grief they cannot admit.'

Roman paced in front of the fire.

'You must learn to forgive and start with yourself. Then Mother. Then me.'

'Words come easily to you, Elouna, but what if my heart has been so shattered it may never heal again?'

'You must try.' Elouna sat back in her seat and rested her head. How small the room was compared to their childhood home. There were no signs of Roman's past life. It was unfamiliar and alien, just like Scotland. The thought she ran from erupted again. *You will never have a true home again. You will never belong.*

'You know, Elouna, I've experienced guilt and shame, which sometimes overwhelmed me. And other times, I've boiled with rage and hatred against those who hurt me. There was no one to share it with apart from Andrej because he was with me in that camp.'

Roman's face altered as darkness passed over it. 'I tried to forgive you and Mother, but the thought of it drove me crazy. You lived with the enemy. The very people who destroyed my life. How could you? How could my so-called loving Mamushka?'

'Roman, listen, please. She had her reasons.'

'Really, what were they, Elouna?'

She heard caustic bitterness in his voice.

'She tried to protect you after you escaped Warsaw and searched all over for you. She bribed people for information. Paid to get forged papers to travel to find you, wherever you were.'

'I don't care. You're avoiding the truth.' Roman spat out his words.

'The truth hurts. It has already hurt.' Elouna nodded sharply.

'So, tell me this truth,' Roman said.

'In 1937, our parents changed their surname. Have you ever wondered why?'

'Papa said our name sounded rude. Made people laugh.'

'He lied. Hitler was going from strength to strength, and it was clear what would soon happen. He publicly ranted about ridding Germany of Jews and declaring war on Europe. To be Jewish was to be vulnerable.'

'We lived in Poland and were not Jewish?'

'Well Roman, here's a surprise. Your maternal grandmother was. Her family name was Frank, but she married out and assimilated.'

'We have Jewish ancestry?' Roman stared at Elouna, picturing his grandmother.

Elouna nodded. 'Yes. Our parents changed their surname to break the connection.'

'You're losing me, Elouna.'

'Their marriage certificate identified grandmother's maiden name as Jewish. Our parents were protecting themselves and us from a future of persecution. They knew what was coming. Even then, the Germans traced people's backgrounds to gather evidence.'

'How is that mother's reason for living with you and Schutt during the war? For approving her daughter's marriage? It's absurd.'

'No, it's not. In 1943 our maternal grandparents paid for a fake certificate to prove they married as practising Roman Catholics. They'd been married since 1889.'

Roman looked at Elouna and slowly nodded his head. 'I've seen that certificate; in Mother's suitcase. I thought it was a replacement for a lost document.'

'It's evidence of a frightened couple in their late sixties desperate to avoid ending up in a concentration camp.' Her voice faltered.

'Mother was arrested shortly after us. She was in Pawiak, where her husband, son, and daughter cowered in the cells below. Schutt visited Papa to interrogate him, and I was there. Schutt, the pig, who sent our father to his death, decided he liked the look of me.'

Roman groaned. 'That terrible day. Papa, broken, but fighting.'

Elouna continued. 'Schutt arranged I would become his children's nanny. He suspected my Jewish heritage but turned a blind eye. And later, he used it against me.'

'That's hardly believable. Surely that's a massive risk for someone in that position?'

'Yes, it was. But Schutt was obsessed with me. It was a way for me to hide in plain sight, Roman. Untouchable while I was with him. Mother hated the idea but prayed the situation would buy me time.' Elouna stood and grasped Roman's hands to stop him from pacing the room.

'A mother's instinct is to protect her children.'

'Even after Victor, you could have tried to get away?'

'It was too dangerous. Schutt threatened to expose me. Oh, God, I hated the bastard but grovelled to get mother to live with us before I went mad.'

'You think you *saved* her?'

'Yes. But Schutt was posted back to Germany. Mother wouldn't come with us. She wanted to stay and continue her search for you. She begged me to stay, but I was too afraid. I had a baby. There seemed no way out of Schutt's control.'

Roman put his head in his hands. Muffled gasps escaped from him. 'I don't know what to think.'

'Mother lived on the streets in Poland but got word to me. Schutt arranged her passage to Germany, but she didn't stay long. One night she left while we slept. Her note said to continue searching for you. Roman, she was a woman possessed.'

Roman lifted his head. Tears dribbled down his chin.

'Later, Schutt heard our mother was arrested again in Poland. The Germans discovered her false documents. They transported her to Bergen-Belsen. By then, it was only a few months before liberation, and things were falling apart at the camp.'

Elouna watched Roman pull his collar away from his neck. 'I can't breathe.' He opened the window and leant out, taking huge gulps of cold air before turning back to Elouna.

'When I visited her in Scotland, mother told me she was in Bergen-Belsen as a *displaced person after the war*. She emphasised it had become a transit camp. She showed me a card that certified she worked as a camp teacher, part of the Polish Union of School Teachers in Germany. Was she lying to me?'

Elouna felt helpless and exhausted. She flopped onto the sofa.

'There are some things we will never know, Roman. Whatever happened, mother survived her ordeals and continued searching.'

Roman slumped down by her. 'The Germans took everything from us - destroyed our lives. The terrible things they did – unspeakable, unthinkable. The bitterness grew in me and hardened, day-by-day, year-by-year. I have hated deeply.'

Roman closed his eyes. 'But forgiveness is a treacherous journey.' He rested his head on the scratchy nylon sofa.

'I don't ask for it, Roman.'

'But I can see what will happen if I don't find peace.'

'What do you think that is, Roman?'

He opened his eyes and turned to Elouna. 'I will lose everything dear to me. All that I live for: Bridget and Janek.'

Elouna reached for Roman, but he put his hand up to stop her.

'I do not say I can forgive you.'

Elouna understood Roman; he would be forever suspended, unresolved like her and clamped in the jaws of an irreconcilable past. They sat in complete silence until the fire's embers turned to ash. Until he said, 'I must speak to Bridget.' He jumped up and bolted upstairs.

Bridget rested on Janek's bed after she had nestled him under the covers. He was tired from the afternoon of playing games with his newfound cousins and fell asleep at once. Outside, the dying light fanned into wispy layers across the inky blackness that descended. The twilight chirps of birds had settled into a frozen quiet, and Bridget felt suspended in time. Her emotions halted at a towering grey bank that, to her, was impenetrable. She needed to talk to someone badly but could not face Elouna's evasiveness. What were they hiding? Her face flushed at remembering their first date when she didn't even know his surname. What madness had possessed her? Had she been naïve – a trusting Irish lass awash in a complex world she could barely understand, let alone navigate?

She kissed Janek's soft forehead, wrenched her coat from the wardrobe and tiptoed down the stairs. The house was utterly silent, with only the clock ticking in the kitchen—the second hand moving in tiny jolts to an unknown future. Bridget prised the front door open, stepped onto the chilled path, and ran to Kay's house. Although Gillian lived nearer, Bridget needed to talk to her old friend to cling to stability in her upturned world.

She reached the house just as Kay stood at the window to close the curtains. Kay spotted her scrambling up the path. Bridget stumbled over on her weakened ankle and fell to the ground, letting out a wail as her hands slapped the gravel. The front door swung open, and light poured out. Kay rushed towards her.

'Bridget, whatever's the matter? Here, girl, get up now and come inside.'

Kay bent to settle on her haunches and pushed Bridget's hair back from her face. Bridget smiled weakly as Kay helped Bridget gently up and led her into the front room, where a log fire spat and crackled.

'Before I ask what's happened, I'm getting you a glass of whisky.'

Kay settled a cushion behind Bridget, then disappeared into the kitchen. Bridget could hear cupboard doors creaking open and closing, then the tap running. Comforting domestic sounds. Kay returned with two sloshing tumblers she set down. She eased onto the sofa and handed Bridget a glass.

'Sláinte,' she said and took a large mouthful.

'Slainte!' Bridget rasped.

'Now, what on earth is going on?'

Bridget sipped at the fiery liquid, frightened to let go of herself. 'I don't know where to start. I'm sure Elouna is hiding things from me, saying to ask Roman. And he's been hiding things from me.' She looked down at her lap, feeling stupid.

'What things?'

Bridget's rib cage rapidly rose and fell.

'Things about the war. I don't know.' She shrugged. 'Jesus!' The rough whisky burned her throat.

Kay turned to her. 'Listen to me; you need to hear it from Roman, whatever it is. Bridget, people don't always tell the whole truth now, do they? They have their reasons.'

Bridget pushed forward in her seat. 'I do! I tell the

truth.'

Kay rubbed her forehead. 'Is that so? Did you tell Roman your alcoholic father ruined your family, and you wound up living in a slum?'

'Well, no, but that's different.'

'How is it different, Bridget?'

'It was merely omitting something.'

Kay snorted. 'Really! And why did you do that?'

Bridget took another swig of whisky. 'Because I felt ashamed. But why are you putting me on trial, Kay?'

'I'm not. But we all have secrets.'

'Holy Mary, mother of Jesus, why is life so complicated?'

Kay swigged back the last of her whisky. 'More?' She hurried to fetch the bottle. On returning, she said, 'What did Roman have that attracted you so much?'

Bridget remembered when they first danced to Glen Miller in an environment alien to both of them. They were immigrants from foreign lands. Roman held her close, and the feeling of safety engulfed her. He defended her from a leery Czech and took control of the situation. He was hot-headed, which excited her. She'd rushed away that night but pined to see him again. Being with him was like bathing in a sea of light.

She finally answered Kay. 'It was his compassion and forthrightness. I could tell he was a good man, an honest….' Her last word hung in the air as she broke off to gulp more drink.

'I was madly in love with his mystery and charm. When I told him I was pregnant, he proposed. I'd expected him to reject me. It was clear that he would take care of the baby and me.'

'And he did.'

'Yes.' She nodded. 'Roman found us a home, worked hard, put food on the table, and all he seemed to care about was looking after us.'

'That's accurate enough, Bridget, but you knew something had happened to Roman because of the nightmares and excessive drinking with his Polish friends.'

Bridget filled her glass. 'I thought when we moved here, he would change, being away from the influence of his community.'

'Oh, sweetie, we all think we can change our man, but people only change if they want to.'

'But Roman got better away from his buddies, and I learned to live with his occasional outbursts because he didn't direct them at Janek or me.'

'No, but it frightened you, you told me yourself.'

'I didn't know how to deal with him. What to do about it, but the night of the storm, well, that was more than I could stand.'

'It must have been frightening,' Kay stretched for Bridget's hand. 'I know you've had it hard. It all happened so quickly between you and Roman.'

Bridget picked up Kay's wedding photo from the coffee table and peered at it, lost in time.

Kay continued. 'But Roman's had it tough as well. He loves you and Janek. If the doctors say they can help him, there's hope for the future.'

'Kay, I don't know what I want anymore.'

Kay shook her head. ‘I think you need some sleep. I’ll fetch a blanket, and you can grab some rest. Things will seem much better in the morning.’

## Roman

I wake fitfully this morning, hearing voices in the kitchen and the unmistakable sound of Bridget talking with Elouna. She's come back—my heart is fit to burst. The rich, romantic voice of Mario Lanza drifts upstairs from the kitchen radio. It calms me. I dress, splash cold water on my face, and dash down to them. Bridget and Elouna stand by the cooker as I fling open the kitchen door. Steam rattles from the kettle's spout before the piercing cry of its whistle at boiling point. Elouna lifts it from the leaping flames of the gas. Bridget and I move towards one another and fall into each other's bodies. She leads me to the dining room table, where breakfast awaits. Bridget is lovely, and her green eyes radiate warmth. We sit down, holding hands. I can't let go. I can never let her go again. Elouna slips in with a plate of toast. I look at it, but I don't need food right now—I, who starved and scavenged black bread from the pockets of the dead.

'Where were you last night?' I ask her. She looks me directly in the eye with such force I feel overpowered with remorse.

'I slept on Kay's sofa to clear my head. I felt bewildered, Roman, and I hope you know why.'

I nod and try to gulp down the lump forming in my throat. 'Bridget, there are things I have not told you.'

'I know, and you need to. Otherwise, I can't trust you, and that is too terrible for me.'

I stare at the soft curls on her shoulders and imagine her running on the shores of the Atlantic Ocean as a child, the salty wind tangling her thick locks. A free, wild spirit with no terrible memories to haunt her. How could I have recounted the horror of my life to her when we first met? It would have changed her view of me forever, and I could not bear to live without her love. She interrupts my thoughts.

'I share my life with you, but you are a stranger in many ways,' Bridget says.

I stroke her soft cheek. 'I will tell you. All of it. We go for walk.'

We leave the house swaddled in coats and head to the railway embankment to scramble up, where the view stretches to the blue horizon. I say, let's sit down. A train is chugging along the tracks. It carries coal to the town centre to be gobbled up in the industrial furnaces. We watch it pass, the fat white curls of steam trailing behind it as it disappears around the bend. Traces that soon evaporate as though they were never there.

I take Bridget's warm hand and begin my story. The actual story. I start with my arrival in Krakow.

## Roman Krakow 1940

The sky darkened as Roman finally arrived at his relative's house on the outskirts of Krakow. He was young, robust and resilient. His uncle Teofil had given him the address and sworn they would keep him safe during the war, and when it was over, his family would reunite. There was a faint light in the upstairs window of his relatives' house. As he approached the doorstep, a dog began barking, and he heard the thud of its paws as it jumped at the inside of the door and growled. He knocked loudly, then stood back to peer at the upstairs room; his heart beating like a trapped bird.

The shutters opened, and an unfamiliar man looked out.

'Who's there?'

'Sir, Teofil Sobotniki gave me your address. He's my uncle, you see.'

'Who did you say?'

The man raised a hand to his ear, and Roman realised he must be hard of hearing.

The figure of a woman appeared behind him. What's going on?' she said as she peered over her husband's shoulder at Roman, who stood shivering below, terrified of what might happen next.

His mind raced with a million possibilities, and he wondered if it would be better to run and try to make it on his own. What if Teofil had the wrong address? What if these strangers turned him into the Germans?

'Hold on, and I'll be right down.' He disappeared from

the window, but his wife's silhouette remained. Roman glanced over his shoulder to check he hadn't aroused suspicion through shouting in the street. The dog ceased barking as the man opened the door a fraction, a hand hooked under the dog's collar as he assessed Roman. The dog strained but didn't growl. Roman could see its tail wagged and was relieved.

'You better not be bringing me any trouble.' The man stared hard at Roman, then stepped back to open the door fully. 'Who did you say you are again? '

Roman's voice trembled. 'Teofil Sobotnicki's nephew.'

'Don't you have a name, lad?'

'Yes! I do. It's Ro…' He remembered his new identity.

'Get in here now,' the man said as a car crept from the end of the street with its headlights dipped.

He pulled Roman into a darkened room lit only by the flickers of a dying fire. Along a wall, a set of stone steps led upstairs. The man held a candle and gestured to Roman.

'Follow me.'

The candle glow threw wavering shapes on the wall. His bare feet made the slightest of sounds as he climbed the narrow stairs. At the top, he pushed open a door and led Roman into a tiny room with a single bed and chair. He set the candle down on the floor and pulled the curtains tight.

'It's curfew time, and we don't want to attract attention to ourselves.' He turned. 'Sit down there,' he said, pointing to the bed. Roman sat obediently, and the springs creaked beneath him. He was overcome with exhaustion and hunger.

‘Why are you here?’ The man balanced on the chair and placed his hands on the knees of his pyjamas.

‘Uncle Teofil said you could help me.’

‘Did he? I wonder why?’

‘He wrote you a letter.’

‘I haven’t received a letter from him. How do I know you are who you say you are?

Roman smiled helplessly.

‘And what’s your name again?’

‘I have papers…’ Roman trailed off as he realised the forged documents bore a different name, and without the backing of Teofil’s letter, his story would not stand up. But he reasoned with himself that his relative had already allowed him into his home and had taken him upstairs, so he must trust Roman somehow.

‘How is Teofil’s wife?’ He peered intently at Roman.

Roman was confused for a moment, then realised what was happening.

‘Teofil doesn’t have a wife, sir.'

‘Ah, yes. Then Teofil’s sister, Elouna. How is she?

‘I think you’ve made a mistake. Teofil’s sister is my mother and is called Anya. Anya Kozynska. It’s her daughter that’s called Elouna.’ Roman’s palms were damp by now.

The man nodded and relaxed a little. ‘So, you are Roman, then?’

Roman exhaled loudly. He pulled his identity card from his pocket and handed it to the man. ‘This is who I am now. Teofil arranged it.’

The man examined the forged document. ‘Well, Josef

Rogalski, you can stay here for the night.'

Roman let out a massive sigh of relief.

'And my name is Janusz, by the way. I'm your mother's cousin. Are you hungry?'

* * *

As the cock crowed, Roman was shaken awake by Janusz. 'It's time for breakfast.'

As they gobbled potato pancakes, Janusz told Roman that Krakow was not safe. The Germans had cordoned off an area of the old town, as a Ghetto and people were trapped there. Uncle Teofil had misjudged things.

'I have a better idea for you. There's a group training in the forest. Young men, some younger than you.'

Roman put his fork down. 'Training for what?'

Janusz's wife raised her eyebrows.

'To defeat the Nazis. You could join them?'

'You mean to fight?'

'When it's time.'

The dog began barking. Janusz's wife stood up. 'They're here.'

'Whose here? 'Roman said.

She opened the door. A gangly youth slid in. Handsome with razor-sharp cheekbones. He glanced at Roman and winked.

'I'm Andrej, and I hear you're joining us.'

'Andrej will look out for you. What do you say?' Janusz touched Roman's shoulder.

'I'm in.' Roman stood up to shake Andrej's hand.

## Roman

My Krakow story is easy to tell. Bridget dabs her eyes. I think she's relieved, but I am not. There is more. I'm glad we are sitting down because my whole body shakes with fear and remembrance. I tell her I am ashamed of what comes next. It's about the work Andrej and I had to do in the camp. I will look away at this part because I can't bear to see her shrink from me. *Only a monster would have done that,* she would think.

'I understand shame. Roman, I do.' She hugs me tight as she says this, unaware I am to shatter her world.

I hold my breath without realising it—my face flames. Hot tears flood my eyes. I gulp in the fresh air, then tell Bridget about pulling gold teeth from corpses. I look away but then back because I must know what she feels. Her face is rigid, her eyes wide, and she bites her bottom lip. The longest of silences follows, broken only by the shrill hoot of a train.

'That's terrible. Roman. I'm staggered. People like me could never understand what you've endured. I would never judge you until I stood in your shoes.' She lets go of me to place a warm palm against my face.

I gaze at her through my blurred vision. I can hardly believe the compassion and sincerity in her lilting voice. She speaks from her heart; it shines in her eyes.

She leans in and kisses me with such force I think I will dissolve. But now I must tell her the other part from which I have been running scared for so long.

'I got away from the camp,' I say and look at her.

'Did you escape?' She looks even more relieved, and I see her shoulders relaxing.

I tell her flatly, 'No.'

'Then how did you get away?' she asks.

I breathe in until my lungs feel like they will burst. 'When I was old enough, the Germans conscripted me into their army from the camp. In 1944.'

There's a sharp intake of breath. 'What?' Bridget says.

I confess I had to fight with the German army. I rush to say I changed sides in Italy. But Bridget pulls away from me to stand up. She wraps her arms around her body and hugs herself. Bridget stares into the distance as I recount my shock about mother and Elouna.

She doesn't look at me as she says, 'Jesus, Roman, you're such a hypocrite. You did the same thing.'

Her words slice through me, and cold floods in. We are both silent for a while. Bridget sits down again. She reaches for my hand and says how hurt she is because Andrej knows my history, and she doesn't. I talk of my fears of being discovered, of the constant conversations in the mill canteen concerning beating the Germans. Hatred burned in their eyes. They would direct it at us if they'd known. I am sadder than ever, but the weight is lifting. Eventually, I can say no more.

Bridget turns to me and says, 'Let's go home.'

As we enter the living room, Janek is there. He's wearing his favourite patterned pyjamas, rubbing his eyes, his soft hair fluffed like a baby bird. He runs to me. I grab him and swish him up to kiss him. Suddenly, I have an idea. I call Elouna and tell her to sit down as I announce my plan.

I will speak in English so Bridget and Janek can understand.

I remind them we were poor when Mother died in Scotland. And they buried her in an unmarked grave, courtesy of the parish. The fact pains me each day, but life has been so full of money demands I've pushed this to the side. I propose Elouna and I buy a headstone to stand at Mother's grave. I say I have an idea for some words to engrave on the stone. Bridget squeezes my hand, and there's a light in her eyes. Janek looks from me to her, half-smiling, puzzled by what I say but instinctively knowing it is something that makes us feel glad. I pass Janek to Bridget and tell them I'll be back in a minute.

I take the stairs in giant leaps. Try to remember where my mother's suitcase is. The stool I stand on to push back the hatch wobbles beneath my feet. Dust drops on my face, but my fingers find the solid corner of the case, and I tug it towards me. A curled dead spider falls out as my fingers grasp the handle, and I pull it over the cobwebbed lip to swing it to my knees.

Downstairs, I open the suitcase. Elouna's face fills with heaviness as she recognises her mother's case. But I tell her it's okay. I'm looking for the letter from her to me, written on Christmas Eve from the hospital in Ballochmyl. She was ill, tired, sad, and losing hope for our reunion. She did not post this letter but saved it probably because it contains such devastating news.

I first read it to Bridget on our first Christmas Eve with Janek, but she'd fallen asleep after our celebrations and too much Polish cherry brandy. In her letter, Mama also wrote of the circumstance of my father's murder. Shot and buried in a mass grave, they were forced to dig themselves with others as punishment for their resistance. I will tell Bridget the truth of his death later and Janek too one day, when he can understand this awful moment and not have it stain his soul. The moment now is for Anya.

The small sea of ageing letters and frayed-edge documents give way to the one I seek. I prise it out and lay it on the table. Elouna and Bridget stare at me, but neither says anything. I unfold it carefully, scan the contents, and try to blink the tears away from my eyes. On page four of her letter, I spot the poem Mother included, one of her own.

'Here is what we should have written on her gravestone,' I say and read out the lines:

*Please give me wings to fly from this troubled earth,*

*to speed over the tumbling blue seas; on my way*

*to soar over the green mountains that pierce*

*the icy clouds, up and over the sad black forests,*

*and back to you.*

I pass the letter to Elouna.

'How beautiful, Roman,' Bridget says.

'It is,' says Elouna, nods, then puts her head down to conceal her grief.

* * *

In early November, I received a letter to say the headstone was finished and placed at Mother's grave. Bridget, Janek, and I planned to go to Scotland, meet Elouna in nearby Glasgow, and travel to the hospital cemetery to lay flowers by the stone.

After the train and a bus ride to Ballochmyl, we walked towards her final place of rest. We had a cemetery map and took in the many Polish names carved on the small stones as we passed. Finally, we found the place where she lay. It was unadorned. As we approached, we grabbed each other's hands and crunched gravel and withered grass underfoot. We'd chosen a headstone with little ornamentation to keep costs low due to the length of the engraving that, to us, meant everything. The soft sandstone scattered with tiny white particles which twinkled like stars when caught by the afternoon's ebbing light was a gift to us all.

We four reached the edge of the plot and halted. Elouna placed a wreath of white winter roses by the pristine stone.

Bridget kneeled and said softly to Janek, 'This is where your father's mother is buried. She's your *other* grandmother.'

Janek smiled shyly, a little uncertain of the meaning. We stood in silence for some time; each lost in their thoughts until the bitter day gave way to fat white flakes bursting from the open sky. When I looked back, everything was locked in a blinding white silence. As we said our last goodbyes, the snow fell thickly, and we turned towards the open gates into the swirling, glittering mass.

## About the Author

*The Suitcase of Secrets* (formerly *Northern Pole*) is Julie Fearn's first novel. Previously she has published short stories. Julie was born to Polish and Irish immigrant parents in West Yorkshire and jokes that she is 'Poirish'. She now lives in the historic city of York, North Yorkshire, with her dog Poppy and is immensely proud of her heritage, family and late parents.

You can learn more about Julie and her writing at her website: **JulieFearn.com**

Printed in Great Britain
by Amazon